Raves for James Patterson

"Patterson knows where our deepest fears are buried...
There's no stopping his imagination."
                              —*New York Times Book Review*

"James Patterson writes his thrillers as if he were building roller coasters."   —Associated Press

"No one gets this big without natural storytelling talent—which is what James Patterson has, in spades."
                              —Lee Child, #1 *New York Times* bestselling
                              author of the Jack Reacher series

"James Patterson knows how to sell thrills and suspense in clear, unwavering prose."   —*People*

"Patterson boils a scene down to the single, telling detail, the element that defines a character or moves a plot along. It's what fires off the movie projector in the reader's mind."
                              —Michael Connelly

"James Patterson is the boss. End of."
                              —Ian Rankin, *New York Times* bestselling
                              author of the Inspector Rebus series

"James Patterson is the gold standard by which all others are judged."   —Steve Berry, #1 bestselling author
                              of the Cotton Malone series

ESCAPE

ESCAPE

JAMES PATTERSON
AND DAVID ELLIS

GRAND
CENTRAL

NEW YORK BOSTON

Copyright © 2022 by James Patterson

Hachette Book Group supports the right to free expression and the value of copyright. The purpose of copyright is to encourage writers and artists to produce the creative works that enrich our culture.

The scanning, uploading, and distribution of this book without permission is a theft of the author's intellectual property. If you would like permission to use material from the book (other than for review purposes), please contact permissions@hbgusa.com. Thank you for your support of the author's rights.

Grand Central Publishing
Hachette Book Group
1290 Avenue of the Americas, New York, NY 10104
grandcentralpublishing.com
twitter.com/grandcentralpub

Originally published in hardcover and ebook by Little, Brown & Company in June 2022
First oversize mass market edition: January 2024

Grand Central Publishing is a division of Hachette Book Group, Inc. The Grand Central Publishing name and logo is a trademark of Hachette Book Group, Inc.

The publisher is not responsible for websites (or their content) that are not owned by the publisher.

The Hachette Speakers Bureau provides a wide range of authors for speaking events. To find out more, go to hachettespeakersbureau.com or email HachetteSpeakers@hbgusa.com.

Grand Central Publishing books may be purchased in bulk for business, educational, or promotional use. For information, please contact your local bookseller or the Hachette Book Group Special Markets Department at special.markets@hbgusa.com.

ISBNs: 9781538752913 (oversize mass market), 9780316499477 (ebook)

Printed in the United States of America

OPM

10 9 8 7 6 5 4 3 2 1

*To attorney extraordinaire Dan Collins
and the amazing Collins family—
Kristin, Riley, Declan, and Aidan Collins*

APRIL 8

CHAPTER 1

HE'S HERE somewhere. I know it. And the girl might still be alive.

The girl: fifteen-year-old Bridget Leone, abducted off the streets of Hyde Park forty-four hours ago.

Bing. Bing. Bing. Bing.

The ALPR sounds on the dashboard of our unmarked car, registering every license plate we pass, searching for any plate beginning with the letters *F* and *D*. But our witness told us the letters might have appeared the other way around, *D* and *F,* and maybe not even next to each other.

If we have this right, the same man who kidnapped Bridget Leone has abducted four other girls between the ages of thirteen and sixteen, all African American, around the Chicagoland area over the last eighteen months. None of those four girls has been found. All four of them were runaways, homeless—meaning they were easily overlooked and forgotten by overworked and understaffed suburban police departments dealing with cold trails of girls gone missing.

Bridget Leone was different. African American and

age fifteen, yes, but far from homeless or a runaway. Still, her parents said she dressed "way too provocatively" for her age and often ran with some "wild kids," typical teenage rebellion stuff that her abductor could have misconstrued. And just before she was abducted, we eventually learned from her reluctant friends, she and some classmates had been smoking weed in an alley only a few blocks from the elite magnet high school she'd attended.

When Bridget disappeared, her father—a real estate developer worth millions—called his good pal Tristan Driscoll, the Chicago police superintendent, who in turn immediately deployed the Special Operations Section to find her. That meant my partner, Carla Griffin, and me, at least as the lead detectives.

The computer mounted on the dash buzzes. A hit. Carla leans forward in the passenger seat and checks it. "False alarm," she says.

These automated license plate readers aren't perfect, natch. Sometimes a *D* is mistaken for a zero or an *O,* or an *E* is mistaken for an *F.*

Bing. Bing. Bing. Bing.

"I feel like I'm in a freakin' arcade," I say as I pull our unmarked car into a heavily wooded subdivision called Equestrian Lakes. Giant houses; wide, grassy lots.

Carla smirks. "Well, this is definitely a game of luck, not skill."

She's right. We have so little to go on. Nobody saw the direction in which the offender drove his car after he scooped Bridget off the street. The route he took didn't hit any PODs—our police observation cameras mounted in various places along the streets. The only witness was a homeless guy who had no phone, so he couldn't snap a photo or call it in. And he could only recall two possible digits of the license plate on a "dark"

SUV and give us a vague profile of a white male who is "slightly hunched," probably five nine or five ten, with a long scar on the left side of his face and wearing a baseball cap.

We have AMBER alerts, community alerts, investigative alerts, and flash messages on every cop's screen in northern Illinois. The Illinois State Police are patrolling the highways. The night Bridget was abducted, we ran a check of ALPRs for those letters *D* and *F,* next to each other—and picked up a Ford Explorer on South Archer Avenue. The registration traced to someone in Missouri who died six months ago.

We've cleared every registered sex offender in the area. So far, nothing. Nothing but hope for a little luck. Unless by some chance my gut call was right and he's here, on the southwest end of unincorporated Cook County.

My thinking: this largely vacant area would be close to the place where the ALPR picked up the Ford Explorer. There are some nice subdivisions, sure, but it has a rural feel, lots of woods and houses set back deep into the lots, no sidewalks or curbs or streetlights. Lots of privacy. Perfect for a predator.

So instead of running everything from the Special Operations headquarters, at North and Pulaski, Carla and I are here, taking phone calls and issuing orders while patrolling in an unmarked vehicle—unmarked unless you notice the tiny camera, the ALPR, on the roof.

Nothing unusual in Equestrian Lakes, a fancy subdivision, so I get back onto the main road, Rawlings, and follow the bend, the ALPR *bing-bing-binging* as cars pass.

The terrain gets more remote, more wooded. It feels like lake country out here, reminding me of the trips we'd take to Michigan when I was a kid. It's not yet dusk when I take a left turn down an unmarked narrow dirt road, hooded by tall trees, PRIVATE PROPERTY signs nailed to the trunks, glimpses of houses down paths. Beams of sun so infrequently break through the trees that my headlights switch on automatically. I'll do a quick tour before I—

A quarter mile ahead, a white van turns toward us onto the road. Carla's on her phone, talking with the state police, but she drops it from her ear and goes quiet.

I slow the car. The van continues to approach, going the speed limit, its headlights on us.

Bing. The ALPR picks up the plate.

"Commercial van," Carla reads off the mounted computer. "Registered to LTV, LLC. Registration's up to date."

The van moves slowly, giving us a wide berth, nearly driving onto the uneven shoulder.

I stop my car entirely, putting it in Park, and put on my hazards. Just to see what the driver will do.

The van seems to slow but doesn't stop. Carla and I lean down to look out the window at the driver, who's up higher than we are in his van.

White guy, roughly shaved, dark-framed glasses, baseball cap, bandage on his left cheek. Both hands gripping the wheel. His eyes stay straight forward, not even sneaking a peek in our direction, despite the fact that we have stopped in the middle of the road and put on our hazards.

Carla's voice is low. "That look like a white guy, five nine, hunched, scar on his face?"

Yeah, it sure as hell does. Not a Ford Explorer, no *F* or *D* on the plates, but a guy fitting the description in a creepy van. "Let's check it out."

I put the car in Drive and do a U-turn, following the van.

CHAPTER 2

THE VAN rolls along the dirt road, slowing even further as we pull up behind it. So far, it's guilty of nothing. Not speeding. No busted taillights. No apparent malfunctions that would warrant a stop.

"No PC," Carla says. A summary and a warning. We stop the car. Without probable cause, we have a problem in court.

But we don't need probable cause to follow it for a while. It's a free country.

I figure he's headed for the main road from which we just came, Rawlings. But he isn't. The van turns left down an unmarked path. Another dirt road.

No crime in that. And he used his blinker.

Still. I glance at Carla, the expression on her face probably the same as mine, gearing up.

"Baird Salt," she says, noting the logo visible on the side panel of the van when it turned.

I follow the van onto the turnoff. It hardly qualifies as a road—it's more like a clearing through the foliage and heavy tree cover, enough for a single lane of traffic, barely. The bumps are enough to challenge our Taurus's suspension and the fillings in my teeth. The canopy of trees keeps it dark, but the piercing beams of the lowering sun manage to penetrate here and there.

The van keeps moving at a normal clip down a path that wasn't meant to be noticed, much less traveled. I feel like I'm driving through a jungle, overhanging branches tapping our windshield and scraping the sides of the Taurus.

We still haven't taken any official police action, but there's no longer any doubt that we're following. If this guy's innocent, he has to be wondering about our intentions.

But he's not, I think, my pulse banging. *This is our guy.*

And he knows we know.

"Sosh, where are you?" Carla says into her radio. Another SOS team, Detectives Lanny Soscia and Mat Rodriguez, are in this area doing the same thing we are.

"West of Archer near…Hogan?"

"We're just south of Rawlings, traveling westbound on an unmarked dirt road. We're following a white van, driver fits the description. We need assistance."

"Where on Rawlings?" Sosh calls back.

Carla cusses at the GPS, which is spinning right now, unable to connect. "We're at the first turnoff west of the Equestrian Lakes subdivision, south side. West of… Addendale, I think."

"On our way."

I keep a distance of two or three car lengths as the van bounces along.

The van begins to slow. I nudge Carla, who nods.

Up ahead, a clearing, sunlight blanketing the ground. No tree coverage.

A road of some kind? An intersection?

"What's that up ahead?" I ask Carla, not wanting to take my eyes off the road.

"Can't get GPS to pull up yet," she answers. Then, into her radio, she calls to the state police chopper: "Air 6, this is CPD 5210. Do you copy?"

"Air 6 to 5210, what's your twenty?"

These state troopers and their formality. Carla repeats our location, best she can.

"We'll try to find you," the pilot calls back. *"GPS is a nightmare out here."*

No shit. The van slows still further, so I do, too.

Then the van reaches the clearing, suddenly cast in the glow of sunlight, while we remain in the darkness of the trees.

The van rolls carefully up onto a small incline, a tiny hill, then comes to a complete stop.

"He stopped," I tell Carla, who's busy banging the GPS on the laptop. "What the hell's he doing? What's he on? Are those…" I lean forward, squinting.

"Wait—GPS is up," says Carla.

We say it at the same time: "They're railroad tracks."

Not a public right-of-way. No crossbucks or gates or flashing lights. "One of those old crossings, out of use for decades," says Carla.

"So what the hell is he doing?" I mumble.

"Parking on the tracks."

Then we both hear it, from our right, the north. The rumbling sound of a train coming.

"Shit."

"He's done, and he knows it," Carla says. "Suicide by train."

And possibly with a fifteen-year-old girl inside.

We burst out of the car.

CHAPTER 3

WE RUSH toward the van, feeling the vibration of the oncoming train underfoot, fanning out on each side as the train horn bellows its warning. The screeching sound of metal on metal as the train tries in vain to halt ahead of the van stopped in its path.

"Chicago police! Chicago police!" I shout as I approach the driver's-side door, emblazoned with the salt-company logo.

In the rectangular side mirror, I catch sight of the man's face, his eyes intense. The van's tires screech as they spin into motion, blasting the vehicle off the platform and over the tracks—just as the train barrels past us, the deep blare of its horn, sparks flying, a high-pitched screech from the brakes.

I'm blown backward and almost lose my balance. Carla is calling into her radio to the state police chopper, to all units, as we lose sight of the van on the other side of the tracks, blocked now by the freight train.

The train shudders to a halt. "No!" I yell. "Keep moving! Clear this crossing!"

That will take forever. The conductor has protocols.

And he's well down the track. He probably can't hear me. He's probably cursing the idiot van driver who just played chicken with him.

Carla drops to the ground, looks under the train. "Can't see anything underneath!"

I look around me, a tree branch raking across my face. A tree.

I grab onto the thickest low branch I can find and do something I haven't done in twenty-five years. I pull myself up onto the branch and look out. No view. Still blocked by the idled train. I find another branch, pull myself up, and straddle it. There.

I spot the van just as it's turning left through what looks like a cornfield. "He turned south a few hundred yards up!"

I lose sight of him. But at least I know the direction he's heading. I climb back down, jumping from the branch and scraping my hands, falling face-first into some foliage that may or may not be poison ivy. "C'mon," I shout, heading back to the car.

We get into the car. I drop it into gear. I turn in the same direction the van is headed, south, and drive along the sloped gravel right-of-way next to the train tracks on my right.

"Air 6, you got this asshole?" Carla shouts. "We're near Rawlings and the train tracks! A white van. It's heading south now, probably a half mile southwest of the tracks and Rawlings."

"CPD 5210, we are responding."

We race along on the sloped gravel, our tires slipping and sliding.

"Twelve o'clock," Carla says to me.

I see it: a large structure on the right-of-way, a big black junction box mounted in the gravel. I can't plow over it. To the left is unknown terrain, and we could be screwed. Only choice is to go right, nearly hitting the train tracks. Carla braces herself.

"Hope all those years of video games paid off," I say.

I speed up and swerve to the right, the angle dangerously sharp, Carla nearly falling into me from the passenger seat. We scrape the embankment of the railroad tracks, bouncing downward against the junction box, but the momentum carries us past, the Taurus nearly nosediving into the very terrain I wanted to avoid to the left. We kick up rocks and dust, but the Taurus rights itself, and we barrel forward again.

"Air 6 to 5210, we have a twenty on the white van."

So do we. Up ahead, maybe a hundred yards. Flying across the train tracks again, back to the side that we're on, the Baird Salt logo unmistakable.

He's driving in a square. He's heading back where he came from.

"CPD 5210 is in pursuit," Carla says.

"CPD 5210, we can't track him in those woods."

Which is why he came back. He knows these woods. He knows where to hide.

We're on him, at least. But he has a head start. I can only go so fast without losing control of the Taurus on this uneven gravel.

After ninety seconds that feel like an hour, we reach the road where the van crossed back over the tracks. Carla is cool and calm as she relays the developments. "All units, we need to seal off this perimeter. Sheriff 1, you call it; you know this area."

I floor the Taurus, which responds with its souped-up police-model engine. At least this road is paved, so we can make progress. But so can the van. With the cherry lit up on the dashboard and the siren blaring, I hit nearly ninety miles an hour, hoping nobody or no *thing* jumps out into our path. I can't afford to lose the van.

We've probably got it pinned down now, but that's not the problem.

The problem is the girl and what he'll do to her if he feels cornered.

"There, Harney, there—"

We catch a glimpse of the van, turning left yet again. Completing the square.

He's going back home?

"Suspect is heading north," Carla calls in. "Air 6, you got it?"

I push the Taurus as hard as it can go, then skid into a left turn onto a dirt road, nearly wiping out. "This is the same road," I say. "The same one where we first saw him."

Carla calls it in, now on familiar ground. But the van driver has the advantage.

We see the van make its final turn up ahead.

"He did all this just to circle back and get home," says Carla. "What's so special about back home?"

I pound the brake as we slide into a turn, reaching the turnoff the van just took.

"We're about to find out," I say.

CHAPTER 4

WHEN WE reach the turnoff, we see a DO NOT ENTER sign chained across the path. That makes no sense. How did the suspect get through it and reattach it?

Whatever. I blast the Taurus through, the sign splitting apart before I could hit it.

"Some kind of automatic gate," says Carla, checking her weapon, adjusting her vest. "Who the hell *is* this guy?"

We follow a winding road, slowing to navigate the turns. Too slow to overtake the van.

"C'mon…"

Up ahead, the van pulls up to a house of brick and stone, the garage door opening. The van roars inside. Behind us, the sirens of law enforcement—state, county, city—come blaring from Rawlings Road.

The van screeches into the garage. The man pops out. The van's back doors open. He reaches in and pulls out…

…a girl, African American, tied at the hands and feet. Bridget Leone.

Carrying the girl in his arms, the man rushes into the house as we reach the property and squeal to a halt.

I run into the garage, seeing the door to the house ajar. My Glock out and high, I push the door open and shout, "Chicago police!"

I'm in a kitchen, red light flashing in a high corner. An intruder alert?

We race into a sparsely furnished family room—a couch and chair but not much else. A door to the left. To the right, a sliding glass door onto a patio.

And another red light flashing in the corner.

"Bridget! Bridget Leone?" Carla calls out. She tries the door. It opens into a staircase leading down.

Out of the corner of my eye, I see a figure running through the backyard. It's our offender, the ball cap and build matching the description.

"Bridget!"

A faint but clear "Yes!" comes from the basement.

"I got the perp; you get the girl," I say to Carla.

I push open the sliding glass door and leap off the patio onto the grass a good ten feet below. I ignore the pain in my ankle and start running.

It's a thick net of trees, a natural fencing, but I saw where he went in, and I see his hat on the path. I run with my Glock at my side. The path is narrow, the footing uneven. I try to watch for an ambush while running at top speed in an area this asshole knows and I don't.

Advantage: asshole. But I have some wheels when I'm motivated, and I get the sense this guy does not.

Then I hear him up ahead, his labored breathing, the sound of his footfalls. He comes into my view, running with all he's got, but it isn't enough.

"Police!" I shout as best I can while sprinting, my chest burning, my ankle throbbing. I make a decision, stop, aim, and fire at a tree in front of him.

The wood splinters. The man cowers, slowing down. Then he stops.

"Hands up and turn around!" I shout, shuffling toward him, both hands on the Glock.

He raises his hands. Turns around.

Beady eyes, greasy dark hair, thick nose. A large head rising from a long, skinny neck and sloping shoulders. Big ears protruding off his head like those of some cartoon character. The bandage dangling from his face, the sweat overpowering the adhesive, revealing a decent scar.

"Drop to your knees!" I command.

He doesn't. Instead, with a poker face, he makes a word with his lips.

"Boo."

Then he looks over my shoulder, past me.

"Drop to your—"

Then I realize he wasn't saying *Boo*.

He was saying *Boom*.

My phone buzzes in my pocket.

Behind me, a deep, thundering explosion. I turn to see the roof blowing off the house, a massive ball of orange and black, the sides of the house caving in.

The entire house, reduced to ash and rubble within five seconds.

I turn back. The suspect has started running again, turning into the thicket of trees and disappearing.

I look back and forth, then holster my weapon and start running back to the house.

CHAPTER 5

I BAT away tree branches and stumble over a hole along the path as black smoke fills the sky. I feel the searing heat before I reach the clearing.

When I push through the final branches into the backyard, I'm hit with an oven blast of heat and dark soot and dust. I nearly stumble over a young African American girl lying in the grass, facedown, wearing a T-shirt and shorts.

"Bridget?" I bend down, touch her neck for a pulse. "Bridget Leone?"

She opens her eyes, nods, looks up at me.

I cover my mouth with my hand so I can breathe. "Are you okay? Can you move?"

She manages to nod, squint at me, cough.

Around the other side of the house, a state police trooper and a county sheriff's unit come running. I flag them down. Eventually, they see me through the smoke. "This is Bridget," I say, while my eyes whip back and forth for Carla. "Get her out of here!" But before I do, I lean into her ear. "Bridget, where's my partner?"

Still dazed, she shakes her head. She doesn't know.

The troopers gather her in their arms and rush her away from the blaze, the poisonous soot, the scalding heat.

"Suspect went through that clearing!" I shout to the sheriff's deputies, pointing. "I don't think he was armed, but I can't be sure! Go! And get the chopper on him! Go!"

I push them as I soldier forward, my mouth covered by the crook of my arm, taking quick, greedy breaths as I move forward. "Carla!" I shout. "Carla!" Each time breaking into a coughing spasm.

By now, more than a dozen officers are on the scene in their various uniforms. I grab two and yell, "There's a Chicago police detective here somewhere!"

Mini fires are scattered around the rubble, but the house was all brick and concrete, mostly stamping them out. The real problem is the air quality—beyond treacherous and making it almost impossible to see through the thick blanket of dust and soot.

What I can see: a house, leveled. Parts of a roof and walls scattered about. Utter wreckage. Carla could be anywhere.

"Carla!" I call out, and others join me, calling her name. Knowing without acknowledging it that if she was still inside the house, she has no chance. But the girl got away, so she probably did, too.

It gets darker by the second. I pull out my Maglite and shine it around. A rescue squad is spraying the remaining fires.

"Billy, you okay?"

I turn. Lanny Soscia, part of the SOS squad. "Can't find Carla!" I shout.

We look through the debris, pieces of roof, wall, furniture. I break into another coughing spasm. Someone hands me a gas mask.

Then I remember my phone, buzzing just before the

explosion. I check it; the call came from Carla. I press the button to call her back and look around.

Through the darkness, only a few feet to my right, a phone lights up.

"Over here!" I rush over, slide down. Carla is lying underneath a slab of concrete that covers her body up to her shoulders.

Her eyes are shut. She looks...she doesn't look...

"I'm here, kiddo, I'm here." Her face is painted soot black. I touch her neck and feel a faint pulse.

"Over here!" I yell. "Officer down! We need a medevac!"

Carla coughs, spraying blood, and opens her eyes. I put my hand over her face, trying to shield her as I lie down on the ground next to her. "You're gonna be fine," I lie.

Her eyes narrow, a smile without a smile.

Sosh runs up with several officers.

"We gotta get this thing off her," I say. I try to push on it. Heavy is an understatement, but all we need to do is raise it enough for someone else to pull her out.

"Should we be moving her?" Sosh asks, bent down.

He might be right. You don't move someone with suspected spinal injuries if you don't have to. "We can at least get this thing off her," I say. "Everyone at once; we can do it."

I bend down to Carla. "Put on this mask, Carla, so you don't have to breathe this shit."

I lower the mask to her face. In her weakened state, she manages to bat it away. "Tell Darryl...I love him and I'm...counting...counting on him now."

"*You* tell him," I say. "When you see him later."

Even in her dazed, battered condition, she manages to shoot me a knowing look. "Tell my baby...his mama loves him."

"He knows that," I say, choking up. "Samuel knows, but you're gonna tell him yourself, goddamn it!"

Officers scramble around us, trying to figure out how to remove this massive concrete wall off Carla's body.

She winces. "Did the girl…did…"

"The girl's fine," I tell her. "You saved her, Carla."

She closes her eyes.

"Put on the mask," I say, "and we'll get this thing off you."

Officers have placed tire jacks on each side of the concrete slab while the others prepare to move it.

Carla wets her lips and tries to speak. "Come… closer."

I get as close as I can, practically nose to nose on the grass. My hand wiping the soot from her face, caressing her cheek. "I'm here," I manage, hardly able to speak.

"You saved…my life," she whispers. "You…know that." She grimaces from the pain. Tears well up and fall sideways to the grass.

The concrete slab starts to lift, the tire jacks raising it off the ground and a dozen officers struggling to get purchase under it.

"You saved mine, too," I tell her, making my voice work. "That's what partners do. We stick together." I take her hand in mine. "We're always gonna stick together. You think I'm gonna let you off this easy? You and me, we're gonna retire together. You and me and Darryl, we're gonna sit in rocking chairs and tell war stories."

With the help of the tire jacks, the officers get enough momentum, pushing the concrete up to a ninety-degree angle and then toppling it over in the other direction.

Revealing an area of grass untouched by the soot. But covered with Carla's blood.

"That's better," Carla whispers, her eyes closed.

"Good," I say. "Medevac's on its way. Hang with me, kid. C'mon, hang with me."

She doesn't answer.

She doesn't open her eyes.

"Carla!" I shout.

"Carla," I whisper.

CHAPTER 6

DARRYL GRIFFIN sits in a chair, stoic, dazed, three hours after arriving at Our Lady of the Cross. His face is cast in shadow: the hallway lighting is weak, and there is no natural light, because we're in the basement.

The hospital's morgue.

"I just got her back," he whispers. "We were finally a family again."

After three years of being divorced, he means. Darryl and Carla reconciled after Carla got clean. He moved back into the house with Carla and their boy, Samuel, and Darryl's elderly mother. Carla had never looked happier than in these last few months.

I sit next to him, still buzzing, still in disbelief. "You're still a family," I say. "You still have Samuel. Carla told me to tell you she was counting on you."

Darryl leans forward, his head dropping into his rough hands, and bellows in pain. I place my hand on his back, but there's nothing more for me to do or say. He's been repeating this cycle the last few hours, crying himself to the point of exhaustion, then going cold and silent.

The door to the observation room opens. Samuel, who just turned eleven, steps out into the hallway and stops. He'd asked for some time alone with his mother. He was in there for thirty minutes. The only good news is that the injuries to Carla affected her from the shoulders down; her spine was broken, and she suffered massive internal injuries, but because she was lying on her back on the stainless steel bed, covered to her neck in sheets, all Samuel could see was his mother's unblemished face and peaceful expression.

Once in the hallway, he looks around as if he has no idea where he is, no idea what to do next. I walk over and put my arms around him. He doesn't hug back, doesn't move.

"Your mother is always your mother," I whisper. "All her love, all her hopes and dreams for you. They'll always be inside you, Sam."

For a heavy moment, he remains silent and still. Then he speaks, slowly, cautiously, warily, in a gravelly voice. "Was...she in...pain?"

"No, no, no," I say. "She never felt a thing."

I wish I could be sure of that. One of the paramedics told me that her spine probably snapped on impact, all feeling from the fracture down lost. But he might have been saying that for my comfort, just as I'm saying it for Samuel's.

"She saved a young girl's life," I whisper. "She's a hero."

His gangly little body starts to tremble.

His father comes over and takes over my position. "Let's go home," he says. It's well past midnight. I wave to one of the uniforms and tell him to get the family home safely.

"I'll be by in the morning," I say. I hug each of them, and then, because there's nothing else to do or say, I watch the two men in Carla's life limp down the hallway, shell-shocked. One phone call from me, and their lives have been turned upside down.

Detective Lanny Soscia walks over and leans against the wall, his eyes bloodshot. He holds up a phone and shows me the headline from the *Tribune*: POLICE RESCUE LEONE GIRL.

"You're famous," Sosh says without feeling.

I snap out of my trance. Darryl and Samuel are gone now. I got time of my own with Carla, too, and I have a feeling I'm going to be talking to her in my prayers for a very long time.

But for now, it's time to do my job. It's time to worry about the subheading beneath the headline: ABDUCTOR STILL AT LARGE.

"Let's go find this asshole," I say.

CHAPTER 7

SOSH AND I take the elevator up to the third floor of Our Lady, filled with cops from every jurisdiction involved in the abduction—the state police and the county sheriff, local cops and CPD. A measure of quiet falls over them as I walk down the hallway, respect for my fallen partner, some handshakes and back slaps out of condolence. Someone directs me to the door I'm looking for.

I see Sosh's partner, part of our Special Ops team, Detective Mat Rodriguez, standing outside Bridget's hospital room. "No sexual assault," he says. "No abuse of any kind."

That's good. Whatever Bridget went through, whatever terror and trauma she experienced, at least it didn't get that far.

"She was scooped off the street, thrown into a trunk, and driven to the home where you found her. The guy locked her in the basement, but he didn't hurt her. Didn't touch her. Gave her food and water. A bucket to piss in. He even put *makeup* on her, she said, and did her hair up fancy."

"Jesus."

"Yeah, I know, dolling her up. But he hadn't touched her yet, at least not in that way." Mat shakes his head. "She didn't move until he came down and put her in the back of that van. That's when you spotted him."

"He was moving her," I say. "That basement wasn't her final destination. He got her out of the city, took her to this unincorporated area, waited a couple days for everything to die down before he moved her in a different vehicle."

"Looks like that, yeah."

"Anything else, Mat?"

He makes a face. "In the van, during the chase? She was in an enclosed compartment in the back, but she heard him yelling to her. She said she couldn't make out most of what he was saying, but she heard him telling her to hum. He shouted that at her a couple of times, she said."

"He told her to...*hum*?"

Mat shrugs. "That's what she said."

"Okay, Mat." I push through the door into the hospital room. Bridget Leone, looking younger than her fifteen years, sleeps peacefully in a bed inclined at forty-five degrees, an IV in her arm, machines humming. By her side are her parents. Jackson Leone, the real estate developer, rises from his seat in a button-down shirt and jeans and expensive shoes. His wife, Martha, huddled over the bed holding her daughter's hand, notices me and gets up as well.

"I don't know how to thank you," says Jackson, shaking my hand. "Words can't convey—"

His wife wraps her arms around me and hisses an urgent "Thank you so much for bringing her back to us."

"I'm so sorry about your partner," Jackson says. "What can we do?"

I raise a shoulder. There's nothing he can do.

"I understand she had a little boy. Is there…we were thinking…could we set up something for him to help with college? Anything like that?"

I start to answer, feel the emotion returning. I nod and put a hand on his shoulder. "Something like that…would have meant a lot to Carla," I whisper.

Some more crying all around. When we get ourselves back together, we turn toward Bridget. Her eyes are half open now; she looks drugged but aware of us.

"I need to ask her a few questions," I say.

They nod and give me space. I force a smile and walk up to her. "Hi, Bridget."

She slowly blinks. "You're the one…that fou— found…"

"Yeah, that's me. Can you tell me about the man who took you?"

It comes in starts and stops. And it tracks with Mat's report in the hallway—the guy scooped her off the street and threw her in the trunk, drove her to that remote location, locked her up, but fed her, clothed her, put makeup on her, and washed and styled her hair. He wore a ski mask at all times except when he first abducted her, but that's not a problem—I saw his Howdy Doody face and won't ever forget it.

Then we get to the van.

"I was…tied up," she says. "My wrists and ankles. In the back. I couldn't see him or really…hear. It was bumpy."

Calling that path in the woods bumpy is like calling a hurricane breezy.

"Then we went up a little hill and stopped."

Right—the abandoned train crossing.

"I heard…" She swallows hard. Bridget's mother steps forward to give her some water through a straw. "Heard a train. Felt the…"

"You felt the vibration of the train coming."

She nods.

"What do you remember next?"

"He…called to me," she manages. "He told me…to hum."

"To hum? Like, hum a tune?"

She nods, finding a nonverbal response easier. We've been talking a good fifteen minutes now, and her energy is waning.

"So…then what?"

"I didn't know…y'know, what to do. But then I heard…someone shouting, 'Chicago police.'"

That was me, as Carla and I fanned out on either side of the van.

"And then?"

"Then the van…took off real quick. Like, we went real fast over that hill and kept going."

I give her a smile. "You're doing great. Can you tell me anything else you heard the man say?"

She shakes her head no. "When the van drove ov— over the hill—the, the tracks, I rolled toward the back of the van."

"The momentum carried you toward the back doors," I say. "Away from the cabin."

She nods. "I couldn't hear him then." She coughs, a deep, hacking cough, having inhaled some of that polluted air after the explosion.

I give her a minute while she finishes coughing and takes more water from her mom.

"Bridget," I say, "tell me again about humming. Tell me exactly what he said. Quote him."

She closes her eyes, recalling it, reprising it, taking a breath.

"'Hum! Can you hear me? Hum!'" A heavy blink of her eyes.

"And that was it."

"I...that was all I heard. That was wh——when the van started going fast and I rolled toward the...back doors." Her head drops on the pillow. I've used up her energy.

I look at Bridget's parents. They don't know any more than I do.

I look at Sosh, now in the room as well.

He told her to hum?

FIVE WEEKS LATER: MAY

MONDAY

CHAPTER 8

VERONICA TRIES to concentrate.

She hears: The hum of the car engine. A car horn. The screaming inside her head. *Please, God, don't let him hurt me, don't let him kill me*.

She feels: The bump over a pothole, the twist of the car as it rounds a corner. The sweat dripping from her forehead, though it never reaches her eyes.

She tastes: the knot of rope in her mouth, wrapped tightly around the back of her head.

She sees: nothing. Not since he made her put on the blindfold.

The stops and starts, the bumps and turns, subside after a while, blending into a smooth, even ride. She tries to calculate. No matter how hard her heart pounds, no matter the mounting terror, she tries to have some idea of the direction they're headed while she lies, hog-tied and blindfolded, in the trunk of the stranger's car.

She figures around forty, forty-five minutes. She figures he navigated the streets on the South Side and has now reached the highway. But she can't tell if he's taking the Kennedy or the Edens, whether he's headed north or south.

Veronica doesn't know why he's doing this or what he wants. She doesn't know who he is, couldn't see his face. All she knows is that the man showed up in her bedroom at about two o'clock on Monday morning, wearing a ski mask and holding a gun.

He put the gun against her forehead. He slowly moved his other hand under the bedsheet, put his hand between her legs. He didn't move his hand, didn't use his fingers in the way she feared he might. But he told her he could.

I can do anything to you I want, he said. *And I will, if you don't do what I say. I'll do whatever I want, and then I'll put a bullet through your brain.*

So be good, Veronica, and this will be over soon.

She estimates that another thirty minutes has passed. She hasn't been able to silence the screams in her head or calm the panic overtaking her ability to reason and calculate. She doesn't know which direction they traveled, and the mileage, at best, would be a big guess.

She could be anywhere in the greater Chicago area.

She hears much of the outside noise stop, the soft grind of machinery, the car slowing nearly to a stop.

A garage. The door lifting upward, the car entering.

The car stops. The engine dies. Footsteps. He's coming for her now. Her heart racing so fast she can't think, can't speak—

Bright light colors her blindfold.

"Well, hello there, Veronica," the man says. "I'm going to untie your ankles, so you can walk. Nod if you understand."

She nods.

"I'm going to get you out of the car and walk you

inside the house. I'm not going to hurt you as long as you cooperate. Nod if you understand."

She does.

"I still have my gun. Would you like to feel it against your head again?"

She shakes her head no.

"Would you like me to put my other hand where I put it before?"

No, she thinks, shaking her head.

"Do what I say, Veronica, and neither of those things will happen."

He pulls her out of the car. Her legs freed up now, she stands with difficulty, her knees nearly knocking together with fright. He pushes her forward, his hand on her shoulder. She walks, still blindfolded, taking tentative steps. He leads her up two steps and through a door. The smell of gasoline is replaced with the smell of microwaved food. A floor with linoleum. A kitchen.

She keeps walking, turning a corner, then her feet are on carpeting.

They stop. The stranger keeps a hand on her but seems to be tapping the wall. She hears a hydraulic hiss, feels a rush of air.

He pushes her forward. For an instant, she thinks he's pushing her into nothingness, to her death, but her feet make contact with a steel floor a half step down. She stumbles forward into glass, banging her cheek but keeping her balance.

"I should've mentioned: watch your step."

She hears the push of a button, then doors clicking shut. Then they plummet downward with another hiss.

An elevator.

The ride doesn't take long, what would normally pass as maybe a floor or two on a standard elevator. Then she hears the doors slide apart.

And feels the gun against her neck.

The man unties her hands. "Listen carefully, Veronica. I want you to keep this blindfold on for sixty seconds. I want you to count to sixty. I will be watching you. If you don't keep on that blindfold until the count of sixty, I will be very upset. You don't want me to be upset, do you?"

She shakes her head.

He pushes her out of the elevator. She catches her balance as, behind her, the doors snap shut. The elevator hums upward. Other, thicker doors close with a heavy thud.

She counts to sixty. Then she pulls down on her blindfold.

She looks around.

And screams.

CHAPTER 9

"FAR AS anyone knows, he's dead. Looks like a dead end." The patrol officer, a kid named Walden, drops the file on my desk.

I pick it back up and swat it against his chest. "Find him," I say. "And then you can tell me if it's a lead or a dead end."

"He's a homeless junkie sex offender, Billy. He's probably OD'd by now under some bridge. We've looked everywhere we can think."

"Look harder," I say. "Think harder."

"Detective, all I'm—"

"Or we can give this assignment to someone who gives a shit that a cop killer is still at large, sucking oxygen and living the life of Riley, while a decorated detective is six feet in the dirt. Is that what you're telling me, Walden? That you don't give a shit?"

"Hey, hey, hey. Hold on a sec. Lemme see that." Soscia reaches our desk and grabs the file from Walden, reads it over. "So what, some guy who sleeps under Lower Wacker thought he recognized a composite sketch of the offender, and now we're looking for everyone who sleeps under Lower Wacker? Which is about a hundred people, give or take, on any given night?"

"Yeah," I say, "and if you got a better lead, I'm all ears."

Sosh puts a hand on the patrolman's shoulder. "You're good, Walden. We'll take this one from here."

I watch Walden make his exit, then I turn on Sosh. "What the fuck?"

"What the fuck is you've got people chasing their tails," says Sosh. "The offender's in the wind, kid. The trail went cold." He holds out his hands, like *Forgive me for breathin'*. "We'll find him. We're looking everywhere we need to look. We've got every alert out known to man. He's gonna turn up. You know he will. But you're running yourself and everyone else ragged—"

"Harney!"

"—for over a month now. It's time to ease it up, Killer."

"I'll decide when it's time," I say.

"Harney!" comes a voice from behind us. "Jesus, am I still in charge around here or did I miss a memo?"

We both turn. Lieutenant Wizniewski is standing at his office door, having called my name twice.

"You're still in charge, Lew, last I checked," Sosh says. "Did you remember to wash the supe's car this week?"

"To be continued," I tell Sosh.

By the time I make it into the Wiz's office, he's back behind his chaotic desk. No unlit cigar for now; he's been chewing gum lately to keep his mouth otherwise occupied.

He gives me a big wide grin, a wedge of gum showing through his teeth.

"What are you so happy about?" I ask. "Did you get some new body spray?"

"Nah," he says.

"Have you done something different with your hair? Cuz I gotta tell you, Lew, you've never looked better."

He shakes his nearly bald head, his chubby face lighting up. "Okay, Harney. You done?"

"I don't want a new partner," I say.

"Didn't say you were getting one."

"Okay, then what?"

"Let me be the first to offer you congratulations," he says. "Once again, your hard work and excellent results have earned you commendations."

I make a point of looking behind me, above me.

"The fuck are you doing?"

"Looking for a knife," I say. "Or a guillotine."

"Relax. We're starting a new task force within SOS."

I make a face. "The whole point of Special Ops is that it's a special unit. Now we need a *super*-special crew?"

"Apparently. And you're gonna be running it."

I consider that. "I'm in the middle of something," I say.

"You're supposed to be in the middle of taking down the Imperial Gangster Nation," he says. "You know how many people the Nation's whacked just in the last month?"

"Six."

"Cor-*rect*," he says. "And we got cases on a grand total of none of 'em."

"We're close, Lew. You know that. Any day now—"

"Yeah, I know, Harney, but you know how this goes. Another shooting on the West Side, the press shits on the mayor, the mayor shits on the supe, the supe shits on me, and—"

"And I'm downhill of you."

He points at me. "That you are, my friend. The mayor wants to tell the public that we got a brand-new task force devoted to crushing the gangs, so the supe says we're gonna do it, and you're gonna run it. And that means your whole focus is on that. Your *whole* focus."

"Meaning I can't keep looking for Carla's killer," I say. "I can't do both at once."

"'Fraid not."

"The message being, we don't care if someone kills one of our own?"

"The message being, we have a massive multijurisdictional squad of coppers looking for that perv, and we're gonna find him. But you, Mr. Super Cop, we need on the Imperial Gangster Nation and one Jericho Hooper."

"I'll keep on the Nation and Jericho," I say. "But I'm gonna catch the perv, too."

The Wiz leans back in his chair, eyeing me, chewing like he's punishing his gum. His prominent forehead starts to glow. "See, you get a lot of rope, Harney," he says, smiling. "You got a huge save with that girl Bridget. And you lost your partner. But that rope don't go forever. You're being reassigned."

"I'm not taking it."

"I just said you are."

"Yeah, I heard you just fine. I'll do it after I catch the pervert."

"You'll do it now," he calls to me as I'm leaving his office.

CHAPTER 10

"THE HELL'S wrong with *you*?" Sosh is throwing on his sport jacket when I return to my desk.

"Just got my nuts clipped."

"Sorry for your troubles. We're riding with Winters on a search warrant. Come with."

"Pass." I look to my right, to an empty desk, a clear, polished wood surface. No photos of Samuel and Darryl. No leather work bag on the floor. No smart-ass remarks.

I could've been the one who went for Bridget in the basement. Carla could've chased the perp. She'd be alive right now, with her young son and her rekindled relationship with her ex. With her family, who needs her. I'd be the one in the dirt. The one without a spouse, without kids depending on me.

That one decision, that split-second division of responsibility. Whoever gets the wrong end of it: *Sorry for your troubles*.

"Billy, come with. Ride with us. Be good for you."

I snap out of my fog. I didn't realize Sosh was still standing there. He knows where my head is, staring over at Carla's desk. He's given me the speech a dozen times. *Ya never know. One of those things. Hazards of the job. She knew the risks. She'd want you to keep doing the job.*

"I'm good," I say.

"If I don't see you, come to the Hole tonight."

"Sure; see you there."

I head to the john and splash water on my face. I look in the mirror, then wish I hadn't. I think of Samuel, a great little kid whose whole life was Carla. All I can do is check on him. He seems to be doing relatively okay, especially with his dad back in the picture. But he's going to have to grow up a lot faster than he should.

All because some pervert likes to kidnap young girls and get his jollies.

That fucking perv, that smirk on his face as he mouthed *Boom* to me.

And I'm supposed to stop chasing him?

I punch the wall of the bathroom stall, because there's nothing else to hit, until my knuckles are bleeding. Then I take a deep breath and leave the john, having taught that stall a lesson it'll never forget.

My phone rings in my pocket. The call's from a cell phone with an 812 area code.

I recognize the code. The only person I know in Terre Haute could not possibly be calling me from a private number.

"Harney," I say into the phone.

"The fuck you doing?"

It's him. The deep, scratchy voice, the down-to-business lack of a greeting. It's Pop. My father, the convicted felon, residing for the rest of his life in the federal supermax penitentiary in Terre Haute, Indiana.

"What do you mean?" I say. "Where are you calling from?"

"Me? Oh, I'm sipping banana daiquiris in the Caymans. Where the fuck you think I am?"

Pop and I don't have, let's say, a warm relationship. I've made it clear that I don't want to talk to him again, and he's made it clear that he doesn't give one shit what I want.

He calls me once a week. I always know it's him by the caller ID from a restricted phone service operated by the BOP. At first, I just let it go to voice mail, so he'd take his allotted time and preach to me on whatever subject. And I'd listen to the voice mail. Despite everything—call it morbid curiosity or the mystery of familial bonds—I'd listen.

He called after Carla died, over a month ago. For some reason, I answered. Probably feeling sentimental after a tragedy. I don't know. But I answered the call. And I started bawling like a child. I hated the fact that I gave him that…that intimacy, that connection with me again.

"I mean the cell phone," I say. "What happened to the calling card?"

"Never mind that. Here's something you should know by now. It's better to work for yourself than someone else."

I pass by the Wiz's office. "Okay, well, thanks for those words to live by. Anything else? Should I take time to stop and smell the roses, too?"

"Always that attitude. All you kids, but mostly you."

"Yeah, I can't imagine why I'd have an attitude with you." The reservoir of hatred and anger starting to refill inside me. It doesn't take much.

"Take the promotion," he says. "Run your own task force."

I stop cold, halfway to my desk. Glance back at Wizniewski's office. It was only, what, fifteen minutes ago that the Wiz pitched me the assignment.

What the hell? How did he—how could he—

But before I manage to speak, he does.

"Trust me," he says. And the line goes dead.

CHAPTER 11

"HAVE A look around, Veronica, if you wish."

The stranger's voice crackles through a speaker that Veronica traces to the corner of the ceiling. She walks on shaky legs, taking small steps, afraid of anything and everything.

The room looks like a dressing area. A full-length standing mirror. A makeup table with cosmetics and a chair with a lavender cushion. Closet doors on one side. Looks like a small refrigerator, too, with cabinets above it.

And a chain bolted to the wall, connected to a pair of handcuffs.

It smells like bleach and disinfectant. Like someone scrubbed this room within an inch of its life.

She looks back at the spot from which she entered the room, blindfolded. It looks just like part of the wall, save for a slight parting in the woodwork that reveals two doors, now closed, that must slide apart for the elevator.

That's worth remembering, she decides, but she turns away so as not to signal her thoughts. Because there's a camera in the ceiling's corner, next to the speaker.

"You see the closets. Go ahead—you can open them."

She walks over, reaches for a handle, her hand trembling.

"For goodness' sake, Veronica, it's just a closet. No scary monsters, I promise."

No, she thinks, the only scary monster is the one talking to her right now.

She opens the closet door, sees a lengthy space inside.

Costumes, dangling from plastic hangers, spaced out evenly. Cheerleader outfits of various sizes—children's 11, 12, 13; adult 1, adult 2. Schoolgirl outfits, the white tops and plaid skirts and stockings—same variation of sizes. Pajama tops depicting female Disney heroines, also in the same sizes.

Below them, in a clear plastic box, underwear, children's panties, running the same gambit of sizes.

She stifles the urge to vomit.

"We'll need to find you something that fits, I realize. Keep going, Veronica. Go to the next room."

All she wants to do is collapse to the floor, squeeze her eyes shut, fall asleep, and wake up back home.

"Veronica!"

She jumps, turns, finds a sliding wooden door to the next room. She slides it open with caution, as if something might jump out at her.

A classroom. A chalkboard, erased clean, and chalk. Three rows of chairs and desks for the students. A teacher's desk. A yardstick.

A violent shudder races through her. The screams drown out everything else. She can't stop the tears.

"This, quite obviously, is the classroom. Please keep going."

Shaking so hard she can hardly keep her balance, her eyes clouded with tears, Veronica forces herself forward, to the next room. She slides the door open.

A bedroom. Murals on the walls, in purples and pinks and light greens, the stuff of fairy tales—princesses and wands and fairy dust and castles. A king-size bed with a hot pink duvet and a dozen pillows.

"Oh, my God," she whispers.

"*And of course a full bathroom attached,*" the voice squawks. There's a speaker in every room. And a camera in every room.

"*Now listen, Veronica. You may not have noticed, in the dressing room—there is a small fridge and a cabinet above it. There is some fresh milk inside. And in the cabinet, you'll find some bowls and plates and plastic spoons, a couple of boxes of cereal and power bars and granola bars. And a case of bottled water. There should be more than enough to sustain you for a week. But you should conserve it. Be smart.*"

Why? she wonders. What is he going to do to her for a week?

And what's he going to do *after* a week?

What is this place?

She thinks through the possibilities. None of them good.

She's seen the news. She and everyone else in Chicago read all about that girl, Bridget something, who was abducted in Hyde Park a month ago. One of a series of girls kidnapped around Chicago over the last year and a half.

That girl Bridget was rescued by the police, something else that was splashed all over the news. But the kidnapper got away.

And the other girls—was it four others or five?—have never been found.

Is she the next one?

Did they, like her, all come here?

"I can't be here," she says.

"I understand you're upset——"

"No, you *don't* understand! I can't be here! I *can't.*"

"Veronica, I'm afraid you don't have a choice. Now be a good——"

"I . . . never s-saw your face," she manages to say, trying to keep her voice even. "If you let me go, I could—couldn't identify you. I wouldn't say anything."

"I'm not worried about being identified, Veronica, but thank you for your concern."

Her head drops into her hands. She can't hold it back any longer, sobbing and trembling and gagging. Please let me fall asleep and wake up at home, she prays. Please let this be a nightmare.

"You don't understand!" she shouts through her hands, choking out the words through her sobs, quivering like jelly on the floor.

She hears a *click,* the speaker shutting off, and cries harder still.

She's going to die down here. She knows it. One way or the other.

The speaker clicks back on. She lifts her head.

"Okay, Veronica, explain this to me," the voice says. *"What don't I understand? Why can't you be down there?"*

CHAPTER 12

SOSH PUSHES me up on stage, if you can call it a stage—more like a corner of the bar with a light and a microphone and a speaker resting on top of an old crate so whoever's holding the mike can be seen from the other side of the bar. The Hole in the Wall, on Rockwell on the northwest side, has been a coppers' hangout since coppers bought it and started giving discounts to the boys and girls in blue. The open-mike thing has become something I do every night I'm here—which is most nights: a few minutes of stand-up, which people seem to enjoy or at least pretend to. But I haven't taken the stage since I lost my partner.

And everyone in the joint knows that, which is why the noise quickly simmers down to utter silence as I raise the mike. We're a family, and when one of ours goes down in the line of duty, we all show up. The entire force was at Carla's funeral, in full dress uniform, the honor-guard procession, the gun salute, the whole nine yards. People who'd never known Carla cried and hugged me and threw in some money for an informal fund for Samuel.

Usually when I take the mike, you'd better watch out if you're standing close by, because I'll start giving you shit. Your personality, your clothes, your wife, your life—nothing is off-limits. But the idea of humor right now...I'm not feeling it.

"Someone once told me your life is a book," I say. "Carla's book was about two things: her family and the job. She loved this job. She put everything into it. She went undercover and risked her life. She took on corruption and risked her life. She saved a young girl from a kidnapper...and lost her life.

"But if she were here right now..." My throat catches. I take a moment. "If she were here right now," my voice heavier now, full of gravel, "she'd tell me to shut the fuck up. She'd tell me to man up and go out every day and be the best cop I can be. There's no better way to honor her memory, boys and girls. Keep doing the job. Keep loving it. Even when—*especially* when—it doesn't love you back.

"Here's the thing," I say. "Carla went through some rough spots on the job, but she never quit, because she couldn't quit, because she loved this job. So her book? It was a good book. A great book. And like any great book, it felt like it ended too soon."

I raise my bottle. "To Carla Griffin, one of the best damn cops I ever knew."

The crowd, a hundred strong, responds to the toast. I step off the stage and shake hands with a few people, get a few slaps on the back. What I said was right. Carla would smack me if she thought I was wallowing in guilt or even sadness. *Get your head out of your ass,* she'd say, *and do the job*.

"That was nice." My twin sister, Patti, also a detective, fist-bumps me by the bar while she sips from a Jack and Diet. The low-carb thing is part of her weight-loss, body-is-a-temple transformation, which also includes marathon running, her body trim and hard as a rock.

"How are the Russians?" I ask. Patti caught a case of a Russian dissident, Dmitri something or other, found dead in his home. It made the news because the guy was a critic of the Putin regime, but Patti doesn't buy the international-conspiracy theory. Turns out her victim had a pretty colorful life, plenty of things that could've gotten him in trouble here in the States.

"Not getting much," she says, "other than compiling a freakin' encyclopedia of Russian mobsters in Chicago."

Wizniewski waddles past me, a cigar back in his mouth, though unlit. Winston Churchill without the courage or smarts. But probably better political instincts.

"I'll do it," I say to him as he passes.

He stops, turns back, processes that. Even removes his beloved cigar from his mouth. "By 'I'll do it,' you mean you'll accept an order from a superior officer?"

"I guess so."

"Well, Detective Harney." He brings a hand to his heart. "Never have I been so fuckin' *honored*."

CHAPTER 13

"I'LL HAVE one more. Nurse! One more, if you please."

The Hole has a 4:00 a.m. liquor license, but most of us don't stay nearly that long unless we have the next day off or at least the morning shift off. I don't have tomorrow off, and I don't have shifts anymore; SOS doesn't work like that.

But tonight's a night for drinking. I've been putting my head down and focusing on catching the pedophile who killed Carla. The last month's been a whirlwind like that, intentionally so. I haven't given myself time to think too hard about her.

Now, per orders, I'm off that assignment. I'm out of excuses. So the memories of my dead partner are hitting me head-on. And the last thing I feel like doing is going home, lying in bed, and remembering. Remembering how she saved my life. Remembering how hard she worked to get back on the force. Remembering how fiercely she loved that little boy.

Which is why I'd really like another bourbon, and I'm getting annoyed that I have to ask more than once.

"Jesus, did this place close up and nobody told me?"

A woman appears from behind the staff-only door. That's the bartender, but it's the first time tonight I'm really noticing her. The White Sox jersey tied at her navel, ponytail through her ball cap. Great eyes, big blue eyes. Red hair and blue eyes. I might be in love. I might be drunk. Her eyes are blue, if I didn't mention.

"Pardon me, miss," I say, faux polite. "Do you guys sell alcohol here?"

"I heard you," she says, grabbing a glass off the bar and dumping it in the washer. "I was giving you time to reconsider."

"Why would I reconsider?"

"Drinking can affect your decision making," she says, a wry poker face.

"You may be right," I say. "I can't decide."

She looks down, a broad smile. "Dudley Moore," she says. "*Arthur*."

"You're too young to know Dudley Moore. Shit, *I'm* too young."

"I'm old enough to recognize when someone's had enough to drink."

I try to focus on her. Athletic and youthful. But mature, too, more poised than I'd expect of someone her age, if I knew her age. If I could see clearly. I can see clearly now the rain is gone. It's possible I've had too much to drink.

"You're eighty-sixing me," I manage to say.

"I'm exercising my discretion to ensure the well-being of a patron." She slides a glass of water in front of me. "I'm sorry about your partner, by the way. That speech was very sweet."

I focus on her, best I can, through the fog. "You're new here."

"I've been working days," she says. "Just switched to nights for a couple weeks."

"For the pleasure of hanging out with drunk cops?"

"Oh, no, I got those during the day shift, too. No, it's for final exams," she says.

"Ah, you're a student. You're just a kid."

"Not that much of a kid. And I'm still eighty-sixing you."

I lean back, which is a bad idea, a wave of nausea passing over me. "You realize I have the power to arrest you," I say.

"I'd argue justification," she says. "Defense of another."

"You're saving me from myself."

"Something like that."

"You're a law student?"

"Guilty as charged."

I raise a finger. "I thought the first thing we were supposed to do is kill all the lawyers."

"Only if you want to suspend all constitutional protections and let the government take over. That was Shakespeare's point. Lawyers are the last guard against government oppression. It was a compliment."

I throw my hands down on the bar. "I can see I'm not going to win this argument. Or probably any argument with you. You're too smart for me."

"I'm just more sober."

"Then...have a drink with me."

"I'm on the job."

"Then quit!" I throw up my hands. "Throw caution to the wind."

She leans forward, as if to confide in me. "Don't take this the wrong way," she says, "but that sounds like a dramatic step for someone I don't know very well."

"Then you leave me no choice," I say. I get off the bar stool. "We must marry at once!"

She shields her face with her hand, starts laughing.

"I'd drop to a knee, but I'm not sure I'd get back up."

"That would be problematic, yes."

I turn and head for the door, my feet heavy as anchors. "Jilted and heartbroken," I say, "he has only his dignity...if that."

Something tells me I'm going to be embarrassed tomorrow.

TUESDAY

CHAPTER 14

"THE IMPERIAL Gangster Nation," I say to the conference room. "I shouldn't have to say more than that."

I don't. Everyone in this room knows the Nation. Biggest street gang in Chicago, these days around three thousand strong. Drugs, guns, prostitutes. Started on the West Side, Austin neighborhood, and gradually expanded east and south, taking turf away from other gangs. They don't ask nicely. They don't negotiate peace treaties. They go in hard and take what they want. And apparently they don't care who they kill in the process.

"And you all know this asshole." I point to the photograph at the top of a chart pinned to a wall of corkboard. Jericho Hooper, known by the humble moniker King Jericho to his troops. Just turned forty-three, Jericho has a long face with gray braids tight across his head. He dresses in long, flowing garb, like he's some kind of urban messiah, not a ruthless leader responsible for the deaths of over a hundred people at this point.

"Jericho didn't get where he is by being stupid," I say. "He's smart and he's cautious personally. Anyone talks, they get the full treatment—torture and death, for the informant and for his entire family. They've raped and butchered eighty-year-old grandmothers of snitches. They've burned down houses with the snitch's family still inside. So the best we can do is get a few scraps here and there from CIs." Confidential informants, I mean, but they are few and far between in the Nation. "And nobody, but nobody, will go on the record. He's gotten to people even in protective custody.

"So," I continue, "we decided to borrow from an old playbook. We're going Al Capone. We're going after his money." I point to Marsha Flager. "Detective Flager from Financial Crimes."

Marsha gets up, puts on her reading glasses. "The federal government used to estimate Jericho's net worth at twenty, twenty-five million," she says. "But our numbers say it's probably closer to fifty. Yeah," she agrees when someone whistles.

"He launders the cash. He does it in several ways. First, he runs cash through the businesses he owns, which have multiplied just over the last year. He owns three nightclubs, one strip club, and a string of laundromats, believe it or not." She looks at us over her glasses. "Cash-dominated businesses. They all have bank accounts. He pumps cash into them every day in small increments, well under the ten-thousand-dollar threshold—usually like four or five grand a day.

"He flips real estate with the money, too, so the transactions end up totally legal.

"Then there's the casinos. He or someone he trusts takes large sums of cash to two different casinos that we know of. They cash it in for chips, gamble, win some, lose some—whatever—and then cash in their chips at the end of the night, washed clean."

She walks over to the corkboard wall and the chart

showing Jericho's holdings and people. She points to a photo of a young African American man, caught on camera on the street, staring vacantly forward.

"This is the man who makes it happen for him," she says. "His name is Mason Tracy. Age twenty. A child prodigy, they say. He dropped out of high school his junior year, by which time he was so advanced in mathematics that nobody in the school could teach him; they had to send him to UIC, where he was taking graduate and PhD-level courses in"—she reads from her sheet—"differential equations, nonlinear dynamics, and advanced algorithms."

"I don't even know what that means," I say.

"None of us does." Marsha shakes her head. "Anyway, this kid grew up poor, dirt poor, living with his mother and his younger sister. His mother died three years ago, when Mason was seventeen. He and his sister were orphans."

"Enter Jericho Hooper," I say.

"Enter Jericho Hooper. He takes Mason under his wing. Even though Mason has scholarship offers coming out of the woodwork, he drops out of school and starts working for Jericho. He's a numbers savant. He helps Mason diagram a web of financial transactions that are so complex that the money's untraceable. The guy doesn't even have a high school diploma, but he's got more smarts than a NASA engineer. I mean, this kid should be a code breaker for the NSA, but instead he's advising a criminal warlord."

"If he's so good," says Sosh, who's on our team, "how do we bust Jericho?"

"Good old-fashioned police work," she says. "We have a guy on the inside."

The guy on the inside is Ronnie Lester, who's worked undercover for us going on four years inside the Nation organization. But Ronnie's not here, and his name won't be mentioned. Not even Marsha knows his identity.

"Our guy," I say, taking over again, "has been trusted enough that he's doing the money runs. He's depositing drug money into the banks for the small deposits. He's taking the drug money to the casinos. And he knows Mason, too. He can testify on personal knowledge to the money laundering.

"Combine that," I say, "with grand-jury subpoenas we've served on the banks without notice to Jericho, and we go a very long way toward showing that the money he's depositing into those accounts didn't come from legitimate businesses."

I take a moment with that. "Guys, if we get something solid on Jericho, the whole game opens up. Nobody wants to talk because of Jericho's wrath. But if we show them there's blood in the water—if we show them the King is dead—people won't be afraid anymore. We can take down this whole freakin' organization, domino by domino, if we can get King Jericho."

I clap my hands. "So that's exactly what we're gonna do. This is the first step. And we do it today. Let's go arrest some bad guys."

CHAPTER 15

"WE'RE GONNA hit 'em at the same time," I tell the room. "One crew grabs Jericho; one takes the boy wonder, Mason Tracy. Soscia will take the lead on Jericho." I nod toward Marsha. "Flager and I will lead on Mason."

Against my better judgment, I glance at Sosh, who's wearing a smirk. I know what he's thinking. I've heard his side-of-the-mouth comments about Marsha all day. *Looks like she's been taking care of herself. She's laughing pretty hard at your jokes. You know she's divorced now, right?*

He edges toward me as the team breaks up, ready to move.

"Don't even," I say.

"No, I think it's a wise division of responsibility," he says, deadpan. "Marsha can watch your back, and you can watch hers."

Here's the thing: Marsha and I, back in the day, before either of us was married, went a few rounds. Sweaty, greedy sex but not much else. Went our separate ways when she was reassigned. Some fun, no hard feelings.

We both got married, then she left the street altogether once she started having babies, deciding to put her finance degree to use and mostly sit behind a desk in Financial Crimes.

So yeah, I'm a widower now and she's divorced. But that's not why I'm taking her with me. I'm taking her with me to arrest Mason because Mason is the key to all this. Yeah, King Jericho's the guy we want, but he would never keep anything incriminating in his house. He's way too cautious. He doesn't even use a cell phone. His communications are old-school Mafia—whispers in his ear, nods of his head.

But Mason? If we're taking down Jericho on money laundering, Mason is how we get there. He'll have the data, the records, the incriminating information. And Marsha's the financial expert. She'll know what to target in the search.

Mason will be the bookkeeper to Jericho's Al Capone. The child prodigy will take down the King.

But I'm not getting into it with Sosh. It will only encourage him. Somewhere along the line he appointed himself as my life coach, and now he seems determined to put Marsha and me together.

"Go get the King," I tell Sosh. "Try not to fuck it up."

Marsha and Mat Rodriguez ride with me, a patrol unit following. Mason Tracy lives out west in the Austin neighborhood, where Jericho used to live and where the Imperial Gangster Nation was born. It's a decent ride from our headquarters, on Pulaski.

"Pretty geared up to arrest a math nerd," Marsha says.

"You never know." Which is true. Mason Tracy doesn't have a FOID card or a concealed-carry permit, so at least officially, he doesn't own a firearm. And from everything we've looked at, this guy is harmless, a bespectacled, introverted genius.

But you never know until you're knocking on the door. Or busting through it.

I curb the unmarked car on Thomas, around the corner from Mason's house. The area is crowded, mostly mothers pushing strollers, enjoying the late spring. We walk down Leclaire, a sunlit street of brick walk-ups. Mason lives halfway down the block on the bottom floor of a two-story building.

The patrol unit drives down the alley to the rear of Mason's building. "Mat," I say, "take the alley, wouldja? Just so none of those uniforms gets an itchy finger. We need the boy wonder alive."

So it's Marsha and me in the front. We pass through the gate and take the concrete stairs up to the porch. I press the button labeled TRACY and wait.

It takes so long that I reach for the buzzer a second time before a voice comes through the speaker. *"Yes?"*

"Mason Tracy, we're Chicago police detectives. We'd like to speak with you."

A pause. Then, *"Why?"*

"Open the door, please, Mr. Tracy. We have a warrant to search the premises."

"But…why?"

"Mr. Tracy, we have the right to use forcible entry. I'd rather you open the door and let us in. None of us wants your door busted down."

"Um…o-okay…hang on."

"Mat," I say, turning my back to the door and speaking into my collar, "heads up in the alley."

"Roger that."

I look at Marsha. "This more fun than reading financial statements?"

She smirks, but she's keyed up, sensing the tension. She leans forward, bangs on the front door. Shakes her head.

"Let's force it," I say, stepping back. We can give this

guy a second to put on his shorts or turn off the stove before reaching the door, but anything more than that and the possibility of evidence destruction, or his going for a weapon, is too high.

"Back door, back door," Mat calls into our radios. *"Mr. Tracy—"*

Marsha and I are already off the porch, fanning out to the north and south sides of the building. I take the north side as Mat's commands buzz in my ear.

"Police—don't move!"

"Hands where we can see them—"

"Coming your way, Billy, coming your way!"

Bounding around the corner, heading squarely toward me, a young African American man in a cotton undershirt and cargo pants.

"Don't move, Mason!" I shout, my hand out, but not my gun.

He stops when he sees me, looks back as Mat Rodriguez comes around the corner with a couple of uniforms. I have my hands out now, for both Mason and Rodriguez.

"Mason, we have a warrant for your arrest. Let's do this nice and easy."

"No," he says, looking away, shaking his head, squeezing his eyes shut like he's trying to shut out the noise. "Not now! You can't do this now!"

We close in on him from both sides.

"No! No!" he shouts. "Not now!"

"It's okay, Mason. I'm going to take you into cus—"

"No!" he says, less of an objection and more a plea. "Not...not now."

"Mason, c'mon. Make this easy on yourself. Easy, now."

His head turned away, as if considering. His right hand dangling out from his body.

Then he reaches into his pants pocket, fixing on something.

"Don't move!" I shout, drawing my Glock. "Do not move that hand or I will shoot!"

Rodriguez and the uniforms yelling as well. Behind me, Marsha has come around from the other side, shouting the same stuff at Mason: *Freeze! Don't move! Show us your hands!*

Through the chaos, Mason, barely twenty and looking more like a young teenager, seems entirely lost in his own thoughts, his breathing escalating, his own personal horror show inside his head.

"Wait a second!" he shouts.

My heart pounding now as his right hand inches upward from the pocket.

"Mason, don't do it! Do not move!"

"Hold on a second!" Mason shouts, still not looking at us, staring into the brick wall of the building. "Hold on!"

His hand starts upward again, out of his pocket.

I'm not gonna shoot an unarmed kid.

Unless he's armed.

I holster my weapon and break into a full sprint as Mason's hand comes free of his pocket.

CHAPTER 16

I BARREL into Mason like a middle linebacker but focus on his right forearm and hand, falling on top of him while disabling his right arm. We land hard, Mason grunting with the pain both from hitting pavement and landing awkwardly, his right arm extended out.

A phone, I see immediately, lying in the grass next to the pavement. He pulled out a damn cell phone.

Rodriguez cuffs Mason and searches his person. I walk over and pick up his phone, the postaction adrenaline overtaking me.

After the pat-down, Rodriguez stands Mason up.

"You know how close you came to getting shot?" I yell at him. "Over a *phone*?"

"I need that phone. I need…you can't…I can't…" Mason shakes his head, looking at the ground, his voice shaking. "No," he pleads. "No!"

"You're under arrest, Mason, for money laundering and conspiracy to commit money laundering."

"Money—no! No, you…you don't under—understand…"

"The best move you can make is to cooperate with us, Mason."

Rodriguez Mirandizes him while I put my hands on my knees, replaying it, thinking how close five cops came to shooting an unarmed kid.

The uniforms walk Mason to the squad car in the alley while Mason screams and complains about his phone and shouts varying refrains of *No, not now, you can't.*

"Another satisfied customer." Marsha smacks me on the arm. "That's the most excitement I've had in years."

I call Sosh on my cell. "His Highness, King Jericho Hooper, is on his way to the station right now," he tells me.

"He won't talk," I say. "Maybe Mason will. I'm gonna stick around for a little bit of the search here. Hang tight and I'll be there in an hour."

"So let's do it," Marsha says. "Let's see what Mason has for us."

The actual search doesn't take as long as you might think. This isn't a crime scene, so we don't need Forensic Services for prints or fiber collections. We just want information. Our search warrant gives us broad authority, and we always err on the side of inclusion. Mason has a laptop computer. That's automatic; the uniforms wrap it up while Marsha inventories it on the receipt. After she takes about five minutes reviewing a large file cabinet in the corner of Mason's office area, she nods and tells the uniforms to take the whole cabinet.

We check for loose floorboards, hidden compartments in the walls, false-bottom drawers, but find no indication he was hiding anything anywhere.

There is one bedroom with two beds, neat and orderly to a fault, as if someone with a type A personality tidied it up. Several prescription bottles rest on a nightstand between the beds, lined up perfectly. "Photograph the drugs and log them, but leave them here," I tell a uniform. "If he needs them, he'll tell us."

The uniforms put everything into a police truck parked in the alley behind Mason's house. We lock the house up behind us and walk around to the front.

"Think we'll get Mason to talk?" Marsha asks.

"Dunno. He seemed pretty spooked. That can work both ways. Is he, like, autistic or something?"

"Not that I know of," she says. "He wouldn't make eye contact. But the situation wasn't exactly normal."

"Well, let's see what he's willing to tell us. And after you get through his computers and files and see how much evidence we have, his tongue will loosen even more."

She rubs her hands together. "Can't wait to get my hands on 'em."

We make it to Thomas, where our car is parked. I glance to my left, where someone is walking on the sidewalk, heading east toward us. White guy, baseball cap, long-sleeved shirt and jeans.

I do a double take and stop. Look back again at the man.

His head is down, earphones in, passing a woman pushing a stroller.

No. It...no.

His hair, peeking out from under his hat, is dark as ink. And his ears aren't sticking out. No scar, either. So...no.

But the long neck. The slope to his shoulders. You can change your hair color. You can surgically cover a scar and even pin back your ears. But the neck and shoulders...they don't change.

"No way," I mumble, brushing my hand against my holster, my pulse ratcheting up.

The man walks out from under the shadow of a tree,

nearly reaching Leclaire, opposite side of the street from us. Then his eyes trail up to meet mine.

He stops, does a double take of his own. Making me. Recognizing me.

"What—what's up?" Marsha asks, just noticing that I'd stopped.

I can't believe I'm saying it.

"That's the guy who killed Carla," I whisper.

The man turns and breaks into a sprint.

CHAPTER 17

"GET THE car!" I yell to Marsha as I run after the suspect.

He has over half a block on me, but he couldn't run as fast as I could last time, and he can't now, either.

"All units, all units!" Marsha's voice in stereo, shouting only a few yards from me but also crackling through my radio. "Plainclothes detective in pursuit of a homicide suspect on foot. Heading west on Thomas Street past Leclaire. Suspect is on foot, Caucasian, blue baseball cap."

The man runs along the sidewalk on Thomas, heading west, then turns left, heading south down Leamington. Smart move, I realize as I reach the corner, because the street's one-way north, making it hard for Marsha to pursue by car.

As I close the distance, running all-out with my weapon holstered, the suspect crosses over diagonally to the opposite side, the west side of the street, an oncoming car screeching to a halt and blaring its horn. I cross in front of the car, trying to keep the suspect in my line of sight.

Once on the other side of Leamington, he turns right between two houses and disappears. I call it into my collar, not knowing the name of the next street over.

I reach the two houses he split when he turned, drawing my weapon for the possibility of an ambush. The space between the houses is empty, a thin walkway and grass on each side. It ends in an alley between the two streets.

As I race toward the alley, I hear shouting—a woman's, then a man's, then a scream.

I reach the alley, weapon up, and pivot to my right.

A woman flies backward from an SUV, falling into an open garage as the SUV's driver's-side door slams shut. "My kids are in there! My kids!" she screams as the SUV's tires burn rubber, gaining purchase to motor forward.

I drop to a knee and fire at the rear right tire—one, two, three shots—until the tire blows out with a loud, hissing pop. The SUV, in the midst of acceleration, fishtails to the right, exposing the rear left tire—close to the screaming mother, but my only choice. I aim and fire four times and blow out the second of the rear tires.

The SUV, disabled and rear-heavy, tries to accelerate, the hubcaps scraping up sparks on the alley's asphalt, but it's not going to make it. It stops only a few houses down from the place where it started. I'm already coming around to the driver's side, seeing a flash of the suspect as he jumps out of the passenger's side and into a passageway between two houses facing the next street over.

But I can't get to him. The SUV is blocking the space between the two houses.

"Flager, he's heading to the next street west of Leamington, halfway down the block."

"Got it."

As the woman rushes to the SUV and opens the rear passenger door to two young kids in car seats, I move past her, climb onto the hood of the SUV, then spider-walk up the front windshield and onto the roof.

Below and in front of me, the suspect has stopped halfway down the passageway between the two houses, having reached a large wooden fence blocking his progress. There's a door, but it's locked. It's too tall to hurdle, nothing to grab on to to help him climb over.

He's cornered.

Careful with my weapon, I jump off the SUV's roof onto the pavement in the passageway. Land in a squat. Pop to my feet. Aim my Glock at the suspect.

Don't move, I'm supposed to say. *Hands behind your head. Slowly turn around and drop to your knees.*

I say none of those things to the man who killed Carla.

He senses me even before he turns. Shakes his head. Turns around and faces me. Shows me his hands, waves them like jazz hands. Smirks at me.

The asshole is smirking at me.

Peeking up from his waistband as his shirt lifts, a revolver.

Hands behind your head, drop to your knees.

But I don't say that. I don't say anything. I just look at the revolver at his waistband.

After a moment, he follows my line of sight to his weapon. A weapon he could probably pull out on a count of one, two, three. Then he looks back up at me again.

I lower my weapon to my side and nod to the man who killed an eleven-year-old's mother.

"I don't have him!" Marsha calls through my radio. *"Do you?"*

"Unit 15-12 responding."

"Unit 15-8 responding."

With my left hand, I lower the volume on the radio. No more Marsha. No more responding patrols.

Just me and the man who killed my partner, one of the best people I ever knew.

"Here's your chance," I say.

It's a fair deal, and he gets it. I can't shoot him unless he draws on me. And I really, really want to shoot him.

But he gets a chance, too. If he's the better man, he puts me down and still has a chance to escape. What's the downside? He's already a cop killer, already looking at a life sentence. What's killing a second cop going to get him that he won't already get?

His hands poised out in front of him, his body coiled, his eyes intense.

"Now or never," I say.

He pauses, looks down and up.

Then his shoulders relax. He gives me a broad grin. Drops to his knees. "I surrender, Officer!" he shouts, his arms extended upward. "I surrender!"

I shuffle toward him, ready for him to make a move. "Lace your hands together behind your head," I say.

"Yes, sir!" He complies, elbows out.

I reach him, remove the gun from his waistband, and kick him in the stomach.

He doubles over, wheezing, falling face-first to the pavement. I put my knee on his back and cuff him. "Get up, asshole," I say. I pull him to his feet as he begins to catch his breath again.

"You're a cop killer," I say. "The prison guards are gonna love you. And you're a pedophile, so you're gonna have a lot of friends in general pop, too."

He makes a noise, something that sounds like a low giggle. He turns his head to the side to glance back at me.

"We'll see," he says.

CHAPTER 18

INTERVIEW ROOM 3, less than an hour later. I walk in and close the door behind me.

"I want a lawyer," he says.

"And I want a Maserati," I say. "Looks like we're both gonna have to wait. What's your name, guy?"

He smirks. Again.

I pull his wallet out of my back pocket. The wallet is a bright purple job with a white star. It looks like a wallet more appropriate for a teenage girl.

"Donnie Delahunt," I say. "Two busts for child indecency, but charges dropped both times. How the hell'd you pull that off?"

I walk over to him. He's in a chair, locked to a table. His beady eyes, narrow face, scumbag expression.

I lean in close to him, look him over. "You clean up good," I say. "Dyed your hair. Plastic surgery. Some skin grafts on that scar." He recoils, turns his head as I touch the place where he had a scar on his cheek. "And those big ears of yours that stuck out, now pinned back against your head." I look behind his ear, see fresh surgical scars.

I handle his ear, and he howls in pain. "That hurt, Donnie?" I reach around with my other hand and grip both ears and yank down hard. He screams like a wounded animal.

He writhes and groans in his chair, unable to move much with the shackles on his wrists, bolted down to the table.

"Who did your surgery?" I ask. "Just curious. I was thinking of having my chin done."

He eventually recovers. "I want…a lawyer," he snarls.

"Yeah, I heard you the first time." I sit down on the table. "I should've shot you, you piece of shit. You killed my partner. But you pussed out. You had the chance to go one-on-one with me, and you chickened out. You're a real tough guy with young girls, but not so much with adults who can fight back. Hey, I'm talking to you."

I grab his face and turn it toward me. His face pinched between my hands, his lips pursed, he manages only, "I don't gotta say nothin'."

"That's true, Donnie, you don't gotta," I say, nose to nose with him now. "But understand something. You killed one of our own. There's not a single cop out there that will give a rat's ass if I work you over in here. I'll say you fell down the stairs on the way to processing. Or I'll make up some story about how you got banged up on the street when I chased you. Or you resisted. We'll reshoot the booking photo. Cops'll be getting in line to back up my story over yours."

I watch the fear grow in his eyes. He believes me. He shouldn't. It's been known to happen, of course, but beating up suspects was never my thing. It wasn't Carla's, either, and as much as I'd like to pulverize this guy, Carla wouldn't approve.

But Donnie Delahunt doesn't know that.

"You have one chance to avoid a beatdown," I say. "You need to answer me one question."

He shuts his eyes, but he's thinking about it.

"That house where we caught you, that you blew up, was temporary, a holding station," I say. "Where was the final destination?"

He slowly shakes his head, wincing, ready for my punch or slap.

"I'm getting that information one way or the other, Donnie," I say. "It's just a matter of time. You have a burner phone. You probably think it can't be traced, right? But you're wrong. Every phone, even a burner, has an ID number. It's called an IMSI. I'm going to pull the cell-tower records and find out where your phone's been. You think I won't figure out where you've been stowing away those girls? I will. You gonna piss me off and make me wait a week to get those records? Or you gonna tell me right now and save yourself a trip to the emergency room?"

CHAPTER 19

SOSH AND Marsha Flager are standing outside the room when I come out. Sosh gives me a high five and pulls me into a half hug. "You did it," he whispers. "You did your partner proud, brother."

Sosh is kind of a softie deep down. Carla wasn't his partner, but we did plenty of work together, and he took her loss almost as hard as I did.

"I mobilized all my skills as a police detective," I say.

A multijurisdictional task force, over two dozen cops chasing leads all over the state and the Midwest, trying in vain to locate this creep, and Donnie Delahunt practically walks right up to me on the street.

"Better to be lucky than good," Sosh says. "He give you anything in there?"

I shake my head no. "I tried to spook him, but he called my bluff. Marsh, how quickly can we get our hands on Delahunt's phone records from that burner?"

"A week, give or take."

"Okay, let's get on that, can we?" I clap my hands. "So where are we on our friends with the Imperial Gangster Nation?"

"Jericho Hooper's lawyered up, like we figured. He's got a fancy lawyer—"

"Elan Tenenbaum," I say.

"You know him?"

"Yeah, we've worked together a bit."

"Anyway," says Sosh, "he's representing both Jericho and Mason Tracy."

I was afraid of that. "So Mason won't talk, either."

"Actually, the lawyer says he wants to make a deal."

"A deal with Mason Tracy?" Marsha says. "He can walk us through this whole thing. We make a deal with Mason, Jericho's toast."

This thing could be wrapped up that easily? "Lead the way," I tell Sosh.

CHAPTER 20

MASON TRACY is just down the hall from the interview room holding Donnie Delahunt.

"Detective Harney!" Elan Tenenbaum is looking sleek as always, an alpha male in Armani attire, the baritone voice, the ego. A pink tie perfectly knotted, a striped shirt, and a thousand-dollar gray suit, dark hair combed back.

"Hey, Elan." We shake hands, and I introduce him to Marsha, who comes along with Sosh. "Your client's in a lot of trouble," I add.

His eyebrows arch. "Money laundering? What is this, Al Capone?"

"Remind me," I say. "Didn't Capone spend the rest of his life in prison?"

Tenenbaum beams. "He didn't have me for a lawyer."

"So what's the deal here, Elan?"

I look behind him. Mason Tracy is not locked down, because he's not that kind of risk. But he's handcuffed. He is looking down at the table, rocking back and forth, mumbling to himself. Looking very concerned.

"My client wants his phone," he says. "Five minutes."

"I want to be six five and throw a ninety-five-mile-an-hour fastball," I say. "But I'd like it for five years."

"Well, only one of those things can happen."

"That phone is the subject of a search warrant," I say. "I can hold it for thirty days. And if we determine that it's evidence—which we will—we can hold it indefinitely."

"I'm aware of your rights." Tenenbaum doesn't hide his opinion of them, either.

"And what do I get in exchange? He pleads guilty?"

"Please, Detective." He smirks. Everyone's smirking at me today. "He'll give you the password to his computer," he says.

"We don't need the password," Marsha says. "We can get in."

"My client says that isn't so."

"We'll take our chances," I say.

"My client…" Tenenbaum lifts a shoulder. "He's not a neophyte. If he says you won't be able to get into his computer, I'd believe him."

I look at Marsha, think it over. "Tell you what," I say. "Your client wants to make a phone call on that phone of his, I'll let him. Under supervision."

"That's ridiculous."

"It's not, Counselor. He doesn't have a privilege except with you. Anyone else he's calling, we have the right to listen. You let us listen, we have a deal."

Tenenbaum glances back at his client, mulls it over. "What if it's not a phone call?"

"He—oh." That makes more sense, now that I think about it. If all he wanted to do was make a phone call, he could use a landline here at headquarters.

"Last I checked," I say, "there's no constitutional right to an email."

"I didn't know we were talking about constitutional rights. I thought we were making a deal."

And, he could have added, he never said it was an email. Who knows why Mason wants to use that phone?

"Give us the passcode to the iPhone," Marsha says.

That's a good idea. Our people can hack into computers. But getting into an iPhone without the passcode when it's not yours? Probably beyond our capacity. It would take a court fight, and we'd probably lose.

"I'd take that deal," I say.

Tenenbaum says, "Give me thirty seconds with my client, if you could."

We step outside, close the door.

"What's he want with his phone?" I whisper to Marsha.

She shrugs. "Could be anything. I'm not keen on letting him. But if he gives up the passcode and we can access his iPhone, it'll be worth it."

We pop back in.

"My client," says Tenenbaum, "is not willing to give you the passcode to his phone. But he assures me that giving you his computer password is something of real value."

"Great," I say. "So we have the assurance of someone who's been laundering drug money for a brutal gang leader."

"Give us a couple days," Marsha says. "If my people can't get inside his computer by then, we'll rethink your offer."

Tenenbaum pauses. "Unfortunately, time is of the ess—"

"I need it now. I need it now. Now." Mason, his eyes shut, is rocking so hard it looks like he might fall out of his chair.

Tenenbaum gestures to his client. "So there's that."

"Can't help you, Elan," I say. "Not unless your client

gives me more than a computer passcode." I direct the line to Mason, not his lawyer.

Mason stops his rocking, turns his head in my direction. Still no eye contact. But listening.

"He agrees to walk us through how he laundered the money," I say. "I guarantee I can get an ASA to give your client immunity if he does that."

"No chance," says Tenenbaum.

But his client, Mason, is nodding.

"Two, three hours, probably all it will take for him to walk us through the basics," I say. "He never serves a day in prison, and he gets his phone back before dinner."

"Okay," says Mason.

"No chance," says his lawyer.

I look back and forth between them. "Is that your client sitting over there you're representing, Elan? Or is it your other client down the hall, Jericho?"

"We're done," says Tenenbaum. He waves his hands: show's over.

"You sure you don't have a conflict of interest, Counselor?"

"We. Are. Done." Tenenbaum angles himself to block my view of his client.

"Sounds like your client likes my offer."

"It's not for you to decide. I need to speak with my client alone. This conversation is over."

"No," says Mason.

"Please leave, Detectives. I have the right to speak with my client in private."

"Unless he fires you, which he can do," I say to Mason more than Tenenbaum.

"Please leave now!"

"Unless he fires you," I say as loud as I can, "I guess we have no choice."

We step out. I really *don't* have a choice, and

Tenenbaum is a topflight defense attorney. He'll make hay out of anything that happens in here.

"Maybe Mason *will* fire him," says Marsha once we're outside.

"Don't count on it. Jericho Hooper is Tenenbaum's golden goose. He won't let Mason say anything to hurt the King."

"His phone records are no help," she says. We already got Mason's records from the phone company, courtesy of a grand jury subpoena. "His text messages didn't tell us anything. We know who he's called but not what anyone said."

I shake my head. "I don't think it's an electronic communication. It's something else. Something else on his phone."

I look at the door, wishing I could go back in.

"I just don't know what," I say.

CHAPTER 21

"THIS IS a bad idea," I tell Pete Parsons, the assistant state's attorney. "This could kill our case."

"No choice," Pete says. "Nan is insisting. We don't do it, she'll shove it up our ass at the arraignment tomorrow."

"Oh, c'mon. The judge won't let Delahunt out. We've got my ID. He's accused of killing a cop and of child abduction. He won't get bond."

Pete grimaces. "Suddenly you're an expert on bond? Listen, Nan is one of the best defense lawyers around—"

"He's completely changed his appearance," I say. "The scar, the ears, the hair color."

"Didn't stop you from ID'ing him, did it, Billy?"

"Well…" He's got me on that, I guess.

"It won't stop Bridget, either," he says. "Besides, most of the time, he wore a mask. She only saw his face when he scooped her off the street, right?"

"Yeah. That's what she said."

"Okay, so—if she can't ID him, it's not fatal." He drives a finger into my chest. "But what *could* be fatal, at least for the arraignment, is if Nan gets up there and says she demanded a lineup and we refused it. Trust me, Detective, we do not want to start this case by looking like we're hiding something. Now let's go." He opens the door. "It's happening."

Outside the interview room where Pete and I were debating, Delahunt's lawyer is looking at her phone. Nancy Carpenter is wearing a pin-striped blue suit and heels, blond hair pulled back in a bun. She cross-examined me once. She was good. I had a solid case on the defendant, but she managed to isolate a few details and harped on them like they were the only things that mattered. Kept her cool the whole time, too.

"Ready, boys?" she says without looking up.

"Let's do it," says Pete.

"And have we had conversations with the victim, gentlemen?" she asks as we walk.

"I notified the Leone family that we had a suspect in custody," I say.

"And that's all?"

"You mean did I tell Bridget that he'd look completely different when she saw him this time? Did I tell her that your scumbag client clipped his ears back and covered up his scar and dyed his hair? No, Counselor, I did not."

"You didn't tell *Bridget*. What about her family? Did you tell *them*?"

"Hey," I say, and stop walking. She stops, too. "I wasn't playing word games with you. I don't do that. That's *your* job. You look for any technicality to free low-life pedophiles and cop killers. You play with words. I do not."

"Okay, okay," says Pete.

I step closer to Nancy Carpenter. "I did not tell Bridget *or* her family that your client changed his appearance. This lineup is totally unfair, and you know it. It has nothing to do with truth or with justice. It's all about you trying to gain an edge. So that's your job, and fine, whatever. But lady, do not ever speak to me like you're wearing the white hat here. Your client killed a good cop with a young son. If I could bring back the death penalty in Illinois, I would. Just for this case. That's what this guy deserves. He preyed on young girls, and then when it looked like he was gonna get caught, he didn't hesitate to try to kill that girl and the cop who rescued her. So go ahead, with your fancy suit and expensive briefcase, and do your job, but get off your fucking high horse."

Carpenter isn't moved in the slightest by what I'm saying. She must tell herself what defense lawyers tell themselves all the time—they're defending the Constitution, the guardian of civil liberties, whatever. Nothing I'm saying is going to penetrate that veneer.

She makes a point of turning her head away from me. "I don't want him in the room," she says to Pete.

"He won't be."

"I have a demand of my own," I say. "I want him to talk."

Carpenter looks at me as if I just quacked like a duck.

"He shouted to her, 'Hum! Can you hear me? Hum!' Bridget will recognize his voice. Unless he surgically altered that, too."

"It's a reasonable request, Nan," says Pete.

"No. Absolutely not. My client doesn't have to speak, and he won't speak."

Pete looks at me, raises his shoulders, a *Nothing I can do* expression.

The lawyers leave. I assume Bridget and her family are already inside the room down the hall, waiting for the curtain to slide open for the lineup. Pete won't let me within a mile of the room. He doesn't want anyone claiming I steered her toward an ID.

If he could be made to speak. If everyone in that lineup had to shout, "Hum! Can you hear me? Hum!" Then it would at least be a fair identification procedure.

I take a stab at the paperwork on my desk. All the shit that's happened, there's a mountain of it I need to get to so lawyers like Nan Carpenter can pore over it looking for mistakes.

Too anxious to fill out forms, I walk over to the desk of another SOS detective, a guy named Freeman who came from the Twenty-First. I'm there because you can see the hallway from the place where he sits. "Hey, Freeman. How are the hemorrhoids?"

He hardly looks up at me. "Shoot anybody today, Harney?"

"Day's not over yet."

Then a door opens down the hall, and three people pop out. Bridget, sandwiched between her parents, huddled over her while she sobs uncontrollably. They hustle her to the stairs and out of my sight.

Shit. *Shit*.

Then Nan Carpenter walks out, cell phone to her ear, and turns in the other direction, showing me her back.

Pete Parsons walks out last. He looks at his phone as he comes toward me. When he looks up at me, he shrugs, tucks in his lips.

Shit.

Then a smile breaks across his face.

"Positive ID," he says.

CHAPTER 22

I WALK into the Hole in the Wall about eight that night. I get a howl from the cops in the bar—which is pretty much everybody—who call me the "TV star" and "Eliot Ness" and variations of that theme. They must have watched the press conference that the supe and Wizniewski made us attend announcing the arrests. The takedown of the top gang leader in Chicago got top billing, followed by the arrest of the guy who kidnapped Bridget Leone, which seemed more important to the press than the fact that he killed a cop, too.

The supe, taking up most of the airtime at the presser, glossed over the circumstances of Donnie Delahunt's arrest, saying officers "spotted Delahunt on the street and apprehended him." Technically true. I guess nobody wants to admit that it was pure dumb luck.

"Some would say it was pure dumb luck," I say into the mike on the stage, after I've had a few bourbons. "But it's part of my new strategy: stand around and wait for the offender to walk past you on the sidewalk.

"It's a variation on a strategy Detective Soscia's been

using for the last twenty years. He's still waiting for some perp to walk into a bar.

"Not that Sosh drinks too much. Why, just the other day he read this article about how too much booze can hurt your liver. He swore, right then and there, to give up reading.

"Seriously, though, he's cutting back. He's vowed to drink only on days beginning with the letter *t*. Today and tomorrow."

I spot the bartender to whom, if foggy memory serves, I proposed marriage last night. This time it's a Bears jersey she's tied off at her midsection, again the Sox hat with her cinnamon-colored ponytail protruding out the back.

"And how about our new bartender?" I say, but the owner of the bar, a former copper who's also serving drinks tonight, happens to come into my line of sight at that moment and salutes me. "No, Morty, not you. I don't think you qualify as new. Morty's about as new as an eight-track tape player.

"When Morty's grandkid Jimmy showed him a picture book of dinosaurs, Morty thought it was his grade-school yearbook.

"When little Jimmy says it's time for a diaper change, Morty isn't sure which one of them he means."

"Don't push your luck," Morty says to me afterward, when I hit the bar for my complimentary drink. "This old fart still has a couple moves left."

"I've seen you bolt for the john pretty fast."

The Hole, midweek, clears out close to midnight. I'm at a corner booth with a couple of patrol rooks and Soscia when I amble up to the bar, my turn for a round. And there is the bartender, an expectant look on her face as she pulls on the tap for a pint of Guinness.

"There she is," I say. "The lawyer in the making."

"There he is, the stand-up comic in the making."

Those blue eyes again. The quick retort again. That something-about-her again.

I order the round. "I was serious about that marriage proposal, though," I say. "I think it's time. Don't you? No," I add, raising a hand. "Don't say yes right away. Wait until you're absolutely sure."

She places the drinks on a round serving tray. "That might be a while."

"No problem. I'm here at least another hour. That enough time?"

She winks at me. "I think I'll have an answer by then."

I walk away with the tray.

"Congratulations, by the way," she says to me.

So she wants to talk some more. I'm surprised at how happy that makes me. It's not like this is going anywhere. I'm not looking for it. Not ready for it. I lost a wife, then three years later another woman. Two women I loved, two women dead. Being in love with me is an ultra-hazardous activity.

I'm not once bitten, twice shy. I'm twice bitten, *thrice* shy.

Yet here I am, wanting to make nice with the bartender lady.

"Sounds like you win the prize for cop of the day," she says.

"Got lucky."

She wipes the counter with a rag. "And modest, too."

"No, it really was luck. But I'll take it." I'm standing here holding a tray of drinks. Do I put them down? That's a commitment to talking longer. But then again, she's the one who roped me back in for more conversation.

Why are you analyzing this, shithead?

"Can I ask you a personal question?" I say.

She looks up at me. "I suppose that depends on how personal."

"Oh, this is deep, soul-bearing personal," I say. "What's your name?"

"Everyone calls me Mia," she says.

"They call you Mia...because that's your name?"

She smiles, takes a breath. "Let's just say it's the only name I answer to."

I laugh. "You're definitely a lawyer in the making." I put down the tray. Okay, so I did it. I put the tray down.

"Listen," I say, "if this marriage is gonna work, we have to trust each other."

She seems to like that. Billy hasn't lost his charm.

"Plus," I add, "how am I gonna fill out the marriage certificate?"

"That's fair," she concedes. "Tell you what: at some point before the wedding, I'll tell you my full name."

"So it *is* short for something."

She grants me that, shakes her head. "You're a seasoned interrogator, I see."

She moves across the bar to take another order, a few coppers from the Fifteenth ordering beers. Soscia starts barking at me for his drink.

The bartender known as Mia returns. Not because it's the spot at the bar where she's dunking glasses into the soapy water, I decide, but because I'm such a joy to converse with.

"Wilhelmia?" I try.

"You nailed it," she deadpans. "My full name is Wilhelmia. Please start calling me that."

"*O sole mia?* Mia Francesca?"

Her eyes narrow. As much as I enjoy those large blue eyes, I'm liking that probing look, too. "I'm not telling you my full name, Detective."

"Well, that's just not fair."

"The Fifth Amendment is fundamental to our liberties."

So I've heard. "A woman of mystery," I say. I decide to cut my losses. Pick up the drinks and head back to the booth. Soscia's never looked happier to see me.

WEDNESDAY

CHAPTER 23

"MR. TENENBAUM," says Judge Bonnie Jorgensen, looking over her glasses, "do you have anything further to add?"

The courtroom is standing room only, reporters and sketch artists taking up the front half of the peanut gallery. I'm in the front row just in case I'm needed. Pete Parsons is there for the people of the state of Illinois. Elan Tenenbaum, dressed to the nines again for this well-publicized court appearance, is there for Jericho Hooper and Mason Tracy, who are standing next to Elan in shackles.

"Nothing further," he says, having given an impassioned plea for bond for his two clients, each of them, he repeatedly emphasized, having been charged with the nonviolent crime of money laundering.

"I find the risk of flight to be more substantial than the defense would have this court believe," says the judge. "I'm going to deny bond for each defendant."

"Your Honor—"

"Mr. Tenenbaum, I've made my ruling. Preliminary hearing will be scheduled for next Monday. Get a time from the clerk. I'll revisit bond at that time. We're adjourned."

It's been a good morning for the good guys. Donnie Delahunt was denied bond, but that was never in doubt after Bridget identified him. Jericho and Mason, though—that could've gone either way. Pete Parsons figured we had less than a fifty-fifty chance of holding these guys without bond.

I pull down on my tie and open my collar. I hate wearing ties, but I thought I might have to testify. I make it back to SOS a little before lunch, fortified by the rulings of the court today. Jericho Hooper, Mason Tracy, and Donnie Delahunt will all sit in county while they await trial. All is right with the world.

Vitrullo, at intake, frowns when he sees me walk into the station.

"Why the long face, Vin? The genital warts acting up again?"

He rolls his eyes but gets back to the frown. "Girl was looking for you."

"Don't tell me—another supermodel? They won't leave me alone."

He stares at me like he's not in the mood. "A teenager," he says. "She was in here asking for you. I told her SOS wasn't the standard police headquarters."

"It's for elite cops like you and me."

He shakes his head. "Anyway, she lives in the Gold Coast, so I told her to go to the Eighteenth. But she wanted you."

"She wanted the best cop Chicago has to offer?"

"No, she wanted you."

"You sure know how to hurt a guy's feelings, Vin." I look around. "Is—is she still around, you think?"

Vinny doesn't know. "Saw her standing outside once. Dark hair, wearing jeans and some top."

"Some top? That'll narrow it down." I walk outside. A bus hisses at me as it stops at the intersection. The smell of tacos from Querida's, my favorite Mexican restaurant in the city, located just two doors down, makes my stomach growl. I could eat some Mexican.

A young woman wearing jeans and, yes, some top has her elbows on her knees, her face in her hands. I walk over but don't get too close.

"Excuse me," I say. "I'm Detective Billy Harney. Were you looking for me?"

She looks up at me like I'm a creep. Seeing her face, I realize she's not a teenager, either.

"Sorry, my mistake."

"I thought you were a lawyer."

I turn around at those words. Leaning against our building, her arms crossed, is a dark-haired girl in jeans. A top, too. Like every other teenager in the city, she's clutching her phone.

"I'll try not to take that as an insult," I say.

She gestures at me. "The…suit and tie."

"I had court. You're looking for me?"

I make the girl for fifteen or sixteen, old enough to have a little poise and maturity. She's put on some makeup to make herself look older. Her high cheek-bones and long, lean build give her the makings of a future beauty. She has good bones and money to pay for fashionable and expensive clothes. Her ripped jeans are cropped just above her ankles, as if someone took a chain saw to them, which must be the look these days.

"I thought you'd be older, too," she says, pushing off the building and squinting up at me.

"I'm old enough. Why did you want to talk to me? Are you okay? Do you have a crime to report?"

"I'm fine," she says in that insolent, duh way, like I'm an idiot for even asking.

"Okay, well—did something happen?"

"Nothing's happened yet."

I take a breath. I'm not in the mood for twenty questions. This meeting was her idea, not mine. But I remind myself I'm talking to a teenager. And a wealthy one, to boot, if Vitrullo's reference to the Gold Coast, the city's swankiest neighborhood, was accurate. Meaning: Lots. Of. Attitude.

"You think something's going to happen?" I try.

She nods, suddenly gets quiet. As if rethinking this whole thing.

"You came all the way here to tell me," I say. "Why don't you tell me?"

She looks away when she speaks. A gust of wind blows a strand of her hair in her face. "Do you know Henry Arcola?" She sneaks a peek at me.

"Don't think so. Doesn't ring a bell. Who's Henry Arcola?"

She tucks her hair behind her ear. "He's my dad," she says.

"Is he okay?"

"He's—well…I'm not sure I'd…it's not him I'm worried about."

"Who are you worried about?"

"My—" She loses it after that word, her face contorting, tears coming. She covers her face with a hand as her narrow shoulders tremble.

"Hey, it's okay." I touch her arm but go no further, being twice her age, not too comfortable putting my hands on her at all.

After a few minutes, she takes a deep breath. She wipes her face, shields her eyes with her hand, and finally blurts it out.

"I think my dad's gonna kill my mom," she says.

CHAPTER 24

WHEN SHE was eight, dressed in a leotard, dancing to "Viva La Vida" while Daddy beamed at her from the front row.

When she was nine, kissing his tombstone, laying a flower by his grave.

Fifteen, before the homecoming dance, Mama kissing her on the forehead, holding her at arm's length to look at her in the emerald-green dress she'd recycled from Cousin Rita.

And the pain, the gnawing, searing pain—

Veronica opens her eyes, raises her head off the pillow, waking from the ache spreading through her abdomen. She blinks, looks around, orients herself, looking for any marker in this dimly lit underground dungeon.

He hasn't returned. The monster, the man in the mask who put his hands on her, who put a gun against her head and abducted her from her warm bed, who threw her down into this creepy place with the staged classroom and kid's bedroom and the wardrobe full of children's clothes, hasn't returned.

The thought of his coming back fills her with dread.

She fears sleep, fears that she'll awaken with him standing over her, leering, his hands out, a greedy smile on his face, showing jagged teeth. But as much as she fears his return…

…she's been waiting for him to come back. She *needs* him to come back.

And he said he would.

It's been…two days? Four days? There's no clock down here, no outside light signaling daytime and night, no change in lighting from the dim overhead illumination. Just one long, dreary, foggy passage of time.

Her mouth dry as sand, the faint onset of a headache coming. She always knows when they're starting, when the needles are beginning to scratch, warming up their spiky tips before plunging into the nerve endings inside her head.

She looked all over this creepy place, pulled open every door. He left her bottles of water, a jug of milk, two boxes of Cheerios, power bars, and granola. But he didn't leave her any ibuprofen or acetaminophen, much less anything stronger. No salt. And the water? Not nearly enough of it. She's already blown through three-quarters of the supply.

She drops her feet to the floor and tries to push herself up. Already the fatigue is setting in. She stands up, moves on shaky legs toward the small refrigerator. Opens a bottle of water and gulps it greedily, unable to moderate.

Only four bottles left. The monster said she had a week's supply. But it's nearly gone. And the demanding *thirst,* the craving for water, is only getting worse.

She struggles her way into the bathroom, fights the urge to vomit. Vomiting is the absolute last thing she should do, the worst thing for someone already dehydrated.

She pulls up her pajama top, pulls down her underwear—the same clothes she was wearing when she was put here—and pees.

She can hardly push herself up off the toilet. She washes her hands, looks at herself in the mirror. Deep circles like bruises beneath her eyes, hair standing everywhere. She feels as tired as she looks.

"You've got to…keep it together," she says to herself.

But she doesn't have much longer. She can already feel it setting in.

She hears a popping sound overhead, a soft crackle. Her head twists up toward the speaker in the corner. She holds her breath, listens.

He's back. He's here.

She tries to speak, tries to tell him what she needs to tell him, but the fear chokes her throat. Her heart pounds so hard she can hardly stand.

Then: *"Veronica."*

She startles from the voice, nearly loses her balance.

"How are you holding up?" he says.

How is she holding up? The question is so ridiculous that under any other circumstance she would laugh.

The man's voice is different. Different from the way she remembers it, at least. Before, he was confident, cocky, condescending.

Now the voice is…a whisper. A whisper into a microphone.

Why whisper? She can't see him. She's never seen him, not his face.

"Did you…did you bring—"

"No. No, I did not," the voice whispers. *"I need you to hold out a little longer."*

"I…can't."

"You must, Veronica. Hang in there. I need a few more days."

"I can't…I need more…more water. And my—"

"You have to make do with what you have. Drink water out of the sink if you must. You'll be fine."

Woozy, feeling vertigo with her head turned upward, Veronica drops to the floor to preempt a violent fall.

"But I need my—"

"Patience, Veronica. I need some time. You have to give me time."

Her head drops to the tile floor. Her eyes flutter to a close.

"I don't…have time," she says, a whisper, just like the voice from the speaker.

CHAPTER 25

SO NOW, apparently, this girl, who came to SOS to see me, is going to tell me why her father wants to kill her mother.

I could kick this to the Eighteenth, where the girl lives, like Vinny said. Maybe I will. This isn't my jurisdiction. But there's something about this kid, presenting herself as cocky and confident but choking up the moment she mentioned her mother. And I admit, I'm curious why she came to me, of all people.

And hey, my grumpy-old-man stomach needs some food, so there's no harm in hearing this girl out over some tacos.

We've ordered at Querida's. A red plastic container of fried salty tortilla chips resting in wax paper, already stained with grease. Large bowls of salsa, green and red, mild and wicked hot. The smell of the sizzling chorizo on the grill.

My mom always said that 99 percent of the secret to appeasing your kids is either sleep or food. This girl, the daughter of Henry Arcola (whoever that's supposed to be), drops a straw inside her can of Coke and takes a long sip. It seems to perk her up.

While we wait for the food, she checks her phone, the default move for a teenager. "Omigod, Greta is *such* a psych job."

"Why don't we start with your name?" I say. "You're Henry Arcola's daughter."

"You don't know him?" She reaches for a tortilla chip, glances at me.

"Never heard of him," I say. Second time she's asked, second time I've answered. Does she not believe me?

"I'm Logan," she says.

"Okay, Logan. And you're how old?"

She says, "Fourteen," like it's obvious.

"Four—you're only *fourteen*?"

"But I'm wise beyond my years."

Apparently so. "Careful with that sauce," I say. "It'll put hair on your—well, it's hotter than it looks."

She raises her eyebrows. "I've had *salsa* before." She dunks a chip into the red salsa, tosses it into her mouth, her face blushing as she tries not to let on that it's a lot spicier than she expected. She skips the Coke and goes for the tall glass of ice water, takes a long sip.

"Anyway, Logan—tell me what's going on."

She grabs another chip, goes for the milder green sauce this time. "I saw your name in the news," she said. "You caught the guy who took Bridget Leone."

I nod. "We got lucky. He was a bad guy."

She watches me, like she's waiting for me to elaborate. But I won't.

"And you, like, totally broke open this big scandal in the police department. You took down a bunch of bad cops. You were sorta famous."

I'm not sure if it's fame or infamy. It depends on who you ask. But she's done her research.

"Feels like a long time ago," I say. "Anyway, Logan, tell me about your father."

"I already talked to the FBI," she says.

"The FBI? About your father?"

"Yeah. Is that, like, a problem?"

I shrug. "Not with me it isn't. I'm not sure the FBI would handle—"

"I told the agent everything I'm gonna tell you," she interrupts. "And I gave her a copy of my audio files."

Her audio files? "Okay," I say, though I'm not sure why she's telling me all this.

She sounds like the protagonist in one of those cheesy movies, warning the villain, *If my people don't hear from me by midnight, that letter gets mailed to every news station in the city.*

Come to think of it, thus far Logan hasn't told me much of anything.

It feels more like she's been interviewing me. Testing me.

And warning me.

CHAPTER 26

"TELL ME about your father," I say to Logan Arcola.

She tucks a strand of hair behind her ear. "I mean, he has this, like, hedge fund? He manages people's money. He's made—I mean, I don't really know how much money, but a lot, obviously. People say he's a billionaire." She shrugs. "He doesn't really tell me. I mean, why should I know? I'm just the daughter."

"So—"

"But he's always out there giving out money. Like, to causes. Charities. Stuff like that. He's got his name on a school on the West Side. He, like, endowed—I think that's what they call it—some 'chair' at UIC? Whatever that means. But stuff like that. He likes the cameras. He likes reading about himself and putting up pictures of himself with famous people. The whole...like, high-society thing. Marlene pretty much likes that stuff, too, but...not lately."

"Marlene...is your mother?"

Duh, apparently, from the rise of her eyebrows.

If I'd ever called my mother by her first name, she would've knocked me sideways.

"So Henry and Marlene are pretty much just like companions, right? They pretty much, like, ignore each other."

"Not a good marriage," I say.

The food comes. Chorizo tacos for me, a plate of nachos for her.

She grabs a chip that threatens to break under the weight of the load of ground beef, melted cheese, beans, guacamole, and sour cream. Pops it in her mouth. Puts a hand over her mouth as she chews. "If Hope saw me, she would totally freak. She's, like, a way-militant vegan."

I let her eat awhile. I grew up with Brendan and Aiden, two older brothers who considered mealtime a contact sport. I don't know how Patti ever managed to eat a morsel. So I'm accustomed to eating competitively, but before my three-taco plate is halfway done, Logan has devoured the entire plate of nachos and wiped up lingering cheese and guac with her finger, leaving nothing but orange grease smeared across the plate.

She goes quiet. The food put her at ease. The basic background wasn't hard to discuss. But the rest of the story, apparently, is.

"So what's happened recently to change your parents' relationship?" I ask.

She looks away, as if people-watching or admiring the blue-and-yellow murals on the walls. "I don't know. I just know it's different. She, like, keeps a distance from him. Sometimes he stays over in the condo and doesn't even come home. I've heard her say things to him—I mean, that's the thing, I don't *hear* it, but I hear it, y'know?"

"I actually have no idea what that means."

She gives me one of her eye bulges, like she can't believe how dense I am. "Like, I hear her saying things to him like real harsh, right? I can't really hear the words. She doesn't want me to hear. But harsh, right? Like, he's the lowest form of pond scum. Not like they're arguing but like…he's a horrible person."

"Well, harsh words between spouses—"

"So, okay." She looks up at me. "I did hear her say one thing. I think—maybe she didn't know I was in my room. Or maybe she was so mad she didn't care."

I lean forward. "What did she say, Logan?"

She looks away, closes her eyes, remembering. "She was like, 'What will happen to us? Did you ever think about what would happen to us if anyone finds out?'"

If anyone finds out. That doesn't sound good. It sounds like something a lot worse than basic marital problems or even infidelity.

"And no," she says, "I don't know what she meant. And Marlene won't tell me."

"Okay," I say, "but why do you think that means your father's going to kill your mother?"

She chews her lip, fiddles with her phone. Nervous habit, maybe. A comfort device. But then I realize she's poking and sliding and sweeping her thumb across the phone.

"You mentioned audio files," I say.

She nods and hands me the phone, faceup. Pulled up on the screen is, yes, what looks like an audio file. I press the triangular icon for Play, and a series of horizontal lines dances before me as a man's voice comes on:

> *No, no, no! You're not hearing me. My wife is a problem…yes…yes, Strazo! Just like dimes. If she starts talking, I'm toast. It's over. Everything's over! Make it happen, Strazo!*

The recording ends. I play it again. The man is speaking just above a whisper, but his tone is harsh and urgent, and the enunciation is clear.

I look up. Logan is watching me closely, the most direct eye contact she's made, her body still.

"This is your dad, talking to someone on the phone?"

She nods. No smart-ass *duh* expression.

"Talking to someone named Strazo?"

A shoulder rises. "Apparently. I don't know that name. But it's not like I know anything about Henry's business."

"What does 'Just like dimes' mean?"

"No idea."

"Well, when did this happen? When did you record this?"

"I don't know the exact day," she says. "It doesn't say the date and time. But recently."

"Did you talk to your dad about this?"

"God, no."

"Your mom?"

"I haven't seen Marlene for a couple of days."

Whoa. "You haven't seen your mother in *days*?"

She rolls her eyes, lets out a sigh. "Marlene sometimes goes up to the cabin to chill. Lake Geneva," she adds before I can ask.

"When's the last time you spoke to Marlene, Logan?"

"Well, like, texting—yesterday. She just says everything's fine."

"So it's just you and your father at home?"

"When he's even home. He's been staying at the condo downtown a lot. No, no," she says, seeing my alarm. "My grandmother lives next door. She sleeps over when my parents aren't home."

I hand the phone back to Logan. "Call your mother right now," I say.

CHAPTER 27

LAKE GENEVA, Wisconsin, high noon. The warm weather bringing out the vacationers in full force already.

"I don't care how 'rock solid' the prenup is. Henry won't enforce it. He'll be too afraid of my going public with what I know." Marlene Arcola drums her fingers on the steering wheel of her Mercedes coupe while pedestrians cross the street at the crosswalk toward the boats along the lakeshore. She breathes in the smell of the lake, lets the sun wash over her face. Calms herself. Finally, the road opens, and she speeds forward.

"I can't be part of it, Marlene." The voice of her lawyer, Allan Camus, through her earbuds. "That has to be an off-the-record conversation between you and Henry."

"Meaning I have to do all the heavy lifting."

"If what you've told me is true," says Camus, "the lift won't be that heavy."

She lets out an annoyed sigh. These lawyers and their faux ethics. A divorce lawyer, of all people! Claiming he can't threaten Henry to get him to cough up more money than that lame prenup would give her? That it's beneath his *ethics*?

Well, so be it. As usual, men are totally useless.

"It's not like I want half," she says. "He can easily afford it. It's the timing I care about. The timing is everything."

"You want the money up front. I understand."

"Damn right I want it up front. Wouldn't you, if you were in my position?"

If Henry's secret ever comes out—*when* it comes out—he'll be ruined. His money will dry up overnight. Marlene and Logan have to get out now, with as much as they can.

Marlene maneuvers her car around the bend, turns down the long private drive to her lakeside home, flower beds lining the way. She punches the remote to open her garage.

She removes her earbuds, places them in their case. Gets out of the car as her phone rings in her hand, a chipper, singsong ditty. She checks the face of her phone as she enters her home, the gleaming white kitchen.

Caller ID says Logan. She doesn't have time for Logan right now.

She breathes in a powerful scent of aftershave. She almost doesn't see the man, standing so still that he almost blends into the kitchen. A large man with a scowl, the face of a bloodhound.

He takes a step toward her before she can take one backward. His hand flashes up so quickly that she doesn't see it coming, the *whump* from the force of his fist splitting her lips, the crack of her front teeth breaking.

She flies backward, her head smacking against the door to the garage, stars dancing in her watery eyes. Somehow, she keeps her balance.

Another large man, a brute like the first guy, walks into the kitchen as well.

She looks at each of them. Brings a trembling hand to her mouth. When she pulls it back, it looks like it was dipped in red paint.

Her phone sings again, this time from the floor, where she dropped it.

The man moves toward her, Marlene freezing in terror. He bends down and picks up the phone. Looks at it. Waits for it to stop ringing.

"What's the passcode, Marlene?" he says, his voice deep and flat.

She shakes her head.

The man holds the phone up to her face. Her mind racing, reeling with shock and fear, she doesn't understand at first.

Then she sees the phone's screen change, and she gets it. The facial-recognition ID unlocked it.

The other man, the one not holding the phone, circles around her, browses through the knife block on the kitchen island, and removes the butcher knife.

"Two calls in a row from Logan," says the first man. He looks up at her. "How much does she know, Marlene? And how many times you gonna make me ask?"

CHAPTER 28

"NO ANSWER." Logan stands up as we head back to the station. "But that's totally her. If she's in the middle of something, she won't answer."

Sounds like she's trying to convince herself as much as convince me.

"Text her," I say. "Tell her it's urgent."

She nods. I'm not trying to make her nervous, but she's starting to make *me* nervous.

She texts her mother as we enter the department. We head up to my desk. Lanny Soscia is typing up a report on his keyboard.

"Sosh, you know cops up in Lake Geneva?" Soscia knows everybody. His tentacles—uncles, cousins, friends—run through the Midwest.

"Detective sergeant up there's a buddya mine."

"Help me out here," I say. "I need a welfare check on a woman up there. Logan—this is Logan; Logan, this is Detective Soscia—give him the details."

"Wait." Logan looks up at me, a look of relief on her face. "She responded."

Logan shows me the text:

No need to worry, Flower. I'm doing fine. In the
middle of a treatment n then cocktails w some
friends. Will call u later, ok?

I look at Logan. "Flower?"

"It's what she calls me." She tucks her hair behind
her ears, a look of total relief in her expression. "She's at
the spa. *So* Marlene."

"Okay, well, that's good." I nod to Soscia. "All the
same, Sosh. Make the call to your friend in Lake
Geneva, wouldja?"

Because something about this gives me a bad feeling.

CHAPTER 29

THREE HOURS later. I sink down into a chair with a velvet cushion, which may be a first for me. The secretary hands me a glass of water with a slice of cucumber in it. Another first.

Music plays softly in the office, sounds of the ocean, a harp, a wind chime. I feel like I should be wearing a terry-cloth robe.

The office is spacious but minimalist, large enough to park three cars in but containing only a single sleek desk of steel and two chairs on the other side, one of which I occupy. The decor is a soft purple, though there's probably a fancier name for the color—mauve or periwinkle. The only thing interrupting the serenity is the ego wall, one that's better than most: framed photos with three presidents, celebrities, governors, and mayors, along with awards from various groups for philanthropic service or contributions.

I'm on the phone with Marsha Flager while I wait.

"Haven't gotten into Mason's laptop yet," she tells me. "He wasn't kidding. He's got, like, a Jedi force field around that thing. Maybe we should've cut that deal and given him a few minutes with his phone in exchange for the password."

"Yeah, but what was he going to do on that phone? If he's so into technology that you can't hack into his computer, what did he have on his phone? The code to the nuclear arsenal?"

"Yeah, I don't know."

"Marsh, we need more to hold Mason. The judge gave us the first week. But she won't let us hold him indefinitely, until trial, unless we come up with more. Jericho, we're probably okay. Judge knows he's a vicious killer. But Mason? He's just the money guy."

"I know. I'm on it. I'll get in. Give me time."

"They're holding him at Dunham, right? The new place?"

"Right," she says.

"But he's segregated from Jericho?"

"Yeah, he's in PC." Protective custody, she means.

"Good. I don't want Jericho getting to him."

"Hey, Wizniewski's asking where you are."

"Yeah? What'd you tell him?"

"What you told me to tell him—that you're getting a pedicure. He didn't see the humor in it. Why are you there, anyway? It's not SOS. Kick it to the Eighteenth."

"It's just a quick visit." I check my watch.

"Why'd this girl come to you? Why you, of all people?"

"Obviously, Detective Flager, she wanted the best."

"But she settled for you."

Everyone's a comedian all of a sudden. I punch out the phone and look at my watch again.

Just as the office door opens. Good timing. Or maybe he was listening.

"Music off," he says, and the sound of crashing waves abruptly ceases. "Sorry to keep you waiting, Detective."

Henry Arcola doesn't look like a billionaire, at least not one from the old school. He is medium height, slim, with a dark goatee and a full head of silver hair brushed back. Silver, that is, not reflecting old age but hair dye. This guy colors his hair.

He is wearing a silk collarless shirt buttoned to his neck and untucked over trousers, sandals with no socks. He's a hotshot hedge-fund guy, apparently, but he seems to fancy himself some kind of artist. I guess people can tell themselves whatever they want, and if they have enough money, they can buy other people who will repeat those things.

He sits behind his shiny sliver of a steel desk, facing only a laptop computer. This is where he performs his magic, I suppose, undisturbed by any distractions like family photos or memorabilia.

"Is everything all right?" he asks. "I confess I was surprised to hear that a police detective wanted time with me today."

"I'll get to the point, Mr. Arcola. I spoke with your daughter, Logan. She's concerned about you and your wife."

He cocks his head, his expression more one of curiosity than surprise. "Logan went to the police? Why would she do that?"

"She thinks you have some reason to want to do harm to your wife."

He looks up at the ceiling. "Now, if that isn't my passive-aggressive daughter, I don't know what is."

"Was she wrong?"

He shakes his head, lowers his gaze to me. "Ever been married, Detective?"

"Yes."

"But not now." Noting the lack of a ring on my finger.

"No," I say, "not now."

"So you know."

He's assuming I'm divorced, not a widower, and that we're on the same page about what a pain in the ass wives can be. I play along. No reason not to.

"My wife can be dramatic," he explains. "And my daughter inherited that trait from her." He opens his hands. "I wouldn't say that we have the most traditional of marriages. The last I checked, that isn't a crime."

He rocks in his chair, shaking his head some more.

"My wife is not happy," he says. "I know that. Maybe she wishes she'd kept working. She could have. I've worked very hard to provide her and Logan with a comfortable life. She's never had to work. But she could have, if she'd wanted. And now I suppose it's my fault for making so much money. And of course Logan will take her side every time. There's no pleasing some — well, anyway." He looks at me. "Marlene drinks too much. And she takes antidepressants. So yes, I worry about her, too. But I can assure you that *I* am no threat to her whatsoever."

I open my cell and find the recording Logan transferred to my phone. She told me I could use it. She wanted me to, in fact. I press Play:

> *No, no, no! You're not hearing me. My wife is a problem…yes…yes, Strazo! Just like dimes. If she starts talking, I'm toast. It's over. Everything's over! Make it happen, Strazo!*

Henry loses his smirk, his jaw tightening. He goes to considerable effort to control his reaction. But he can't stop the color from leaving his face. He's completely off his game now.

"That's you on the phone, isn't it?" I say.

He looks at me. Off his game, yes, but he hasn't lost his senses. He's not going to volunteer anything to me.

"Mr. Arcola? That's your voice on the phone."

He takes a deep breath and pops out of his chair, looking out a massive window that frames views of the city's West Side.

"Who's Strazo?" I ask. "Who were you talking to?"

His head shakes. Still with his back to me, he clears his throat.

"If there's nothing else, Detective, I have another appointment."

"I'd like an answer to my question, Mr. Arcola."

"I think we both know I don't have to answer you."

I get out of my chair. "If anything happens to your wife or your daughter, I'll be the first to know," I tell him. "And you'll be my first visit."

CHAPTER 30

SIX HOURS later. Ten o'clock.

The wind whips up with a fury, carrying the stench of death, along with soil and other debris from the mound of dirt. Tech officers move about in hazmat suits with the awkward gait of astronauts. Giant machinery, rigs with monstrous, earth-scooping claws, tires like a tank. Small hand-propelled devices for ground-penetrating radar that look like nothing more than fancy lawn mowers. Large spotlights beaming down from platforms, lending a theatrical quality to the horror show.

A giant truck stretches its mechanical arm over the gaping hole, a cable lowering down, the latch at its end disappearing into the darkness. Techies in their hazmat suits climb up ladders placed into the hole, having secured the latch to the bed they have placed under the cadaver.

We wait in respectful silence, as if it were a ritual, while the pulley on the rig's arm rotates, slowly retracting the cable from the burial site with a steady, whirring hum. The body appears, cocooned in some kind of tarp, a bed beneath it, rising from the massive hole. The arm of the rig pivots and deposits the body gently on the ground nearby, one of the techies taking it to cushion the landing, as if for the comfort of the deceased, though in reality the preservation of her remains—of the evidence—is the reason.

I stand behind a rope as another gust of wind, another temper tantrum from Mother Nature, whips against my face, carrying the putrid odor of decomposing flesh. The smell is expected, no matter how neatly wrapped she was, no matter how far into the ground she was buried.

She's been dead, after all, for four months.

"This seems to be the last of 'em," says a techie next to me.

The last of four girls, all buried behind a hill less than a hundred yards from the house where we caught up to Donnie Delahunt, on the southwest side of unincorporated Cook County. Less than a football field from the house he blew up. Where Carla died.

We'll need DNA to identify them, but there's no real doubt. These are the four girls who went missing in the Chicagoland area over the last eighteen months before Bridget Leone became the fifth. He brought them here initially, just as he did Bridget, to stow them away and out of sight. Then he transported them somewhere else, as he was doing with Bridget when we caught him, to get his sick, twisted jollies with them. He returned here to kill them and bury them.

"I want DNA right away," I say. "Right away. Call your guy at the lab."

"Will do," says Sosh, next to me.

"I don't just mean DNA of the victims."

"I know," he says.

Yes, I want DNA of the victims for identification, to give some measure of closure to the families. But what concerns me most is trace DNA on their bodies from Donnie Delahunt. We have enough on Delahunt just based on Bridget Leone, but I want him on all these murders. The girls, their families, deserve that.

My phone buzzes. I fish it out of my pocket.

"Marlene hasn't called back," Logan Arcola says. "I think something's happened."

THURSDAY

CHAPTER 31

IT'S NEARLY one in the morning before I get there. I show my credentials to get past a blockade and park half a block away, the street littered with patrol cars from two different jurisdictions, the local Lake Geneva cops in their navy uniforms, the county sheriff's deputies dressed in olive.

I throw my star around my neck and approach the house. Can't make out much of it this time of night, but it's clearly a grand spread, a mansion on the shoreline of Lake Geneva.

"Harney? Sergeant Murray, with the detectives' bureau."

We shake hands, and I thank him for the call. He's younger than I'd imagined, probably midforties, broad-shouldered with a thin beard, dressed in uniform.

"Thinking homicide?" I ask as we walk up the long driveway to the pungent smell of fresh flowers.

"Keeping an open mind on that," he says. "We'll rush the tox screen and have a better idea. The injuries to her face are a question, though. And luminol picked up some blood in the kitchen and staircase."

So not ruling out homicide. That's good. I don't know if this is going to be our case or theirs, but I don't need an ME fucking up my case with a hasty conclusion of accidental death or suicide.

He steers me up the front walk, which bisects a magnificent front lawn, and ushers me in through the front door. I snap on latex gloves and put covers on my shoes. Inside, forensic officers are doing a full workup.

"Husband here?"

"Husband and daughter," he says. "And the victim's mother."

"Logan's grandmother."

"Yes, sir. Logan came with her grandmother. She doesn't want to be in the same room with her father."

"I'll bet."

It's a gorgeous home, but it's a lake home and feels like one. Pinewood, not marble; generous windows, some expensive artwork on the walls, but mostly nature shots and photos featuring boats and fish.

Sergeant Murray takes me up the carpeted stairs, where I step over and around spots that have been identified as bloodstains, most too microscopic for the naked eye to register. At the top of the stairs, we turn left into the master suite.

The bathroom is predictably huge, newly renovated, gleaming white. About three steps away from a massive claw-foot tub is the body of Marlene Arcola.

She is prone, lying on her stomach in bra and panties, a bottle of red wine shattered on the tile floor. Her face, turned in profile, is bloodied and beaten. A reddish bruise under her eye, the first signs of swelling. Her nose is busted. Her mouth is a bloody mash.

"The idea is, what, she was intoxicated, stumbled, died from the fall?" I say.

"A preliminary idea," says Murray.

"Looks like the early stages of bruise formation and swelling. Those things don't happen after death."

"Nope, they sure don't. Maybe she didn't die right away."

True enough.

I bend down, examine her face more closely. Her front teeth are busted. Trickles of blood from the nose. Traces of dried blood, looks like, on her cheek. "There's a lot of blood in a person's head," I say. "This much violence to her face, she'd have bled a helluva lot more than this."

"Maybe she did die right away. Heart stopped pumping."

I look at the sergeant. He acknowledges the contradiction with raised eyebrows. The bruising and the minimal blood tell incompatible stories.

"You think this was staged?" I ask.

"Good a guess as any." He reached the same conclusion.

"Agreed," I say. "Falling to the floor didn't cause these facial bruises. Not all of them, at least. Somebody hit her. More than once. She started to bruise, started to swell up, and bled like hell. But not here. Not in this bathroom. The kitchen, the staircase. They tried to clean it up, but that's nearly impossible to fully hide."

Murray nods. He doesn't get a lot of murders in Lake Geneva, but he's worked this up well so far, and he's proud of it.

"How long has she been dead?" I ask. Marlene Arcola was the prototype of a billionaire's wife, hard-bodied and pretty though so skinny as to almost look unnatural.

"The ME thinks she died this morning, maybe early afternoon."

So by the time I was interviewing Henry Arcola, in the

late afternoon, Marlene was already dead. And he knew it. That gives me an idea of who I'm dealing with.

"What does the husband say?"

"He was at his condo in the city when he got our call. He says he was at work all day. He says his wife drank too much and took antidepressants, which checks out."

Convenient, though.

"He told us you came to him today with concerns he might hurt his wife."

"Right," I say. "After talking to his daughter."

"You wanna talk to Mr. Arcola?" he asks me.

"I would, Sergeant, if that's all right."

"Sure, no problem."

"But first I want to talk to Logan," I say.

CHAPTER 32

THEY LEAD me into a family room on the ground floor, where Logan sits on a couch, head in her hands, her grandmother's arm slung over her.

Logan doesn't get up when she sees me but grabs my arm and puts her face against it. I don't say anything for a long time. She may be privileged, but she's still just a kid, a kid who feared the worst for her mother and turned out to be right.

"I knew it," she whispers. "I knew it. I should've done something sooner—"

"Hey—"

"—and I was sitting there eating lunch with you and texting with my friends like everything was fine—"

"Logan—"

"—I didn't think it was a matter of *hours* or something. I mean, I wasn't even sure it was going to happen at all, I just—"

"Logan." I put my hand on her shoulder, bend down. "None of this is your fault."

She looks up at me, her face streaked with tears, her eyes bloodshot, her mouth quivering.

"This is absolutely not your fault, Logan."

She falls against me, sobbing, while her grandmother rubs her back. We make eye contact, her grandmother and I, and she nods as if she wants a private word with me.

"I know it was him," Logan says, her voice muffled against my chest. "I *know* it."

After a while, the grandmother and I steal into the hallway. "Marilyn Ashe," she says by way of introduction. She has much of the beauty of her daughter Marlene — fine features, an etched face softened a bit by age but still striking.

I flip open my small notepad. I still use paper. Carla had switched over to typing notes on her phone so she could paste them into emails or download them. A couple of clicks on her computer, and all her investigative notes from multiple interviews were in one document, while I'd have three or four different notepads going. Old Man Harney, she called me.

This, I realize with a twinge, is my first homicide call without my partner. Now begins the rest of my career.

"You're the policeman from Chicago, the one Logan went to see," she says.

"Yes, ma'am. I'm very sor—"

"She was going to divorce him," she says. "She was drawing up papers."

"Marlene was divorcing Henry? Okay. Logan didn't mention that."

"Logan didn't know."

"Any particular reason," I say, "besides your basic bad-marriage stuff—"

"Fraud," she says. "He was cheating his investors. That's what she told me. She said she didn't want to be around, and she didn't want Logan around, when the bubble burst."

That squares with what Logan overheard Marlene say to Henry—*What will happen if they find out?* Yeah, that's a secret you'd want to keep.

That's a motive to kill.

"He wasn't a good husband. They'd drifted apart. But she would have stayed married, at least until Logan was out of the house. When she learned about the fraud, though, she decided it was time to get out."

"Okay—"

She takes my arm, looks into my eyes. "He did this. Henry did this."

"I'll look into it."

"Will you?" She shakes my arm.

I do a double take. "Of course I will." Why is everyone questioning that?

"You don't have to leave the room to talk." Logan's voice is a low croak. Her life, privileged in so many ways, complicated in others, now completely upended. "Henry would never get his hands dirty," she says. "He has all the money in the world. He'd have someone else do this."

I pat her hand. "Let me go do my job now," I say. "Do you know the passcode to your mother's phone?"

She does. I find Sergeant Murray again. "Can I see the victim's phone?" I ask.

Murray sends an officer, who brings it to me, bagged as evidence. "Mind if I check it?" I ask, still cognizant of interdepartmental boundaries. Murray doesn't seem troubled with any of that, gives me the green light.

Still wearing my latex gloves, I type in the passcode and open the phone. I go straight to her call log. The last eight calls, none of which she answered, came from Logan. Two while we ate lunch together today and six others as the night wore on and Logan's fears grew.

The last call before that was one Marlene made, a call to Camus, Allan, that lasted thirty-nine minutes. It ended at 12:11 p.m., which would have been while Logan and I were at the Mexican restaurant, talking.

She was still alive when Logan and I were eating lunch.

I press the number and wait. It's near two in the morning, so the voice that answers is hoarse, groggy.

"Is this Allan Camus?" I ask.

"Yes. Who's calling?"

"Sir, my name is Billy Harney. I'm a detective with the Chicago Police Department."

That usually wakes people up.

"Is—is everything okay? What happened?"

"Sir, a woman named Marlene Arcola was discovered in her home in Lake Geneva tonight, dead. You were the last person who talked to her on her cell phone."

"Marlene is dead? Oh, Jesus."

"Sir, could—"

"I'm her lawyer," he says. "I'm a family law attorney."

"Divorce," I say. "Marlene was getting a divorce from her husband?"

He pauses, lets out a breath.

"I'm investigating a possible murder, Mr. Camus. I understand the attorney-client privilege, but it would—"

"No, no, it's not that. I—Marlene told me that if anything happened to her, I could tell the world what he was doing. I mean, people say stuff like that sometimes, but I didn't—Jesus, she didn't think it would actually *happen*."

Same basic thing Logan said. People don't actually want to believe that someone they've lived with is capable of murder.

"Sounds like you have authorization from her to tell me what you know," I say.

His throat clears. The man is definitely wide awake now.

"Henry was defrauding his investors," he says. "He was running a Ponzi scheme."

Just like Marlene's mother said.

"Marlene told you that?"

"Marlene *showed* me that. She downloaded a spreadsheet off his computer. I can—I could bring it to you."

"Any chance she emailed you a copy?" I ask. "Any chance I can see it now?"

He pauses. "As a matter of fact, she did," he says. "I'll email it right over."

CHAPTER 33

"I'D NEED to know more," Marsha Flager says to me an hour later over the phone. "But if this financial statement is accurate, then Henry Arcola was running a blatant Ponzi scheme. He was paying dividends to existing clients with seed money from new clients. And pocketing most of the principal. He was keeping the thing afloat on fumes and siphoning off tens of millions of dollars at a time."

"We're talking Bernie Madoff?"

"Yeah. A smaller scale, but exactly like that. I need all his records, though, Billy. This is one spreadsheet from last week."

"Got it. Go back to sleep."

"No, I'm awake now, thanks very much, Detective."

I punch out the phone and head into what they call the parlor room, lushly carpeted and filled with expensive antique furniture. For moments when they want to forget about that whole lake atmosphere, apparently.

Henry Arcola sits alone in the room, dressed in a button-down shirt and jeans, elbows on his knees, feet drumming the carpet. He looks up at me like he's bored, made more so by my showing up. "You again," he says.

"Yep, me again. Sorry to interrupt your grieving."

He rolls his eyes. A small smirk makes an appearance on his face.

"This is the part where you tell me that people grieve in different ways," I add.

He adjusts himself, sits back in the chair, crosses a leg. "I don't have to justify myself to you. And I don't have to say anything to you." He flicks his fingers at me, like I'm a gnat in his face. "Why don't you run along now, Detective, and leave things to the first-rate professionals in Lake Geneva?"

Like he's daring me.

"You have nothing on me, and you know it." He puts his head back and closes his eyes.

"I think I do," I say. "Not as much as the FBI, SEC, and the US attorney's office, but a fair amount."

He opens his eyes, loses his smirk, but tries to hold it together. It's a thing for him, I could tell earlier today. The poker face, never letting them see you sweat. It doesn't usually last. Especially when you start playing federal alphabet soup.

"What in the world," he says, forcing a chuckle, "could the FBI or the SEC or the US attorney possibly have on me?"

I shrug. "I'm just a city cop, Mr. Arcola. I don't deal with financial crimes."

His eyes narrow. That not-letting-them-see-you-sweat thing is getting tougher.

"The Bureau, though, they have a whole department. And shit, that's all the SEC does. They're pretty excited about you. How many investors have you ripped off in your Ponzi scheme?"

He forces a smile, like he's receiving a shot in the arm and refuses to wince.

He could lawyer up at any minute. He knows that. So I might as well cover my bases and Mirandize him, just in case some judge would say he's technically in custody right now, which under the law, he probably is.

"I know my rights," he says after I give him his warnings.

"Marlene knew about your scheme," I say. "She knew, and you knew she knew."

He watches me, thinking, while trying to read me.

"What you didn't know," I add, "is that she downloaded documents. And told lots of people about it."

"Bullshit." He blurts it out with a laugh, more hopeful than certain. "That's not how she'd play it."

"How *would* she play it, Henry? Threaten you as leverage in a divorce? She keeps your secret, you give her a nice payoff?"

Yeah. I can tell from his expression, that's exactly what he thinks. And he's right.

"The thing is, Henry, she'd want insurance," I say. "She gave financial documents to her divorce lawyer just in case. And her mother, too."

Jackpot. He hadn't figured she was that far along in her planning. He thought he killed her before she had the chance to do anything. But it makes perfect sense, and he knows it.

He wipes at his face and pops off the couch. I reach for my weapon, startled by the movement, but he walks toward the window, runs his hands over his slick silver hair.

"If there's another side to the story," I say, "now's the time—"

"I need some time to think," he says.

"Mr. Arcola, what you need—"

"You can give me ten minutes right now," he says, finally letting his emotions get the better of him, "or you can go fuck yourself, and I keep my mouth shut. Leave me alone for ten minutes, all right?"

He's right. He has that over me. I gain nothing by forcing the issue.

"I have to frisk you first," I say.

He raises his hands, an invitation. I pat him down. He's clean.

"I'll be right in the hallway," I say. "Watching you."

"Good for you, Detective."

As I leave, he bends over, hands on his knees like a third-base coach. Sweating a lot more now. I can see that I'm not off base with the Ponzi scheme. I don't know the details, but the mention of it decidedly moved the needle.

He's nothing if not smart. He's been thinking about this since our visit earlier today. Maybe it's all finally crashing down on him, and he can't bear the weight. A lot of people can't. I once interrogated a defense lawyer on a homicide. The guy had spent every day of his career advising clients not to talk to the police, but before I had so much as sat down in the interview room, he was spilling his guts to me. Some people just can't hold it in.

Is Henry Arcola that kind of guy? I don't think so. But you never know.

After eight minutes, Henry stands up straight and nods his head. I reenter the room.

"So what's it gonna be, Henry?" I ask.

"I might be willing to talk," he says. "But not here. I don't want to spend another fucking second in this town."

"What a coincidence," I say. "I happen to be headed back to Chicago myself."

I check with Sergeant Murray, who reluctantly gives

me the okay to take Henry back to Chicago, with the caveat that he be kept in the loop.

I lead Henry out of the house, sheriff's deputies and forensic techies and local cops lining the path as we pass.

Henry looks up and says, "I want a lawyer! I am invoking my right to counsel!"

I don't get this guy. Or maybe I do.

Either way, it should be an interesting drive back to Chicago.

CHAPTER 34

THE RIDE back starts quietly. Henry is handcuffed in the back seat of my SUV, restrained by the seat belt. He looks out the window and keeps his mouth shut.

Sometimes a car ride is a good way to do it. The opposite of a sweaty, in-your-face confrontation. Sometimes they start the conversation, sometimes you do.

But I'm reading Henry as a classic psychopath. This guy talked with me in his office this afternoon, knowing that his wife was already dead, and was cool as ice. He's feeling no guilt, no remorse.

Not to mention that he invoked on his way out of the house, announcing that he wanted a lawyer to anyone within shouting range.

As I'm hitting the interstate, he breaks the silence.

"You said you were married once."

"Yeah, I did, Henry, but I can't talk to you now."

"Because I invoked?"

"You seem to be pretty familiar with police procedure there, Henry. And yes, because you invoked."

"Then consider me uninvoking. I no longer want a lawyer. I can change my mind."

That he can. But why?

"Yes," I say, "I was married once."

"Divorced?"

That's what he assumed when we talked in his office earlier. That seems like the better play here than telling him the truth—that my wife, Valerie, died five years ago.

"Yeah," I say. "I'd rather not think about it."

"Did she leave you or did you leave her?" he asks.

"I'd say it was mutual." Winging it, but a safe play.

"That means she left," he says. "But you're too proud to admit it."

I chuckle. "Whatever you say."

"Did she fuck around on you? Was that it? Was she opening her legs for other men while you were toiling away at work to put food on the table?"

"Nothing like that," I say.

"I only ask because I had a one-nighter once with a cop's wife."

"Yeah?" I look in the rearview mirror. The first hint of a personal reveal. A guy like Henry, that's all that matters to him. All roads in a conversation lead back to him. Every comment a segue back to Henry Arcola.

"I met her at a bar," he says. "She was . . . God, she was hot. Sexy. On the prowl. I mean, she came on to me. I took her back to my condo, and we fucked all night. Some of the shit I did to her you couldn't do to a circus animal. I tied her up, I smacked her around. She was ravenous. She couldn't get enough. She said she couldn't get off with her husband, so when he was working the overnight beat, she'd go out, meet some stranger, and fuck him senseless."

What the hell is with this guy? Well, you never know where these conversations—

"She was a lawyer," he says. "Her name was Valerie. Valerie Blinderman."

I swerve my SUV off the road and screech to a stop. Put the car in Park. Get out, walk around to the passenger side, open the door, and drag Henry out of the car. He falls to his knees, his arms still cuffed behind his back. Still a smug look on his face.

I grip his shirt, get up close to him. "You looking to get beaten, Henry?"

"Are you going to violate my constitutional rights, Detective? Beating a defenseless suspect?"

He couldn't look more pleased, his eyebrows raised.

"You say one more word about my wife, I'm putting you in a coma."

His smile widens. "Well, at least now we're being honest, Detective. Divorced? C'mon, Billy. You're a widower. Your wife died the same day your poor little daughter died, isn't that right? That must have been awful. Jane, wasn't that your daughter's name?"

I raise my hand, ball it into a fist. God, I get so close.

But…then he wins. There's no fucking way I'm letting him win.

"Tell you this much, though," he says. "I saw a photo of Valerie online. I know a cheater when I see one. That woman fucked around on you. Are you even sure you were Jane's father? You ever think maybe that's why Janey died at age three, as some kind of punishment for her mother's sins——"

I pull him to his feet so we're face-to-face, my jaw so tight it hurts. "So we're being honest now, Henry? Okay, then let's be honest. You couldn't cut it as an investor, so you cheated your way to the top. And you couldn't make your wife happy no matter what you did, cheating or otherwise."

His eyes turn to fire. "Attaboy, Detective. Now you're getting the hang of it."

"She found out you're a fraud, a phony, and you

couldn't have that. Not the great Henry Arcola, investor to the stars. In reality, a big phony con artist."

"Right, right." He nods. "So then what?"

"So you killed your wife to keep her quiet. But you didn't have the balls to do it yourself. You had to hide behind some tough guys, some thugs."

"Yeah?" He laughs. "Did I?"

"Yeah, you did. Because you're a fucking coward."

He loses his smile. Appraises me. Works his jaw. Makes a *tsk, tsk* noise.

Then he nods at me, motioning to me to get closer.

I take another step forward, nearly nose to nose with him, his breath on my face.

"Closer," he whispers. "I won't bite."

My heart pounding, not sure I'm reading this right but not caring, I lean my ear into him.

"Not a coward, just smart," he says. "But just between us girls, Detective?"

I don't say anything.

He leans up on the balls of his feet, so his mouth is nearly caressing my ear.

"I killed that whore wife of mine," he whispers. "But you'll never fucking prove it."

CHAPTER 35

Billionaire charged in wife's death.

An irresistible story, the lead on every local and national news show. Photos of Henry with Marlene, with mayors and governors, with celebrities, at black-tie galas and celebrity-studded fundraisers. People love to see the elite brought down.

Outside the courtroom, a mob of reporters and photographers, B-list journalists who couldn't score a seat inside for the standing-room-only arraignment.

Down the hall, Pete Parsons, the assistant state's attorney, closes up his file. "You always bring me the fun ones, Harney," he says. "Remind me again why I was so honored to be assigned to SOS."

"Pete, listen—"

"You have an audio recording of him referring to his wife being a problem, and you have some evidence of financial fraud from a spreadsheet. Oh, and a tox screen of the victim that's more consistent with an overdose than homicide. I mean, shit, Billy, props to you for getting that rush on the tox screen, but Marlene had taken three times the amount of antidepressants she was prescribed and had enough booze in her to get a DUI twice over."

"There's a trail of blood from the kitchen up to her master bathroom," I say. "Unexplained bruising. They beat her, forced her upstairs, forced her to take drugs and drink. Probably at gunpoint. Tried to make it look like an overdose."

"And you—"

"And he confessed to me, Pete. The circumstances might've been weird—"

"Weird? You pull him out of the car on the side of the highway, and he picks that moment to confess to you. Oh, and only after he invoked his right to counsel in front of half the cops in the state of Wisconsin. But we're asking the judge to believe that he suddenly had a change of heart, voluntarily, of his free will, on the shoulder of Interstate 94."

"He set all that up," I say. "He invoked for cover. He confessed under circumstances that sound unbelievable."

"If he's that careful, that manipulative, then why confess at all?"

"Because he couldn't stand *not* telling me, Pete. The guy's a psychopath. If you don't believe me, why'd you approve charges?"

"I—of course I believe you, Billy." He hits my arm. "But the dream team of lawyers Henry's going to assemble will have a field day with that in front of the jury."

"We're a long way from a jury. Give me time. I can make this case. And shit, after he spends a week or two in the Dungeon—they'll eat him alive in there. He'll be dying to cooperate."

He allows for that. "Dunham *is* a hellhole. Jesus, how'd those guys ever talk the state into letting them build a private jail in Cook County?" He shakes his head.

"I don't know, Pete. Good lobbyists, I guess. You wanna talk about that? Or you wanna talk about this case?"

He lets out a sigh. "You have to be prepared for the fact that Judge Patton won't no-bond him. Not on evidence like this. Maybe—maybe the confession will do it. But if he has any kind of a decent lawyer, and you know he'll have the best, he'll bond out."

"And he'll be gone," I say. "He'll flee."

"He'll have to surrender his passport."

I shake my head. "Won't matter. He's too smart for that. He's thought this through. He has a getaway. I know he does."

"You know him that well, do you?"

"I know him well enough. Hey, what lawyer did Henry hire?"

"Don't know. Nobody's reached out yet. Which is weird." He shrugs. "Anyway, he, she, or more likely *they* will be the best lawyers money can buy."

We head to the courtroom, approaching the herd of media awaiting outside.

"We gotta hold him," I say to Pete. "He gets bond, we'll never see him again."

CHAPTER 36

WE ENTER the courtroom of Judge Catherine Patton, cramped and sweaty with the standing-room-only crowd of media on hand for the circus.

Sitting near the front, with her grandmother, is Logan, who looks exactly as you'd expect—wearing a dulled, washed-out, sleep-deprived expression, darkness framing her eyes. She is drained of emotion at this point, but her eyes still show fire.

"How ya doin', kiddo?" I whisper.

"You're not gonna let him out of jail, are you?"

"We'll do our best." I head up to the front of the courtroom, ready to testify if it comes to that.

Judge Patton, who runs a crisp courtroom, efficiently disposes of two remaining arraignments—indigent defendants represented by the public defender, a man named Will Hastings. The judge has saved the best for last, the one that will probably take the longest: the arraignment that everyone in the courtroom's waiting for.

"People versus Henry Arcola," the clerk calls.

Pete Parsons rises for the people. I look around for a heavy-hitter attorney like Elan Tenenbaum or Nancy Carpenter. I don't see any. The spectators' gallery is packed, but the front rows, for the lawyers, are empty.

Henry Arcola is led from the holding cell and approaches the bench in shackles.

"Good afternoon, Your Honor. Pete Parsons for the people."

"Will Hastings for defendant Arcola."

Wait. Henry is using Will Hastings?

A guy worth billions is using the public defender?

"Mr. Arcola," says Judge Patton, looking down over her glasses, "is not represented by private counsel?"

"Judge," says Will Hastings, "he's in the process of retaining counsel but has not yet done so."

"I see." Judge Patton tucks a strand of gray hair behind her ear.

"We waive reading of the charges, Your Honor, and my client pleads not guilty."

"All right," says the judge. "Does the state wish to be heard on bond?"

Pete goes through his spiel. The charge of first-degree murder of his wife. A recitation of the evidence, in only pro forma fashion for the time being. A confession to Detective Billy Harney. A statement recorded by his daughter. A pending divorce. The victim in possession of incriminating information that, if made public, would have caused embarrassment.

Pete stops short of detailing that incriminating information, the Ponzi scheme. His only hope is that Henry won't want it out yet, either, and he'll lie down on bond rather than risk a fight that will force Pete to talk about it publicly.

Then Pete turns to the risk of Henry's flight. High,

he argues, given Henry's vast resources, his ownership of a private jet, and houses on three continents.

"Given the crime and the risk of flight, the people request a no-bond hold."

The judge nods. "Mr. Hastings?"

"Judge, Mr. Arcola informs me that, other than waiving reading and the not-guilty plea, I am not authorized to take any further action on his behalf. I am not authorized even to argue against a no-bond hold."

Judge Patton does a double take. "Mr. Arcola, is that true?"

Henry, looking the worse for wear, still wearing the same clothes from last night, clears his throat and stands at attention. "Yes, Your Honor."

"The state wants to lock you up pending trial, Mr. Arcola. You have the right to challenge that. I submit that you probably should."

"I will, Your Honor," he says. "When I get my lawyer."

The judge leans forward. "Mr. Arcola, given the seriousness of the charge, I would typically deny bond unless the defendant could challenge the strength of the evidence or assure me that he's not a flight risk. But you have to say something."

"I will, I will." He nods. "When I get my lawyer."

"But not now?"

"Not now, Your Honor."

The judge leans back. She looks as surprised as I am.

"Very well," she says. "Defendant will be held without bond and remanded to Dunham Detention Center. Bond will be revisited one week from today."

The sheriff's deputy takes Henry by the arm and leads him out of the courtroom. We all rise as the judge steps down from the bench and disappears out the back door of the courtroom.

And that's it. Five minutes, no arguments, and Henry

Arcola is denied bond. He will be locked up in pretrial detention in one of the worst jails in the state.

Pete turns and looks at me, pleased but shocked.

I shrug. I have no freaking idea, either.

What the hell just happened?

CHAPTER 37

WHEN I get off the elevator, my sister, Patti, is coming out of a different elevator. I'm still not used to her new look, even after a year. She was never in her life over-weight, but since she's running every day and cutting carbs, her body has turned into a rock, the skin on her face so taut it looks like it was carved from a mountain. She has some of that unnatural bodybuilder look to her. I'm not sure it's an upgrade. But nobody asked me. I'm her twin brother, not her mother, and it seems to make her happy.

She looks at me with a question. When I see her up close, the lines by her eyes are more apparent. We're aging, and she's tired.

We hit our stride together and head out toward the parking lot across the street.

"The billionaire," I say.

"That guy Arcola on TV? That was your collar?"

"Yep. You?"

"Had to testify in a prelim," she says.

"Your Russian dissident case? Gorbachev or something?"

She laughs. "Baranov. And I *wish* I was far enough for a prelim in that case."

"No good leads?"

"I'm thinking of going with your strategy. I'm gonna stand on the sidewalk and hope the perp walks up to me."

Always the jokes. I get lucky one time, and that's all anyone remembers.

"I have a decent lead," she says.

"Run it by me." We often bounce stuff off each other. We haven't done it in a while.

Outside, the sun is high, the air wet with humidity. Patti throws on shades as we cross California Avenue.

"Dmitri Baranov," she says. "What do you know about the guy?"

"Human rights advocate in Russia," I say. "Outspoken critic of Vladimir Putin. Putin trumped up some charges against him for child molestation or something and threw him in the clink. Amnesty International and all those human-rights groups went nuts, so Putin eventually let him out and expelled him. He came to Chicago and kept up his criticisms of Moscow. A few weeks ago, someone whacked him in his home on the North Side. How'm I doing?"

"Good, except the part about the charges being trumped up."

"Our good Mr. Baranov was a deviant after all?"

"He got pinched three months ago for indecent solicitation of a minor."

"Yeah? I didn't know that. Must've missed it."

"It was in the news. Baranov said it was a frame-up, the work of Putin, trying to discredit him."

"That's possible," I say.

Her nose crinkles, meaning she doesn't buy it. "Anyway, he got bond conditioned on home confinement. So he got the ankle bracelet and everything. That's where they got to him."

"They?"

"More than one person. Baranov was tortured inside his home. They broke every one of his fingers on each hand. One by one."

"Yowza."

"Yeah, his pinkie finger was at a ninety-degree angle from his hand."

We reach the parking lot, the good news being the shade, the downside the smell of urine.

"That doesn't sound like a professional hit by the Kremlin," I say.

"I don't think so, either," says Patti. "Neither does the FBI. No, I think someone had questions for Baranov and didn't like his answers."

"What kinds of questions?"

We stop at my car.

"Baranov was into young girls," says Patti. "It's all over his laptop's browser history. And we know he paid for underage prostitutes on Craigslist."

"I'm feeling less and less sorry about the death of Mr. Baranov."

"Right, but who gained from his death?" she asks. "I'm thinking, depending on how deep he was into that sick, perverted underground world, he might have had a card he could play with the state's attorney to get leniency on the indecent-solicitation charge."

"A name he could give up," I say. "Or information of some kind. So that was the torture part before they killed him. They were trying to find out if he'd told the cops anything."

Patti nods. "That's the only string I have right now. So I'm pulling on it."

"Bring a raincoat," I say. "And a vomit bag." The

seamy, disgusting world of human trafficking. I've had more than my fair share of contact with it. They should bring back the death penalty just for those monsters who prey on children.

"*Was* Baranov trying to cut a plea deal on the indecency charge?" I ask. "Was he willing to give names? It would be a start—"

"Wasn't my collar," she says. "But no. Apparently, he lawyered up right away with big-time private counsel. She shut him down. I reached out to her after Baranov was whacked, and she told me, in her polite, lawyerly, a-thousand-words-or-less legalese, that I should go fuck myself."

Sounds about right. "Who was the lawyer?"

"A real shark," says Patti. "Name was Nancy Carpenter."

"Nancy—" I stop in my tracks. "Nancy Carpenter?" Same lawyer Donnie Delahunt hired.

"Lawyers usually have more than one client," Patti deadpans when I explain my reaction. "Besides, Baranov was an international celebrity. A hero to a lot of people. Published that memoir that was on the bestseller list. I wouldn't expect him to hire some knuckle dragger."

"True," I say. She's probably right.

It's probably just a coincidence.

CHAPTER 38

"NOTHING," MARSHA Flager says to me. "This massive house, and there's nothing here."

We're inside Henry Arcola's enormous home in the Gold Coast, executing the warrants we obtained this morning to search both his residence and company.

Henry lives in two brownstones put together, over six thousand square feet. He opted for minimalist decor in his downtown office, but not here, where he is surrounded by opulence: polished marble, chandeliers in every room, a kitchen you could land a plane in, furniture so expensive you'd be afraid to sit on it, museum-quality artwork.

"He cleaned everything out?" I ask, walking with Flager.

"Looks that way. He had a head start on us."

"Don't remind me." When I paid Henry a visit yesterday, I was trying to warn him off harming his wife. But by then, she was already dead. And Henry knew that, once she was discovered, he'd be the first suspect. So he had time yesterday to clean house, literally, and remove anything incriminating. I gave him that head start.

"Our only hope is his home office," she says. "First place we searched, but we've hit a problem."

"What's the problem?"

"I'll show you."

Tucked in the corner of the downstairs, Henry's home office is all dark oak, bookshelves from floor to ceiling on three sides, classics like Homer's *Iliad* and nonfiction about finances and start-ups, biographies of great historical leaders. *Look at me and how sophisticated I am,* he's saying.

The U-shaped desk is in matching oak and is, of course, custom-made. A power cord pops out of a hole on the top, but there's no computer to which it can attach. "I take it Henry ditched his computer," I say.

"I'd guess, yeah," says one of the forensic techies, a guy named Grundy, whom everyone calls Grungy, with his ponytail and shaggy beard. "But here's the problem. The desk drawers don't open."

"They're locked?"

"There's no lock," he says.

I walk around to the front of the desk. "They don't just push open?" I ask, pushing on one of them myself but getting no response from the drawer.

"Gee, why didn't we think of that?" Marsha says.

"Okay, okay. So—what's the deal?" I bend down to get a closer look. On each drawer, a small charcoal-colored square, smooth to the touch, something metallic. A square approximately the size of a—

"It's thumb-activated." This from Logan Arcola, standing in the doorway, still dressed as she was for court today. Eyes still bloodshot, expression still pale. "Only Henry's thumbprint can open those drawers."

I press my thumb into the metallic square. A soft grinding, whirring sound, but no movement from the drawer.

"Okay, well." I look up at Grundy. "Can we pry 'em open?"

"Don't see how," says Grundy. "They're flush. No place to insert a lever."

I stand up again, look at Logan. "Do you know what he kept in here?"

She shakes her head. "Sensitive information," she says, making air quotes.

I put my hands on my hips. "He had this custom built to respond only to his thumbprint," I say. "And the rest of the house, there's no financial records at all?"

"Correct and correct," says Flager.

I walk over to the work bag the techies bring with them to every search and fish through it.

"So what do we do, boss?" Grundy asks me. "I suppose we could try to superimpose his thumb—"

Wham.

I slam a sledgehammer I pulled out of the bag onto the desk, splintering the top, the legs buckling. Flager, who'd been looking the other way, nearly jumps out of her skin at the sound.

"Fuck his damn thumb," I tell Grundy. "Break this thing to pieces. Let's find out what's so important."

CHAPTER 39

"I'LL SHOW you," Logan says to me.

Behind the desk in Henry Arcola's home office is a set of French doors. Logan slides open the curtains and pushes open the doors onto a small rectangular balcony, all marble, big enough for three people at most, with a view to the west, four stories off the ground.

My stomach flips as I get my bearings, separated from the ground sixty feet below by only this tiny waist-high balcony.

"This is one of those, like, Juliet balconies," I say.

"It's *the* Juliet balcony," she says. "Henry re-created it exactly from the one in Verona. He imported the same marble and everything."

I smooth my hands over the white-and-tan marble. I'm pretty sure this balcony cost more than my town house.

The wind lifts Logan's bangs, but she doesn't react. She is all business now, which for her is surely a relief, a brief vacation from the grief. "Henry's office was private. He used to sweep it for bugs all the time."

"Yeah?"

"Yeah. He said he was worried his competitors were listening."

"Competitors. Okay."

"But whenever Henry came out here on the balcony, you knew it was *really* private."

Behind us, inside, the banging sounds of tech officers smashing open the desk.

"There," Logan says, pointing back at the French doors, still swung open. The doors, on the interior side, have motion sensors, small white squares with a tiny eye, ready to scream out if anyone were to breach the doors while the house alarm was set.

That itself feels over the top. How could anyone climb up four stories to break into this home office? Or what—they were going to rappel down from the roof?

Henry must have really wanted privacy.

"No, the outside part of the door," she says.

I pull back the French door to my right. "What am I looking for?"

Then I see it, up in the corner. Another small white square, painted the same color as the door. "That's the recording device?" I ask. "Looks like another motion sensor."

"If Henry even bothered to look," she says. "But he doesn't. He never even sees that side of the door. He pops out here when he wants to talk, but he doesn't usually close the door all the way. And even if he did, he'd be facing out, looking at the view."

Hmm. That makes sense. Smart of her.

"And he swept the interior of his home office for bugs," I add, "but it never would have occurred to him to sweep the exterior, out on his balcony."

She shrugs.

"Remind me never to piss you off, Logan Arcola."

She hands me a small flash drive. "Those are all the recordings downloaded. The device is voice- and motion-activated. Sometimes, once in a while, a bird might land out here and make enough noise to activate it. So you'll hear a little bit of that. But mostly, it's Henry coming out here and talking on the phone."

Jesus, it's scary what people can buy nowadays online.

"Audio only," she says. "No point in trying to get video."

I look at the flash drive in the palm of my hand. "You said you gave a copy of this to the FBI?"

The wind blows again. She swipes her bangs off her face. "Did I?"

"Yes, you did. You made a point of telling me that you'd already given a copy to the FBI."

"Oh. Well, I didn't."

"But…then why did you say you did?"

"I…I don't know."

"You don't know? Of course you know." That came out too harsh. This girl's world has just crashed.

"I guess I just wanted you to take me seriously." Her eyes drifting off, distracted, her voice croaky with exhaustion. "Just listen to the recordings," she says.

Fine. I let it go. She needs some rest.

She heads back into the house. So do I. The techies didn't take long, with their crowbars and hammers, to reduce the desk to rubble.

But no papers inside those drawers. No files. Nothing but the remnants of the desk. A great big bunch of nothing.

"Empty," says Grundy. "Not one thing inside. Nothing in this whole room, either. Not a single document."

Flager claps her hands together. "So that's a big fat zero for the whole house."

"Because I gave him a head start," I say. "He probably

spent all afternoon yesterday cleaning up his trail. He did everything he needed to do."

"Except call a lawyer," Flager says. "That's why he got denied bond, you said. Because he didn't have his lawyer yet and wouldn't let the PD speak for him. Right?"

"Right; that's what happened."

She shrugs. "So he knows he's gonna be arrested, he goes to all this effort to clear out anything incriminating, but he can't take two minutes to call a lawyer and get ready for an arrest and an arraignment? What kinda sense does *that* make?"

Huh.

"None at all, Marsh," I say. "That doesn't make any sense at all."

CHAPTER 40

PATTI FEELS the adrenaline course through her. You never know. No matter how many times you do it. You just never know.

She checks herself in the rearview mirror, adjusts the brown hat. She puts the truck in gear and pulls away from the curb.

Her shirt practically sticks to her chest with sweat. She's had to sit in this damn truck for the last half hour without AC.

"They're in the house," says Riordan, watching the alley, into Patti's earpiece. *"Homeowner's wearing a white shirt; visiting male's wearing a black shirt."*

Makes things easy.

"And the girl. She doesn't look of age."

"Then we have to hurry," says Patti.

Patti turns the corner and drives halfway down the block of Georgians and A-frames, small homes with humble plots. She parks outside number 1742.

She hops out of the truck and goes to the rear of the vehicle. Unlatches the double doors. Inside is a single package. And four tactical officers, ready for her call.

She picks up the package and winks at the four officers.

"How come *you* got to drive?" asks her partner, Mickey Stanton, vested and geared up, sweating up a storm. "We're baking back here. Another few minutes, we'd be a fucking casserole."

"You wanna dress up in this stupid outfit next time, Mick, be my guest."

"I'd pay green money to see that," one of the other tac officers says.

"What's the color of the day?" Patti asks. "Yellow?"

"Right."

"Then go on my yellow," Patti says. She walks the package up to the front porch. Glances through the picture window. Nice furniture, TV on the news, but nobody in that room.

She rings the doorbell. Nobody answers. She rings it again.

She steps back off the porch. Sees a man peeking through the picture window at her. He sizes her up, sees the package in her hand, the stupid all-brown uniform.

The man is white, on the young side, a bad complexion with hair greased back off a generous forehead. No neck or chin. Busted nose. Black button-down shirt hanging over a gut. Not the homeowner, then; the one who brought the girl.

And not a guy you bring home to meet the parents.

He motions to her to leave the package on the porch. She signs her name in the air, points at the package. Signature required.

She hears them calling to each other inside the house. A moment later, the door cracks open. Same man. The pockmarked greaseball.

He takes his time appraising her, a hardbody in a

little brown uniform. Doesn't even try to be subtle about checking her out, scumbag that he is.

"Need you to sign for it." She hands him a clipboard. Always easier if his hands are occupied. Slows his reaction time, makes it harder for him to access any weapon he might have.

But he doesn't take the clipboard. He doesn't say anything to her. He looks over her head, past her, toward the street.

"I need you to sign for this package, sir."

Sound bored, she thinks. *Sound annoyed. You hate your job, and you have an attitude.*

Don't sound too eager.

The man doesn't move. Patti's spidey sense tingles.

"Sir?" she says. "You need to sign this. Hello?"

They both hear it from the street. The rear doors of the truck popping open with a bang. Tac officers spilling to the street.

The man grabs the front door and slams it closed, only Patti manages to wedge in her foot, catching the full force of the door against her left running shoe. She elbows the door, but it opens again easily, without resistance.

The man has backpedaled from the door, a gun now in his hand.

Patti dives to the right as bullets sail overhead, others splintering the door frame. She lands hard on the porch, pops up, draws her weapon from her rear holster as Stanton and the other tac officers rush toward her.

"Breacher up! Breacher up!" Patti shouts for the rear-entry team. "Suspect is armed!"

She gets to her feet, enters the doorway in a crouch. Shuffles to the hallway, head low and gun high. Sees two things: a battering ram breaching the back door and the man turning halfway down the hallway into a bedroom.

She reaches the bedroom, bracing for more gunfire.

A man, the homeowner in the white shirt, pants at his ankles, hands in the air, scared as shit. The underage girl, skirt off, shirt unbuttoned, crouched in the corner.

The man in the black shirt doing a header through the bedroom window, smashing through the glass, his feet catching on the windowsill but ultimately clearing.

Followed by a single shot of gunfire.

"Perimeter west!" she shouts. She shuffles to the window, ready to shoot, and sees the man trying to get back on his feet.

Trying, but stumbling back to his hands and knees, panting. The gun in the grass, a few feet away. Something…dripping from the man's chest.

Blood.

By now the inner perimeter has closed in, two detectives with guns drawn, shouting their IDs along with Patti.

The man collapses to the grass, rolling over on his back. A massive bloodstain by his left shoulder.

One of the perimeter officers secures the man's weapon in the grass. The other cuffs the man's hands, now resting on his navel, and calls for an ambulance.

Her adrenaline decelerating now, Patti uses her weapon to clear out the remaining shards of glass from the windowpane. Then she carefully steps through the window, weapon down, and jumps onto the grass.

"I'm…shot," the man calls out, out of breath.

This asshole shot himself while jumping out the window. Didn't stick that landing.

You never know.

Other tac officers surround the man, securing the scene and tending to his wound.

Patti leans back against the house, the aftershock settling in, her pulse throttling, her limbs quivering. Not every day you get shot at.

Stanton comes through the window. "You're not hit?"

She shakes her head.

"Who put him down?"

"He put himself down," she says. "Landed on his gun."

"No shit."

No shit.

"The fuck happened?" Stanton says. "How'd he make you?"

She breathes in, breathes out. "He didn't. He made you guys."

"He made us? But you called—"

"I said *Hello,* not *Yellow,*" she says.

CHAPTER 41

"YOU'RE NOT in trouble, Sonia," Patti says. "You're the victim in all this. But I need your help."

Sonia, sixteen, sits in a conference room at headquarters, sipping lemonade from a paper cup. A recovered junkie, she says—recovered by the age of sixteen, having started scoring when she was *twelve*.

It's enough to make Patti want to cry, if not shoot somebody. This girl, born into abuse, turning later to drugs, then running away and becoming a prostitute by the ripe old age of fifteen.

"Remy's not gonna like it," says Sonia, shaking her head slowly.

"Remy? The guy who brought you to the house? The one who's gonna have trouble using that arm for a long time? Let me tell you something about Remy, Sonia. He's not only looking at child-prostitution charges but also at the attempted murder of a police officer. So I'm pretty sure *Remy* is gonna spend the next forty years behind bars."

Those words make less of an impact than Patti would expect. This young girl, pretty but weary, deep circles under her eyes, spit on at every phase of her life, probably figures that one abuser will beget another. If it's not Remy, it'll be someone else.

Patti shows her a photo of the Russian dissident Dmitri Baranov.

"Yeah, he's a client."

Patti already knew that from a review of the burner-phone calls Baranov made; it's how they made the bust today. But good that Sonia admits it outright. There's trust.

"How many times?"

"Um, well…" Her eyes rise to the ceiling. "Five, I think? Six?"

"Where'd this take place?"

"His house. He lives up by, I think it's north of Lawrence?"

That checks out. "Just you and Baranov?"

"Who's Baranov?"

"Sorry—just you and the man in this photograph?"

Sonia stares at the photo. Peeks at Patti. Her expression goes from seen-it-all to worried. She scratches her cheek. "Yeah. Yeah, just us."

No. No way. Patti hit a nerve.

"Nobody's gonna know you told us, Sonia. I promise."

"Why?" she asks, crossing her arms, her shoulders hunching together. "I mean, what's the difference?"

"I don't care about the man in this photograph," says Patti. "I care about the man or men who were with him."

"Why?"

"Why doesn't matter." It does, of course, but Sonia's scared enough already without Patti telling her that the people she's interested in are probably murderers.

"This will never come back to you, Sonia. Really."

She chews on a nail as her eyes drift away. In

most ways, she looks far older than sixteen, but at this moment, caught up in the gears of something that could jeopardize her life, she looks younger than her age.

"Those gunshots today," Sonia says. "You were the one Remy shot at?"

"Yeah. Yeah, I sure was."

Sonia blinks, glances at Patti. "Were you scared?"

Patti nods. "Terrified."

"You didn't…seem like it. You were all business."

"I had to be. At that moment. But trust me, I about peed my pants."

Sonia looks into Patti's eyes, holds her stare, before dropping her head and running her fingers through her hair. Then she freezes, hands gripping her hair, eyes squeezed shut.

"Two men," she whispers. "Sometimes there'd be two men with him. Russians, like him."

"Tell me about them."

Sonia drops her hands on the table, drums her fingers. "They were scary. They had…"

Patti reaches across the table and takes Sonia's hand. "What did they have, honey?"

She takes a breath. "Weapons. Guns and…brass knuckles and knives."

"You saw them?"

"Did I *see* them?" She lets out a chuckle. "You could say that."

"Tell me, Son—"

"They'd threaten me with them. They'd put the guns in my mouth. They'd move them in and out, like I was, y'know, giving—"

"I understand."

"They'd play…Russian roulette with me. They said they'd killed a bunch of people and they could kill me, too." With that, she bursts into tears.

Patti comes around and puts her arm around Sonia's shoulder. "It's okay, honey. I'm going to get you help. And I'm going to find these men and put them away. Without you ever having to testify. You'll never have to see them again."

She holds Sonia a long time, as the girl lets it all out, crying years' worth of tears, hugging Patti back. Someone from Social Services is already outside, waiting to help. Whether Sonia will accept it is another question.

Another girl lost.

But at least Patti can do something. Not everything, but something.

She can find these men and put them out of business for good.

Eventually, Sonia wipes at her face and takes a deep breath. "Since this guy died," she says, pointing to Dmitri Baranov's photo, "they call for me on their own."

"You've gone to see them since then?"

She nods. "Usually on Fridays. They say I'm their Friday night date."

Friday. That means tomorrow.

Maybe this Friday night, Patti thinks, *I'll be their date.*

CHAPTER 42

"WE NOW go live to Miriam Polsky at the criminal courts building for the latest."

"Amanda, over an hour ago, a judge denied bail for Henry Arcola, the billionaire investor and philanthropist charged overnight with the murder of his wife, Marlene Arcola, at their home in Lake Geneva...."

A hoot goes up throughout the day room in Dunham Detention Center's Housing Unit A, usually known as A Block.

Their reaction doesn't surprise Jericho Hooper. Most of the inmates in A Block are minorities and poor, unable to afford bail or charged with offenses so severe that bail is denied. It's not often they see the same fate befall a privileged white man like Henry Arcola. Misery, at least in this place, definitely loves company.

They reacted the same way earlier, when the morning shows were covering the overnight arrest of the billionaire. But hearing that Arcola is now headed to Dunham—and A Block, no doubt, given the charge of first-degree murder—is like icing on the cake for them. It will be the first time they're mingling with someone so prominent, and they aim to enjoy themselves.

"That brother's comin' to the Dungeon," says one inmate, sitting on one of the couches around the television.

"Boy best get protection," says another. "That motherfucker's gonna be fresh meat."

Jericho is seated at the couch directly in front of the television, flanked, as always, by other members of the Nation. A chief never goes anywhere in jail without his crew. And nobody ranks higher in Dunham than Jericho Hooper.

Jericho turns as his top lieutenant, Tyrone Minter, comes down the stairs from the cells and approaches him. A hard-ass among hard-asses, a Nation enforcer for years, Tyrone's in for a double murder set to go to trial in three months. More valuable than his physical attributes is his loyalty. Jericho has cared for Tyrone's family—his mother, wife, and daughter—since Tyrone got pinched nearly a year ago. Rent for the apartment, a monthly stipend. That's Jericho's deal: you do your time like a man and keep your mouth shut; I take care of you and yours.

But you turn on me, I *fuck up* you and yours.

Tyrone leans in and whispers in Jericho's ear. "G's here," he says.

Jericho gets up, Tyrone leading the way, the remainder of Jericho's crew trailing him.

They walk through a corridor, past central security, to the law library in E Wing. Stacks of books from floor to ceiling and wall to wall. Long tables of pinewood. Two computers, used for legal research, placed precariously on tiny desks.

Sitting at one of the long tables in the corner is a young man dressed in gray who pops up, standing at attention, as Jericho enters the library.

The only other two men in the library, a white guy in an orange jumpsuit and a Mexican man from

B Block, require no prompting. They get up and leave immediately.

"Stay here," Jericho tells his men. He walks up to the young man dressed in gray. Gray, meaning he's in D Block, the protective-custody unit for detainees at high risk of danger in jail. He's Nation but low on the totem pole; Jericho didn't even know him before arriving at the Dungeon.

G-Ride, they call him, supposedly because he once jacked a state police car and took it for a spin. He's twenty-four, in for possession with intent, probably will get pleaded down to simple possession.

His head is shaved, not uncommon in here. Hair is a liability, something that can be grabbed in a fight. Jericho kept his dreadlocks, because he doesn't have to worry about such things. Nobody would so much as give Jericho a nasty look.

G-Ride, nervous, claps his hands behind his back and bows his head. "King," he says.

"How you doing, G?"

He looks surprised at the question. "Oh, it's all good, King. Sir. Yes, sir."

"You enjoying D Block?"

"Yes, sir. Kinda different. Kinda boring, know what I'm sayin'?"

"Sure. And how is Mason?"

Mason Tracy was immediately assigned to D Block — protective custody — when he came to Dunham along with Jericho. It wasn't hard to figure out why. The cops don't care about Mason. They want Jericho. Mason is the one person who can deliver them Jericho. He could give them a road map to Jericho's money laundering. So they had to protect Mason from Jericho, keep Mason segregated from the general population.

Which, of course, is how G-Ride found himself in

D Block. He'd spent the last four months assigned to medium security—B Block—but Jericho needed eyes and ears on Mason, so he called in some favors and had G-Ride transferred to protective custody, too.

And put in the same cell as Mason.

"Scared, King," says G. "Mason's real nervous."

Jericho had heard as much from the COs in his pocket. But he wanted to hear it from G-Ride directly.

"He wants to get out?"

"Yeah. Yes, sir. Like, he just keeps sayin', 'I gotta get out. I gotta get out.' That's about all he says, know what I'm sayin'? That, and he wants his phone."

"And you told him I'd take care of things?"

"Yes, King. Yes. I did."

Jericho nods. There's no chance G-Ride would bullshit him. The penalty would be death.

"Has he talked to anyone else?"

"Only me, King. Like you said, King."

"Not the police?"

"No, King. He ain't never left my sight. We eat chow together, we hang in the day room together, we hit the yard together, we even piss together."

"All right. Very good." Jericho lets out a breath. "Tell him I'll fix our problem very soon. Very soon. Tell him it'll all be okay. He just has to let me handle it. Okay? Will you tell him that, G?"

"Yes, sir, King. Yes, sir."

"Good. You're doing very well, G. I'll remember you helped me when I needed it."

G-Ride lights up with that promise. "Thank you, sir. Thank you."

As soon as G-Ride leaves, Jericho bows his head, blows out a nervous sigh.

This is bad. Mason could turn into a very big problem for Jericho.

Jericho loves the kid, truly. He's family.

But there's family, and then there's business.

Mason knows all Jericho's secrets. He could take Jericho down. He could give the government every single detail.

And he will. Under the circumstances, Mason will do anything, including giving up Jericho.

King Jericho's running out of time.

CHAPTER 43

THE SUN beams down on the jail yard of dead grass and concrete, surrounded by twenty-foot fences topped with coiled wire, its three hundred detainees in their orange jumpsuits. A Block's one hour outside for the day.

Some lift weights. Some kick around a soccer ball or a Hacky Sack. Most just hang out and jaw within their groups.

The typical divisions of men, first by race and then by gang affiliation. The Blacks on the west side of the yard, divided into multiple gangs but primarily the Insane Posse, the K-Street Hustlers, the Cermak Kings, and of course the big one, the Imperial Gangster Nation. On the east side of the yard, the Latinos, divided into Los Depredadores Latinos, the Almighty Kings, the Maniac Disciples, and their spin-offs.

The Blacks and Latinos generally have a truce in A Block. You stay out of our way; we stay out of yours. You don't sell dope to our people; we don't sell to yours. Don't start nothing with us; we won't start nothing with you.

The same goes with the intraracial gangs. The Posse,

the Hustlers, the Kings, and the Nation have generally agreed to work together, rivalries only occasionally coming to the surface.

None of these truces is durable or perfect. Fights break out. Inmates get beatings. Some get cut. But nobody's died in the last eight months. And there hasn't been a full-on war for over a year.

Things got tense when Jericho Hooper, the King himself, arrived a couple of days ago. Nobody was sure what his arrival would do to the fragile peace treaties. But Jericho made it clear that he wanted peace inside the Dungeon. Whatever deal had been worked out among the Black gangs, he said, would be fine with him for the time being.

The band of white detainees in A Block is smaller, most of them belonging to some version of a white-power gang, generally locating in the middle of the yard, outnumbered.

Then there's the new guy, the one they saw on TV this morning, the billionaire, Henry Arcola, looking meek and overmatched in a jumpsuit two sizes too big for him. He is standing even a bit apart from the other white detainees, looking like he could use a friend.

He probably could. It will be rough for him in here.

Corrections officer Korey Heppner patrols the yard, one of a handful of COs out here, not counting the snipers in the two towers at each end of the yard. "How we doin', Luis?" he calls out to one of the Latino detainees, trying to spin a soccer ball on his finger. "Gonna be late for roll call tonight?"

"You fucked me, *ese,*" he complains.

Right. Always the same story. It's never the inmate's fault. It's always the asshole CO.

But Korey Heppner has come to like his job, which he's held since Dunham opened, two years ago. It works.

At age thirty-four, living in Oak Forest with his wife and three sons, he needs the steady paycheck and the pension.

And he needs Jericho Hooper.

On the books, Korey is clean. Off the books, he is not. Korey is a violent man. And he has unique sexual interests that involve violence and do not involve his wife.

How Jericho Hooper learned that about him, he'll never know. Well, that's not entirely true. Jericho learned about him because Korey frequented a couple of his girls. But how Jericho managed to learn what Korey did for a living—that part, he must admit, was impressive. Jericho must run a good intelligence operation.

And the deal Jericho offered was too good to pass up. All the women he wants, whenever he wants, however he wants, and a small monthly stipend on top of that. And in exchange, Korey does Jericho's bidding inside Dunham. Protect the drug trafficking. Protect the Nation members. Keep an eye on 'em, too, in case any of them is considering flipping on Jericho in exchange for a plea deal.

Intelligence, mostly. Just be Jericho's eyes and ears.

But on rare occasions, use a little muscle on Jericho's behalf, too.

He sees Tyrone Minter, Jericho's top guy, moving across the yard toward him. Tyrone was the Nation's shot caller inside here before Jericho showed up, which makes him Jericho's right-hand man now.

"Still pissed I wrote you up last week, Ty?" Heppner says. "Remember, FFC."

The motto here at Dunham—firm, fair, and consistent.

"Fuckin' faggots and cunts," Ty says.

"The mouth, Tyrone, the mouth."

Took some balls to write up Tyrone. Heppner thought

twice about violating Ty, at the time the Nation's top dog in here. He wanted to let Tyrone and everyone else in A Block know: this is Heppner's jail. They can work together. There's plenty of room for everyone to get a taste. But this is Heppner's jail.

Tyrone stops short of him. The man's gotta be six two, six three, probably two buck fifty of pure muscle. Heppner's seen Tyrone put up four hundred pounds on the bench in the yard. Heppner's no petite guy himself, and he's the one with the uniform, the badge, the gun, the Taser, the stick, and at least five other COs watching his back right now—but his heart still ratchets to the next level as Tyrone sizes him up.

Tyrone glances around. "King needs to talk to you," he says, hardly above a whisper.

A jolt runs through Heppner. Jericho wants to see him. That's what he was afraid of. Jericho's been worried about his boy Mason Tracy in D Block, protective custody. He told Heppner to "be ready" because "something will have to happen soon."

Apparently, soon is now.

Fuck.

Heppner nods, glances around. Wary of cameras. Wary of fellow COs monitoring from the security pod. Wary of the other detainees.

"When?" he says, looking away, his best attempt at casual. "Where?"

CHAPTER 44

THE CHAPEL in E Wing is supposed to be locked at 6:00 p.m., after the nightly service. Tonight, it's been left open.

Jericho lets his men, led by Tyrone Minter, scope it out first. Jericho isn't expecting an ambush for this meeting, but that's why ambushes work.

Tyrone comes back out, nods.

"He's in there," says Tyrone. "Front pew."

"Alone?"

"Yeah, just him."

Jericho walks in alone. The room is dark, illuminated only by the hallway lighting.

But it's enough for Jericho to see him sitting in the front row.

The jail chapel isn't much to look at. The cheap-asses at Dunham didn't wanna spring for more than one chapel, so they kept it nondenominational. As many Muslims as Christians come here. No crucifixes or stained glass. Only white walls and pinewood for the pews. The so-called altar is a podium. On the wall behind it hangs a quilt that reads REVERENCE IS SANCTUARY.

This place could just as well be a location for an AA meeting. Which is a function this room happens to provide every day at 3:00 p.m.

Jericho remembers the church he attended every Sunday growing up with his grandmother. The battered red carpet, the stained-glass windows, the oak pews, the ornate altar, the massive choir in their red robes behind Reverend Cole. Singing until his voice gave out, standing for three, four hours, his feet aching in those too-tight dress shoes his grandmother made him wear.

How he would complain every Sunday morning as she made him put on that seersucker suit, the pants stopping short of his ankles, and those size 6 shoes on his size 8 feet. "Boy," she'd say, "you get out here right now 'fore I hit ya where the good Lord split ya."

She was the only one, his grandmother. The only one who could smack any sense into him.

Jericho takes a seat in the second row of pews.

"I got a big problem," says Jericho. "Which means *we* got a big problem. And I wanna hear how you're gonna fix it."

CHAPTER 45

SIX THIRTY. Mason Tracy sits on the bottom bunk in his two-person cell in D Block, the protective-custody housing unit.

Elbows on his knees. Hands covering his face. Rocking back and forth. A small hum coming from his throat. Shit, the boy won't stop with that rocking and humming. It's gotta be autism or something like that. It'd be enough to drive G-Ride crazy if he didn't have other shit on his mind.

From the top bunk, G-Ride calls to him. "Mason, man, you gotta chill."

"I gotta get out. I gotta—"

"King knows that, Mace. King's gonna figure this out. He gave his word."

"I need my phone. Need my phone. Need—"

"King's gonna take care a alla that."

"Not soon enough," says Mason. "It's…it's gotta be now. It's gotta be tomorrow."

G-Ride nods to himself.

Don't worry, Mason, he thinks. *It will be sooner than that.*

CHAPTER 46

QUARTER TO EIGHT. Corrections Officer Korey Heppner makes his final rounds before his twelve-to-eight shift ends.

"Leo, you causing trouble again?"

Leo, a pudgy middle-aged African American, was convicted of murder four years ago, but his conviction was overturned on appeal, and he was granted a new trial, which meant a transfer from the penitentiary back to jail. Somewhere in the interim, he found Jesus, became born again. He's the easiest inmate in here, always reading the Bible, always preaching peace and love.

"You know me, Mr. Korey: can't help myself."

"You have a good one."

He moves to the next cell, to Pietro, midtwenties, a member of Los Depredadores Latinos who tuned up a cop while resisting arrest, buying him an aggravated battery along with residential burglary. Inside his cell, he's got earbuds and is drumming his feet to some music, but he's holding one hand in the other and grimacing.

"Petey, whatsa matter?"

He removes his earbuds and shows him a bloody palm. "Smashed my fuckin' hand, Hepp."

"You should get that looked at. You ask for the nurse?"

"Yeah, yeah, I asked. When you figure she comes? A week from now?"

"I'll mention something to the supe before I leave."

And then Heppner passes across Jericho's cell.

They lock eyes. Jericho nods slowly. Heppner nods back. Feels a shot of adrenaline.

"Jericho," he calls out, "I'm on the way out. Denny has overnight. You doing okay?"

Jericho points his finger at Heppner. "Ask me tomorrow," he says.

That's about right.

When his rounds end, Heppner heads to the locker room, where he changes out of his navy uniform, replacing it with a T-shirt, sweats, and an old pair of running shoes.

Then he throws a windbreaker over his head.

He gathers his tote bag, big enough to hold two meals' worth of food when he has extended shifts, and empties its contents into the trash.

He walks over to the concession area and shovels several scoops of ice into his tote bag. Then he walks into the bathroom and looks at himself in the mirror.

Sees the fear in his own eyes.

He leaves the locker room and heads toward the exit. He swipes his card at the exit and nods to the CO manning the post, waves a good night at him.

He pushes through the door and feels the warm evening air on his face. His car, an old Suburban, is in sight, not more than twenty yards away in the parking lot.

But he doesn't go to the parking lot. Instead, he

turns and walks around the side of the jail, to the exit by D Block. The door is always closed. But tonight, it is not. A well-placed brick has kept the door ajar.

Heppner enters through that back door, careful to keep the brick in place, the door slightly cracked.

He takes a deep breath and heads into D Block.

He slips into the laundry room, down a long hallway off the day room. The room is wall to wall with shelves of linen and towels, the pungent smell of chlorine and detergent.

He walks over to the first washing machine and opens the lid. Reaches in. Finds the bottle of chloroform.

Pulls out the meat cleaver, too.

Heppner draws a heavy breath. His body shaking with anticipation. Now it's just a matter of listening and waiting.

And hoping that G-Ride holds up his end.

CHAPTER 47

G-RIDE PACES the day room in D Block, unable to sit still. Isn't like G-Ride never planned anything—but nothing like this, nothing with the stakes so high. You don't disappoint the King.

His eyes on the clock, his mind on the sequence of events.

Two dozen inmates in the day room right now, meaning just as many are already in their cells, hunkering down for the night.

But G-Ride only cares about one of the inmates.

Mason is playing checkers, as usual beating every other detainee in protective custody. It's given Mason something to do, something on which to concentrate so he doesn't drive himself—and G-Ride—bat-shit crazy.

G-Ride runs through it again.

In exactly six minutes, there will be an altercation. Not some huge dustup, not a riot, just a sharp elbow to the nose. Enough to ensure bleeding. The blood is the key. The COs will look past an occasional fight, but blood is different. Blood must be cleaned up right away. And blood means a towel, packed with ice.

And the towel means the laundry room.

CHAPTER 48

THE THING about protective custody. It protects you from everyone outside the wing, in general population. But it doesn't protect you so much within the wing.

Standing behind the door in the laundry room, Korey Heppner finally hears it—the altercation. Some shouting from the detainees. Most of the inmates in protective custody are pretty meek and mild and want no trouble. Most would retreat in the face of a fight between detainees, keep their distance and say nothing, wanting to stay away from harm or blame. But these guys being who they are, some of them love a good dustup and hoot and holler like spectators.

So this is happening now. He can feel his pulse banging in his throat.

Heppner's nervous, sure. *Scared* is a better word, if he's honest. But yeah, being honest, he likes the violence. Usually with a woman, but a man will do tonight.

From the laundry room, Heppner hears the CO's voice blaring from the speaker. Then a CO coming into the day room, yelling at the detainees to break it up.

Heppner hears footsteps. And the CO's voice, closer.

"Where the fuck *you* going, G-Ride?"

"You said to clean this shit up."

"Clean it with a mop, dumbshit. In the kitchen. *He's* the one with the bloody fuckin' nose."

"Wasn't me who started—"

"G, brother, you already got one violation. You wanna test me? Go get the fucking mop!"

"That's some bullshit."

"And you—you'll be okay. Bloody nose ain't gonna kill you. Get yourself cleaned up. Grab a towel from laundry and head up to your cell. You're done for the night."

Heppner on high alert, his pulse now a steady drumbeat, the towel dripping with chloroform in his right hand, the meat cleaver gripped in his left. Remembering Jericho's words.

It's gotta look angry, Hepp. Gotta look violent. Like rage. Not professional. Not like a hit.

Jericho told him that with a trace of apology, as if that would make the hit even harder.

What Jericho didn't realize is, that's the part Heppner will enjoy.

FRIDAY

CHAPTER 49

"AND NOW, without further ado, the cop who keeps getting his name in the papers for solving crimes that are handed to him on a silver platter—the notorious, the one and only...well, shit, you know him." Morty hands me the mike, and the cops at the Hole bellow out cheers and jeers, as drunk cops will do.

It's past two in the morning. Anyone with any sense is long gone from this place. My team—Flager, Sosh, Rodriguez, and a few others—made a midnight arrival to the Hole, having killed the evening at the station, going over the contents of our searches today. We got diddly-squat out of Henry's home, but there were plenty of records at his downtown office.

Drinks, multiple, were waiting for us when we arrived, with coppers showing me video of the press conference and noting how uncomfortable I looked. Next thing I know, I'm four bourbons down, and I've had a few shots of unknown origin, colorful and spicy. And then I'm being pushed to the stage.

"That's not fair, Morty," I say, taking the mike. "It took some real police work to not be noticeable to that pedophile when he walked up to me on the sidewalk.

And that billionaire? Sure, his daughter told me it would happen, and she recorded him making incriminating statements, but I put the handcuffs on him all by myself."

The crew seems to like that. I'm on stage later than I normally would be, so the coppers are even drunker than normal. Easy crowd.

"But hey, that's why they put me in SOS," I say. "I get the cases that are 'so obvious, stupid.'

"Tell you this, though. One thing I learned today from that billionaire. Money can't buy you happiness. It'll give you a much better set of memories, but not happiness.

"I mean, what am I gonna do with a million dollars?" I look around. Usually, I'm okay on my feet, winging it with a mike in my hand. Right now, though, I got nothing. A total blank.

But I'm bailed out by a couple of detectives from Wentworth, who don't make it up this way all that often and who are way too far into their pints. They start singing that song "If I Had a Million Dollars," by that quirky band whose name I'd remember If I Had a Clearer Mind. Something about a naked lady. Figures I'd remember that part.

"Yeah, there you go, a little song to spice things up."

Then their singing spreads, and before long, half the cops are bellowing out that song. To make matters worse, all of a sudden I'm kicking my leg out and jerking it around, the twist or something. "Some of you may know I dabble in interpretive dance. I call this the middle-aged white man's spasmic twitch."

I work my arms in a bit, too, throwing elbows. I have no idea why.

"Or maybe I'm having a seizure," I say.

And now it's a full sing-along in the Hole in the Wall,

butchering the lyrics without apology, while I do my best imitation of a mental patient trying to escape from a straitjacket.

My eyes wander over to the bar, where my favorite bartender, the lovely and mysterious Mia, is covering her eyes with her hand.

"I think I've embarrassed myself enough for one night," I say. "Tomorrow, we conga!"

"You are now officially my hero," says Mat Rodriguez, slurring his words, when I step off the stage. "When I grow up, I wanna be just like you."

"A drunk cop? I got some news for you, Matty…"

I make my way to the bar, to Mia, feeling a little wind in my sails. I don't know why. It's not going anywhere. She's dressed in the same basic bartender garb, this time an orange Bears jersey, ponytail looped through her cap again. If there's a way to dress like that and still look classy, Mia's figured it out.

Some rookie's trying to make her laugh, as men do. She humors him, but I know that, deep down, she's awaiting my arrival with great anticipation, because, hey, what woman wouldn't want to be hit on by a drunk cop who just made an ass out of himself?

"Barkeeper!" I yell out. "A lager of your finest ale. And fresh horses for the men!"

She drops a cup of ice water, which, apparently, she had ready for me, on the counter. "Okay, *Dancing with the Stars*."

God, I like her.

"It's just a side gig," I say. "My real passion is ice dancing."

"I could see that. You're very graceful." Delivered with her customary deadpan expression, a great poker face. She pulls on a lever, filling a pint of Guinness. "Are you thinking Olympics? Or turning pro?"

I drop onto one of the bar stools. "I hear Disney on Ice is looking for a Pluto."

She takes money from someone I don't recognize, maybe a civilian—they're occasionally allowed in here—and gives him change. Then she drops her elbows on the counter. "Well, sir, you've had a busy week," she says. "You seem to have put a lot of people away."

The water tastes good. I down the cup and chew on the ice.

"Now I just have to keep them there," I mumble to myself.

CHAPTER 50

I SIT at the bar listening to some baby cop telling me how he collared a purse snatcher on Ashland Avenue, and I'm nodding along and acting like I'm fascinated as hell, when really I'm feeling the start of a hangover, and all I can think about is a teenage girl who just lost both her parents, her mother dead because her father killed her, and four dead girls dredged up from a burial site in the wake of a pedophile's crime spree.

Leave the job on the street. Don't take it home with you. That's the rule. That's what they always tell us. Everyone wants to believe that. Everyone tries to do that. But no cop can. You don't just shower this stuff off. It sticks to you. It seeps inside you. It becomes you. You can have a few drinks and make a few jokes and blow off some steam; you can kiss your loved ones and hug your children; but you can't brush off what you see every day any more than you could peel off your own skin.

How do I just ignore the fact that Logan Arcola's entire life has been turned upside down?

How do I forget that Carla's boy, Samuel, will grow up without a mother?

What about those four girls that Donnie Delahunt abducted, sexually assaulted, and murdered?

And what do I do about it? I catch the perps. I put them in prison. But I don't bring back the dead. And catching the bad guys doesn't seem to be preventing more people from doing bad things. The cycle never ends.

I get morbid like this sometimes when I've had too many drinks, feeling like I'm swimming helplessly against the current.

Or maybe it's just a case of it's-3:00-a.m.-and-I-must-be-lonely.

Great—now I have *that* nineties pop song in my head.

"You doing okay?" Mia says to me after the rookie who was bending my ear heads for the exit. The place is all but empty now, just past three.

"Me? I've never had it so good."

"You didn't hear a word that guy was telling you."

"Sure I did. The…purse snatcher on Ashland."

"Damen," she says. "And he was a pickpocket."

"Right—that's what I meant."

"Those young cops admire you," she says. "You know that, don't you? They want to impress you. They want to be like you."

A smile slowly spreads to her cheeks, her blue eyes narrowing. A soft, gentle smile.

I like her cocky, deadpan, sarcastic routine just fine. But that smile—not a beaming, toothy grin, not an accommodating smirk, but a real smile—I like that best of all.

Because sarcasm and humor are fronts. They're shields. I use them all the time. A smile like that—that's Mia letting down her guard. More intimate than anything I can imagine. Sexier than if she'd leaned over and brushed her lips against mine.

I start to speak, think better of it. She watches me.

Reacts when I pull back. As if she put out her hand but I decided not to take it.

"In the past forty-eight hours," I say. That's all I can say before my voice chokes up, before I feel the heat rise within me. I break eye contact and tap my fingers on the bar, as if for luck.

"In the past forty-eight hours," she says, "you found a dead woman in a bathroom in Wisconsin and you dug up four young girls who were buried behind the house where your partner died."

I nod. Tears well up in my eyes.

"And you aren't human if it doesn't affect you," she adds. "All the jokes in the world can't make it go away."

No. No, I decide. This is a bad idea.

Run away, Mia. Don't get your hands too close to the cage.

"Ah, I'm just tired." I wipe at my eyes and take a deep breath. "Just tired, that's all. I should probably go."

She holds her look on me a beat longer. Not buying my act, but not having a say in the matter.

"You're probably right," she says. "You should—"

"He kidnapped those girls off the street," I blurt out. "He bound them and gagged them and took them to some location and raped them repeatedly. Girls who'd barely reached puberty, for Christ's sake." I throw up my hands. "How does somebody do that?"

She shakes her head, having no better answer than anyone else.

"How does somebody *do* that?" I repeat, this time as a whisper, losing steam, dropping my head.

"He's sick," she says. "Probably something in his childhood. Or maybe he's a modern-day Humbert—"

I raise my head.

"—who justifies his actions by believing it's some kind of twisted romance initiated by the young—"

"What did you say?"

She stops, draws back. "What?"

"What—did you say 'Humbert'?"

"Well—yeah. Humbert. You know—"

"I don't know. What do you mean?"

"Humbert," she says. "From *Lolita*. The man who slept with Lolita."

"And his name was...Humbert?"

"That was the character's name: Humbert Humbert," she says. "It was the pseudonym he used, I think. But—why?"

Hum! Can you hear me? Hum!

The words Bridget Leone heard while she was in the back of the van Donnie Delahunt drove during the chase, before the vehicle took off over the tracks and she was hurtled back toward the rear doors.

Hum! Can you hear me? Hum!

I pop off the bar stool so fast I almost fall.

"I don't understand," says Mia.

I didn't either. But I do now.

It never made sense, why Donnie Delahunt would have told Bridget to hum. But he wasn't talking to Bridget at all. He was on his phone.

Donnie Delahunt had a partner.

CHAPTER 51

I MAKE it to the station at eight thirty, exhausted and energized at the same time. Exhausted because I couldn't sleep, even after hitting my pillow close to four in the morning. Energized because of what I figured out while talking to Mia.

When I walk into the detectives' room, the buzz evaporates in an instant. Eighteen, maybe twenty pairs of eyes fall on me.

"Morning," I say, looking around.

Two more detectives walk in from the coffee room and stare at me.

What, did I forget to wear pants or something?

"Is this an intervention?" I ask. "I promise I'll stop drinking bourbon. I'll stick to vodka."

Mat Rodriguez, standing at his desk, plays with his phone.

Next thing I know, music is playing from his phone. An acoustic guitar strumming, some piano, a catchy beat. I recognize it just as the lyrics begin.

"If I had a million dollars..."

"Oh, shit."

Rodriguez nods, and then nearly in sync, they all jut out their elbows, kick out their left legs, and start twitching and twisting to the song.

I have sinned often in life. But I figured my penance would await me in the afterlife, not this morning.

Some of the uniforms come up from downstairs and join in, too. Everyone wants a piece of this. Elbows out like they were in some vaudeville routine, legs kicked out like they were having an uncontrollable seizure. If I didn't know better, I'd think I was watching a senior citizens' jazzercise class.

To their credit, most of them keep a straight face.

I'm armed, but so are they, so my only option is to take it like a man.

Eventually, Rodriguez shows me mercy, cutting off the song at the point where the singer says he'd buy his woman a fur coat—but not a real fur coat. That's cruel.

The place erupts in applause. I bow. "I'll be here all week," I say.

"Forget all week." Marsha Flager walks up to me. "You're forever now."

She hands me a phone. A YouTube video of me last night at the Hole, up on stage. The elbows, the leg twitch.

The title under the YouTube video: "The Billy Goat."

"You're viral," Flager tells me. "Over ten thousand views this morning."

I look up at her. "You've got to be fucking kidding me."

She looks at her phone and starts reading the information below the video. "Chicago supercop Billy Harney—"

"Oh, Jesus, enough already."

I look toward Sosh's desk for help. He's waving me over. I'll do anything to change the subject.

"Who took fucking video of me last night?" I ask him. "I'm gonna pistol-whip him."

"Like I know. Wasn't me." He hands me a file. "I promised I'd get back the DNA on those victims at the burial site right away. I had to call in some favors, but here you go."

I take the folder. "What's the punch line?"

"It's the four girls we thought, the four who went missing," he says. "And Delahunt's DNA was found inside their vaginal cavities."

"Good."

"But," says Sosh.

"But there was someone else's DNA found, too," I say.

"Yeah. No match in the database." Sosh cocks his head. "How'd you know?"

"Delahunt had a partner," I say.

"Looks that way, yeah. How'd you know?"

I fill him in on what Mia told me last night.

"Humbert?" he says. "Okay, his partner used a code name. Pretty appropriate one, sounds like. So...you and Carla were chasing Delahunt in his van. Bridget hears him on the phone with his partner."

"Exactly," I say. "Hum was his partner's name."

"And I take it we have no freakin' idea who Donnie Delahunt's partner is?"

"Correct," I say. "Not yet."

CHAPTER 52

PETE PARSONS, the assistant state's attorney assigned to SOS, stands with me over a speakerphone in one of our conference rooms.

"You're not honestly asking me to answer that question," says Nancy Carpenter, the heavy-hitter lawyer who represents Delahunt, through the speakerphone.

"No, we're expecting Delahunt to answer it," says Pete.

"And assuming that your premise is correct," she says, *"and my client had a partner, why would it be in his interest to identify him, Pete?"*

Pete looks at me. "I'd be willing to discuss how we could make that worth his while."

"If my client admits to having a partner, he's admitting to the crimes himself. He's copping to the murder of a police officer, the rapes and murders of four girls, and the abduction of a fifth girl. What are you going to offer him—only one life sentence instead of five?"

I pick up my notepad, scribble down the words *She's not denying it,* and show it to Pete. He nods.

"You know your boy's going down, Nancy. C'mon.

We have his semen inside the dead girls. No way he walks on that. And both Billy and Bridget Leone put him at the scene of the escape where Detective Griffin died. He's going down. It's just a matter of waiting for the trial."

"I still haven't heard an offer, Pete."

"I don't have authority yet on a number. But what if I could give you a number that gave Delahunt the chance to get out at some point in his life?"

"A number such as?"

"I don't know. We're just spitballing, but—maybe fifty? At 85 percent, that's forty-two years and change. He's out when he's seventy."

I push down on the Mute button on the speakerphone. "Fifty years for killing Carla and four young girls?"

"You want this information or not?" Pete says. "Anything more than that is the same thing as the life sentence he's gonna get anyway."

"Pete, I have a call that I have to take. They say it's urgent. Would you mind holding one second?"

"We'll hold, sure."

Some classical music comes on the line while we hold.

"It could be more than one other person," Pete says. "It could be a pedophile ring."

I nod. "I thought about that, too. There could be a girl out there right now in their clutches."

The music stops.

"Pete."

"Yeah, I'm here, Nan."

Lanny Soscia pops into the room, looking alarmed. "Did you hear?" he asks.

"I just got a call from Dunham," Nancy says. *"Donnie Delahunt is dead."*

I pound the table. "You're kidding. Fuck!"

Soscia nods. "We just got word, too."

"I thought he was in protective custody at Dunham," I say. "Every pedophile goes into protective—"

"He was," Sosh says. "He was in D Block. They got to him in the laundry room. Hacked him into pieces."

"Kinda…takes the 'protective' outta 'protective custody,'" says Pete.

And leaves us back at square one.

CHAPTER 53

DUNHAM DETENTION Center. The first and only private jail in Cook County, built two years ago, a massive campus spanning the block of 3100 South California, replacing vacant lots and junkyards with a series of sleek steel structures.

D Block, like inmate blocks A through D—and like E Wing, for social, medical, and religious services—branches off central security, in the middle of the facility, like the spoke of a wheel.

The camera in D Block caught the initial tussle in the day room, where an inmate threw an elbow into the face of Donnie Delahunt, causing a gusher of a nosebleed. Delahunt was sent to the laundry room down the hallway for a towel, and nobody ever saw him alive again.

Soscia, Rodriguez, and I are walking with officers from the Tenth District and with Cook County Sheriff's deputies through D Block's day room. The inmates are on lockdown, stuck in their cells, catcalls and insults and threats pouring down on us as we head to the laundry room, where Delahunt met his maker.

"This private fucking jail," says Detective Ellie Shurtleff from the Tenth, who has the lead. "They cut costs everywhere, including guards. They think they can monitor this whole thing with cameras."

"Speaking of," I say. "The video of that fight in the day room. Who was the inmate who elbowed Delahunt?"

"Name of William Avery," she says. "Goes by G-Ride."

"Is he affiliated?"

"He's Nation."

I look at Sosh, who purses his lips. The Imperial Gangster Nation. This just got more interesting.

"You like G-Ride for this?" I ask Shurtleff.

"Hard to say," she says. "Everyone wants a shot at a chomo. Could be nothing more than that."

She sounds like the inmates. Chomo, short for "child molester."

"But all G-Ride did was throw an elbow," she says. "Can't prove more than that. And he ain't talking to us."

"What's G-Ride in for?" Sosh asks.

"Possession with intent. So now you're gonna ask me why he's in protective custody, right? He requested it two days ago."

"So Wednesday," says Sosh. "Same day Mason Tracy arrives. What a coincidence."

The CO leading us to the laundry room, down a long hallway off the day room, stops short. We can smell the stench from here.

"Hope you had a light breakfast," the CO says.

The laundry room is floor to ceiling with shelves of towels and linens. Large industrial washing machines occupy one end. But this place looks more like a slaughterhouse than a laundry room. Whoever did this to Donnie Delahunt took his time and enjoyed himself.

"We're still looking for some of the body parts," Shurtleff says.

Blood everywhere—in spatters on the floor and ceiling and walls and many of the towels; in thick dried pools on the floor. The carcass, Delahunt's torso, lies like a hunk of beef in the center of the room. His legs have been cut off at midthigh. His left arm is missing from the elbow down. His right arm is largely intact, though half of his hand and most of his fingers are missing. And what the offender didn't hack off he sliced and diced in the midsection, probably thirty, forty swipes with whatever ax or butcher knife he used.

Delahunt's severed head rests on top of a washing machine, his vacant eyes staring at us.

Sosh leans into me. "If someone wanted to take him out for professional reasons, there's easier ways. A shiv in the shower'd do the trick. This looks like hate."

I nod. "Unless it's a cover."

Shurtleff takes me out in the hallway to talk. "Forensics aren't gonna get us anywhere. Anyone can access this room. We probably have the prints of half the D Block population in here."

She points down to the exit. "Guard at the desk said he didn't hear anything. When those washing machines are running, they make a lot of white noise."

"You believe him?"

She makes a face, shrugs it off. "My problem is the rear exit door. Day room video doesn't catch anyone going into this hallway who didn't come back out. Besides Delahunt, obviously."

"So whoever did this," I say, "came through the rear exit door."

"Gotta be. Inmates don't use that door. It's only there for the fire code. And guards only use it to step out for smoke breaks."

She opens her notepad. "But that door was last opened at 6:32 p.m. last night. And that was two hours before Delahunt took that elbow to the face and got sent to the laundry. And nobody left again through it."

"The guard watching the door would have the opportunity," I say. "He wouldn't need the door."

"Yeah, but he'd be covered in blood," Shurtleff says. "You saw the scene. And his uniform is pristine. It'd be too obvious, anyway. He'd know that he'd be suspect number one."

"Okay, so that exit door," I say. "You said it last opened at 6:32 p.m.?"

"Right."

"Who used the door at 6:32 p.m. last night?"

"Some guard name of…Cunningham," she says, checking her notepad. "I interviewed him. He's assigned to D Block. But we have him on video. He leaves the day room and walks into the hallway, where the video loses him. But the key-card record shows him going out that door at 6:27 p.m., then coming back in at 6:32 p.m. after finishing a cigarette, then he's back in the day room."

"So he's not the offender."

"Well, he didn't do Delahunt, no. He was in central security when that kid G-Ride hit Delahunt in the face, and he was there for everything afterward."

I look around, take it all in. "You think he left the door open?"

"I do," she says. "There'd be no record of it. The only record is the card swipe. You come back in at 6:32 p.m. and stick a wedge in that door, it stays open without any record of it remaining open. Another guard could come in from outside and wouldn't need to swipe it with his card."

"He could come in from the outside," I say, "kill Delahunt, then sneak back out. No record of his coming or going."

"Exactly," she says.

"But the CO manning that door would see it."

"He sure would. He says it wasn't open. He says he'd never allow that. But what's he *gonna* say? 'Yeah, I left it ajar so someone could sneak in and kill Delahunt'? He'll never come off that story if he wants to keep his job and avoid trading his CO uniform for a prison jumpsuit."

"Yeah. You'll need more before you could sweat him."

The rest of the team shuffles out of the room, probably trying to hold in their breakfasts. You never get used to seeing carnage like that.

"Ellie, I don't think this was random," I say. "Delahunt was part of a pedophile ring. Someone wanted him dead before he could give up his buddies."

"And you're thinking Jericho Hooper," she says. "He used a low-level Nation kid and a jail guard he compromised."

That's the thinking. Hard to imagine this was a coincidence.

But why would Jericho Hooper want Delahunt dead?

Unless Jericho was Delahunt's partner.

Unless Jericho is Humbert.

CHAPTER 54

"I WANT Mason Tracy fully protected." I thump a finger into the warden's chest. "He so much as chips a nail, it's on you. Do whatever it takes. Put him in a fucking suite at the Ritz-Carlton if you have to. Nothing happens to Mason Tracy."

"I understand." The last thing the warden wants is another murder in his jail. He'll be lucky to keep his job as it is.

A CO escorts us from D Block down another hall toward the admin facilities. Coming toward us, also under escort, is Nancy Carpenter, Delahunt's lawyer. She looks ready for court in a crisp gray suit, hair pulled back, leather briefcase.

"Detective," she says to me. "You've seen him?"

"What's left of him, yes. I don't recommend it."

Her eyebrows rise. "Well, duty calls."

"What duty is that, exactly?" I say. "He's dead. He won't be needing your representation at this point."

"The family's asked me to look into this," she says simply enough.

My guess is she's thinking of a lawsuit for wrongful

death. She's a criminal-defense lawyer, but she can pawn it off to one of those ambulance chasers and get a finder's fee, a third of a third of the recovery.

"Hey, I hear you also represented that Russian dissident guy, Bara-something."

"Baranov, Dmitri Baranov. Yes, I did."

"That's two pedophiles," I say. "And two pedophiles dead. Quite a coincidence."

She gives me an expression like she doesn't have time for this. "Dmitri Baranov was only a pedophile if you believe Vladimir Putin's government."

"Or the charges filed here in Chicago," I say.

"If that's all, Detective…"

I step in front of her. "That's not all. Delahunt had a partner. I know it; you know it. Maybe it was Baranov. Maybe it was someone else. It was probably *ten* someone elses. I want to stop them. If they're still out there, then more girls are in danger."

"You're assuming a lot, Detective. You're assuming my client had partners. You're assuming he told me about them. And you're assuming that, if he did tell me, I would tell you. Even if your first two assumptions are right, your last one most certainly is not."

"You have no reason to protect them any—"

"There's something called the attorney-client privilege," she says, "and it survives the death of the client. I don't get to pick and choose when I honor it."

"Even if other girls die," I say. "You're willing to have that on your conscience."

Her eyes go cold, her jaw set. She steps around me, but I move and block her.

"Billy, c'mon," Sosh says to me, but when he reaches for my arm, I knock his hand away.

"There could be a girl right now, the next victim. Already hidden away somewhere or about to be taken off the street. You can stop that, Nancy. Right now. Just give me a name."

She looks up at me, her face hard as stone, a sheen across her eyes. "Get out of my way," she hisses.

"This is life or death," I say. "Give me a—"

"No!"

She tries to brush past me. I grab her arm.

"Really?" she shouts. "I'm being falsely imprisoned by a police officer?"

Soscia puts his hands on my shoulders.

"You're choosing a dead client over innocent girls?" I say to Nancy. "How do you sleep at night? How the fuck do you look at yourself in the mirror?"

"Let go of me right now," she says, "or I'll haul you in on a section 1983 lawsuit before you can say *police brutality*."

"Right, 'cause it's all about money for you. You don't care how many innocent victims will suffer or die. As long as your clients pay, right?"

"Oh, and you have the right to judge." She squares off on me. "You put your hands on my client and threaten him with violence if he doesn't give you a name. Now you do the same thing to his lawyer. They give you medals, Harney, when they *should* pull your damn badge."

"Let's go, Billy. This isn't worth it." Soscia pulls me away.

"This is on you, Counselor!" I shout. "Another girl dies, it's on you!"

CHAPTER 55

THE MONSTER has wings. The monster hovers over her bed, his long spiky tongue lashing out, his eyes on fire.

The monster is a serpent, crawling into her bed, wrapping his torso around her neck, slowly compressing her throat, depriving her of oxygen, while his face moves close to hers, his beady eyes on hers, his rancid breath as his mouth opens and snaps shut—

Veronica gasps for air, her eyes popping open. She props herself up on her elbows on the bed.

"You were sleeping. It was…just a…dream." Her mouth so dry, her tongue so heavy, it's as if she has a speech impediment.

Water. She needs water. A while ago—last night? Earlier this morning? She has no sense of time down here, no idea of the rising or falling of the sun in this time warp of a dungeon—

A while ago, she filled up the empty bottles with water from the faucet. The man who spoke to her through the intercom, however long ago that was, was right. Unlimited water is one thing she does have down here.

It feels darker now. Darker and hotter. Water. She needs…she needs…

She tries to sit up. The needle pricks inside her head so piercing she hears herself moan. She struggles to remain upright.

She finds a water bottle on the floor. Tries to unscrew the top. Takes her a few tries. She begins to sob. Why won't you open why won't you—

She gets it unscrewed, pours water into her mouth, much of it dripping down her cheek and dousing her shirt.

There. Better. A little better.

"Where are you?" she shouts up at the ceiling. "Why won't you come back? Don't leave me down here!"

Please don't leave me down here to die.

How long…how long has she been down here? Five days? A week? She has no idea. When sleep overtakes her, she never knows whether she's slept for fifteen minutes or eight hours. And the fatigue, the overwhelming exhaustion, keeps her in a fog even when she's awake.

The whole thing, one long nightmare.

She forces herself to her feet. Trudges along like she's dragging barbells behind her. The shooting pain in her head, the searing ache in her abdomen.

She makes it into the bathroom, to the pedestal sink and mirror. Puts her hands on the sink to brace herself, looks at herself in the mirror. She looks like…

…like she's already dead.

"Let me out!" she cries. She pounds on the sink. "Let me out of here!"

She pounds again and again, losing control, screaming and crying and shouting, until she loses her balance and falls to the bathroom's tile floor. She lashes out with her foot, kicking at the metal leg of the sink. Kicking and kicking and kicking, her head exploding with each thrust. Kicking and kicking and kicking until her foot screams out in pain. Kicking and kicking and kicking until her leg feels like it's on fire. Kicking and kicking and kicking until—

Until the sink's leg gives way, snapping out from under the basin.

The sink buckles forward. A crack ripples across the wall.

She freezes. Waits. Rests.

Gives herself time to regain her strength. Time for the screaming inside her head to subside, just for a while.

Then she starts kicking the sink's other leg.

CHAPTER 56

"HE'S NOT safe," I say to the prosecutor, Pete Parsons, back at SOS.

"What do you want from me?" says Pete. "I'm not a warden."

"No, you're a lawyer. Figure it out."

Pete falls into his chair. They don't give the ASAs much of a space here in SOS, just a small office that barely holds a desk and file cabinet.

"You want me to transfer him out of Dunham? I could try to do that."

"I want you to spring him," I say. "And put him in WITSEC."

He looks at me like I just told him I'm wearing edible underwear. "WITSEC? We don't give witness security to people who don't cooperate."

"We do now," I say.

"No, actually, we don't. I'll check again, but I don't remember anything in the regulations about hotshot cops getting whatever they want."

"This kid." I shake my head. "This kid is the ticket to taking down the biggest gang lord we've had in Chicago—"

"I *know* what this kid represents, Billy."

He reaches into his drawer and pulls out a tin of Skoal. Pinches some tobacco and throws it into his cheek.

"You're a dipper," I say. "Didn't know that."

"Closet dipper," he says.

"Well, we're pretty much in a closet."

"Quit smoking a year ago," he says. "It's a bitch. Once in a while, I get weak. Like when I'm feeling a lot of stress because some cop thinks I'm personally responsible for the safety of an inmate in the county jail." He finds an empty Starbucks cup and spits a stream of tobacco juice into it.

"Look," I say, "can we get creative? Can we—I dunno…can we say we're hoping for his cooperation and we have to show him he's safe to ensure that cooperation?"

Pete, the bulge in the side of his cheek, looks calmer now with the nicotine flowing through him. "I'll try," he says. "But listen, Billy. It's Friday afternoon. And Mason's bond revisit is Monday morning. If the judge decides to bond him out, and I think she will—"

"That's what you really think?"

"Yeah. Kid has no record, he's charged with a paper crime, and there's no particular reason to think he's a flight risk. The judge gave us a gift for a few days. But she's gonna spring him.

"And here's the thing," he goes on. "If she lets him out, we have no authority over him. We could offer protective custody, but he doesn't have to take it."

"But if I can build up my case some more," I say, "the judge might hold him. And then we could do what I'm saying."

Pete smirks. "Ifs and buts, and if the queen had nuts, she'd be king."

"Give it the old college try, Peter."

"Only my mother calls me Peter." He leans forward. "I'll see what I can do," he says. "And you better get a lot more than you currently have on young Mason between now and Monday morning."

I knock on his office door. "That assumes he survives until Monday."

CHAPTER 57

"OKAY," I say once my team is in the conference room. "The judge is revisiting bond on Jericho Hooper and Mason Tracy on Monday morning, which, today being Friday, gives us the rest of the afternoon and the weekend to make a stronger case against them. I don't want them out. Jericho gets out, he'll ghost us. Mason gets out, they'll whack him." I nod to Marsha Flager.

"Still can't penetrate Mason's phone or computer," she says. "We brought in the FBI to help. So far, no luck. We still have our undercover who delivered the drug money to the banks—"

"But he's only one of many," I say. "The amount our UC alone can testify to laundering isn't enough to get more than maybe a class 3 felony. Jericho wouldn't serve much time at all, even with the record he already has. And the other confederates we think he used to launder his cash—Mat, we getting anywhere on that?"

"Not so far," Rodriguez says. "We've pulled in six of them. Everyone has lawyered up. They're still afraid of Jericho."

"Right, so the key to this is Mason. Or at least Mason's

computer. We get into that computer, we lock down millions and millions in ill-gotten gains. We lock up Jericho for twenty years."

"I understand," says Marsha. "We're working on it."

"Do more than work on it. Get it done," I say. "Before Monday."

I rub the back of my head. "Marsh? Anyone? From everything we know about Jericho, any reason to believe he's a pedophile?"

"A pedophile? Not that I know of. Why?"

"The murder of Delahunt," I say. "If that was just a child molester getting whacked, it's nothing new. But I'm thinking maybe he was silenced. And if so, who wanted him silenced? We know the guy who started this whole thing, this kid they call G-Money or something—"

"G-Ride," Rodriguez says.

"Right, G-Ride's the guy who threw the elbow in Delahunt's face in the day room and got him sent down the hall to the laundry room for a towel. And G-Ride is Imperial Gangster Nation."

"You think Jericho called the hit," says Sosh. "Because he's part of the pedophile ring with Delahunt, and he doesn't want Delahunt flapping his gums?"

I shrug. "Good a guess as any."

"Emphasis on *guess,*" Marsha says. "I haven't seen anything in Jericho's background that says he likes young girls."

I look at her. Think it over.

"Or boys," I add.

CHAPTER 58

EVERYONE HAS the will to win. But few have the will to *prepare* to win.

Words from Jericho's mentor, Christian Lemore, the founder of the Insane Gangster Mafia. Listen before speaking. Plan before acting. Let all those mother-fuckers strut and boast and act like assholes. But you? Show as little as possible, say no more than you must. Your silence will keep them wondering. It will amplify your words when you choose to speak.

It was four days after Jericho lost his grandmother when he met Christian. Age eleven, lost and hurting, he found himself on the wrong side of the street, didn't follow his grandmother's advice to keep his head up and eyes open, and before long he was surrounded by six men in the middle of 69th Street. They didn't even ask for his money. He probably would've handed it over. They wanted to beat him first.

They did for a while, with their fists, with their feet, one of them with a baseball bat. Until everyone stopped at once and backed away from Jericho like he was contagious. Jericho, curled up in the fetal position, blood dripping from his mouth, his world spinning. His eyes finally fixed on the man, the reason they stopped beating him. Probably no more than twenty years old himself, with dreadlocks to his shoulders, a plain white T-shirt stretched over his wide chest, hardly containing his massive biceps.

"Boy just lost his grandmother," the man said. "Give him back his money and help him up."

Two of the punks who jumped him helped him to his feet. Handed him his cash, wadded up.

"Now give him *your* money, too," the man said.

Christian took Jericho to his house on Paulina, cleaned him up, fed him, and drove him home. Told Jericho that if he wanted, he'd come see him tomorrow.

Christian didn't let on back then that he already knew all about Jericho. Actually, he *never* admitted that, but Jericho figured it out later, after he was fully recruited into the Gangster Mafia, after years of watching how Christian operated. Yeah, in hindsight, Jericho realized, Christian probably orchestrated that entire event so he could come to Jericho's rescue.

Christian kept a very close eye on the neighborhood. He knew Jericho was a straight-A student, that he could fight when necessary but never provoked it, that he stood by his grandmother's side, waiting on her hand and foot, even skipping school sometimes, while cancer slowly ravaged her body. And he knew that, with his grandmother dead and his mother a crack addict, Jericho was, for all intents and purposes, now an orphan.

Christian wanted boys like Jericho.

Monday, Jericho thinks. *Monday, I'm getting out of here.*

A Block is noisy right now, the inmates restless during lockdown, the guards shouting back at them, warning them not to make a mess of their lunches, don't give the mice and roaches another reason to visit their cells. This entire jail isn't yet three years old, and already these cells feel like they've received a lifetime's worth of abuse—blood and urine and fecal stains scrubbed but not entirely removed; pockmarked walls; a floor with visible cracks; the toilets barely functional.

The din of the complaints and threats makes it harder for Jericho to hear the key inserted into his cell door. He raises his head off his bed as he hears the first set of doors slide open. Then the second.

He nods to CO Korey Heppner.

"Good news, bad news," Korey says. "Good news, everything went as planned."

"So I heard." The word around A Block, passed down from cell to cell, is that the reason for the lock-down is that a new inmate, a pedophile in D Block, was found chopped into a hundred pieces.

"G-Ride's keeping his powder dry," Korey says. "Mostly, people figure this was just a chomo getting his due. The cops are still asking a lot of questions. But G-Ride's cool. He won't say a word."

"And what about you, Korey?"

"Me? I'd already left for the night. My shift was long over." Korey tries to smile, to show what a tough guy he is, how cool he's operating, but Jericho knows better. Korey is nervous. They're going to sweat the corrections officers hard. Who else could have killed Delahunt?

Jericho will need to do something about that.

"The bad news," says Korey. "Mason got isolated. They put him up on level 3 of D Block. Food will be brought to his cell. No yard time. He can't leave the cell."

Jericho sits up on the bed. "That's not bad news."

"It's not bad?"

"It's not *news*. It was an obvious result. We've rattled

their cages. We got to someone in protective custody. And Mason is the prize jewel right now. They'll do anything to keep him safe."

"Okay." Korey doesn't really understand the long game here. That's fine. He doesn't need to. Don't tell him any more than he needs to know.

"But...you can't get to him now," says Korey.

Jericho stands up. Korey takes a step back. That's good to see. Good to see Korey still fears him.

"Sure I can," says Jericho, placing a hand on Korey's shoulder. "Because I have you."

CHAPTER 59

DON'T STOP don't stop don't stop no matter how much it hurts

Ignore the pain keep going this is your only chance

You don't wanna die do you so keep going keep going

Veronica, lying on the bathroom floor in her dungeon, exhausted and depleted beyond any definition of those words. The stabbing pain in her abdomen. The needle pricks inside her head intensifying with each thrust of her leg.

But she can't stop. The second leg of the sink, more stubborn than that first leg she kicked out, is finally starting to give.

She takes deep breaths, ignoring the nausea, ignoring the intense thirst. The sink has buckled forward slightly, causing a rip along the wall.

"Keep...going," she orders herself.

She kicks and kicks and kicks at that second leg. Kicks and kicks and kicks.

The sink jerks slightly downward. The rip along the wall grows wider and deeper.

No, she can't, she has to stop, so tired, she has to stop, she can't—

She lets out a primal scream and kicks with everything she has left.

The second leg flies out, clanging against the shower door.

The sink drops down a good inch or two, an audible rip across the wall. Veronica pushes herself backward on the tile to avoid the sink's fall.

It doesn't fall.

She gets to her feet using the wall for support, her legs quivering, her head screaming. She walks over and places her hands flat on the edge of the sink's basin. Pushes down with all she has left, leaning on it with her body weight.

It starts to give. Crackling and snapping behind the walls.

She lets her feet leave the floor, suspended in the air while her chest and elbows press down on the front of the sink's basin, allowing every ounce of her body weight to do the work. Her legs dangling, she hears groans and pops and waits.

Getting there. Not enough. Not enough force.

She puts her back to the pedestal sink, puts her hands on the ceramic basin, and jumps up and lands her butt hard on the basin.

A loud snap: large chunks of plaster fly from the wall as the sink rips away, tumbling forward and downward, crashing to the floor, smashing the tile in the process. A stream of water shoots upward. The mirror on the wall above the sink slides straight down and shatters into pieces on the floor.

Veronica finds the water valve on the wall and twists it off. The stream of water shuts down with a loud cough.

She steps back and takes a look.

The wall is now giving her a devious smile, a wide but

narrow and jagged horizontal hole where the pedestal sink had once been attached to the wall. Maybe three feet wide, probably no more than a foot in height.

She doesn't have the strength to smile back.

She carefully steps toward the hole, around the large shards of glass, around the naked plumbing protruding from the wall. She squats down, looks inside the hole.

The plaster wall runs something like four or five inches in thickness. Behind that, she can't see. There is nothing but blackness.

"Hello!" she yells. "Hello?"

She hears nothing in return. She slides her hand through the hole and extends her arm as far as she can. She feels nothing but cold air.

"Hello? Hello? Can anyone hear me? Please! I need help!"

No response.

She grips the jagged edges of the hole in the wall and tugs. The wall is too thick; it won't give. At least not with the amount of strength she has remaining.

She steps back. Looks around. Thinks, or at least tries to think with the pain in her head, like cymbals clashing together over and over.

She picks up the metal leg and stabs it against the plaster wall.

CHAPTER 60

PATTI HARNEY paces the hospital room. The pimp she arrested, the idiot who shot himself while jumping out the window—Remy—sits upright in the hospital bed, his arm in a sling.

On Remy's lap, his cell phone. Waiting for the call from the Russians for their "Friday night date" with Sonia.

The phone buzzes. Patti and her partner, Mickey Stanton, snap to attention.

"Answer it," says Patti.

He does. "Yeah, go," he says.

His eyes light up, and he nods to Patti.

"Okay, we can do that. Where? Okay. Yeah, I guess. Okay, let me know."

He punches out his phone. "It was them."

"You're sure?" Patti asks. "It was the Russians?"

"It was them. They want Sonia again tonight."

Patti feels an adrenaline kick. "Where? What time?"

"Seven o'clock," he says.

That's three hours from now.

"But he wasn't sure where yet," he says.

"He didn't say where?" says Mickey.

"He said he'd call with a location an hour before."

Stanton shoots a glance at Patti and mouths the word *fuck*.

That is not good news. They need time to set up on these guys. There's a house on the north side of the city that Sonia showed them last night, a place where she and Remy met the Russian goons a couple of times. They've had eyes on that house ever since, but nobody has shown up.

That house is owned by a man named Jurek Svoboda, a naturalized citizen originally from Russia. Svoboda has a FOID card in Illinois and owns four different handguns, along with a concealed-carry permit. And he has an out-of-state license for an AK-47 assault rifle.

But they haven't seen hide nor hair of Jurek Svoboda since they found that house last night. Patti even got a BOLO—a be-on-the-lookout order—on his credit cards, but he hasn't used them so far.

So they don't know where Jurek Svoboda or his pedophile friend are at this moment. And they're not going to have a location until a mere hour in advance. One hour's notice.

Stanton leans into her. "This just got twenty times harder," he says.

CHAPTER 61

"OKAY," I say to my team. "Next up is Henry Arcola. We have a few more days before his bond hearing, when he'll be lawyered up to the hilt. Are we getting anywhere on the financial stuff?"

Marsha Flager flips open another file. "We got diddly-squat from his home, but the office search yielded some fruit. It's obvious now that Henry Arcola was running a Ponzi scheme. He had a commercial-factor company that supposedly was buying receivables from third-party—"

"Time out, time out." I raise a hand. "Marsh, do me a favor: dumb that down so Soscia can understand it."

Sosh makes a face. "Oh, but you're a captain of industry, right?"

Flager sits back in her chair. "You're company A. You sell widgets to company B for a million dollars. But the industry standard is, company B doesn't pay you for sixty days. That's an account receivable for a million dollars. Only company A, it needs liquidity. It doesn't wanna wait sixty days for the million bucks, right?"

"Right. They want the money up front."

"As much as possible, at least," she says. "So that's where a commercial factor comes in. Basically, it's a private financing company. It says, I'll give you a bunch of that money up front—like, say, eight hundred thousand—and you transfer to me the account receivable. And when that debt gets paid to me in sixty days, I'll give you the rest of the million—the other two hundred thousand—minus a fee for my services."

"Like interest."

"Yeah, interest, a fee, whatever. So Henry Arcola, not only does he run a hedge fund, he also has one of these commercial-factor companies. It's called Logan Financing."

Logan. He named the company after his daughter. Or his daughter after the company.

"He doesn't tell his investors that it's his company, of course. He just tells 'em he's got a sure-thing investment. So he invests his clients' money in Logan Financing."

"So what's the problem?"

"The problem is that Logan Financing is a sham. It's not buying debt. It's not doing business with vendors. It's not doing anything. It's a shell. Henry's sending his clients' money into a black hole. More specifically, into his own pocket."

"How does he pay back the investors?" Sosh asks.

"Well, that's what a Ponzi scheme is. Henry gets you to invest a million dollars in his hedge fund, right? He puts it all in Logan Financing. He pockets, say, seven hundred thousand and keeps three hundred thousand to spit back to some of the earlier investors and call it a dividend. The earlier investors like that dividend. It's a great return on investment, so they keep their principal invested with Henry. And they tell their friends about Henry. As long as Henry keeps getting new investors, his scheme will work. He'll get new money, pocket most of it, and kick some of it back to the older investors."

"Sounds like a house of cards."

"It is. That's what a Ponzi scheme is. It works until you run out of new money to placate the older investors. It works until either you stop getting new investors or the current investors decide they want their principal back."

"So that's what happened?" I ask. "Henry ran out of investors?"

"Well, actually, no," says Marsha. "He was still going strong. But six days ago—last Saturday—twenty million dollars disappeared from his account. And that more or less bankrupted his funds."

Sosh winks at me. "Twenty million dollars suddenly disappears from that account? Sounds to me like he was worried about his wife, Marlene, giving him up. Sounds to me like he was planning a getaway. And that sounds to me—"

"Like a flight risk," we say together.

I turn to Marsh. "That'll be great for the bond revisit," I say. "Judge hears that ol' Henry was stashing away most of his money, the risk of flight will be too high. She'll never let him out. Are you a hundred percent certain?"

"That the money disappeared?" she says. "I'm a hundred percent certain. But that's not what bothers me."

"What bothers you?" I ask.

Marsha leans back, looks up at the ceiling.

"I have no idea where that twenty million dollars went," she says.

CHAPTER 62

"HARNEY," LIEUTENANT WIZNIEWSKI calls out, waving me to his office.

When I walk in, I see an African American woman sitting across from him. She looks as hard-ass as she means to, with her hair buzzed on the sides, shit-kicker boots, and a tight shirt revealing chiseled arms.

"Detective Harney, Detective Regina Turner."

"Hey, Gina," I say.

"Hey, Billy."

She doesn't smile. I've actually never seen her smile. Not that I know her all that well. I saw her at Carla's funeral, where nobody was smiling, but I've only worked with Gina Turner once, when she was a rookie. We were part of a stack that took rear entry on a drug bust. She disarmed a drug dealer with a judo kick to the stomach that put him in an ambulance. Never even drew her gun. I made a mental note never to get on her wrong side.

She knew Carla from Undercover. Carla worked one of the Latino gangs, while Gina, like a lot of young African American cops, got assigned as UC on one of the Black street gangs. Carla flat-out said that Gina was the best cop she ever knew.

"As you know," says the Wiz, "Detective Turner was just assigned to SOS. And as Detective Turner now knows, Detective Harney has requested that you join his, um, elite squad."

"Yeah," I say, "I want you on my team, if you want."

"I have a choice?"

"Of course."

Gina nods, not as a yes but considering.

I don't know Gina well, but I do know her file. She grew up in the Henry Horner Homes, a housing project best known for violence and gangs. She lost one of her brothers to a drug overdose and the other to the Gangster Disciples, where he served as an enforcer until he was convicted of murder and sent away for sixty years. But Gina kept on the straight and narrow, graduated from high school, and put herself through NIU.

Her record as a cop is stellar, but what really caught my eye, beyond my experience with her on that drug bust, and besides Carla's glowing opinion of her, is that two years ago, she jumped into the Cal-Sag Channel to save a little boy who had fallen in. That's heroic enough, but come to find out, Gina performed the rescue without ever having learned how to swim.

"Mostly we focus on the West Side street gangs," I say. "We also have that case with the billionaire who killed his wife."

"But primarily the street gangs," says the Wiz.

"Lieutenant Wizniewski wanted me to focus only on the gangs. But we collared the billionaire, and that made our superintendent very happy, so I got kept on that case. It's a sensitive thing for Lew, so I don't bring it up that often."

"I'm still sitting here," says the Wiz.

"So what do you say, Gina?" I ask. "It comes with a car and driver, expense account, and free membership to the East Bank Club."

That actually makes her smile. A little.

"Okay, it comes with none of those things. But the hours are long and irregular, and the pay sucks."

"I'll do it if you stop talking," she says.

So I don't say anything. I put out my hand.

"One thing," she says. "Why me? Am I just for optics? You check three boxes, a Black female who's gay."

"I didn't know you were gay," I say.

"But you did know I was a Black woman."

"Yeah, that much I figured out."

She's still waiting for an answer.

"Gina, I want you on my team because I trusted Carla. And Carla said you're the best cop she knows."

"Funny." She stands up and shakes my hand. "She told me the same thing about you."

CHAPTER 63

I'VE JUST finished introducing Gina Turner to my team when my phone buzzes. I recognize the caller ID this time, the Terre Haute area code. My father. Apparently, he's done with the prison phone altogether. But how the hell does a federal inmate have access to a cell phone?

"The Billy Goat?" he says to me, when I answer. "You fuckin' kiddin' me?"

That stupid YouTube video. I'm never living that down. Even inmates in a maximum-security federal penitentiary in Indiana are watching it.

"What the fuck you doin', boy? Prancin' around like that."

"What am I doing? I'll tell you what I'm doing. I'm getting lectured on behavior by a guy serving a life sentence for corruption and murder, that's what I'm doing."

"Maybe so, but I never acted like a jerk in public."

"That's true, Pop. You kept your misconduct private. I'll try to remember the difference."

"You got eyes on you, kid. You don't wanna fuck up right now."

I duck into an empty interview room for a little privacy.

"What do you know about eyes on me? And how'd you know I was getting promoted to run this task force before even *I* knew?"

"I know things, that's all. I still got friends. Something your generation never learned. Friendships that last through everything."

"Okay, hooray for you. Are we done?"

"You caught a big fish, son. You gotta keep him in the net."

"Jericho Hooper," I say. He could mean Henry Arcola, too.

"Who'm I talking about? Yeah, Jericho. You got a good case on the money laundering?"

"Not bad," I say.

"Tell me."

"Tell you? I'm not gonna tell you. You're not a cop anymore, Pop. And you'll forgive me if I don't exactly have a lot of trust—"

"Tell me, boy. I'm tryin' to help."

I sigh. I don't know what it is with this guy. Wasn't a year ago I told him I never wanted to speak to him again, that he was no longer my father. But he kept calling, and I kept listening to his voice mails, and then I started answering his calls. I guess it's as simple as blood. He's my father. He gets me to do things.

"We got someone close to Jericho who helped him launder the proceeds," I say.

"A gangbanger? No way. Nobody flips on Jericho."

I don't say anything. I've said enough.

"Oh, you got a UC in there? You got a cop close to Jericho? Yeah, yeah, that might be enough. But how

much could one guy launder by himself? Not much.
So you got a problem, see, because you gotta show the
money was illegally obtained in the first place. Your UC
can testify to the amount *he* laundered, but I bet it ain't
that much—"

"I already know that—"

"—by itself. So that's gonna be a low-level felony—"

"I *know* that, Pop. I didn't just fall off the truck."

I put the phone at my side. We're talking over
each other. My father, unsurprisingly, is quite the expert
on laundering money. He managed to hide bribes and
extortion payments from the eyes of the federal government for most of his career.

"We got his bookkeeper, too," I add, the phone back
at my ear. The arrest of Mason Tracy is public knowledge. I'm not giving anything away. "He could testify to
all the proceeds. Millions upon millions."

"Yeah, that's this kid Mason, right?"

So he did already know. Those must be pretty well-
informed friends he has.

"Mason won't flip on Jericho," he says.

"He seems pretty eager."

"Never. That ain't gonna happen, son. What Jericho'll
do, he'll have his lawyer represent Mason, too, and make
sure he keeps his trap shut."

Yep. Yep, that's exactly what Jericho did. Elan Tenenbaum has stood between Mason and me every step of
the way.

"Lemme give you some advice," he says.

"Hey, Pop? You aren't Hannibal Lecter, and I sure as
shit ain't Clarice Starling. This isn't happening."

"I'm still your pop, though."

Always with that ace up his sleeve.

"I gotta go," he says. "You want my advice or not?"

"Okay, I'll bite," I say. "What should I do?"

"Oldest line in the book. Follow the money."

"We're trying," I say. "Jericho tied all his money up in—"

"Then try harder," Pop says before cutting off.

CHAPTER 64

SIX O'CLOCK. Patti isn't in the hospital room anymore. She's gathered her team at headquarters. The two Russians promised Remy the pimp that they'd call at six to tell him where to deliver Sonia. A patrol officer is sitting in the hospital waiting for that call, which he will relay to Patti at headquarters.

Patti's cell rings at 6:06 p.m.

"Harney," she says into the phone. She listens. Closes her eyes. "You gotta be kidding me. Okay, stay there in case they call back and change the location."

She puts down her phone. God, if they didn't have bad luck in this investigation, they wouldn't have any luck at all.

All eyes in the room are on her. Her lieutenant, Andy Moss. Her partner, Mickey Stanton, and three other detectives. Patrol officers ready to provide inner and outer perimeter. SWAT, geared up with their full-auto SMGs, led by Commander Richard Lincoln.

And HDU, the Hazardous Devices Unit, led by Sergeant Janet Clancy, if the bomb squad is necessary. Patti thought it might be. Now she knows for sure.

"Templeton, Arroyo, Reynolds," Patti says to three of the detectives. "Our subjects are at the Wainwright Hotel, room 1614."

The reaction in the room is expected. *Fuck. Jesus Christ. Shit.*

"It's one of those hotels in the Gold Coast, a little north of the Mag Mile," she tells the three detectives. "Go!"

The three detectives leave the room.

"A freakin' *hotel,*" says Mickey Stanton. "I was afraid of that."

Patti glances at Rick Lincoln, the SWAT commander. She knows what he's thinking. A hotel-room breach sixteen stories up is a SWAT team's worst nightmare.

"Sonia says these guys get off by putting their guns in her face," says Patti. "So we should assume they'll be heavily armed. Jurek alone has an AK plus four hand-guns. His partner—who knows?"

Lieutenant Moss runs his hand over his face. "Best thing we can do," he says, "is get them coming in or going out. Sounds like they're already checked in. So what about getting them on the way out?" Moss is a good lieutenant, a good boss—decisive, respectful, no bullshit—but he doesn't have tactical training, so he defers to the experts.

"We can't take them in the hallway on the sixteenth floor," says Lincoln from SWAT. "We can't exclude civilians, other people on that floor. And without any idea when they're coming out, we'd have to basically set up shop there. We'd expose ourselves."

"When Sonia doesn't show tonight, they're gonna be paranoid," says Patti.

"Why do you say that?" Moss asks.

"Because they're paranoid generally. Why are they meeting at some hotel? Why not their home? These guys are staying on the move. When Sonia blows them off, they'll wonder if they've been made. So then, whenever it is they leave, they'll be on high alert. If we try to take them in the lobby at that point, whenever it is— later tonight, tomorrow morning—we could end up banging it out in front of twenty civilians."

Lincoln nods in agreement. "Not feasible. Plus, then they control the timing. *We* wanna control the timing."

"We take them in the room," says Patti.

Lincoln takes a deep breath. "That's the least shitty among shitty options, yes."

Patti looks at Clancy from HDU. "I'm thinking a double explosive breach," she says.

"What's your second point of entry?" Lincoln asks. "The room door and what else? The balcony's sixteen stories up."

"We can't breach the next-door wall," says Janet Clancy from HDU.

Patti gives a half smile.

"But we can port it," Patti says.

"Oh, Jesus, Patti," says Moss. "Are you sure?"

CHAPTER 65

SURPRISE, SPEED, violence of action.

Patti checks her watch: ten minutes to seven.

She'd like to do this before seven, before the Russians are expecting someone at the door, before they start looking through the peephole impatiently.

Inside room 1612 of the Wainwright Hotel, Patti puts her ear against the wall. She can hear them next door in 1614, talking to each other in what sounds like Russian, or certainly an eastern European language. They are laughing. They are probably drinking, too.

As far as she can tell, she hears only two voices. Two men speaking.

They've had zero intel on this room. They know only this: room 1614 is a corner suite, basically two separate rooms converted into one, with two king beds. They know the room's layout, fortunately an open-plan design, with no interior walls. They know that the man who checked in paid in cash and did not identify himself as Jurek Svoboda, though the hotel clerk ID'd him from the picture the detectives showed him.

That's what they know. What they do *not* know: how

many people are in that hotel room. The hotel clerk gave out only one room key and didn't pay attention to who was traveling with Svoboda.

Patti only hears two voices. But you never know.

Sergeant Janet Clancy from Hazardous Devices carries over a large duffel bag. "Who's providing lethal cover?" she whispers.

"I am," says Patti. She could have delegated it. But she wants first eyes in that room. She wants to issue the commands.

"You've got tactical training? Good for you, girl." Clancy sets the bag down and removes three large black bladders made of PVC, all of them filled with water. One in the shape of a circle, one a square, the last a thin rectangle.

"You want round, square, or narrow?" Clancy asks Patti.

"Didn't realize I'd have a choice," says Patti. "Last time I did this, we attached a det cord to an IV bag of water and taped it to the wall, then covered the whole thing with a lead pipe."

The last time she did this. The only time, in fact, outside of tactical training.

Clancy smiles. "I used a soda bottle once. But hey, technology. These babies hold the charge and about three gallons of water. One-stop shopping now." She nods at Patti. "The SWAT boys usually like the square. It's a bigger port, easier to rest your weapon, more range."

"How big?"

"Two feet wide, two feet high. Not enough to crawl through—well, for a tiny thing like you it might be—but you'll like the range of motion."

"Okay, let's go with the square bladder."

She checks her weapon, a Rock River fully automatic submachine gun. It has an eleven-inch barrel with

EOTech red-dot sights. She fell in love with this baby when she did her refresher on tactical training a year ago; the red dot remains internal and doesn't project onto the target.

Meanwhile, Clancy gets to work on the bladder—a shaped charge that focuses its energy into a square-shaped blast trajectory that will put a two-foot-by-two-foot hole in the wall, giving Patti a gun port from which she can aim her weapon into the room and see what's happening. They use water for the noncompressible fluid to mini-mize fragmentation, so the only thing that will blast into the room is a heavy splash of water, nothing lethal.

The second point of entry will be the hotel room door, but those things are nightmares, usually made of steel, thanks to fire codes. SWAT will be able to breach it by taking out the dead bolt, then ramming it, but that takes time—how much time is unclear.

Surprise, speed, violence of action. The credo of tacti-cal training. Create conditions so intense that the targets don't have a chance to react.

The surprise is the easy part, the simultaneous breach. The speed is the bitch here, the nightmare for a tac team because of the difficulty posed by the front door and the lack of a second full point of entry. The gun port is the best they can do for a second point—immediate eyes in the room with an automatic weapon for lethal cover as SWAT comes through the front door.

She plays out her training in her head, envisioning the simultaneous explosions timed to blow the dead bolt (with any luck) and the wall port, which she'll man with her weapon while SWAT breaches the door and bangs the room. The flashbang will knock those Russians side-ways, temporarily blinding them, shutting down their hearing, and fucking with their inner ear and balance, all for a good ten to twenty seconds.

If this goes right, before these guys know the difference between up and down, they'll both be in custody.

But you never know.

God, she wishes they'd had time to set up on that room and get some intel.

But they don't, so it's time to go to work.

"We good, Janet?" Patti whispers.

Clancy gives a thumbs-up, the breach bladder attached to the wall between the studs. She walks over behind the "blanket"—the tall officer holding the ballistic blanket in case of blowback—and picks up the cap, ready to detonate with the push of her thumb.

"Commander?" Patti whispers to Lincoln from SWAT.

"We have the C-4 on the door. My stack is ready on my command."

Patti nods, the in-the-shit adrenaline pumping, focusing on her training. Checks her Rock River SMG one more time. Gets in line behind the "blanket" and Clancy, the detonator. Takes a breath. Says a prayer.

"Call it, Commander," Patti says.

Lincoln nods, speaks to the room and into his earpiece. "Breaching in 3...2...1...breacher up!"

A muted explosion, a blowback of dust shooting into the room. Patti waits until the count of two for the dust to clear—not as much as she'd like—and drops into position, slipping the weapon through the makeshift hole in the wall, the gun port, resting the barrel of the submachine gun on the base, a bit of insulation in her way as she looks into room 1614, the carpet wet from the blast, one of the Russians on the ground but crawling toward the far end of the suite—

"Chicago police: don't move!" she shouts.

Can't see the second man.

SWAT banging at the door, a problem, a delay for some reason—

Shouting in Russian.

Another bang at the door.

And a wail. A small wail growing louder.

"Oh, no." Her eyes whip to the far left, by the balcony.

The wail of a baby crying.

CHAPTER 66

PATTI YANKS her weapon from the port, tosses it, and goes headfirst through the square port, banging and writhing through the tight space.

"Baby, there's a baby, don't bang it, don't bang, do not flashbang!" she calls, even as she realizes that she lost her earpiece while scraping through the hole and nobody can hear her.

She falls to the wet carpet of room 1614. She gets to her feet and rushes toward the crib, one of those portable jobs.

The hotel room door bursts open.

Patti scoops up the baby without breaking stride, like she's fielding a ground ball, tucks the child against her vest, smothers her in her arms, and races toward the sliding glass door to the balcony, pulled open to let in the warm breeze.

She crashes through the screen, twisting so she hits it back first to protect the infant. She flies against the balcony's barrier with her back and smacks her head but manages to stumble to her left.

A deafening blast and searing light fill the hotel room

as Patti falls backward to the balcony's concrete floor, the baby on her chest, the sliding glass door softening a deafening blast into a really loud one.

Patti opens her eyes and lifts her head to check the baby, her hands covering the infant's ears, the child writhing facedown on Patti's bulletproof vest, making a noise between a moan and a sob. Patti rolls to her right, her back to the room, shielding the baby. She holds out the baby to size her up, this tiny little cherub in a red onesie, no more than three or four months old, with beautiful eyelashes and chubby cheeks, eyes intact and clear, though too shocked, too dazed, to even cry yet.

"Boo!" Patti says, making a funny face, to check the baby's hearing.

The baby coughs back at her.

Ten seconds have probably passed since the flashbang. Any second now—

Shots fired inside the room. SWAT officers shouting.

Patti places the baby down on the balcony's concrete, checking that the railing is low enough, the bars narrow enough, to prevent the infant from rolling through. She removes her bulletproof vest and drapes it over the child, fully enclosing her, propping it slightly so the infant won't suffocate.

More shots fired inside. She draws her sidearm and crawls toward the open space by the sliding glass door, the screen having come completely off its tracks.

Her back screams in pain. Her head spins. But she crawls toward the open space and does a quick appraisal.

One man on the carpet, same man she saw before, only this time with a wound to his torso, a handgun falling from his fingers. A SWAT officer kicks it away and puts a knee on the man as the other officers shuffle toward a door at the back of the suite—the bathroom.

"Hostage! Hostage!"

The SWAT members backpedal.

The other Russian man emerges from the bathroom, holding a gun to the head of a young woman—the baby's mother, presumably—shouting at the SWAT officers in his native tongue. He must have been in the bathroom with the mother, so the flashbang had no effect on either of them.

Patti holds completely still, her body flat on the balcony, her arms and firearm extended into the room.

The man inches himself and the woman forward, the SWAT officers shuffling backward, their rifles taking deadly aim. A symphony of urgent voices: *Don't move drop the gun don't move*—

The Russian isn't talking anymore, but he's still moving forward, as if planning an exit from this room. That's not going to happen. SWAT will give him a little leeway, but only because they want him out in the open, far from any cover that the bathroom could provide.

The woman, grimacing and crying, can hardly keep her legs. The man has to struggle to keep her going, keep the gun pressed against her temple.

Don't move drop the gun don't move drop the gun—

By now, the Russian and the girl have begun a slow turn toward the front door, which they will never reach.

One of the six SWAT officers covering the man drops to a knee, indicating that the moving part of this ordeal has ended. The man is not going any farther.

Patti wishes she had her earpiece. But the SWAT guys are facing her, and the Russian has his back to her.

She takes one hand off her weapon and waves it.

Their face shields are down, but two of them nod at her.

She readies her aim. The SWAT officers stop yelling.

They subtly reposition themselves out of the line of fire without tipping off the Russian.

For a strange moment, it is all quiet.

"Hey!" Patti shouts.

Instinctively, the man turns toward her voice, the weapon moving off the young woman's head, just as Patti fires one round into the back of the man's thigh. He arches backward, his right hand immediately reaching for his hamstring, the gun falling from his hand. He trips over himself, falling to the carpet, now unarmed.

SWAT officers kick away the gun and pounce on him and whisk the woman from the scene faster than you can say "mission accomplished."

Patti holsters her sidearm and rushes over to the child, lifting the bulletproof vest off her and picking her up. She looks more dazed than anything else, with those wondrous eyes. Won't be long before she's wailing again.

"Let's get you out of here, sweet girl," she says. "Let's get you back to Mommy."

"Ma-ma," she gurgles.

Hearing intact. Thank God. That flashbang could've blown out her eardrum.

She finds the first detective she sees, Templeton, and hands him the baby. "Get her to the ER just in case," she says. "Take the mother, too."

Her heart breaks for an instant, the thought of that little girl and her mother, probably not twenty years old from the looks of her, who undoubtedly was not with these men of her own free will.

Later. She isn't done here.

She wants a word with the Russians first.

CHAPTER 67

THE RUSSIAN whom Patti shot is howling in pain as SWAT officers wrap his thigh to stop the bleeding until the paramedics come. He'll live. She can wait for him.

The other one lies prone on his back, blood trickling from his mouth. Judging from the file photo, she thinks he must be Jurek Svoboda.

The gunshot wound is to his stomach. One officer is monitoring pulse and airway, confirming the radial pulse aloud. Another officer has filled the wound with dressing and applies pressure to it, arms locked, his full body weight down on the wound.

It's necessary to stop blood loss and help clots form, but it should hurt like hell, and Svoboda shows no indication of pain other than a slight grimace. That's not a good sign.

Patti takes a knee near the man, opposite the officer monitoring his airway, who is talking to him gently. Svoboda is moaning, his eyes vacant and wandering, his head moving slightly from side to side. He takes quick breaths and forces words out of his mouth.

"Book…"

"Jurek," Patti says, "can you hear me? I'm Detective Harney."

The officer giving aid shoots Patti a look, but ultimately he relents—closes his eyes and nods his head. They both know how this is going to end.

"Book…"

"Jurek, what about a book?"

"Book-press-cheech-ee-meenya."

Shoot. Russian, presumably, or some such language.

"Jurek, did you kill Dmitri Baranov?"

His eyes close. He grimaces, grunts in pain.

Opens his eyes again. Takes a couple of urgent, short breaths.

He knows it, too.

"Book…mia-less-see-a-dee."

Prayers. Maybe *book* means "God" in Russian. Or something like that.

"Tell me, Jurek," she says. "Did you kill Dmitri Baranov?"

"Pulse is getting weak," says the SWAT officer. "What happened to the paramedics on call?"

Patti leans in closer. "Did you, Jurek? Did you kill Dmitri Baranov?"

Svoboda's head lolls to the left. His eyes focus on Patti. She draws closer still, her nose against his cold, rough cheek.

"Yes," he whispers. "I kill him. And not…not just him. I kill…"

"Paramedics are here!" the officer shouts, as the paramedics skip the other Russian with the leg wound and head toward Svoboda.

"Who else, Jurek?" Patti asks. "Who else did you kill?"

SATURDAY

CHAPTER 68

I LEAVE SOS close to two in the morning, groggy from work, my head buzzing from trying to put so much information together. The city, in the first hours of Saturday, has that uniquely urban kind of tranquillity, a stillness punctuated by the occasional burst of sound from late-night revelers stumbling home from bars and nightclubs, a random siren, the backfiring of a car that could be a gunshot.

I head to the Hole in the Wall as if on autopilot, but I can't deny that I'm thinking of her. Not everything makes sense. Not everything adds up logically. Some things we just do. Or at least I do.

The place is nearly dead when I show up. That's the funny thing about the Hole. Weeknights, it's part of a lot of cops' routines. You do your shift, you hit the Hole before you go home. Maybe you stay for an hour, maybe six; maybe you drink club soda, maybe you raise a few pints, maybe you throw back whiskey. It's understood as part of the day. But weekends are for the families or whatever else a cop has going on.

"She don't work here no more," says Morty, wiping the counter.

"Who?"

"Yeah, right, who." He slides a bourbon across the counter. "She's finishing up law school for the year and then interning at some law firm or something for the summer." He looks at me. "You're gonna pretend we don't both know who you came here to see?"

"I don't know what—" I scratch my face. "You're talking about Mia?"

He likes that, blurts out a chuckle. "Okay, tough guy."

"I mean, she seemed like a nice kid."

He busts out laughing, shakes his head.

"I say something funny, Mort? What's your fucking problem?"

"Nothing. No problem, hotshot." He flips the towel over his shoulder and heads into the back room.

I lift the glass of bourbon but drop it down without tasting it. Fuck. She quit and didn't even mention it to me?

I can't decide if the burn I'm feeling is anger at her or anger at myself. I mean, Christ, what's wrong with me? She doesn't owe me anything. She was a nice woman who did a good job of listening to the drunken idiots who plopped down in front of her. If I had a thing for her, that's my problem. She never gave me any indication that she returned the sentiment.

Except…I thought she did.

Okay, Detective, time to put on your big-boy pants. You're better off without her anyway.

I slap down a twenty on the bar and scoot away. Turn for the door and see a familiar figure leaning against the jukebox, a crooked smile on her face. And those bluer-than-blue eyes.

She looks different out of context, not wearing her standard bartender gear of the tied-off jersey and ball cap and ponytail.

Her hair is pulled up, but strands of cinnamon curls fall just past her chin. A satin shirt and black stretch pants that she fills out quite nicely, thank you very little.

Like a successful lawyer, dressed down.

And those eyes.

"Leaving so soon?" she says.

"Uh, no I—I was just—heading for the john."

"Bathroom's that way," she says. "First time here?"

"I, um, I was—I was just gonna have one drink and take off."

"Looks like you didn't touch that drink."

I take a breath and surrender.

She crosses her arms. "Why is it that a man who faces down the most hardened criminals without flinching is unable to come out and say what's on his mind?"

I raise a hand, like I couldn't possibly imagine what she means. This seasoned cop who faces down hardened criminals without flinching is suddenly finding the English language exceedingly difficult to navigate. And it's my mother tongue.

"I seem like a nice kid?" she says.

"Oh, that? Well, I meant, y'know…"

"No, I *don't* know." She eases over toward me, eyes down, about as slow a walk as she's capable of, or maybe I'm just slowing it down in my head. There should be a movie sound track playing. Are we under water?

"I mean, not a kid…I mean, I don't know your age…"

Still moving toward me. My heart slamming against my chest.

"I figure you for maybe late twenties…"

Her smile growing wider, but a playful smile, her eyes still cast down.

I'm breaking out in a fuckin' sweat over here.

Then she's up close and personal, so close I can smell

her perfume, a flower I can't identify, but if I could, I would buy a million of them and swim in them. I would dive into them headfirst.

Her chin lifts, those eyes in full bloom, at once light as the sky and deep as the ocean, like God invented a new color of blue just for her.

Her lips so close I can feel her breath.

"Do I seem like a nice kid now?" she whispers.

"That's...not the phrase that leaps to mind, no."

Breathe, Billy, breathe. My heart threatening cardiac arrest. Some other parts of my body waking up, too.

She puts her hand on my heart. Feels it drumming.

She takes my hand and puts it on her heart. It feels the same way, pounding against my palm.

She leans into my ear. "Me, too," she whispers. "We'll go slow."

"Slow is...slow is good," I say.

She takes my hand and leads me out of the bar.

CHAPTER 69

"DON'T BE afraid," I whisper, lying next to her, nose to nose.

"Oh, but I am."

"I promise I'll be gentle. I won't laugh."

Her mouth curves, eyes narrow. "You can't promise something like that."

"I don't have all night," I say. I haven't looked at a clock or my phone since we got to her place, in Logan Square, but I'm not sure it's even technically night anymore. We sat down on her couch and opened a bottle of wine and started talking. Then sitting became lying down, face-to-face, still on the couch. I haven't so much as kissed her.

"It's a big step, I realize," I say.

"I don't think I'm ready."

I try to parrot back what she said to me at the bar. "Why is it that someone who plans on stepping up in court and doing combat with the biggest law firms in this city and taking on the biggest global corporate interests can't just—"

"Okay," she says. "Fine."

"Never mind," I say. "Wait till you're ready. You have to want to do this. And for the right reasons. You'll know when the time is right—"

"Shut up already," she says. "But you have to close your eyes. And keep them closed until I tell you to open them. Do you accept those terms?"

"I do." I close my eyes and wait.

And wait.

At this rate, I might be eligible for Social Security before—

"Michelangela," she says.

I hold it in, because I promised.

"You're trying not to laugh," she says.

I shake my head, eyes still closed.

"You can open your eyes now."

I put on my best poker face and open my eyes. "Listen, I'm afraid we can't see each other anymore. I promised myself if I ever started dating again I wouldn't get involved with someone named after a fourteenth-century painter."

"Stop." A blush to her face, giving color to faint freckles across her nose that I hadn't noticed before tonight. "And it's the fifteenth century, for the record."

"I always thought of you as a Renaissance woman—"

"Enough. Don't make me sorry I told you."

"I can't help it. You really painted me into a corner."

"I'm gonna kick you out of my apartment."

"Okay, okay," I say. "So your parents were big fans of the painter or sculptor or whatever?"

"My father was. He had big aspirations for me, apparently. And they thought I'd be a boy. Apparently, my father didn't let my gender get in the way. He put an *a* on the end to make it feminine, and there you have it. Michelangela."

"So what's your middle name?"

"Don't have one. They figured the first name was long enough. Half my teachers thought my name was Michelle Angela. I didn't correct them."

"So why Mia for a nickname?"

"Oh." She rolls her eyes, which make them even bigger. "When I was a kid, a toddler, I couldn't pronounce it. I'd say, 'Mia-la-la.' They liked that. It became Mia."

"Okay, so *that's* your dark secret? Try having a name like Billy. There were always at least two other kids in the class with the same name. I'd have loved to have a unique name."

"I highly doubt you'd have preferred to be named Michelangelo."

"Especially now," I say. "It would make it really awkward for us."

She laughs, the Chardonnay on her breath. "Okay, Detective Harney, your turn for a secret."

"I was afraid you were gonna ask. Okay. Here goes. I've never told anyone this." I take a breath. "My real name is Leonardo—"

"I *knew* you were—"

"—da Vinci—"

"—going to say that, you jerk!"

She jabs at me. I fight her off.

I can't remember ever having this much fun with my clothes on.

CHAPTER 70

I ARRIVE at Northwestern Memorial at noon on Saturday, woozy from lack of sleep but with a spring in my step. The patient has been transferred from the ICU to a traditional room—traditional if you discount the police guard standing outside the door.

Patti is standing outside the room, wearing a jacket and jeans, her shield on a lanyard around her neck.

"What happened to you?" she asks.

"Shoulda seen the other guy." My standard line.

"I think you mean woman," she says. "You get some last night?"

"What? No."

"Yeah, you did."

I didn't, actually. But as usual, Patti knows me. The twin thing.

She leans into me. "Marsha Flager? Going back to that—"

"No, no, no. That was years ago. It's strictly professional between us now."

"Not if it were up to Marsha, it wouldn't be."

Pete Parsons steps off the elevator, looking haggard

and mussed. He greets Patti, whom he's never met in person, though they talked on the phone this morning.

The three of us head into the hospital room.

In the bed, under sheets, with a tube in his arm and shackles around each wrist locking him to the bed rails, sits a Russian man whom, apparently, Patti shot in the leg last night in a raid at a hotel.

Sitting at his bedside are two people. One, some guy from Social Services who can translate Russian. The other is an assistant public defender, name of Rick Diaz, who gets up and shakes hands with us.

"I got the nutshell," says Pete, "but why don't you lay it out for me again?"

Patti summarizes, as she did for me a couple hours ago. The raid last night at the Wainwright Hotel. One suspect, Jurek Svoboda, killed after SWAT officers returned fire. A second one—the guy chained to the hospital bed, a guy named Joseph Ciszewski—shot in the hamstring.

"Before Svoboda died," Patti goes on, "he confessed to Dmitri Baranov's murder. He told me our friend over there in the bed, Mr. Ciszewski, was a part of it. So we have Ciszewski on that murder."

The PD, Diaz, stifles an instinct to interrupt, letting Patti finish.

"These two wonderful gentlemen also were holding a young woman and her baby. They used the woman for sex, but they also used her and the baby as hostages when necessary. So we not only have our good friend over there, Mr. Ciszewski, on murder, we also have him on aggravated kidnapping, aggravated criminal sexual assault, and probably a lot of other things."

"But before he died," I say, "Svoboda confessed to another murder, too. Which is why I'm here."

Patti nods. "Svoboda told me he killed Marlene

Arcola, too. And that Rick's client over there in the bed did it with him."

"But he didn't tell you why. He didn't tell you who hired him." Rick Diaz, playing his card. "If he did, we wouldn't be having this conversation. You want Henry Arcola, and you need my client for that."

"We can put your guy away for life," says Pete. "Baranov's murder alone, not to mention soliciting underage girls, kidnapping, and that stunt he pulled in the hotel room, putting a gun to the woman's head. We'll have a thirty-count indictment."

Diaz concedes the point. Pete's argument will win out sooner or later. The longer Ciszewski spends in lockup, the closer he gets to a trial where he'll probably get a sixty- or seventy-year sentence, and the more likely he'll sing. But Rick knows that we need this information now, not a year from now.

"I want to hear the proffer first," I say. "Before we deal."

Diaz nods. "Simple. My client is willing to testify that he, along with Svoboda, killed Marlene Arcola in her home in Lake Geneva. And he's willing to tell you that he was paid to do so by Henry Arcola. He's willing to explain how they did it to make it look like a suicide."

"Why these Russian guys?" I ask. "How did Henry know them?"

Diaz flashes an unfriendly smile, deadpan. "He'll tell you whatever you want to know," he says, "after you give us what we want."

"Which is?"

"Ten years," Diaz says. "Deportation to follow."

"Ten years?" Patti looks like her head might explode. "For everything he's done?"

"I understand, Detective. You want to put my client away for the rest of his life, then do it. But if you want his cooperation now, the price is ten years."

"Forty," says Pete. "That's a half-off discount."

Rick shakes his head. "I'm not coming off ten."

Shit.

"Hey," I say, "tell me this." I fish into my pocket for my phone, find the audio file that Logan Arcola played for me. "Would his proffer include verifying that this was the phone call?" I play the audio for the room, Henry's voice on his balcony:

> *No no no! You're not hearing me. My wife is a problem...yes...yes, Strazo! Just like dimes. If she starts talking, I'm toast. It's over. Everything's over! Make it happen, Strazo!*

"I've said all I'm going to say," says Diaz.

"Who's Strazo?" I ask. "There was a third guy besides your client and Svoboda?"

"*Strah-zo.*"

We all turn toward the bed, to the Russian interpreter, middle-aged with a round bald head. "*Strah-zo,*" he says again, just as Henry did on the recording, but with a Russian accent, a roll of the *r* with his tongue.

"It's not a person," I say, guessing. "It's a word in Russian."

"It means 'immediately,' 'now,'" the man says. "That man on the tape was saying, whatever it was he needed, he needed it *now.*"

Diaz shrugs it off. "Okay, so Henry was talking to a Russian. That narrows it down to about a million Russians in Chicago alone. Listen, guys, think it over if you want. My client's not going anywhere. You've got Henry's all-important bond revisit next week. And I know you don't want him getting bond. Give us ten years, and we help you put Henry away for life. Otherwise"—he shrugs—"best of luck."

CHAPTER 71

"NO WAY we give that piece of shit ten years," says Patti inside the elevator. "That man has abused underage girls, kidnapped a young woman and her baby, and committed at least two murders."

Pete says, "It's not your—"

"And I don't give a flying you-know-what that your guy is some billionaire celebrity hedge-fund guy. Maybe your bosses at the Daley Center do, Pete, but your case shouldn't get any higher priority."

"Patti," I say, "if we don't put up a stronger case on murder before our bond hearing next week, Arcola will flee. I know it. They can put him on home confinement and confiscate his passport and give him an ankle bracelet—it won't matter. He has all the money and resources in the world. He'll be gone. We'll never see him again. He's already stashed away twenty million that we can't find. He's all ready to flee."

Patti shakes her head, fuming. "You have Svoboda's dying confession, copping to the murder. You have Henry speaking on the phone in Russian. Figure the rest of it out between now and—when's the bond revisit?"

"Henry's is Thursday," I say.

"Great. Today's only Saturday. Look at all that time you have."

I blow out air. I know when I'm beat. And Patti's not wrong: no matter how badly I want Henry Arcola, ten years for that Russian scumbag isn't enough.

"Fine," I say.

Patti plays with her phone. "By the way, little brother—the Billy Goat? Really?"

She shows me her phone, the YouTube video.

I raise a hand. "Yeah, thanks, I've seen it."

"Aren't you the one who told me to always assume someone has video rolling?"

"When you're on the job, out in the street, yeah. I was at the Hole. I didn't think someone would take video of me and post it on freakin' YouTube."

"Okay. Well, don't worry. It's only gotten fifty-two thousand views. There are still a few people living in the greater Chicago metropolitan area who don't think you're a clown."

Nice to know I can count on my sister for support.

My phone buzzes. It's Gina Turner, the newest addition to our task force. I welcome the change of subject.

"Yeah, Gina."

"I've listened to all the audio files that Arcola's daughter recorded," she says. "How quickly can you get here?"

CHAPTER 72

"SO LET'S hear it," I say to Gina Turner when I return to headquarters. She's in front of a laptop, scrolling through the audio files. Sosh and Rodriguez and Flager are all here, too, dressed down for the weekend. I'm liking my team, putting in the extra hours without complaint. And Rodriguez, Flager, and Gina have families, so it's a real sacrifice.

Gina still hasn't fully settled in, a box of her stuff next to the desk. Photos on her desk of what I assume are parents, her partner, and some children.

"We don't have Henry's cell phone, do we?" she asks.

"No," I say. "Never found one. He has one registered in his name, and we've subpoenaed those records. We don't have them yet. But I'm guessing these calls he's making out on the balcony—I'm going to guess he didn't use his normal phone."

"Probably a burner—agreed," she says. "Well, his daughter did a nice job of recording these. Sound quality's pretty good." She squints at the screen. "This is the one and only audio file you've heard so far, right?" She clicks the mouse, and I hear Henry's voice.

No no no! You're not hearing me. My wife is a problem…yes…yes, Strazo! Just like dimes. If she starts talking, I'm toast. It's over. Everything's over! Make it happen, Strazo!

"Right. That's the only one I've heard."

"*Strazo* — that's Russian for 'now,' right?"

Suddenly everyone's a Russian translator. Where were all these people three days ago?

"I was on a joint task force with the FBI," she explains. "We were up on a bunch of Russian mobsters' phones. Two months of wiretaps, you pick up a few words."

I give her the *Reader's Digest* of my last hour at Northwestern Memorial.

"No shit?" she says. "So we know who actually killed Marlene, but we still don't have proof that Henry was the one who hired them. Other than him using a Russian word on this phone call."

"And I don't think we'll get that guy to cooperate," I say. "Which is why I'm hoping these audio files will have more to tell us about the life and times of Henry Arcola."

"Well," she says with a sigh, "I'm not sure I have anything else about his wife. But I can tell you that Henry Arcola was leading a very stressful life."

"Tell me."

"Well, so the challenge here is to create some kind of a timeline," she says. "There's no date or time stamp on these files. They could have been recorded three days ago or three months ago. But that one we just listened to — if Marlene was killed last Wednesday, and Henry's telling them to take care of her *now* — we can probably safely assume that this phone call was made one or two days before she was killed."

"So last Monday or Tuesday," I say.

"Ballpark, yeah. And that recording was audio file

number 15. Now listen to the calls that were recorded before that one. Calls 11 through 14. Here's number 11." She hits Play, and we once again listen to the voice of Henry Arcola on his balcony:

> *Hey, asshole. It's me again. You better call me back. I know it was you, and I know you've been getting my messages. You think I'm someone you can fuck with? I am not. I am not!*

"Henry doesn't sound too happy there. He's practically hissing."

"Same thing," says Gina, "with call number 12." She clicks it on:

> *You think I'm fucking around? Do you have any idea what I can do to you? Call me back and make this right, you low-life freak piece of shit.*

"Okay, yeah, he's stressed."

"Here's the next one, number 13," says Gina. "This isn't him leaving a message. This is him talking to someone on the phone. And definitely not the same person he was yelling at."

> *Hey, it's me. I know, I know, but it can't be helped. Why? Because everything's crashing down all at once, and I don't know where else to turn, that's why. It's gotta happen, and it's gotta happen tonight. Because I'm running out of time, that's why!*

I'm leaning forward now, eyes closed. "Everything is 'crashing down' on him," I say. "He's panicking."

"So here's number 14," says Gina.

Okay, I can talk now—go ahead. So we're good,
mission accomplished? Why, what's the—she
what? Say again? Addison what? Are you seri-
ous? Are you fucking kidding me? I mean, what,
there's not enough shit coming down on me—I
have to deal with this now, too? Christ, I haven't
had my morning fucking coffee and I gotta deal
with this? Okay, just hold on a minute. Just give
me a minute and let me think this through.

A long pause. The sound of a chirping bird. The
sound of a garbage truck dumping a garbage can into its
jaws. I catch Gina's eyes, and she nods.

"I checked with Streets and San," she says. "Arcola's neighborhood gets garbage removal on Mondays.
Usually Monday mornings."

"So this was a Monday morning, probably last Monday, five days ago," I say as Henry starts speaking again,
after taking his moment to think things over:

Well, listen, we have no choice. You're just
gonna have to go back and get it. You got a
better idea? You think I like this any more than
you do? But we don't have a choice. It's not like
we can let her die.

My head shoots up. Gina is looking at me. Now I
understand why she wanted me to rush back to SOS.

"'It's not like we can let her die,'" I say. "He's not
talking about his wife. She's still alive at this point. And
he'd want her dead anyway."

"Agreed," says Gina. "This can't be about Marlene.
This is another woman. Or girl."

"Jesus, this guy had a lot going on. He mentioned a
name on that recording—Addison?"

"Yeah, and I already checked," she says. "We have no reported missing persons with first or last name of Addison."

"Play it again," I say. Gina replays it.

I close my eyes. "He says, 'We can't let her die.' He can't let her die because…"

"Because she's of value to him," says Gina. "Or more to the point, she's of value to someone else."

"And you figure the 'someone else' is the person he was yelling at in the earlier recordings."

Gina nods. "That's the best I can figure. Somebody screwed Henry over in some way. Henry called him at least twice—at least the two times he was on the balcony—but the guy didn't call him back."

"So Henry had to do something else to get that person's attention."

"I think so, yeah," says Gina. "You heard Henry's voice. He sounded desperate. Everything was 'crashing down' on him. So…"

"So desperate people resort to desperate measures," I say. "Like kidnapping."

Gina points at me. We're on the same page.

"It sounds to me like Mr. Henry Arcola took a hostage," she says.

CHAPTER 73

VERONICA OPENS her eyes, raises her head off the floor. She is soaking wet. She takes a moment to get her bearings. The bathroom sink, toppled to the tile floor, leaving the sink piping exposed. The resulting hole torn out of the wall—the horizontal evil smile. The water on the floor from when she busted the piping, before she managed to shut off the water.

She gets up into a seated position, feeling a rush of vertigo.

It's happening. She can feel it. She's crashing.

Next to her, one of the metal legs that once propped up the sink, before she kicked it out from under the basin. She picks it up, gets to her feet, fighting nausea, dizziness, loss of balance, staggering like she's drunk toward the wall.

She finds the area of the wall where she started chipping away and picks up where she left off, slamming the metal leg against the wall like a cop busting through a door. But she only has a skinny piece of metal, not a police battering ram. And this isn't some flimsy door but, from what she can see, a plaster wall around six inches thick.

"I'm not dying," she says aloud. "I'm not dying. Not today."

She slams it again and again. The plaster chips away. It isn't pretty, it isn't fast, but she's making progress.

The dizziness forcing her to vomit more than once in the shower, but progress.

The cramps in her abdomen forcing her at times to double over, but progress.

The pain shooting through her head so piercing that she has to squeeze her eyes shut, but progress.

Her mother singing to her, when she was a girl.

> You gotta be hard, you gotta be tough, you
>   gotta be stronger
> You gotta be cool, you gotta be calm, you
>   gotta stay together

"I'm not gonna die…I'm not…gonna…die…"

Her metal spear breaks through the wall into nothingness, a large chunk of plaster falling behind the wall. A jagged opening in the wall now. Not big enough but close.

She screams and attacks the portion of the wall below it as if it were the enemy and she had no choice but to kill it.

She drops to the floor, catching her breath, and kicks at the wall with her foot.

Another piece breaks off, flying into the darkness. She feels cool air.

She kicks and kicks and—

Yes. Another piece breaks. Big enough. She can fit through it.

"I'm not gonna die," she says, gasping for air.

She crawls through the opening in the wall into the darkness.

The space inside is cool and dark. Dark as pitch. Veronica gets to her feet, realizing the space is tall enough to allow her to stand. Once she takes a step away from the hole through which she crawled, once she's removed from the faint illumination of the bathroom, she can't see a thing. Not her hand in front of her face.

"Hello?" she yells.

Her voice carries, a faint echo.

The air is cool. She looks around her, feels around in the dark. With her left hand on the plaster wall, she reaches her right hand out at arm's length, feeling nothing.

She rubs her foot against the floor. It's paved. Cement.

She steps forward like a blind woman, exactly like a blind woman, her left hand on the plaster wall, her right hand forward. Inching forward into the cool darkness.

Her thirst so intense, and she left the water behind in the bathroom. But she's not going back now.

One step after another through the cool, open space. Calling out but hearing nothing save her own words, echoed back.

Whatever comes, it's better than going back to that dungeon.

She's not going back.

She's not dying.

Her head screaming out in pain, her legs giving out, but she keeps going. *You gotta be hard, you gotta be tough, you gotta be stronger.*

"Hell—hello," she manages, but she's losing strength. She knows it. She ignores the pain in her abdomen, the needles pricking the nerves in her brain, because she's not going to die, not today, she's not—

There. Her outstretched hand hits a wall. Smooth. She knocks on it. Sounds hollow.

There must be something here. A door or something.

She runs her hands along the wall. She hits something. Something hard. Iron or metal. She feels it. An iron bar, vertical. Then another, parallel to it. And horizontal...

Rungs. Rungs. A ladder. A ladder to where?

To somewhere better than here.

Instinctively, she looks up, despite being unable to see. She loses her balance, reaching for the ladder but missing it, collapsing to the ground.

She tries to push herself up, but she has nothing left, no energy whatsoever. She has to get up that ladder. It's her ticket, her only chance. But...she needs to rest first.

She doesn't know if her eyes are open or shut. Just that she's drifting away.

SUNDAY

CHAPTER 74

"DETECTIVES HARNEY, Flager, and Turner," I say, holding up the passes we received at intake.

The attorney-client consultation pod at Dunham Detention Center reminds me of a public bathroom minus the urinals, with "stalls" that serve as conference rooms for inmates and their lawyers. An armed corrections officer sits in a booth behind bulletproof glass with controls that open and close the doors to the meeting rooms. Every ten minutes—or more often if the CO sees fit—the CO announces that the doors will open, and the CO can see into each room to make sure no hanky-panky is taking place.

But otherwise, the meeting rooms are private. The CO can't see in and can't hear what's being said. That change came after civil-liberties groups sued, complaining that the government was trying to eavesdrop on conversations intended to be confidential.

They use this area for us, too, when we want to talk to inmates.

Five minutes after we arrive, Henry Arcola enters the room in shackles, wearing his jumpsuit. It's way too big for him, I notice immediately, making him look even smaller than he already does. I wonder if that was intentional, to diminish him from the outset. He looks like a kid wearing his father's suit.

"Isn't this a nice surprise to brighten my Sunday," he says. The CO puts him down in a seat across from us and shackles him to the table.

Still no lawyer, I note.

"Henry, we've made some good progress on the financial-fraud case," I say. "The Ponzi scheme you ran with Logan Financing. We'll be indicting you on those charges, too. And of course the feds won't be far behind us."

He looks at each of us. "I've seen you," he says to Marsha Flager. "But I haven't seen you."

"Detective Gina Turner," she says.

"Ah, okay." His eyes narrow. He waves a finger between Gina and me. "Are you two, y'know…"

"Shut up, Henry."

He sits back in his chair and winks at me. "But I'll bet you want to, don't you, Billy?" He nods at Gina. "Ever been with a white guy?"

Gina slowly smiles. Baiting him, or maybe her way of telling him he can't get under her skin. "You couldn't handle it, fella. Trust me."

"No? What would you do to me? Tell me, please."

"Why don't we stop talking about her," I say, "and start talking about Jurek Svoboda and Joseph Ciszewski? Y'know, the Russians you hired to kill your wife?"

He blinks and looks away. That trace of a smirk disappears.

"They gave you up, Henry. But here's the good news. You have a chance to avoid life in prison. It won't be easy, but there's still a chance."

"Oh?" Still looking away, trying for the cool-customer thing.

"You need to help us," I say. I hit Play on my phone.

Hey, asshole. It's me again. You better call me back. I know it was you, and I know you've been getting my messages. You think I'm someone you can fuck with? I am not. I am not!

"Explain that," I say. "Who were you calling, and what did they do to piss you off?"

He closes his eyes. Shakes his head. I play another file, skipping ahead.

Hey, it's me. I know, I know, but it can't be helped. Why? Because everything's crashing down all at once, and I don't know where else to turn, that's why. It's gotta happen, and it's gotta happen tonight. Because I'm running out of time, that's why!

"Who were you talking to, and what does this mean?" I ask.

Henry raises a shackled hand, scratching the growth of stubble on his face. Shakes his head again.

"You're sitting there right now trying to remember: 'Which calls did I make from that balcony, and which didn't I?'" says Gina.

"That's exactly what he's doing," I say. I hit Play one more time.

Well, listen, we have no choice. You're just gonna have to go back and get it. You got a better idea? You think I like this any more than

> *you do? But we don't have a choice. It's not like*
> *we can let her die.*

"Shut that fucking thing *off*," says Henry, jaw clenched, a vein prominent in his forehead.

"You have a girl stashed away somewhere, Henry? Because if you do, here's your chance to save her life. And yours."

He drops his head, shaking it. Denial, either to us or himself or both. "Illinois doesn't have a death penalty," he says.

"But the feds do. You kidnapped a girl, Henry. That's a federal offense. She dies, the feds will seek capital punishment. You know they will. But you get ahead of this, help us find her? You avoid the needle. And we can work out a sentence that doesn't keep you in prison the rest of your life."

Henry starts rocking back and forth, humming some tune under his breath.

"I know what you're thinking," says Marsha.

"I'm quite sure you don't." Henry looks up at her.

"Sure I do. You're thinking you're gonna make bail this week and flee the country, right? With that twenty million you siphoned from Logan Financing. You think Judge Patton will spring you after we tell her you've got twenty mil stashed away?"

A burst of laughter from Henry. Either this guy's starting to lose it or he's as stone cold as they come.

"Where's the girl, Henry?" I say. "Who is she?"

He wags a finger at me and grins.

"Her name is Addison something?"

His eyes bug, a broad smile across his face.

"Tell me, Henry. Help me save her, and I'll help you."

Henry clucks his tongue. He leans forward, shaking

his fists. "Oh, Detective, I can just *feel* how much you want those answers. It almost hurts, doesn't it?"

"I want to save a girl's life," I say.

He leans forward farther still, cups a hand around his mouth and whispers. "You do know, Billy, that no matter how many girls you save, your daughter's never coming back."

I take a breath and ignore the rise in my blood pressure. "Henry—"

"I've got it now." Henry points at Gina. "You're gay, right? Yeah. Yeah, you sure as hell are." He wags his finger. "Oh, God, *please* come over here and give me a lap dance."

No way Gina's going to let this guy get a rise out of her. "If it's any consolation," she says, "I'm sure there'll be some brothers in A Block happy to get one from *you*."

"Oh, is that your thing?" He leans forward, elbows on the table, hands on his cheeks. "You wanna hear about the showers?"

"Let's go," I say.

Henry slams his hands on the table. "Well, folks, I haven't had this much fun since— well, since our ride in the police car, Billy. That was pretty fun, wasn't it?"

We leave, having struck out completely.

"Hurry back!" Henry calls out. "I'll be out of here this week!"

CHAPTER 75

"GOD, I wish we had Henry's burner phone," I say.

"Probably at the bottom of Lake Michigan," says Gina Turner.

Gina, Marsha Flager, and I return from Dunham and head for the documents room at SOS, where we're keeping all the stuff we took from Henry Arcola's office and home. We've been focusing on Henry's finances. We weren't looking for any evidence of a missing girl. Now we are.

"I'm not even through all this stuff the first time around," Marsha says. "Much less looking through these documents again to find some reference to a missing girl."

"Hey, Gina," I say. "You have the audio files on your phone, right? Do me a favor and play them for us on speaker. Maybe just listening to them while we're going through the docs—maybe it will jog something."

Gina digs them up on her phone, puts her phone on speaker, and sets it on the table. Henry's voice comes over the speaker—random statements from his end of conversations on his balcony, many of which we haven't been able to place in any helpful context.

> *That's bullshit, and he knows it, but whatever...*
> *If I knew, don't you think I'd tell you?*

Marsha, flipping through a stack of documents, says, "So we're looking for anything about a missing girl, or any reason why Henry might have been really pissed off at something someone did to him. Something that made him kidnap the girl in the first place."

"Pretty much, yeah," I say.

Henry's words from his balcony still playing, one recording after another:

> *That's not how it works. I'm not changing the fucking rules for one guy.*
>
> *I'm counting on you; you get that. Don't make me sorry.*
>
> *Yes, I'm outside now. I can—you're coming in loud and clear, so go ahead, but stop using that name; you're on a cell phone.*

My eyes rise from the documents I'm reviewing as Henry continues.

> *Listen, you have to go back. Right, exactly. Remove all trace, okay?*

"Stop," I say. "Play that last file back from the beginning."

Gina reaches over and grabs her phone. "This is audio file number 6," she says. "Not sure where it goes on the timeline." She starts it over.

> *Yes, I'm outside now. I can—you're coming in loud and clear, so go ahead, but stop using that name; you're on a cell phone.*

A long pause, presumably while Henry listens to the other person on the phone.

> *Listen, you have to go back. Right, exactly. Remove all trace, okay? It's your best bet anyway. Okay. And keep me posted. Fuck. Fuck, fuck, fuck!*

Gina stops it. "That's it. I don't know what he means by 'go back.' Or 'remove all trace.' It would help if I knew when this call happened. For all we know, it could have been two months ago."

I close my eyes. Think it over. And bolt out of my chair.

"It wasn't two months ago," I say. "It was six weeks ago. April eighth."

"What?" Flager and Turner say at the same time.

"How could you possibly know that?" Gina asks.

"Play it again," I say. "The first part only, before the pause."

> *Yes, I'm outside now. I can—you're coming in loud and clear, so go ahead, but stop using that name; you're on a cell phone.*

"Play it again," I say. But before she does, I say the words aloud that, if I'm right, came from the other end of that phone call just before Henry's response:

"Hum!" I say. "Can you hear me? Hum!"

CHAPTER 76

"SO THAT slimeball creepy billionaire," says Gina, "that lowlife we just talked to at Dunham—that guy is your Humbert?"

"I think so," I say. "'Hum! Can you hear me?'—that's what Donnie Delahunt was saying when Carla and I were on him and he had his van parked on the railroad tracks. The girl he had in the back, Bridget Leone, heard him saying that but didn't know what he meant. She thought he was shouting at her."

"But you think Delahunt was on the phone. And the person he was talking to was Henry Arcola."

"Yeah, sure. Reception was bad out in those woods. I remember that well. Our GPS kept going out. It was hard to get a signal at all. When Delahunt calls Henry, it's breaking up. So Henry goes out onto his balcony to get a better signal on his end. Donnie says 'Hum! Can you hear me?,' and this is how Henry responds."

I play Henry's side of the phone call again:

> *Yes, I'm outside now. I can—you're coming in loud and clear, so go ahead, but stop using that name; you're on a cell phone.*

"Then Donnie lays out his problem," I continue. "He's got me and Carla on his tail; he's got Bridget Leone in the back of his van—he's freaking out, right? So what does Henry tell him to do?" I hit play again.

Listen, you have to go back. Right, exactly. Remove all trace, okay? It's your best bet anyway. Okay. And keep me posted. Fuck. Fuck, fuck, fuck!

"He was telling Donnie to return to the hideout, dump the girl, and detonate the place. Which is exactly what Donnie did."

"Wow." Gina sits back in her chair. "The plot thickens."

I point at Marsha. "Hey, when are we getting Delahunt's burner-phone records?"

"Tomorrow's Monday," she says. "Could be then."

"We have to get those," I say. "We can look at that call on April eighth and identify Henry's burner phone, at least his IMSI number."

International mobile subscriber identity, that is. Every cell phone, even a burner, has an IMSI. You might not be able to trace it to a named person, but you can still tell what calls it made and received—and where it made and received them—by the pings on the cell towers.

Smartphones are always searching for the closest cell tower. And every ping of a cell tower generates a time-stamped record. The wireless phone company keeps those records. With a search warrant, we can go back and obtain the CSLI—cell site location information—for any phone. Every time that phone pinged its nearest tower for any reason at all—to make a phone call, send a text message, access the internet, or simply refresh—

we'll know where and when it happened, down to the date, hour, minute, and second.

We can basically retrace Delahunt's steps. But we need those CSLI records.

"And ten gets you twenty," says Marsh, "that if Henry was Humbert, and Delahunt was the guy who abducted all those girls like Bridget Leone…"

"Then Delahunt probably abducted this latest girl, too," says Gina. "Addison or whatever her name is."

That's exactly right. If Delahunt was the guy who scooped those young girls for his own pleasure and that of Henry Arcola and who knows who else, and if Henry needed another girl abducted, why not use Delahunt for that, too?

"Marsh, we gotta light a fire under the phone company," I say. "We issued the subpoena when—last Tuesday or Wednesday?"

"Wednesday morning," she says. "So it's only been three business days. They usually take over a week, but I'll call 'em right now. Not sure who'll answer on a Sunday."

"We'll never get them on a Sunday," I agree. "But tomorrow, Marsh. This isn't just one of thousands of law enforcement requests they get every week. This is an active search for a missing girl."

"Got it. I'll get them tomorrow, Billy. Whatever it takes."

"If Delahunt kidnapped this girl Addison or whatever her name is," I say, "those CSLI records will tell us where she is."

CHAPTER 77

MIA AND I walk along the lake, crossing over at the North Avenue Bridge and heading south. The sun has long since set, but a parade of cyclists and pedestrians and joggers remains. We don't take nice weather for granted in Chicago; summer passes in the blink of an eye, and this May, unlike some, has given us an early start, so everybody's getting outside.

"This is my favorite part of the city," she says, her arm linked in mine, the wind making a mess of her hair. "It's everything I love—the hustle and bustle of the skyscrapers and traffic, the beach and the lake."

"My pop loved the lake," I say. "We used to take a boat off Belmont Harbor. I never knew who it belonged to. Someone let him use it."

"My father always said it's nice to have a boat, but it's nicer to have a friend with a boat."

I chuckle. "Your father was a smart man. But knowing what I know now about my pop, I don't wanna know who his 'friend' was."

She rubs my arm. "Do you still talk to him?"

"He calls me. I can't stop him. I used to not answer. Now I do. Don't ask me why."

She doesn't. I'm sure I'm not the only one with a complicated family, though the Harneys take it to a higher level.

"I never asked you where you're working this summer," I say.

"A law firm," she says.

"Readem and Weep? Woulda, Coulda, and Shoulda?"

"You probably have a lot more of those."

"Oh, I could do it all night. But really."

"I'm working for a civil-rights law firm," she says.

"A civil-rights firm. Is that code for a law firm that sues cops?"

"Well..." Her voice disapproving. "That's part of their practice, sure. They sue school boards, they sue the department of—they sue any governmental agency that violates the rights of our citizens."

"Well, you said you wanted to take on the establishment."

"I also needed a job. The market's tight right now. I wanted to intern for the public defender or the federal defender but didn't get those jobs."

A kid on a unicycle brushes past us, wearing headphones, probably having no idea of the risk he's taking. That's the difference between kids and adults. I look back at some of the shit I did as a kid and can't believe I made it to age thirty-five.

Mia squeezes my arm. "You're quiet."

"Oh, no. Just a lot on my mind. We think we have a missing girl, but we don't have shit for a lead until we get some cell-site data tomorrow for a burner phone. To say nothing of the fact that tomorrow, Monday morning, is the bond hearing for the big gang leader and his genius accountant."

"I thought bond was denied."

"It was, but when you're denied bond, you get a

revisit within a week. Jericho, the leader—I think we stand a chance of holding him. But I'm worried about the kid, Mason. Our ASA thinks the judge'll spring him. Right now, we have him practically quarantined inside the jail. But if he gets out? It'll be open season on him. Jericho will take him out. Mason's the key to our case."

"Let's sit." She takes my hand. We allow a group of cyclists to pass, then we walk up the steps to the promenade, cars behind us, whistling past on Lake Shore Drive, the lake right before us, kicking up waves, as bikers and joggers go by.

I like holding hands with Mia. One of these days, I'm going to kiss her, too. It's almost odd that we haven't done so. We are giving new meaning to "slow." I wonder if that's only for my benefit or if she's cautious, too.

"I thought maybe the reason you got so quiet is that I mentioned the public defender," she says. "I know your wife used to work there."

"Yeah. Yeah, she did. Valerie was a true believer."

Mia swipes hair out of her face. It's an impossible task to fight this wind if you have hair like hers. "You like women who challenge you," she says.

"I guess so." I hadn't thought about it in those terms. I've loved two women in my life. When I married Valerie, I thought my search was over. I thought we'd be together forever. I believed everything I said in my wedding vows. After I was a widower, there was Amy; that was intense but short-lived—literally short-lived. She was killed, and I barely survived a gunshot wound to the head that left me, among other things, with only fragmented memories of that relationship.

Both were lawyers who could kick my ass in an argument. And both are now dead.

"I don't believe there's only one person out there for us," says Mia.

"You don't believe in soul mates?"

"I do," she says, "but I don't think you're just born soul mates. I believe a lot of people can be your soul mate. It's a matter of evolving with someone. Letting yourself be vulnerable. Intimate. But some people think there's only one person put on earth for them. Are you one of the people who thinks that?"

"I've…never really thought about it."

She looks at me. Smiles softly. "Getting pretty heavy on you for a second date, huh?" She nudges me. "Hey, how 'bout those White Sox?"

I smile, but I sense that I swung and missed on her first pitch. She wasn't just asking a random question. She was coming at it indirectly, but she got there all the same.

"And here I said we'd go slow," she says. "I shouldn't have put that on you."

"No, it's okay, it's okay." I take her hands in mine. "I loved Valerie," I say. "I will always love Valerie."

"I'd think less of you if you didn't."

When my mother died, Pop said he'd never so much as look at another woman. He'd loved one woman, he said, and that was enough. As far as any of us kids knew—and we'd know, especially Patti and I, who worked in the department with Pop—he stayed alone until the day he was taken into custody by the feds.

"This is the part," I say, "where one of us says that Valerie would want me to go on with my life."

"Right. Which I'm sure is true."

"I'm sure it is. But you want to know if I'm capable of that."

She nods, looking out at the lake. "That's what I was asking. But listen—"

"Do you want my answer or not?"

She turns, reluctant at first to make eye contact. Shyness is not something I get from her very much.

I put my forehead against hers. "The truth is, I don't know," I say.

MONDAY

CHAPTER 78

MONDAY MORNING. The day we learn whether Mason Tracy and Jericho Hooper stay locked up or get sprung on bond. The day we learn whether Mason Tracy lives or dies, our case along with him.

"People versus Jericho Hooper."

Jericho, dreadlocked and wearing his jumpsuit, stands with his lawyer, Elan Tenenbaum, while Pete Parsons starts his argument to continue the no-bond hold on Jericho. Pete emphasizes the evidence we have—more than enough for probable cause—but glosses over the fact that, since we arrested Jericho, we haven't improved our case. We still can't penetrate Mason's phone or computer, and no matter how many Nation underlings we bring in, they won't say anything against Jericho, even when he's jailed and indicted.

"Why don't you focus on risk of flight, Mr. Parsons?" the judge says.

"Judge, the defendant is the undisputed leader of the most violent street gang in this city. We estimate his resources to be in the millions. He has the people and the resources to flee."

"He's not going to *flee,* Judge," says Tenenbaum. "That's crazy. He's going to fight these charges. At most, right now, the state *might* have a class 3 felony charge on money laundering, a paper crime."

"I assume, Mr. Tenenbaum, that the state is trying to build a much larger case than that."

"And we are confident they will not. Mr. Hooper is going to flee from a minor criminal charge? It's outrageous. Mr. Parsons can disparage my client all he wants, but the fact remains that my client is involved in a number of legitimate ventures and has significant ties to the community."

"Judge," says Parsons, "class 3 felony or not, with Mr. Hooper's criminal record, he's looking at significant time if convicted."

"Which, as things stand now," says Tenenbaum, "he won't be. Frankly, Your Honor, it's a disgrace that my client was even charged. The state has been fishing around, trying to find some charge that will stick against my client, whom they brand as some big-time gang leader. The last I checked, Your Honor, in America, we don't find people guilty by infamy or suspicion."

"Judge," says Parsons, "this paper crime? Money laundering is the instrument of drug dealers. Jericho Hooper is responsible for poisoning thousands of people a day with drugs—"

"Okay, okay, enough of the speeches." The judge sits back in her seat.

"Your Honor," says Pete, "we are concerned that the defendant will take action to retaliate and prevent people from testifying against him, not the least of whom is Mason Tracy, his codefendant."

"But if you're right that Mr. Hooper is the leader of the most vicious street gang in the city," says the judge, "then couldn't he do that from jail anyway?"

"It would at least make it harder," says Pete. "This man has a violent record, and we are concerned he will be responsible for more violence in our community if he is released."

The judge puts up her hand. She's heard enough. She takes off her glasses and rubs her eyes. She doesn't look happy. Whatever she's about to do, she's doing it while holding her nose.

"The no-bond hold is continued," she says. "Mr. Hooper will remain remanded to Dunham Detention Center."

Exhale.

Jericho whispers something to his lawyer.

"Wow, I thought we'd lost her," says Sosh, seated next to me.

"Your Honor," says Jericho. "Can I say something?"

The judge, startled, looks at Jericho. "Mr. Hooper, you're represented by counsel."

"I know that, Your Honor. That's what I want to talk about."

The judge looks at Elan Tenenbaum. "Mr. Tenenbaum, help me out here."

"Your Honor." Tenenbaum glances at Jericho. "Your Honor, my client has just told me that he no longer wants my representation."

"What the fuck?" Sosh whispers.

"He no longer——Mr. Hooper?" says the judge. "Is that correct?"

"That's right, Your Honor. I want a different lawyer."

"Well, you're very well represented, Mr. Hooper. Mr. Tenenbaum is——"

"I want another lawyer. Your Honor," he adds.

"Judge, I suppose—well, under the circumstances," says Tenenbaum, "I guess I would seek leave to withdraw as counsel."

"I think the two of you might want to take a moment to confer," says the judge.

"I don't need to confer, Your Honor. I want a different lawyer."

"I need to admonish you, Mr. Hooper." The judge runs through the rigmarole, advising him of the perils of self-representation while Sosh and I look at each other.

"I understand, Your Honor," says Jericho, when she's finished. "I'm getting another lawyer. I'll have one very soon."

The judge pauses, then shakes her head. "Very well. Mr. Hooper, if you don't have a lawyer by the time you return for the next status, I'll admonish you again about self-representation. In the meantime, Mr. Tenenbaum, you are granted leave to withdraw as counsel."

"I don't understand," I whisper to Sosh. "The fuck is Jericho doing?"

"Call the next case," says the judge.

CHAPTER 79

"PEOPLE VERSUS Mason Tracy."

Mason is brought out of the holding pen, shackled, eyes down, as they usually are. He may have the mind of a computer, but he always wears that seemingly dazed, clueless look. Autism? Asperger's?

Pete, emboldened, goes through his spiel again. The judge doesn't give him very much rope before jumping in.

"Mr. Parsons, am I correct that you haven't uncovered any additional evidence against Mr. Tracy on the charge of money laundering?"

"Your Honor, as we mentioned, we've been unable to access either his computer or his iPhone, and the defendant has not assisted us——"

"Which he's under no obligation to do, Counsel. So I take it the answer to my question is no, you have no additional evidence."

Parsons pauses. "As of this moment, no, Your Honor."

"And I'm correct that Mr. Tracy has no criminal record whatsoever?"

"That's correct, Judge. We are very much concerned about risk of flight, though."

"You are? Why? He doesn't even have a passport."

"Judge, we think the defendant will run. His co-defendant is the head of the Imperial Gangster Nation. We think Mason Tracy will either run or be killed."

"Be *killed*?" The judge looks at Mason's lawyer, Elan Tenenbaum, then back at Pete. "You're saying that you want to lock him up for his own protection?"

"In part, yes, Your Honor."

"Well, that's very nice, Counsel, and you're free to offer Mr. Tracy witness protection, I suppose. But we don't lock people up for their own safety." She turns back to Tenenbaum. "Counsel, are you aware of this concern on Mr. Parsons's part?"

"First I've heard of it, Your Honor," Tenenbaum says. "We find it ludicrous. Mason Tracy will not flee, and he does not fear for his life. Though I must say we do appreciate the prosecution's sudden interest in the well-being of my client."

The judge nods. "This defendant has no criminal record. He is charged with a nonviolent crime. And I've heard no convincing evidence that he's a flight risk. I'm setting bond at one hundred thousand dollars. The defendant will remain in the state of Illinois, will refrain from drugs and alcohol, and will submit to the supervision of Pretrial Services. He has no firearms, correct?"

"Correct, Your Honor."

"Keep it that way, Counsel. No firearms. Any prescription drugs?"

"No, Your Honor."

Wait. Is that right? No prescription drugs? Didn't we see some at his house?

"Mr. Tracy, have you understood the conditions I've imposed?"

Tenenbaum nudges Mason, who raises his head. "Yes."

"Very well. Best of luck, Mr. Tracy."

Parsons glances back at me. He called this.

"Guy's just gonna walk out of here and into the arms of Jericho, or whoever Jericho has waiting for him," says Sosh.

He's right. Mason Tracy is a dead man.

CHAPTER 80

ELAN TENENBAUM drives Mason Tracy home from jail.

"You want some food, Mace?" he says. "You must be—"

"No." Mason's knees bounce up and down, but at least he's out now. He's not helpless anymore. He glances over at Tenenbaum. "Are they...following?"

"Looks like one a few cars back, yeah," says Tenenbaum. "Unmarked car."

"Can you make them...make them...stop?"

"Not really. Not unless they're harassing you. They'll say they're protecting you, not surveilling you."

"Protecting...protecting me."

He looks down at the floorboard. He sees Tenenbaum looking over at him.

"You okay, Mace?"

Mason doesn't answer. He's pretty damn far from okay.

"Take me...take me home. Home."

Twenty minutes later, Tenenbaum pulls up along the curb by Mason's house, on Leclaire. Mason already has the car door open before the vehicle has fully stopped.

Tenenbaum calls out, "Call me if—"

Mason slams the door before Tenenbaum can finish the sentence. He runs to the back of his house, finds the spare key hidden in a crevice beneath the porch, and heads inside, feeling a rush of familiarity and comfort.

Though he can't shake the feeling of being violated by the way the police rummaged through things during their search. The kitchen has been rearranged. Some cabinets are still open, some drawers not fully closed. They tried to put everything back, but they didn't get it right, didn't get it right, it's not right, the plates aren't in the third cabinet and the glasses don't go there and the knives are supposed to be—

No time for that. Not now. He heads to the refrigerator and opens the freezer, finds the package covered with aluminum foil. He opens the fridge and finds the bottle of prednisolone and the steroid shot.

A shiver runs through him.

He closes the fridge and leaves the kitchen. Through the front window, he sees a Chicago police cruiser parked outside his house. Facing north, on a street that's one-way south. They aren't hiding.

The front room has been tossed by the cops, too, cushions thrown haphazardly back onto the couch, books taken off the bookshelf and put back the *wrong way*.

Everything *out of order*.

He heads into the bedroom, which those cops probably also destroy—

A man is sitting on his bed. Mason knows him. His name is Reggie Blake. But everyone calls him Shorty.

An enforcer for the Imperial Gangster Nation.

"Hey, Mason," says Shorty. "Don't look so happy to see me."

CHAPTER 81

TWENTY MINUTES later, Mason Tracy steps out of his house and retrieves the mail overflowing from the mailbox. He is dressed in a Bears jersey, dark blue sweatpants, and an orange baseball cap.

"Look at Mr. Color-Coordinated," says Officer Sams, in the driver's seat of the cruiser.

"Probably couldn't wait to take a shower where he wasn't looking over his shoulder," says his partner, Officer Deering. "And put on some clean clothes."

"Look at that guy," Sams says. "Never looks up. Some kind of *Rain Man* shit."

Deering laughs. "He's some genius, right? He can, like, do the theory of relativity or some shit in his head, but he probably walks into walls in his house."

Sams grabs his radio. "Hutch, you still awake back there?"

"*So far.*" Officer Hutchinson and her partner, Dickerson, have the alley.

"That's why they pay us the big bucks, Connie. Be advised, he's changed into a Bears jersey, orange hat, blue sweats."

"Least it's not a Cubs jersey," she says.

Deering leans back in his seat. "Explain to me again why we fired Maddon? The guy wins a World Series, and three years later, he's gone."

"Four years," says Sams.

"Three."

"Whatever. He does all that psychological guru shit. That stuff wears out after a while."

"And what, you base that on your extensive experience as a major leaguer? No, Theo didn't give him enough starting pitching."

For the third time in a week, they debate the point, as the midday sun drenches the street.

A rusted Chevy with souped-up tires turns off Thomas Street, to the north, and starts heading toward them.

"Hey—"

"—shouldn't be playing third base. Put a guy like him in the out—"

"Check it out, check it out," says Sams.

The Chevy slows as it approaches the police cruiser. The automated license plate reader in the cruiser beeps, registering the plate.

Sams watches the Chevy carefully. It pulls over to the curb only three or four houses to the north of the cruiser.

"Owned by a Gerelle Quadri," says Officer Deering. He pushes a button. "He's got a sheet. He's Nation."

And he has three of his friends with him in the Chevy.

"Hutch, we might have a situation," Sams says into his radio. "We have four males in a Chevy, Nation-affiliated."

Deering grabs the police radio. "Dispatch, this is 15-13 on protective surveillance. Request backup. Suspicious vehicle in the vicinity."

"Copy that, 15-13: 15-11 responding."

The Chevy comes off the curb, rolls toward them.

"Here we go." Deering, in the passenger seat, raises his rifle.

The Chevy approaches the cruiser, moving slowly forward.

His heart banging, Sams nods at the driver and gives him the coolest stare he can manage.

The driver, an African American in a muscle T and a do-rag tied around his head, does a little salute.

"Gerelle," Sams says.

The Chevy stops. The driver says, "Yes, sir, officer, sir."

"I don't wanna see you or your friends on this block again. You understand?"

"Yes, sir, officer, sir." The Chevy moves on.

Sams exhales and watches the Chevy in his rearview mirror, driving south toward Augusta.

"We're okay, Hutch," he says into his radio.

"Cancel 15-13 request for backup," Deering says to dispatch.

"Alley garage is opening," says Hutchinson.

"Say again, Hutch?"

"His garage door in the alley is opening. It's his vehicle backing out. Black Honda."

"Confirm a visual?"

"Visual confirmed. He's on the move, driving toward Thomas in his Honda."

"Hold your position, Hutch. Those're our orders. Jacobs, we're handing off to you. Confirm handoff, Jacobs."

"Confirm handoff," says Officer Jacobs, parked on Thomas. *"Okay, picking up a black Honda. We're on him."*

Sams picks up his cell phone and dials the number. "Detective Harney," he says, "Mason's on the move."

CHAPTER 82

"WHERE IS he now?" Sosh asks after I activate the speaker on my phone in the conference room.

"On the Eisenhower, heading east into the city," squawks Officer Jacobs, the passenger in the squad car following Mason Tracy. *"Or maybe he's taking 90/94; don't know yet."*

Pete Parsons walks in.

"Is he speeding?" Sosh asks. "Is he trying to lose you?"

"Not really."

"What is this?" Pete asks.

"Don't activate your lights unless you have no choice," says Sosh.

"You're—is this Mason's car?" Pete asks. "You're following him?"

"Of course we are," I say.

"Of *course* you are?" Pete flaps his arms. "Was anyone gonna tell me?"

"I hadn't been planning on it, no."

"Tenenbaum's gonna have my ass in a sling, Billy. He'll run to Judge Jorgen—"

"It's *my* ass in the sling," I say. "And I'm not gonna apologize for protecting my star witness. Besides, all we're doing is following him. We haven't pulled him over. We've just been following him at a distance."

"He's taking I-94 east," says Jacobs.

Sosh makes a face. "Taking in a Sox game?"

"He's picking up speed," says Jacobs. *"Traffic's light this time of day. Want me to stop him?"*

"No," I say into the speaker. "But stay with him. Keep a distance, but under no circumstances can you lose him. If you have to light up the cherries, do it—as a last resort only. Otherwise, give him some space. Just don't lose him."

"Roger that. Doesn't seem like he's trying to lose us."

Sosh looks at me. "Where the fuck is he going?"

I shrug. Mason's heading south. From there, he has any number of options.

"We're in the express lane now."

"Billy." Marsha Flager sticks her head into the conference room. "Got a minute? What's—what's going on?"

"Mason Tracy," I tell her. "We're surveilling."

Pete and Marsha take seats. Sosh drums his fingers on the table. I pace the room. Five minutes pass. Ten—

"He's taking exit 71A."

"What's that?" I ask as Soscia pulls up a map on his phone.

"So we're on Sibley Boulevard, Illinois 83. Wait: he's turning left."

"On…Lincoln?" I ask, looking at Soscia's phone map.

"Uh, yeah, yeah. Okay, he turned left."

Soscia moves the map on his phone down and to the right—southeast—and draws a line with his finger.

I see what he's showing me now. Mason is only

a couple of miles away from the state line separating Illinois and Indiana.

"You don't think," I say.

Sosh purses his lips.

"Jacobs," I say, "notify the Indiana State Police and the Hammond police. If Mason drives one inch into Indiana, we're violating his ass."

"Roger that."

I take a breath. "He wouldn't be stupid enough to cross state lines and violate a condition of bond right in front of our faces."

Sosh's eyebrows rise. A wry smile on his face. "Maybe not so stupid."

"Oh. Oh," I say. "You think he *wants* to get violated?"

Sosh raises a shoulder. "Pretty smart move, actually. This is Jericho's show, right? He makes Mason use Elan Tenenbaum for a lawyer, and Tenenbaum keeps Mason's mouth shut. Now Tenenbaum gets Mason sprung, where he'll be easier to whack. Maybe Mason agrees with us that he's safer inside."

"So he intentionally violates his conditions of bond," I say, chewing on that. "Huh."

"Okay, Detective, we're coordinated with Indiana State Police and Hammond."

"Great."

"He just turned right on...on Burnham."

Sosh shows me on the map. Mason is heading due south right now. "He'll be turning left soon," says Sosh.

"He's in the left-turn lane. He's gonna turn left on...River Oaks Drive."

Sosh points to it on the map, scrolls his finger. When Mason turns left, he'll be only minutes from the Indiana state line.

"If he's really doing this," Sosh says, "then he's

going against Jericho's wishes. So maybe he's ready to cooperate."

"Wait. What's he—he's...he's moving over. He's moving out of the left-turn lane."

"Second thoughts?" Sosh says.

"He's moving over two lanes, and he's turning right now."

"West," says Sosh. "Away from the state line."

"Yeah, we're traveling west on River Oaks. Hey, Detectives, technically he violated a traffic law back there, if you want us to pull him over."

Sosh and I look at each other, both of us shaking our heads.

"Just follow him, Jacobs."

"Actually, you think maybe we should reach out?" Sosh says. "Have Jacobs pull him over and get Mason on the horn with us? If he's teeter-tottering, maybe we could tip him over to our side."

It's not a bad thought. I chew on that while the clock ticks. One minute. Two. Three—

"He's turning into some mall. A shopping mall."

"Killing time?" I say to Sosh. "Driving in circles, trying to decide what to do?"

"Stay with him," Sosh says. "Keep it loose."

"He just pulled his car up to the curb by the mall. He's idling there."

Sosh looks at me. "Maybe we should try to talk to him?"

Maybe Sosh is right; that's the way to go. "Jacobs, how close to him are you?"

"Maybe twenty, twenty-five yards? You said not to get too close up behind him."

"Yeah, you're doing fine. But listen—"

"He's getting out," says Jacobs. *"He just got out of his car and...he's jogging inside. What are my orders?"*

"He went into the mall?"

"*Yes. What are my orders?*"

I look at Sosh. "He's free on bond. It's not a crime to walk into a shopping mall. We can't do anything to him."

"We can follow him in, though," says Sosh.

He's right. "Go in," I tell Jacobs. "See what he's doing."

CHAPTER 83

SHORTY BLAKE runs into the shopping mall after parking Mason's Honda at the curb. He jogs down the corridor, passing stores selling health food and children's clothing, then turns the corner, out of view of the door from which he entered.

From their parking space outside the mall, it will take the cops who were watching him at least thirty seconds to pull up, run in, and make it to the spot where Shorty is standing. Thirty seconds at best.

"Hey, baby," he says to his girlfriend, Jasmine, standing there.

He hands her his orange baseball cap. He pulls off the Bears jersey and rips off his blue sweatpants like an NBA superstar. Underneath, he's wearing a bright yellow T-shirt and long black shorts.

Jasmine hands him a slushie and stuffs the clothes into a shopping bag.

Shorty puts his arm around Jasmine and takes a sip from his slushie as he strolls back around the corner. "Say something funny," he tells her.

The cops are inside the mall now, peeking through

the storefront windows, looking for Mason. They barely glance at Shorty and Jasmine, chatting and laughing as they casually walk out of the mall and into the sunshine.

"That's his car?" Jasmine asks, nodding at the Honda on the curb.

"That's it."

"You just drove it here, and they thought you were Mason?"

"Same clothes, same build. They kept their distance. Their mistake."

"So what do we do now?"

"We go home," says Shorty as they reach Jasmine's car. "Jericho said to get the cops off his tail, and I did."

I pinch the bridge of my nose to stifle the headache. "So you're not sure," I say.

"Not for sure, Detective," says Jacobs over the speakerphone. *"Either we lost Mason at the mall or it wasn't Mason at all. Some decoy who dressed up like him and took us on a joyride in Mason's car."*

"And Sams?" I say to the officer at Mason's house, connected on a three-way call. "You're sure you've searched his house high and low?"

"High and low, Detective Harney. He's not here. The open bedroom window is why I think he probably skipped out the side of the house. Must have been while those gangbangers were riding up on us and distracting us. We're busy eyeballing those guys and calling in for backup, and he's jumping out the side window."

Yep, that's probably exactly what happened. It was planned all along. Someone was inside Mason's house, waiting for him. They dressed identically. Mason made sure the cops out front saw him in his new clothes. Then the decoy skipped out the back, got in Mason's Honda, and started driving while the gangbangers drove down Leclaire and caught the attention of the patrol unit. They never saw Mason jump out the side window.

Well executed.

I look at Sosh and Flager. What can we do?

"Stay at the house," I say. "I don't think we'll be seeing him again, but just in case he comes back."

"Detective—I'm sorry about this. I feel like a horse's ass."

"Plenty of blame to go around," I say. "It was pre-planned, obviously. And your job was to protect Mason, not surveil him. I should've seen this coming."

"I appreciate you saying that, Detective. I still fucked up, and I know it."

I punch out the phone and look at Sosh, Flager, and Pete Parsons.

"Nothing we can do," says Sosh.

Pete Parsons agrees. "No crime against shaking a tail. He can do whatever he wants. As long as he stays in Illinois."

Sosh crumples up his paper cup of water and tosses it across the room.

"The worst part," I say, "is that if Mason was trying to lose us, it means he's got something planned."

"At least we have his phone," says Sosh. "That seemed to matter to him a lot."

"Not really," says Marsha. "Now that Mason's out, he'll just clone it."

"Don't you need the physical phone?" Sosh asks.

"Nope. Not these days." Marsha taps her temple. "If Mason memorized the information he needs, he can hack into his phone while it's sitting in our office. And you better believe Mason has that stuff committed to memory."

"Then why didn't he smuggle a phone into Dunham and do it from there?"

"Can't get a signal inside Dunham," she says. "They jam it. Even in the jail yard."

"Bottom line," I say, "Mason's in the wind. We have no idea where he is or what he's doing. Or if he's even alive."

CHAPTER 84

WELL, IT worked. But not without a cost.

For one thing, Mason hurt his knee when he slipped out the bedroom window on the side of his house. He rushed it too much. He only had those few seconds, and he rushed it.

And he left the window open, again, because he had to rush it, jumping out the window and sneaking over into the neighbor's yard, where he hid until Shorty took the Honda and distracted the cops in the alley.

That damn open window. It wouldn't be a problem for most people, but it is for Mason. The thought of that window being open is like torture. He likes things just as they were. He doesn't like mess or chaos.

Which has made this last week like a circle of hell.

At least now he's doing something instead of sitting in a jail cell worrying about it. While the police follow his Honda to wherever Shorty drove it, Mason turns down a winding road on private acreage about forty miles northwest of the city, driving the SUV that was left for him two blocks from his house.

Mason pulls up to the sprawling house and parks

behind a large wooden barn, shielding his SUV from view. He kills the engine and takes his first good, long breath.

He made it.

The new iPhone is powered up now from the car charger. Mason works quickly to install the app and input the credentials. His actual phone is still in the hands of Chicago police, but within minutes, he will have it cloned.

Once that's done, he performs the task he's been wanting to do since the police arrested him six days ago. He knows the account number by heart, of course. He types it in and waits.

The prompt for facial recognition. Mason holds the phone up to his face. A soft beep and a large check mark tell him that it succeeded.

He types in the transaction order. There's an automatic hold for twenty-four hours. At half past noon tomorrow, the money will be ready to transfer.

Okay.

He walks over to the barn, locked with a combination lock and a keypad. He knows the combination and unlocks it. He knows the code to the keypad and types it in.

He slides the barn door to one side, revealing a massive open space. He activates the flashlight on his phone and shines it into the space.

Inside is a flatbed Volvo truck, royal blue, a massive eight-wheeler.

On the wall, hanging from a rack, are handguns. Six of them. Mason doesn't know handguns. He's never held one. But he takes one and stuffs it into his jeans.

So now, only five guns hang from the rack.

On a freestanding set of shelves are several items. First, a large paper shopping bag. Mason opens it and finds multiple sets of uniforms.

Next to the paper shopping bag is a drone, looking like a smaller version of a fighter jet from a *Star Wars* movie. Next to the drone is its remote control.

He'll get to that later. First he picks up a different remote control, a black contraption that looks like it could belong in some family room in front of an Xbox or PlayStation.

He steps back out of the barn, looks around, and sees nobody—nothing but trees and lush grass. The faint smell of manure from the neighboring horse farm.

He studies the remote control. Each of the nodules is marked.

Start Engine. Parking Brake. Release/Engage. Shift Gear. Forward. Reverse. And two joysticks, one for right/left steering, one for forward/reverse.

He clicks the nodule for Start Engine. The large Volvo truck hums to life. His father used to drive a truck about this size when Mason was a kid. His dad would roll over in his grave if he knew that Mason was driving one now, too, but without actually getting inside.

Mason hits the nodule for Release.

The truck starts rolling forward.

He uses the joystick to accelerate. These trucks are usually capped at a speed of ten miles per hour for safety reasons. But not this one.

Mason steps aside as the truck rolls out of the barn. He plays with it, moving the big truck right and left, forward and backward, while he stands flat-footed by the barn.

Okay. Simple enough. Not really any different from one of those toy remote-control cars he'd played with as a kid.

Just a little more dangerous.

Then he takes everything from the SUV and puts it into the flatbed truck.

He takes the drone from the barn, with its remote control, and puts it in the truck, too.

Inside the truck, he flips a switch to take the truck off "dynamic steering"—remote control—switching it to manual driving. He starts to drive the truck forward but sees, in the rearview mirror, the open barn door.

No. He can't leave that open.

He jumps out of the truck, grabs the handle of the barn door, and slams it shut with a *wham*.

CHAPTER 85

THE MONSTER has been waiting for her, waiting at the end of the dark tunnel. She can hear it and smell its putrid breath, but it stays away, eyeing her in the darkness. She can't move, can't do anything; she is submerged in icy water, so cold and shivering so violently, her breath coming in gasps—

And now, finally, it comes for her, but not what she expected, not snarling and hissing but rumbling, coughing, grinding, whining, heavy and bulky in its movements—

Wham.

Veronica opens her eyes into darkness. Where is—

Her heartbeat drumming, she puts her hand on her chest to feel it. She is still alive. Groggy and confused but alive. Shivering in the cool air but alive. Thirsty, so thirsty, her mouth so dry that her lips stick together, her tongue like sandpaper, heavy when she tries to speak.

"Hel—hello?" She looks up into the darkness.

It comes back to her slowly. She can see down that tunnel, ever so faintly, the light from the bathroom, where she broke through the wall.

How long has it been —

It doesn't matter. She heard something up there. It wasn't a hallucination. It wasn't a dream. She knows it. She *thinks* she knows it. A noise from above. There is something up there. Like a...vehicle starting up, rolling forward. And some loud noise.

She reaches out, touches the iron leg of the ladder.

She can't. She can hardly lift her head. However long she's been down in this dungeon, it's been too long. She can't do it. She's out of time.

"You have to," she tells herself. "You have to get up that ladder."

CHAPTER 86

THE BARBER at Dunham Detention Center comes once every two weeks, at least in theory. The detainees with upcoming court appearances get first priority. Again, at least in theory.

But when Jericho shows up for a haircut, he goes first. The COs don't have to adhere to the street-gang hierarchy, but they usually do anyway. They probably think it helps maintain order, keep the peace.

Jericho walks into the room in shackles. The barber's chair is stacked with three cushions, because the barber doesn't have his customary chair he can pump up and down.

"Haven't seen you before," says the barber, an old Black guy named Ozzie. "What do you need, son? Not sure what I can do with dreadlocks."

Jericho takes his seat atop the cushions. The barber hands him a mirror. First time Jericho's seen his reflection in a week. He feels like he's looking at an older man.

"Cut them off," says Jericho.

"Cut off the dreads?"

"Cut them off and shave my head," he says.

"What's the occasion?"

"I'm meeting my new lawyer tomorrow." Jericho hands him the mirror. "Tomorrow's prime time."

CHAPTER 87

"YOU UNDERSTAND," says Pete Parsons into the speakerphone, "that we're talking about an active investigation for a missing person?"

"I understand that now, yes," says the bureaucrat from the phone company. *"That wasn't the original request from your Detective Flager. We'll reclassify it as urgent, but it has to get in line behind others marked urgent. We have to go in order. We get hundreds of urgent requests for historical CSLI records every week."*

If these phone companies could charge by the request, get a nice payout instead of a mere subpoena fee, you better believe they'd churn them out with the highest capitalist efficiency.

"This is life-and-death," I say.

"All missing-persons cases are."

"We have reason to believe this woman suffered life-threatening injuries."

A sigh on the other end. *"Look, I'll—I'll try to get them to you by tonight, okay?"*

"Every minute counts," I say.

I punch out the phone and look around the documents

room, which holds all Henry Arcola's files. Sosh and Gina are still combing through them, looking for information on a missing girl who may or may not be named Addison.

"Nice day," I say. "We lose Mason and get nothing from the phone company." I glance at the clock; it's past four in the afternoon. "We don't get those CSLIs soon, it'll be too late to triangulate, pin down the area, and search it before nightfall."

Gina pulls a document out of a file. "You know Henry served in the air force?"

"Henry? In the *military*? No way."

"Well, this may not be so hard to believe." She holds up a patch, like one you'd stitch onto a shirt or jacket, blue and yellow, with an image of a globe, a key, and some horse-shaped head like one you'd see on a chessboard. Some sort of coat of arms. Curving around the bottom, the words AIR INTELLIGENCE AGENCY.

"Intelligence," I say. "Spy shit. Now, *that* I can see Henry doing. His whole career, making all that money, has been basically a con game, a mindfuck."

"A guy like that would know how to operate a safe house, too, where he stowed away the girls," says Gina. "Not to mention covertly running a sex-trafficking operation."

"Henry Arcola gets more interesting by the minute."

"I was just looking it up online," she says. "The Air Intelligence Agency is the intelligence arm of the air force. It's got a new name now, but basically, it does intelligence, surveillance, and recon. Planes, satellites, drones."

"Drones. Planes. Sounds like Henry. He owns a Cessna we impounded. I could see him having all sorts of gadgets, rich-people toys."

"Looks like they did some on-the-ground intelligence

operations, too. Up-close spycraft. Yeah," Gina says, "I could see him being a spook. Good training for his future career, swindling people with a smile."

"Marsha should know all this," I say. "Speaking of: Where is she? And where's Rodriguez, for that matter?"

"Rodriguez found something in Henry's records about a safe-deposit box at some bank called Marine Commercial or something," says Sosh.

I shake my head. "Never heard of it. Henry didn't bank there. Not that we ever saw."

"No, he didn't, which is why it's so interesting he'd have a safe-deposit box stowed away in some random bank. Something nobody knew about."

"That could be good," I say.

"Mat left a couple hours ago to get a warrant from Judge Palmero. He called the bank and told them to stay open. He should be back any minute with whatever's inside that box."

"Yeah? Great. I could use some good news. And what about Flager?"

"Marsha's on Henry's computer. Not sure what she's doing."

"I'll tell you what I'm doing," Marsha says, popping into the room. "Remember how upset Henry was on those audio files? Calling somebody and threatening them?"

"How could I forget?" I say.

"I was trying to figure out what made him so upset," says Marsha. "And I think I just did."

CHAPTER 88

GINA, SOSH, and I follow Marsha to her desk, where a young woman with large glasses and a buzz cut sits.

"Everyone, this is Sadie from Forensics."

We all say hello and grab chairs.

"I got to thinking," Marsha says. "If Henry's all pissed off about somebody doing something to him, what's that likely to be? For a guy like Henry, I was thinking it was something financial. So I realized we'd been searching his records and his transaction history, but I never had a computer expert actually look for malicious penetrations."

"Okay," I say, "I'll pretend I know what that means just to keep this conversation going."

"I called Sadie here from Forensics to see if anyone hacked into Henry's computer," says Marsh.

"Someone did," says Sadie. "You know much about computers?"

"No," I say.

"So you've never heard of a man-in-the-middle attack?"

"Definitely not."

"A session hijacking?"

Marsha touches Sadie's arm. "I have to help Billy turn on his computer in the morning. Computer hacking 101, Sadie."

Sadie adjusts her glasses. "Basically, the hacker inserts himself between the client and the server. Do you know what spoofing is?"

I drop my head, glance at Marsha.

"I'll try," Marsh says. "Imagine Henry's computer is communicating with another computer's server. Say he goes online to check his bank balance. That's his computer interacting with another computer's server. With me so far?"

"Yeah."

"Okay. The hacker's computer gains control of Henry's computer, disconnects it, and takes over the communication Henry was having with the other server. The hacker spoofs—well, the hacker pretends to be Henry's computer, and he has enough information to make the other server believe the hacker really is Henry. So the other server thinks Henry's issuing it orders, when it's really the hacker doing it. The hacker hijacked the session." Marsha looks at Sadie. "Close enough for government work?"

Sadie nods. "Pretty good, actually."

"Jesus," I say. "Is that hard to do?"

"Usually," says Sadie. "Especially with the level of security Henry had."

"But it's possible."

"Anything's possible," she says. "But it's not only possible in this case. It also happened. I can see it in the encryption files."

"You know that company Henry has?" says Marsha. "Logan Financing?"

"Yeah. That's the company with all the cash. The one he swiped twenty million dollars from."

"Or so we thought," says Marsha.

"Henry didn't siphon twenty million dollars from his account?"

"I think what she's saying," Gina says, jumping in, "is that the hacker stole it."

Marsha nods. "The hacker stole the twenty million. Pretending to be Henry."

I sit back. Wow.

I should've seen that. I knew about the twenty-million-dollar transfer, and I knew Henry was freaking out about something. I didn't put the two things together.

"I thought Henry siphoned off that money for his getaway."

"Oh, I'm sure that was the plan," says Marsh. "But someone beat him to it."

"Who?" I ask. "Where'd the money go?"

"That's the thing," says Sadie. "I can't tell. He—the hacker transferred it to a dummy account. An account that doesn't exist."

"The bank let that happen?"

"The bank thought it was Henry's account. You want me to explain how?"

"No." I put my hand up. "Please, no."

"Suffice it to say," Marsha says, summarizing, "the money went *poof*. The hacker stole it. Sadie thinks we could eventually trace it forensically, but not any-time soon."

"And…when did this happen?"

"Saturday night," says Marsha, looking to Sadie for confirmation. "Not this last Saturday but two Saturdays ago. Nine days ago. Saturday, May 15."

I push myself out of my chair and start pacing. "Jesus—no wonder the guy was panicking. His wife had just discovered his Ponzi scheme and was threaten-ing to spill the beans to get a better divorce settlement.

We had a manhunt under way for Donnie Delahunt that could lead us to him. Then his safety net—that twenty million—suddenly disappeared."

"That would qualify as everything crashing down on him all at once," says Sosh.

Gina says, "And remember, we may not know who stole Henry's money, but Henry did. He called the guy and threatened him, over and over again. Probably a lot more than the two times that Logan recorded on the balcony."

"Okay, so that was Saturday night into Sunday morning. Henry's freaking out and calling the hacker, demanding his money back."

I stop pacing.

So many things happened last week. Now they're all starting to come together and make sense.

Mat Rodriguez walks in. "Back from the bank," he says.

"You find anything in the safe-deposit box?"

"Not really." He pats the bag hanging over his shoulder.

"Everybody come with me," I say. "Let's put some pieces together."

CHAPTER 89

WE ENTER one of our war rooms, the one that Marsha set up for the Jericho and Mason investigation. Bankers Boxes everywhere. Documents marked with colored tabs. But more important for my purposes, a dry-erase board on the wall.

"First, let's see what's inside the safe-deposit box, Mat."

"Basically a safe-deposit box within a safe-deposit box," he says. "Feels empty." He places a paper evidence bag on the desk and pulls the box free.

He's right. It's a small metal box.

"No lock?"

"It's thumbprint-activated," says Mat.

"Like the drawer on his desk at home," says Marsha. "Henry has a real thing for thumbprint security."

I look at Gina. "Spy shit," she says.

Mat goes to work on the metal box with a screwdriver. Eventually, he pries it open. As he thought, it's empty. "Whatever was inside, Henry already took it," says Mat.

"Okay, whatever," I say. "Let's timeline this thing. Let's look at everything Henry knew and did until the time he was arrested. We know that last Saturday, the hacker stole twenty million dollars from Henry. Henry calls the hacker over and over again, threatening him, whatever, frantic to get back his money."

I take a marker and start scribbling on the board.

"And this isn't a good time for Henry, because he also has to deal with his wife, who's just discovered his Ponzi scheme. Everything's crashing down on him."

I point to Gina, who stares back at me.

"When I point to you, that means play the call."

"Oh, okay." Gina finds the file and plays it on her phone.

> *Hey, it's me. I know, I know, but it can't be helped. Why? Because everything's crashing down all at once, and I don't know where else to turn, that's why. It's gotta happen, and it's gotta happen tonight. Because I'm running out of time, that's why!*

"So we think Henry's talking to Delahunt here, right? And we think he's telling him to kidnap someone. Someone close to the hacker, someone who we're calling Addison. Right? Makes sense he'd call Delahunt to do that. Delahunt handled all the other abductions. Agreed so far?"

Everyone agrees.

"Then, on Monday morning—so this is a week ago exactly, May 17." I scribble on the eraser board. "On Monday morning, Henry gets a call that something has gone wrong with the abduction, with Addison."

"Do I play that call now?" Gina asks.

"Yeah, I'm pointing at you."

"How 'bout you just ask nicely instead of pointing at me?"

Everyone's so sensitive these days.

Okay, I can talk now— go ahead. So we're good, mission accomplished? Why, what's the—she what? Say again? Addison what? Are you serious? Are you fucking kidding me? I mean, what, there's not enough shit coming down on me—I have to deal with this now, too? Christ, I haven't had my morning fucking coffee and I gotta deal with this? Okay, just hold on a minute. Just give me a minute and let me think this through.

"So that's last Monday morning. Something's gone wrong with the kidnapping. Something wrong with this woman we're calling Addison. And Gina, if you please, pretty please, with sugar on top, here is what Henry tells Delahunt to do."

Well, listen, we have no choice. You're just gonna have to go back and get it. You got a better idea? You think I like this any more than you do? But we don't have a choice. It's not like we can let her die.

"We don't know exactly what he means here," I continue. "Delahunt has to 'go back and get' something."

"Like an inhaler or something," says Gina. "Like Addison had asthma or something. Some medical problem. She'll die unless Delahunt goes back and gets whatever she needs."

"Right. Yeah, probably something like that. Anyway, now we're still right around Monday or maybe Tuesday, and Henry still has his wife to deal with. So he makes that call to the Russians about killing his wife now, *strazo*."

I wave off Gina; we've heard it a million times. I keep writing on the board.

"So on Wednesday, approximately midday, the Russian guys do just that—they kill Marlene Arcola in Lake Geneva. And later that same day, after Logan Arcola pays me a visit, I go to Henry's office and confront him with the audio file where he's talking about killing Marlene *strazo*. Any disagreement with this timeline?"

There isn't.

"So Henry, at that point, has to be completely freaking out. I've basically told him that if anything happens to Marlene, he'll be suspect number one. And he knows very well that Marlene is already dead, soon to be found. He knows he's going to be arrested any minute now. Agreed?"

"Agreed," says Sosh.

"So what does Henry do?" I ask.

"He cleans up his trail," says Marsha. "He tosses his burner phone. He destroys anything incriminating tying him to Marlene's murder."

"Okay, put it this way," I say. "What *doesn't* Henry do?"

The room goes silent.

Mat Rodriguez finally chimes in. "He doesn't run."

I point at Mat.

"He doesn't run," I say in agreement. "Why not? His whole world, as he said himself, is crashing down on him. Yet he doesn't run. He sits tight. Sure, he cleans up his tracks, tosses his burner phone, whatever—but he stays in Chicago. When the cops in Lake Geneva call him, telling him his wife is dead, he doesn't run. No, he drives to Lake Geneva. Then I show up, and he doesn't put up a fight when I take him back to Chicago. And he even *confesses* to me on the side of the road on the way to Chicago."

Everyone ruminates on that.

"He was practically daring me to arrest him," I

say. "And then what happens at his bond hearing? He might've been able to get bond, right? Our case was circumstantial. Marlene's death arguably could've been a suicide. A judge might have given him bond."

"But Henry didn't even *try* to get bond," says Sosh. "He completely laid down. He didn't even bother to hire a lawyer to *request* bond."

"Which, as we've always said, is weird in itself," I say. "Why wouldn't Henry pick up the phone and call a lawyer if he knew he was about to be arrested?"

Sosh leans back in his chair. "You're saying he *wanted* to be sent to jail?"

I think it through. I think it works.

I can't believe I didn't see it before. Henry Arcola was a sneaky little prick.

"But..." Marsha shakes her head. "How does he get his twenty million back if he's in jail? Jail is the *last* place he'd want to be."

I lean against the wall, stare up at the ceiling. "Unless jail is *exactly* where he wanted to be."

"But why on earth would he *want* to be in Dunham Detention Center?"

I look around the room. Then I smile.

"Because that's where his twenty million dollars is," I say.

CHAPTER 90

"MASON STOLE his money," I say. "Mason hacked into Henry's computers and stole twenty million dollars."

"Whoa. So now Mason's a computer genius?" Gina asks. "I know he's a math savant, an accounting whiz—does that translate?"

Marsha nods. "Billy's right," she says. "That Jedi force field around Mason's computer? No amateur could do that. And a lot of the computer hackers I used to see in Financial Crimes had mathematics in their backgrounds." She shakes her head. "It's why he's so good at money laundering. The reason it's been hard for us to track all the money."

Gina makes a time-out gesture with her hands. "Wait. You're saying Mason Tracy hacked into Henry Arcola's corporate account and stole twenty million dollars. And Henry knew it was him. So…they knew each other?"

"Not that hard to imagine," I say. "Mason belongs to Jericho. Jericho and Henry are both criminals, right? Jericho runs a cash business. He needs vehicles to launder his drug money. And Henry's always looking for new investors in his Ponzi scheme. Maybe they talked about doing business. Jericho would want his numbers savant, Mason, to look into it. Wouldn't you, if you were Jericho? Have young Mason do some due diligence on Henry before entrusting Henry with a bunch of money?"

"Yeah."

"Sure. So Mason investigates. Maybe he hacks into Henry's systems for that very reason, to investigate his finances, see whether he's legit."

"And he figures out that Henry *isn't* legit," says Marsha. "He realizes Henry is hoarding cash, running a Ponzi scheme."

"And who better to steal from than a fellow criminal?" says Sosh. "It's not like Henry could report them to the police. He doesn't want anybody in law enforcement poking around his finances."

"So instead of reporting Jericho to the cops, Henry tries his own brand of justice," says Mat. "He kidnaps someone close to Jericho and Mason. Addison, or whatever her name is."

"Ah, okay." Marsha slowly nods her head. "I think we finally know why Mason wanted his phone so badly. He wanted to perform a bank transaction."

"He was trying to give Henry his twenty million back," I say. "To get the girl back."

"So Henry intentionally got himself locked up," says Gina. "Because he had to get to Jericho or Mason."

"I think so," I say. "He can't just waltz in and visit them. He's not family or a lawyer. He must have felt so desperate to work this out with them face-to-face that he was willing to get locked up for a week in Dunham. And he hoped when his bond was reconsidered a week later, he'd get out."

"Big risk," says Gina. "But he probably felt like he had no choice. He must have been desperate to hatch some kind of plan with Jericho."

"And that plan," says Sosh, "included chopping Donnie Delahunt into a hundred pieces?" Sosh picks up the metal container from Henry's safe-deposit box, plays with it. "Killing him made sense, I suppose. Chopping him up like a dead cow didn't."

Sosh twirls around the metal box absentmindedly, thinking things over.

But I keep staring at that box.

With the thumbprint-activated lock.

I grab my phone and find the number on my call directory for Detective Ellie Shurtleff, from the Tenth. I put the phone on speaker.

"Shurtleff."

"Ellie, it's Billy Harney from SOS. Got you on speakerphone with my team. This a bad time for a quick question?"

"Hey, Billy. No, it's fine. Haven't made much progress on the Delahunt murder. We're trying to get polygraphs on the guards, but it's been a bitch with the union. What's your question?"

"Delahunt's body," I say. "Chopped into thirty pieces or whatever."

"Seventeen pieces," she says. *"Well, technically, eighteen."*

"What does that mean?"

"We recovered seventeen body parts. One's missing. Don't ask me what happened to it. Maybe it fell into the drain or something. Or some inmate's getting his jollies with it. Who knows? We can't find it anywhere."

I look at my team and wink. "Let me take a wild guess," I say. "The part that's missing is one of Delahunt's thumbs."

"For crying out loud," Ellie says. *"How'd you know that?"*

CHAPTER 91

"SO THE hideaway where Delahunt took all those girls," says Sosh, "was accessible only by Delahunt's thumbprint."

"I'll bet, yeah," I say. "Why not? Henry seems to like that security device. And Delahunt was probably in charge of the hideaway. So the only way to get that girl free is through Delahunt. Or his thumb, at least."

"And if you want Delahunt's thumb, you have to go to Dunham to get it," says Gina. "Chop him into a bunch of pieces to distract us, make us think it was a crime of rage. When really it was all about taking his thumb."

"I think that's right," I say. "Henry couldn't get word to Jericho any other way than to go inside Dunham and tell Jericho himself. Jericho took care of the rest. He probably owns half the guards in that place. So he chops off Delahunt's thumb and keeps it on ice somehow, somewhere."

"And you better believe that Mason has it right now," says Gina. "He's trying to find the girl."

"Oh, shit, Harney." Marsha pounds the table. "Mason has a sister."

"Yeah, that's—that rings a bell."

"Can't remember her name," says Marsh.

"Addison?"

"No, doesn't sound right. She's, like, nineteen or twenty. It's in one of those files."

"And the drugs!" I shout. "Remember, Marsh, all those prescription drugs lined up on Mason's night-stand? Lined up in perfect order. We left them there but inventoried them. Mason told the judge at his second bond hearing that he didn't take any prescription drugs. I'll bet he was telling the truth. I'll bet they belonged to his sister."

Marsha sits back. "Oh, my. And here, Detective Harney, I thought you were the luckiest guy on the planet. Delahunt walking right up to you on the sidewalk, down the block from Mason's house after we arrested Mason."

Ah. Well, now it all makes sense.

"Delahunt was coming back to Mason's house to get the prescription drugs," I say. "Because he couldn't let Mason's sister die."

"And we stopped him," says Marsh.

"Right," I say. "We stepped right into the middle of a hostage negotiation and didn't know it."

Marsha reaches into a box. "His sister's name is here somewhere. The list of the medications on the night-stand is in the inventory. That's in box number 1."

Pete Parsons sticks his head into the room. "The CSLI records just arrived," he says. "Flager, I forwarded them to your email."

"Great." Marsha opens her laptop computer. She has software that will take the raw data and allow us to tri-angulate a location based on the cell towers Delahunt's phone pinged when he called Henry about the problem with "Addison."

"Delahunt called Henry on Monday, May 17," I remind her. "Probably morning."

"Yeah, I know, I know…" She squints at the screen. "Not nearly as much data as you'd expect. Which means Delahunt was good. He turned his burner phone off and removed the battery when he wasn't using it."

I look at the clock. It's nearly seven thirty at night. We're already out of daylight for all practical purposes.

"Give me a preliminary, before we triangulate," I say. "Tell me what direction we should head. You can pin it down more while we drive."

"Hang on…" Marsha types furiously and squints at the phone. "Well, Carpentersville. Far west edge of Carpentersville, maybe Algonquin. Head that way, and I'll get it pinned down more."

"Turner, you ride with me," I say. "Sosh and Rodriguez, drive separately and alert the county sheriff that we have a possible search-and-rescue. And gear up, boys and girls. Who knows what traps Henry will have laid for us?"

CHAPTER 92

TRAFFIC IS heavy on a Monday night, even at eight o'clock. We light up the cherry on the dashboard and spend most of the time on the shoulder of the highway, passing the mass of rush-hour traffic leaving the city. Gina Turner rides shotgun and uses the radio to talk to Sosh and Rodriguez, along with Marsha Flager back at SOS.

But we can only go so fast. By the time we're off the highway, it's quarter to nine. This is going to be almost impossible.

"Mason's sister is Veronica Tracy," Marsha squawks. "She's a student at Malcolm X College. I managed to get hold of someone in administration. Last week was finals week, so there weren't classes. She wasn't noticed missing. But their records show that she failed to show up for any of her finals."

"So it's her," I say.

"She has a cell-phone contact. I've called it. No answer. The voice mail is full."

"If Delahunt's as cautious as you say, that cell phone's nowhere near where she's hidden."

"*It gets better. The medication? The stuff Henry told Delahunt to go back and get? We have it on the inventory list from the search of Mason's house. The drugs on Mason's nightstand include things like prednisolone and fludrocortisone acetate. They're used to treat adrenal-gland problems.*"

"And that's life-threatening?"

"*Adrenal insufficiency can be deadly,*" says Marsha. "*Especially if you have a long-term endocrine disorder. Such as…Addison's disease.*"

"Addison." I look at Gina. "It wasn't her name. It was her medical problem. Okay, well, that's her. So we have the whole story. Mason stole twenty million from Henry. Henry had Delahunt kidnap Veronica. She told him she needed medication or she'd die. Henry needed her alive so he could trade her for the twenty million."

"*And when Delahunt came back to get it, we caught him. We stopped him from getting her medicine.*"

"Jeez, talk about the law of unintended consequences."

"*I'm gonna pop the map onto your screens,*" she says. "*It's a big triangle, though. There aren't as many cell towers up there as in the city. It's more spread out up there.*"

"So this triangle covers part of Algonquin and Carpentersville," I say. "Not even narrowed down to one town."

"*The triangle's the triangle,*" she says. "*This is the best we can do.*"

"So…what?" I say. "We go door-to-door? Bring in copters from state police—"

"In two different towns?" Gina says. "At nine o'clock at night?"

"*Carpentersville says no,*" Sosh cackles through the radio. "*Chief says he'll offer patrol support, but there's no way we're knocking on doors and waking up families without a better idea of where she is."*

"Waking up families? It's only nine o'clock."

"Little kids are down for the night," says Gina. "And Billy, look, we don't even know she's here. Marsha said Delahunt was smart—he didn't turn on his phone very often, to avoid tracing. If he's smart, he drove away from the hideaway before he called Henry."

"That's true," says Marsh. *"It's probably not far, but not far in which direction?"*

"The haystack is too damn big for a door-to-door that would stretch past midnight," says Gina. "These are bedroom communities."

She's right. Damn. The records came too late for tonight.

"Marsh," I say. "Talk to me about this illness Veronica has. Addison's disease."

"If she hasn't had her meds since a week ago yesterday— that's, what, eight days? According to what I'm reading online, she could go into crisis. It's literally called Addisonian crisis."

"What happens?"

"I mean, just reading this stuff—without meds, pretty much every bad thing that can happen to you kicks in, to start. Fever, dehydration, dizziness, vomiting, stomach pain, fatigue, low blood pressure. And apparently stress exacerbates the whole situation."

"Stress like being kidnapped from your home and locked away by some psycho."

"Right. Eventually, without meds, it progresses to shock, coma, and death. From what I'm reading, if we're eight days out without her meds, we're right there. If she's not dead yet, she's not far."

"And we do *nothing* tonight?"

I punch the steering wheel. Gina puts a hand on my arm.

"We get the county sheriff and the local cops and ISP and some of our own people," she says. "We start first thing in the morning, going door-to-door, patrols, copters, everything. That's the best we can do, Harney. We're not gonna find her tonight."

CHAPTER 93

MASON TRACY tries to sleep in the truck. It's borderline impossible. He feels safe enough, at least, inside a locked garage on the south side of the city. And he has the handgun he took off the rack inside that barn, though it makes him feel more scared than protected.

He checks the supplies for the twentieth time. The drone, in the footwell of the passenger seat, the remote control with it. The smokeys, six of them.

The prednisolone and the steroid shot, for when he finds her.

And the large Styrofoam container filled with dry ice, holding—under three layers of plastic—the left thumb of Donnie Delahunt, which Mason transferred from his freezer at home.

He checks his phone, getting a weak signal, but a signal all the same, inside this garage. The bank transfer, after the twenty-four-hour cool-off period, will be ready by 12:30 p.m. tomorrow. Henry will have his money back. And, Mason hopes, he'll have his sister back.

"Tomorrow," he whispers aloud. "Tomorrow, I'll

find…find you. Tomorrow. I promise. You'll be…be okay…you—"

He chokes on those last words, his eyes filling with tears. He removes a picture of Veronica from his pocket, places it on the dash. She has to be alive. She has to be.

She was always his rock. After Mama died, Veronica held everything together, even though she's younger than he is by a year.

"Don't…be afraid," he whispers. "I'll…I'll be there."

Henry Arcola puts his feet up on his bed in A Block as the corrections officer slides his door shut for the night.

"Hear you're finally getting a lawyer, Henry," says the CO.

"Yeah, I am. I need a good one. Bond hearing's Thursday."

"Yeah? They're gonna give bond to someone who killed his wife?"

"Allegedly," Henry corrects. "*Allegedly* killed her."

"Yeah, of course, allegedly. Innocent till proven guilty, right?"

"That's the spirit," says Henry.

"We got you down for tomorrow morning at eleven," says the CO. "You sure—you sure you wanna do it at eleven? That's your yard time—"

"Only time he could do it," says Henry. "Not up to me."

"Okay, well, I hope you got yourself a good lawyer there, Henry."

Henry smiles. "Me too," he says.

TUESDAY

CHAPTER 94

THE SKY overcast, a decent wind kicking up, the morning air crisp, the team in place. The sheriff's deputies from Kane and McHenry Counties, locals from the police departments in Carpentersville, Algonquin, and Lake in the Hills, some patrol teams from SOS, and troopers from the Illinois State Police—all gathered in the parking lot of Presidential Park, in the northwestern suburb of Algonquin.

"We go door-to-door," I tell the crew. "You all have the photographs of Veronica and Donnie Delahunt and Henry Arcola. If we're right, this woman was abducted, probably in the middle of the night, and stowed away somewhere around here. So it's unlikely that anyone's seen the girl. Better bet are these two men you also have photographs of, Delahunt and Arcola. They've been around from time to time.

"We're looking for anything at all they might tell you. Anything strange. Vans or trucks coming or going at strange hours. Strange noises at strange hours. Houses that are basically vacant. Anything at all, you call me. You all have my cell in case you need it. But you can get

me on your radio, too. I'll be in the chopper. We're—
we're Air 2?"

"Air 2," says the trooper piloting the helicopter.

"We're Air 2. Anything at all, guys—anything that
raises the hair on your neck, you radio or call me."

I look around. Everyone's ready to rock.

"This girl has a serious medical condition, people.
If she's still alive, it's probably not by much. So let's
find her."

The teams fan out. I blow out air and put my hands
on my knees.

"Whenever you're ready, Detective," says the pilot.

"Great, thanks."

I take a minute with my crew: Sosh, Rodriguez, and
Turner. Marsha Flager's hanging back, working her
computer magic to find some clue as to the whereabouts
of Veronica Tracy.

"Decent chance she isn't around here at all," I say.

"Worth a shot," says Sosh.

"You think Mason's been up here?" Gina asks. "He's
looking for her, too. Do you think he knows where
she is?"

I shrug. "We have a BOLO on all the hospitals, right?"

"Yeah," she says. "I issued it personally. Veronica
shows up at any hospital, we get a phone call."

"Well, this much I know: Henry won't reveal her
location until he has his money back."

"Mason's been out of Dunham since yesterday
morning," Gina says. "That's enough time to transfer
the money back to Henry. Not to an account we're
watching, but somewhere, some Swiss bank account or
something."

"Yeah, maybe," I say. "But I doubt it."

"Why do you doubt it?"

"Because if Henry's already given up Veronica's

location, he's already given up his leverage," I say. "What stops Jericho from killing him inside Dunham? I'm sure Jericho wants to. Henry just fucked with Jericho, and Jericho is not someone to fuck with. Jericho can just say the word, and Henry's dead. No," I say, "Henry hasn't told Mason yet. Henry won't say a word to Mason until he's out of jail. Then he can take his twenty million and put the United States of America in his rearview mirror."

"So that means Henry won't say a word until Thursday, after his bond hearing," says Sosh. "She could be dead by then."

"It's Henry's only shot. I can't see him giving up Veronica's location before then."

"Which means Veronica is screwed," says Gina, "unless we find her first."

I grab my phone. "Maybe I go pay Henry a visit today," I say.

"You think he'll tell you what you need to know? I can't imagine. He'd take tremendous joy in telling you to go fuck yourself."

"Can't hurt," I say. "We have enough manpower up here looking for her." I dial the number for the jail. "Maybe with the detailed information we have now, Henry will see that he's not getting bond on Thursday, he's never getting out of jail, and he's basically a dead man walking if he doesn't help us out."

A woman answers. "Dunham Detention Center."

"This is Chicago police detective Harney for an inmate interview. I need it today, expedited."

"The inmate?"

"Henry Arcola. From A Block."

"Represented by counsel?"

"No."

"One moment."

The sun peeks through the trees. It's going to be hot today. The sheriff's deputies will be sweating their fannies off.

"Detective, Henry Arcola *is* represented by counsel."

"He is? Since when?"

"Since…yesterday afternoon. So you'll have to clear the visit through him."

"Who's the lawyer?"

"The lawyer is…Eugene Cotrillos of Decker, Cotrillos, and Swanson."

"You got a number for me?"

"Sure." The woman reads me the number. I punch out the phone.

"Henry finally lawyered up," I say.

"Getting ready for that big bond revisit," says Sosh. "But with what we know now, Clarence Darrow couldn't get him bond."

I dial the number and get a voice mail. The lawyer may not even be in the office yet at this hour.

"You've reached the office of Eugene Cotrillos…"

I wait for the recording to end and leave my message. "This is Detective Billy Harney of the Chicago police for Eugene Cotrillos," I say. "It concerns your new client, Henry Arcola. Please call immediately. Immediately. It's urgent."

I leave my cell number and punch out the phone.

Then I head to the chopper.

CHAPTER 95

I'M UP in Air 2, the state police chopper, over the northwestern suburbs, working the phones as the calls come in. I can't shake a disconcerting sense of déjà vu, reminding me of a search for another missing girl several weeks ago, which led to the death of my partner.

The clouds are dark, threatening rain, which will make everything more difficult. Winds are starting to gust, too, making helicopter travel harder than usual.

In the cockpit, a two-person crew in olive-green flight suits and white helmets. The pilot, a woman named Mullaney, works the controls while the TFO—the tactical flight officer—a guy named Griggs, sets the course and monitors half a dozen radio frequencies.

These suburbs all blend together from the air, tree-lined streets mostly running in a grid, major commercial arteries, school grounds with baseball diamonds and large playing fields, the Fox River running to the west. I have to check the TFO's monitor just to know which suburb we're over—Algonquin, Carpentersville, Dundee, Lake in the Hills, Middlebury, Sleepy Hollow—the list doesn't end.

"Can you get us closer?" I say. We're right near the boundary between Algonquin and Carpentersville. "What is that?" I say into my phone to a patrol officer from Algonquin. "Some sort of man-made pond?"

"With lots of tree cover," says the officer.

I doubt Henry hid the girls in the woods. He'd want a house. A basement. Something private and soundproof.

But you never know.

"Mullaney," I shout to the pilot in the cockpit, "can we get a camera down in those woods?"

She gives me a thumbs-up and works the FLIR monitor mounted in the cockpit. The forward-looking infrared camera instantly lights up the monitor with glowing white shapes beneath the trees. Little shapes, though—squirrels and rabbits, maybe some deer. "Nothing human," Mullaney shouts back to me.

I relay that info to the patrol on the ground and punch out the phone. It rings again immediately. That's what the last two-plus hours have been like, acting as command central up here in the chopper.

"Harney," I say.

"Mr. Harney? Gene Cotrillos."

"Gene...?"

"You called me this morning? I was in court."

"Oh, right, Eugene Cotrillos. You're Henry Arcola's lawyer, I hear?"

"I'm afraid you heard wrong, Detective. I'm not representing Henry Arcola. I'd be happy to, given what I've heard. Clients with a lot of problems and a lot of money are the best kind." He chuckles at his own line.

"Dunham told me you were listed as his lawyer as of yesterday. Eugene Cotrillos of something, Cotrillos, and something."

"Decker, Cotrillos, and Swanson—that's me."

With my hands free—I'm using earbuds for the

call—I do an internet search for Eugene Cotrillos on my phone. It pulls up the name of his law firm.

I click on Eugene's name on his firm's website. It pulls up a bio—claiming a specialty in criminal defense—along with a photo of a white guy, probably late fifties, heavyset and balding. Not a slick operator like your Elan Tenenbaums of the world. More of a street brawler.

This guy looks like Lanny Soscia in fifteen years.

"But I'm not representing Henry Arcola," he says.

"Is there another defense lawyer with that name?"

"Not that I know of," he says. "Chicago's legal community isn't as big as you might think. If someone else in town had my name, I'd know it."

"Okay. Maybe they transposed your name from another client, some typo."

"Maybe."

Huh. That's weird.

Is it more than weird?

I start to dial Dunham, but my phone's already ringing again, this time with a call from a patrol in Carpentersville.

CHAPTER 96

THE MAN, a tall African American with gray hair and a goatee of the same color, pulls his car up to the gate of Dunham Detention Center. "Counsel here for an inmate visit," he says.

The guard takes his driver's license and bar identification card, checks his name on a clipboard, and waves him through. "Park anywhere in that lot, sir."

The visitor parking lot is segregated, for security reasons, from the remainder of the jail. The visitor entry itself is separated entirely from the jail.

The man takes a moment inside the car and thinks.

He will walk into an entrance marked ADMINISTRATION: VISITOR ENTRANCE. There is usually only one staff member at this entrance, behind a window. Sometimes two. No different from the ticket counter at a movie theater, except the glass is bulletproof.

The staff will ask for his driver's license and bar identification card. They will check his name against the visitor list. When he is approved, they will give him a visitor's pass on a lanyard he should wear, at all times, around his neck.

They will tell him to surrender his cell phone. He did not bring one.

They will tell him to pass through a secure door, down a hallway, past secured key-card-entry doors for the men's and women's staff locker rooms and exits.

They will tell him to walk until he reaches another secured door for detainee visitations. He will hold up his lanyard to the camera. A corrections officer will buzz him through. His briefcase will go through a metal detector. So will he. If he doesn't pass through cleanly, even after he has removed all metal from his pockets, they will wand him.

The wand will alert on his watch. The corrections officer will not ask him to remove it. Smartwatches are not allowed inside the visitation area, but standard wristwatches like his are not considered threats or contraband under Dunham regulations.

Then he will be directed into the visitation area, where he will be sent to the stall where his client will be seated, locked to the table. He will ask that the shackles be removed; under Dunham regulations, that request is to be honored unless the COs believe that removing the shackles is a security threat.

The man gets out of the car, straightens his suit jacket, shoots his cuffs, and removes his briefcase from the back seat. He then walks through the parking lot to the visitor entrance to the administration building.

He walks in and approaches the counter. A man stands behind the bulletproof glass.

"Are you counsel?" the guard asks.

"Yes. Counsel for an inmate visit."

"Name, please."

The man slides his driver's license and bar identification card through the window.

"Eugene Cotrillos," the man says.

CHAPTER 97

HENRY ARCOLA sits quietly in stall number 2 of the detainee visitation room, shackled to a metal ring on the table. The door, controlled by the booth, is open. All Henry can see is the booth, where the officer in charge of the visitation room, CO Korey Heppner, sits behind bulletproof glass, manning the controls.

"All right, Mr. Cotrillos, I'm gonna need to wand you." That's the voice of the other CO in the room, Lou Espinoza. Dunham's regulations require a ratio of no fewer than one CO for every three inmates in the visitation room. There are only two detainees in here right now, so Espinoza is the only CO on the floor, with Korey Heppner in the booth.

"Okay, you're good," Espinoza says. "This your first time here?"

"Yes."

"So let's do some ground rules. You're entitled to privacy with your client. The doors on each stall open and close automatically. The guard up there in the booth, Officer Heppner? He controls everything. He will close the door once you're inside. Every ten minutes, we'll announce the door's opening, and he'll open it. That's for your safety, so we can check on you. Anything makes you nervous, just yell 'Open' really loud, and we'll open it. Okay?"

"Yes."

"Okay, great. You've got two inmates you're visiting. They're both here. Which one do you want to see first?"

It's not uncommon for a lawyer to group all his clients into a single visitation, to save him multiple trips. Dunham typically accommodates those requests.

"Henry Arcola, please."

"He's currently shackled, Counsel. Would you like us to remove the shackles? It's your choice."

"Yes, please."

"We reserve the right to shackle him again for inmate or attorney safety."

"I understand."

CO Lou Espinoza walks into the cell and winks at Henry. "Bringing in the big guns, eh, Henry?"

"You tell me," Henry says. "First time I'm meeting him. He called my family and requested a meeting. I hear he's good."

Espinoza removes the shackles. "If his suit is any indication, the guy's good. Behave, now, Henry." He wags a finger at him.

The man who walks in looks nothing like Eugene Cotrillos of Decker, Cotrillos, and Swanson, whom Henry looked up on the library internet. Cotrillos is a dumpy, balding white guy. This man is a tall, well-dressed Black guy.

"You're Mr. Cotrillos?" Henry asks.

The CO closes the door behind him, leaving them alone.

The man sets down his briefcase, reaches into his pocket, and removes a pair of rubber gloves.

CHAPTER 98

"TELL THEM we're searching for a missing girl, and we'd appreciate their cooperation," I tell the officer on the phone as the helicopter banks west. "Tell them you'll get a warrant if necessary."

I have another call—no surprise—so I end that call and take the new one. It's Marsha, calling from SOS.

"Billy," she says, "this thing you and Gina said about Henry being in the air force? The intelligence wing?"

"The Air Intelligence Agency."

"Right. Well, I dug through his emails and found a message from an old colleague of his, writing about a reunion a year ago. His name is Lucky Anderson. They were in the agency together, and I have him on the phone right now. Mr. Anderson?"

"Yes, ma'am." A bit of a southern drawl.

"Mr. Anderson, tell Detective Harney what you told me."

"Well, listen," says Anderson. "I never had a big problem with Arcola or anything. I wouldn't say we were friends, but still—I'm not trying to, y'understand, testify against him or make trouble or anything. I don't need any trouble with him."

"Not a guy you wanna be on the wrong side of?" I say.

"That's...a good way of puttin' it, yeah."

Marsha says, "Tell Detective Harney what you told me about what you guys did in the agency."

"I mean, we covered a lot of territory. It was recon and intelligence gathering. For example, before an infiltration, we'd get an idea of the aerial capabilities of the enemy. We'd scout targets—"

"Lucky, tell him about the exfiltrations, if you would."

"Okay, yeah. We'd deploy where exfils were required. We'd scout the area, look for points of vulnerability, escape routes, asset recruitment, and we'd usually provide aerial support during the exfils themselves. Henry was particularly good with the asset recruitment. That guy could put on any face he needed. He could talk a mouse into a snake pit."

"Exfils," I repeat. "Meaning you'd get our troops out of enemy territory?"

"Sometimes that, yeah," Lucky Anderson says. "Troops in hostile territory or POWs. Other times— and y'understand, I can't go into specifics—but other times, they'd be peacetime exfils. Political prisoners, people accused of espionage and held by a nonfriendly. With our recon, we basically drew up the PRIME, told them how to execute the PRIME, and provided satellite support while they executed the PRIME."

I sit back in my chair. For just a moment, it feels like the helicopter has stopped moving. Or maybe like the ground has just shifted beneath us.

"Am I hearing this right?" I say. "Are you telling me that you guys used to help people escape from prisons?"

CHAPTER 99

MASON TRACY sits inside the flatbed truck, idling by the curb. Checks his watch.

He picks up the remote control and pushes a button.

In his rearview mirror, he sees the drone lift off the flatbed, rising into the air with the smokeys attached to it. He rolls down the window and looks up to the darkening sky. Sees the drone hovering there, twenty feet off the ground, waiting for his next command.

He works the levers to carefully lower the drone back down to the flatbed.

He wipes the sweat off his forehead with his sleeve. He tells himself, *This will work, this will work, this will work*.

He puts the truck in Drive. Traffic is light. It only takes him ten minutes to reach his destination. He pulls up by the curb.

Across the street, Dunham Detention Center.

More specifically, the jail yard. Where the inmates from A Block have recently begun their hour outside.

He checks his watch. His heart pounding, he waits for the seventy-five seconds to pass. It feels more like seventy-five hours.

Now it's time.

He works the remote. The drone rises from the truck.

Mason puts the flatbed in gear, executes the beginning of a three-point turn, steering the truck perpendicular to California Avenue, directly facing the jail yard.

But instead of completing the three-point turn, he leaves the truck directly aimed at the jail yard. He pushes a button to change the truck to dynamic steering—remote control.

He gathers the remote controls and jumps out of the truck.

CHAPTER 100

CORRECTIONS OFFICER Ken Wittmer works East Tower. Never a dull moment watching the jail yard at Dunham through the bulletproof glass of the watchtower, thirty feet up, but things get especially tense when it's the hour in the yard for A Block, the most violent and confrontational inmates in the jail. Which just began a few minutes ago.

He doesn't have his phone with him. They're not allowed, and Dunham jams the signals anyway, both within the walls and in the yard, a security measure.

So he keeps a paperback book around, usually a thriller he can pick up and put down easily should something come up in the yard. He's really just window dressing up here anyway. The COs in the yard do the heavy lifting; the watchtower looms as a threat that almost never materializes. Wittmer's had to put his sniper rifle through the scope, threatening to open fire, only once in the twenty months he's worked—

"Hey, Witt, what's that?" Coleman, in West Tower, nearest California Avenue, crackles through the radio.

Wittmer looks down in the yard. "Where? I don't—"

"West of the fence. What the…what the fuck is that?"

Wittmer looks down at California Avenue, but then it catches his eye. Not on the ground but in the air. Something flying straight east toward them, something out of a sci-fi movie, with tiny bottles—or something like that—hanging from it.

"Central, this is East Tower. We have an unidentified object over the yard!"

The drone buzzes past West Tower, over the electrified coils, causing an uproar from the inmates below.

"It's a drone, some kinda drone."

"Shoot that thing down!" Wittmer calls out. "East Tower taking mark!" Wittmer slides open the window and ports his rifle, aiming at the drone.

But before he can line it up, the drone practically drops out of the air, nosediving onto the grass of the jail yard only a few yards past the fence line like a pole vaulter wanting only to clear the top before letting gravity take its course.

The drone shatters into pieces on impact but erupts into smoke of various colors, purple and orange and red and blue and yellow and green.

Wittmer aims his rifle downward, but the yard begins to fill with the rainbow cloud, the entire height and length of the electrified western fence disappearing in the multicolored smoke.

"Code black, code black!" Wittmer calls into his radio.

Most of the inmates run away from the smoke toward the detention center, the COs in the yard scrambling to shepherd them back inside.

From his vantage point, thirty feet up, something catches Wittmer's eye to the west, toward California Avenue. He does a double take.

A large blue flatbed truck has driven over the

sidewalk and onto the grass, barreling straight toward the jail yard.

"Central, this is East Tower," Wittmer calls into his radio. "We are code black, do you copy? Possible jailbreak in progress in the yard! We are code black! They're gonna breach the fence!"

CHAPTER 101

HENRY SITS at the table in the attorney-client visitation stall with his "lawyer," a man who identified himself to Dunham as Eugene Cotrillos but who is, in fact, Nathaniel Trainor——Night Train, as he is apparently known within the Imperial Gangster Nation.

They didn't need the full ten minutes——the window of time before the first mandatory check into the stall——to get ready. It only took them about five.

Five minutes, at most, for Henry to strip off his jumpsuit, put on the CO uniform that Trainor smuggled in in his briefcase, and put his jumpsuit back on over the CO uniform.

And a fraction of that time for Nathaniel Trainor to put on rubber gloves, take off his wristwatch, and remove a small patch taped inside the band.

They end up with a few minutes to spare before the next step. Henry watches the clock and waits for it.

There: the siren bellows out, *whup-whup, whup-whup,* shooting waves of red light that Henry can see even within the stall.

The clock reads eleven thirteen and forty seconds.

That gives him five minutes.

Henry nods to Nathaniel Trainor, who scoops up the patch and cups it within the palm of his rubber-gloved hand.

Then the voice through the speaker: *"Code black, code black, jail yard! Proceed to emergency lockdown protocols and report to Central Security. Code black, code black, jail yard! Proceed to emergency lockdown protocols and report to Central Security…"*

"What, they got under the fence?" The voice of the other CO, Espinoza.

The emergency lockdown procedure requires that each pod within each wing be secured by the officer in charge of that pod. Today, the visitation pod's OIC is Korey Heppner.

Lockdown within the visitation pod means that all detainees are secured and locked in and that all civilian visitors are evacuated if possible.

"Evacuate the civilian!" Korey calls out from the booth to Espinoza.

"Code black, code black, jail yard! Proceed to emergency lockdown…"

Every pod will be locked down by the OIC, and all remaining personnel will report to Central Security to address the breach of the jail yard's western fence—on the other side of the jail from the place where Henry now sits.

Trainor, sitting across from Henry, keeps his back to the door as it pops open, hiding his rubber-gloved hands from view.

CO Espinoza rushes in. Henry raises his hands. "We're just getting started, Lou. Gimme a break. We're nowhere near the jail yard—"

"We have to evacuate civilians right now." Espinoza grabs Trainor's arm. "C'mon, sir."

His hand cupped to keep the patch inside the palm of his gloved hand, Trainor spins and smacks Officer Espinoza in the cheek, planting the patch there. The CO staggers backward, eyes widening in horror. He tears at the patch with one hand while reaching for his sidearm with the other.

Henry knocks over the table and hides behind it, just in case the guard gets off a round or two. But the CO doesn't even get his sidearm out of its holster.

Instead, Officer Lou Espinoza seizes up, knees buckling, and collapses to the floor, already dead from the massive overdose of fentanyl.

"Lou!" Heppner calls out. "Espinoza! You okay in there? Shit!"

Well done, Korey, Henry thinks to himself. He won't get an Academy Award, but it's convincing enough.

Technically, Korey's not supposed to leave the booth. He's supposed to radio in for support. But as Korey himself said last night, *Anyone could understand my rushing to the aid of a fellow CO who just collapsed.*

Especially when all available personnel are racing to Central to respond to the breach.

The cameras are watching, Korey told him. *I'll be playing to the cameras.*

"He's having a heart attack!" Henry shouts, doing his part.

When Korey leaves his bird's-eye view in the booth to come to the aid of Espinoza, Trainor will disarm the dead CO, hide behind the door, and point the gun at Korey upon his entry into the stall.

Order me to the floor, Korey said last night. *Disarm me and cuff me with my own handcuffs.*

Korey leaves the booth. Henry nods to Trainor, who removes Espinoza's sidearm and hides along the side of the wall by the door.

Henry stands up, pointing at Espinoza. "I think he had a heart attack!" he shouts.

When Korey Heppner shuffles into the room, weapon drawn, shouting commands, Trainor puts the gun against Korey's ear.

And pulls the trigger.

Loud, yes, but with the siren and general chaos, and the gun muzzled into Korey's ear, probably nothing that would draw the attention of the front desk, two secured doors and a hallway away.

His brains splattered against the wall, Korey collapses, face-planting on the floor, falling only inches from Espinoza, a pool of blood quickly forming under his face.

Watching the clock, Henry reaches for the zipper at the neck of his jumpsuit and unzips to his navel, then climbs out of it, leaving his CO uniform intact.

Trainor drops the gun, carefully strips off the rubber gloves, and dumps them, too.

Henry removes Espinoza's utility belt and puts it around his waist. He hands the keys to Trainor. "Unlock Jericho," he says. "Get him dressed. Fast!"

Trainor runs to stall number 4, where Jericho is shackled, awaiting his "visit" with the same "attorney" as Henry.

After Trainor has left, Henry picks up Espinoza's gun and holsters it.

Henry gets the key card from Korey and swipes his way into the booth. From there, he finds the riot gear. He puts on the Kevlar vest and helmet with the face shield that will obscure his face. He grabs an AR-15 assault rifle. He takes a second set for Jericho and leaves the booth.

While Jericho strips off his jumpsuit and puts on his CO uniform, Henry flips down his face shield and grabs

Trainor by the arm. He swipes his way through the door and rush-walks Trainor down the hallway.

The staff officer at the visitor entrance opens the secured door.

"Evacuate this civilian and lock down your pod!" Henry shouts, anonymous behind his face shield, reciting verbatim the script that Korey fed him last night. "I'll lock down Visitation."

The officer complies, rushing Trainor out to the parking lot. Henry swipes the door and reenters Visitation, where Jericho has his CO uniform on and is grabbing the riot gear. Henry looks at the clock. Ninety seconds remaining before lockdown becomes automatic, before every door locks no matter what.

Jericho has his shirt and pants on. "I need the guard's belt and holster," he says.

"No time. Put on the vest and helmet."

Jericho throws on the vest, puts on the helmet, and locks down the face shield. He picks up the AR-15, too.

Seventy seconds.

Henry swipes through the door one last time. "Central, Visitation is locked down!" he calls into Korey's radio, then clicks it back onto his waist.

"Copy that."

They rush down the hall to the door marked STAFF LOCKER ROOM AND EXIT above the word MEN. Henry swipes through the door.

"All clear? All clear?" Henry calls out, as Korey told him to do.

No answer. As Korey predicted, nobody in the locker room during a late-morning hour such as this.

They jog through the locker room to the exit door. Henry swipes the card, and they're out, the wind whipping up, the sky dark and ominous as he and Jericho enter the staff parking lot.

CHAPTER 102

"HEAD TO Dunham Detention Center!" I shout to the pilot. "South side of Chicago, Thirty-first and California!"

"Roger that. Fasten your seat belt, Harney. We'll be flying into a headwind."

The helicopter angles and turns south, picking up speed, nearly knocking me out of my chair, my stomach doing somersaults.

I dial the number for Dunham again. The phone rings: no answer.

I call Sosh. "They aren't answering the phone," he tells me. "Gina's calling over and over again."

"Tell her to keep calling. And Sosh, call the Eighteenth and tell them to get patrol cars over there if they haven't already."

Shit.

My phone rings. As promised, Marsha calls me back, five minutes after we spoke. "Nobody's answering at Dunham," I say, holding on to my seat with my free hand.

"Because they're in lockdown," she says. "It's

happening. I called over to the Eighteenth. They said they've already received calls for assistance."

"You have any details?"

"They—you know the jail yard's right there on California Avenue?"

"Right."

"They drove a damn truck through the fence and took it down. Knocked out the electricity. And there's a bunch of smoke, too. I don't know if it's a fire or what, but nobody can see anything. They're trying to round up the inmates and do a head count."

"So inmates were in the yard?" But I already know the answer.

"A Block was in the yard," she says.

"Was Henry in the yard?" A man's voice. It takes me a moment to remember: we had Henry's air force colleague on the phone with us, last name Anderson.

"Too early to have that kind of information," says Marsha.

"I doubt he was," says Lucky Anderson. "He's probably clear on the other side of the jail."

"Tell me," I say.

"Do you know where the medical facilities are in the jail?"

"I—not offhand, no."

"Henry would want to be far away from that breach. It's the principles of PRIME."

"You keep saying that word," I say as the ground below me flies by in a blur.

"It's an acronym. *P* is for 'pinpoint the vulnerable exit.' The least guarded. The least secure. That's usually gonna be where there are the fewest inmates. Someplace near an exit, like the medical—"

"Like the visitation room," I say.

"Yeah, could be, yeah, that would work just fine.

The *r* is for 'recruiting assets inside.' A guard would be the best asset."

Jericho probably owns half the guards inside Dunham.

"Or a doctor," he says, "or some vendor who brings supplies—"

"Or a lawyer," I say. "Someone posing as a lawyer to get inside the visitation room."

Eugene Cotrillos. Fuck.

"The *i* and the *m* in PRIME are for 'introducing and misdirecting' a crisis," says Anderson. "Cause a big problem on the opposite end of the prison as a distraction. An inmate riot is the most common."

"Or a truck barreling through the yard fence."

"Exactly. All prisons—or, in this case, jails—are different, but their protocols for this kinda thing are pretty much the same. Issue some kind of lockdown or stay-in-place order for the nonthreatened portions of the facility, then direct all available guards and resources toward the breach. Henry would know that. He probably studied the layout and jail regulations."

"Damn it." I look around for something to punch. "Henry had a guy posing as a lawyer who helped him. Probably had a guard or two inside as well. They breached the jail-yard fence and sent everyone scrambling in that direction."

I look out the window, then look away, immediately hit with nausea. We must be going a hundred miles an hour in the air.

"You might as well tell me what the *e* stands for," I say.

"It stands for 'escape, stupid.' And I'll bet that's what he did," Anderson says. "That's what we used to call the manual. The escape book. And I'll betcha that's just what he did. I'll bet Henry walked right out the side door."

CHAPTER 103

HENRY AND Jericho run through the staff parking lot on the side of the building, fenced in for security. The lot is not monitored by a guard; entry and exit by car occurs through a gate controlled by a key card.

The sound of sirens fills the air as the county sheriff's deputies at the campus up the block respond to Dunham's call for assistance. But the sheriffs will be driving down California, and that's where the action is, where the fence was breached. Henry and Jericho are on the opposite side of the building, where nobody's looking.

They toss their helmets and rifles, strip off their vests, and climb the fence, jumping over to the other side and running south from the campus of Dunham Detention Center toward a vacant lot.

"Where's the van?" Henry asks. "You said you'd have a—"

"Behind the shed," Jericho says, out of breath as he runs, gesturing up ahead to a broken-down, faded shack in the middle of the abandoned lot.

Sure enough, parked behind it, a panel van, where Mason Tracy sits behind the wheel.

Jericho slides open the side panel and jumps in.

Henry pauses, takes a look at the shack, and walks inside.

He comes out a moment later, Jericho waving him inside the van. He jumps in and slides the door closed behind him.

"Go the speed limit, son," says Jericho, putting his hand on Mason's shoulder. He pulls clothes out of a bag and tosses them to Henry. Jericho rummages through another bag, finding a shirt.

Mason puts the van in gear.

"Change outta your clothes," Jericho tells Henry. "Hurry!"

Henry has another idea.

He pulls his sidearm from his holster and shoots Jericho in the head, his brains splattering the other side of the interior panel.

Mason nearly jumps out of his seat, spinning around and crying out, the steering wheel spinning free, the van wandering in a slow circle in the vacant lot.

Henry aims the gun at Mason, who recoils. "Grab hold of the steering wheel and drive!" he shouts. "You wanna see your sister alive again?"

"You *killed him*? You—"

"Drive, Mason!"

Mason grabs hold of the wheel, rights the van, hits the brake, and stops it.

"You killed—killed my—"

Henry jams the gun against Mason's head. "Get my money back!"

"I did. I did. I did." Mason is all blubbering tears now, a freaky puddle.

"Prove it to me! *Prove it to me!*"

Mason hands him his phone. "There's a twenty— twenty-four…"

Henry works Mason's phone, a new one, not password-protected. He finds the app and opens it.

"What are you telling me—there's a twenty-four-hour safety hold on the transfer?"

There it is: Henry sees it now. A transfer of twenty million US dollars from Mason's Swiss bank account to Henry's.

<< Transfer of USD$ 20,000,000 to the following account >>

The words beneath them:

<< Status: Pending validation 12:31 pm CDT >>

So yes—there's a twenty-four-hour hold on the transfer. Not surprising for a transfer of that amount, to make sure no irreversible mistakes are made. Those Swiss are secretive and cautious, too.

So Mason made the transfer yesterday, after getting out, and it takes effect today, when he validates it.

"And what's the validation?"

"Face…facial…"

"Facial-recognition validation?"

Mason nods.

"And it's up today at 12:31 p.m.?"

"Yes." Mason grips the steering wheel, heaving and sobbing.

Henry checks the time on Mason's phone. It's half past eleven.

That means one hour. The money won't—can't—go through for another hour, and then only after Mason validates the transfer. That fucks up Henry's plan, which was to kill Mason right now, along with Jericho, drive straight to his private plane—the one registered under a dummy corporation that the cops don't know about—and leave the country with his twenty million dollars banked.

Mason, he must admit, played that well. He knew the timing of this jailbreak. He knew that once he gave Henry back the money, he'd have no leverage. He bought himself a one-hour window to get his sister back before releasing the money.

So now Henry's stuck with Mason for one more hour.

"I wanna…wanna see her…before I val—validate…"

"Fuck!" Henry shouts, then snaps out of it. This wasn't the plan, but plans change.

He has no choice. They have to go up and get the girl.

Which will probably take an entire hour anyway. He'll get Mason up there, reunite him with his sister, and get his money.

Then he'll kill them.

"Drive the car," says Henry. "Mason! Put the car in gear. I'll take you to her."

The kid's a complete puddle of tears, shivering and blubbering.

"Fuck—I'll do it." He grabs Mason's shirt and yanks him over. Mason moves over to the passenger seat.

Henry climbs into the driver's seat, puts the van in gear, and drives out of the empty lot.

He pulls out onto the street as three police squad cars fly past him, sirens blaring, responding to the jailbreak at Dunham Detention Center.

CHAPTER 104

BY THE time we reach Dunham Detention Center in Air 2, our helicopter is joined by a CPD helicopter in the sky over the south side of Chicago.

On the ground, police squad cars and SWAT trucks are everywhere, roadblocks being set up for a perimeter. Over the jail itself, the remnants of colorful smoke dissipate over the yard, where a truck is parked on top of the fence it flattened during the breach. The yard is empty now, most of the inmates shepherded back inside the jail, but nearly a hundred were in the yard when the truck breached the fence.

"It's goddamn pandemonium here!" says Detective Ellie Shurtleff from the Eighteenth, one of the detectives responding to the jailbreak in her district. "We got six escapees from the yard! And you're telling me I might have two more from Admin? Jericho Hooper and the billionaire guy, Arcola?"

"Call it an educated guess, Ellie. Can you check? I can't get anyone on the line."

"Hang on."

Henry, the billionaire. That was all fluff, the image

he cultivated while he juggled and spent tens of millions of dollars that belonged to other people. And now he's down to his last twenty million, currently held by Jericho and his boy wonder, Mason.

"Take us to the northeast side!" I shout to the cockpit. It's the administration wing, on the other side of the jail from the yard.

In moments, we're hovering over the administration wing of Dunham, including the separate visitor entrance, which I've used several times. The visitor parking lot…next to it, separated by a fence, the staff parking lot…

Besides all the cars, I see something by the fence in the staff parking lot. I use my binoculars to make sure.

Two Kevlar vests. Two helmets. Two assault rifles.

"Billy." Ellie Shurtleff startles me, back on the phone. "You were right. Jericho and Henry Arcola were in Visitation. It was called in to Central Security as locked down and secure, but it's not. The inmates are gone, and two corrections officers are dead."

"They jumped the fence in the staff parking lot," I say. "To that huge vacant lot next door."

The chopper noses forward, only twenty feet off the ground. To the immediate east of the fence is an abandoned lot, nothing but a run-down shack in the middle that looks like it would collapse under a strong wind. Some sort of old fast-food drive-through shack, the kind that used to thrive on the South Side when I was a kid.

"Can you land us in the lot?" I call to the cockpit.

The chopper sets down carefully in the abandoned lot.

I hop out of the helicopter, my weapon drawn, running low to avoid the chopper blades. I approach the shed slowly, weapon up. At least there are holes in this shed, so the sunlight filters in and I'm not walking into darkness.

"Chicago police!" I shout on entry. A rat scurries across the floor. The place is otherwise empty, every appliance, countertop, or piece of metal stripped away years ago.

On the floor, with a rock on top to hold it in place, a piece of paper with handwriting:

Hi, Billy
Are you having fun yet?

"So now I got two more escapees!" says Ellie.

I holster my weapon. "No," I say. "These two are mine."

CHAPTER 105

HENRY PULLS off the highway halfway to the destination and parks the panel van behind a restaurant. "Sit tight," he says to Mason, who's gone quiet, his head in his hands. "Don't forget you need me."

He knows Mason won't forget. That kid's done this much, gone this far, all for his sister. He won't mess it up now.

Henry gets out, goes around to the side, and slides open the panel door. He notices for the first time, on the floor, the sealed plastic—actually, three layers of it—holding Donnie Delahunt's severed thumb. It's been on ice, but Mason's been thawing it, knowing he'll need it soon to get into the basement to see Veronica.

Next to it is the bag Mason brought from the barn. Henry pulls out a blue uniform and throws it up to Mason. "Put this on," he says. "Just in case."

Henry does the same, changing out of his CO uniform and putting on the police uniform. But most important, he takes the belt from the CO uniform and puts it around his waist, including the holster and sidearm.

Henry drags Jericho's dead body out of the van and leaves him behind a Dumpster. When he gets back in the car, fresh tears have fallen on Mason's face.

"You're just go—gonna…gonna leave him…"

Henry doesn't have time for sentimentality. "Change into that uniform, Mason."

Henry puts the van in gear, reverses, and drives out of the restaurant lot, minding the speed limit.

"Look, kid, think of it as self-defense. A big crime boss like Jericho? He'd never forgive me. I could hide on some island without an extradition treaty and be safe from US prosecutors, but I'd never be safe from Jericho. I'd always be looking over my shoulder. But you I have no problem with. You and I can give each other what we want and go our separate ways."

This is probably too much for an introverted genius autistic-or-whatever-he-is kid. It's one thing to have him operate the drones and the remote-controlled truck; a kid like Mason probably sat inside with a joystick in his lap most of his childhood. But seeing someone get shot in the head? That was probably too much for him.

"Give me the burner phone," says Henry. "You remembered to bring me a burner, right?"

Without a word, without looking in his direction, sobbing quietly, Mason reaches into his bag and hands him the burner.

"You should thank me, Mason. Jericho was just using you for your brain. He couldn't have been half as successful without you. You're probably the best money launderer in the country, and you came cheap. What, he paid your rent, put a few bucks in your pocket, and you're supposed to be grateful? I'll bet he didn't give you millions, did he?" He looks over at Mason, deflated and weepy. "Did he, Mason?"

Henry drives toward the ramp back onto the highway. Who knows what kind of bullshit Jericho fed Mason? What did he tell them—they were *partners* or something? Did Mason look up to the guy like a father figure? Probably. Who knows? Jericho played Mason like a fiddle, no doubt.

Well, it doesn't matter. Jericho's dead, and Mason isn't far behind. But Henry needs the money first. So instead of finishing off Mason and being on his way out of the country, Henry has to drive Mason to Veronica.

Still, it nags at him. If Jericho didn't care about Mason, if Mason was just some talented employee but nothing more, Jericho could've just killed Mason in jail, kept the twenty million, watched the criminal case against him fall apart, and let Veronica die.

So why didn't he do that? Why didn't Jericho just kill Mason at Dunham?

Oh. Wait.

"Mason," he says, "don't tell me Jericho…was your father."

Mason bursts into fresh tears, sobbing and wailing into his hands.

"Oh, Jesus. And Veronica, too? She's Jericho's…"

Mason doesn't respond, but now it all makes sense. Henry always wondered why Jericho was so amenable to giving back the twenty million for some girl; he was never sure kidnapping Veronica would work. Turns out he hadn't just kidnapped Mason's sister—he'd also kidnapped Jericho's daughter.

All things considered, this is not a bad development. It makes the stakes even higher for Mason. With his father gone, he'll want to save his sister all the more.

They get back on the highway toward the northwest suburbs. Mason remains mute, rocking back and forth and quietly sobbing. Henry tries to stay focused, driving the speed limit, staying in the middle lane. With one thought running through his mind. Even having to make adjustments, Henry has been ready for every contingency but one.

What happens if Veronica's already dead?

CHAPTER 106

A SECOND CPD chopper—I think our only other one—joins the search for escapees as it expands to include Jericho and Henry. We help coordinate the initial parameters of the search in the area around the jail, accounting for foot speed, but to me, there's no chance Henry and Jericho are still in the area. This was too coordinated. A drone flying into the jail yard with military-grade smoke bombs? A remote-controlled truck with the plates stripped and the VIN scratched out plowing through the jail-yard fence?

They had a car waiting. And I'd bet anything the driver was Mason Tracy.

"We're coming back to the northwest suburbs," I say to Sosh on my phone. "They're long gone, and I'll bet they're on their way up to get Veronica."

"But these suburbs are endless," says Sosh. "We have no idea what kinda vehicle they're in. He'd probably drive the highway, right?"

"Maybe. But he might be careful enough not to."

I sit back in my seat. I'm out of leads. The best thing I can do is just go up there and hope we get lucky or that something clicks.

I look at my phone. It's a quarter after twelve.

"How fast can this chopper go?" I call up to Mullaney. She looks back at me from the cockpit and smiles.

I buckle up as the helicopter slowly rises, the ground nearly disappearing before me, then shoots forward.

The answer is this baby can do about 140 knots an hour, Mullaney shouts to me, which translates to about 160 miles per hour.

"We won't do quite that," she says, "but we'll be there in twenty minutes with this tailwind. You wanna go right back to the place we left? Algonquin, Carpentersville?"

I think about that. "Head that way, yes," I say. But then I dial up Marsha.

"How we doing?" she says.

"Henry and Jericho are in the wind," I say. "Best bet, they're heading for Veronica. I'm on my way in the chopper from Dunham."

"You figure he's going by car?"

"Shit, I don't know, Marsh. With Henry? And a background in the air force? He might be flying a fuckin' drone up there. But yeah, let's assume a car."

"If he's traveling by car, and he's going up to the northwest suburbs from Dunham...hang on, let me check...it's about a one-hour drive with traffic right now."

"The fence breach was at 11:15," I say. "Exactly an hour ago. Henry and Jericho probably busted out a few minutes after that. Add in time to get to their get-away car..."

"Call that 11:25, 11:30," says Marsha. "If it's 12:15 now, he's probably fifteen or twenty minutes from his destination, give or take."

"I'll be up there in twenty minutes by air," I say.

"But the problem is, where?"

"Right. That's why I'm calling," I say. "We

triangulated the area where Delahunt called Henry that night, after he kidnapped Veronica. And we figure he may have driven away from the abduction spot to avoid giving up his location."

"Yeah, he was careful that way."

"Okay, well—we drew, what, a five-mile radius? Did we draw it too small?"

"Sure, that's possible. We had to start somewhere. I mean, those suburbs go on and on in every direction for miles and miles."

"I know, but—look, we're both city kids, born and raised. I don't know these far northwest suburbs. But flying over them today—Algonquin, Carpentersville, Dundee, whatever—they're nice enough places, but they didn't strike me as wealthy. There are rich people up in the northwest suburbs, right?"

"I mean, there's wealth everywhere, Harney. But yeah, you mean like Barrington, that kinda thing."

"Right. We know Henry doesn't personally own land anywhere up there, right?"

"Right. Henry's name isn't on any property other than his home in Chicago."

"So if he owns land through some shell company, he'd probably choose some massive estate, right? Some-place far from neighbors. A bunch of acres. Where he and Delahunt and whoever else was part of that sex-trafficking operation could come and go without notice, cloaked in privacy."

"Then maybe Barrington," Marsha says. "Lemme look at a map."

I don't even dare look down right now, with the ground beneath me whizzing by so quickly. I'm not cut out for this mode of transportation.

"Yeah, Barrington's east but not terribly far away. I mean, the satellite view of it—much bigger houses."

"Okay."

"Hey," she says. "Hey, wait a minute."

"What?"

"Barrington Hills," she says. "Ever heard of it? You should see the size of these estates."

"Big?"

"Yeah, very. Isn't that where Accardo lived after he stepped down from the mob?"

"Fuck, I don't know, Marsh."

"Well, what it says here…hang on…Barrington Hills is known for its horse farms. Massive estates with lots of horse breeders."

"Large estates," I say. "Lots of privacy. No one to see you coming and going."

"And a lot are probably corporately owned," says Marsha. "Some nice, obscure corporate name Henry could hide behind. Equestrian Estates or ABC Corp. or something like that."

Good a guess as any. "Mullaney!" I call up to the cockpit. "Take us to Barrington Hills!"

CHAPTER 107

MARSHA CALLS from SOS, conferencing in Soscia.

"We're here," says Sosh. "Barrington Hills. You're right. These are huge estates. I just drove past a horse farm. I've got five patrols coming. But this area is pretty big."

"About thirty square miles," says Marsha.

"Hey, Marsh," says Sosh. "Can you figure the most logical routes off the highway? We'll post patrols, and maybe we'll pick something up."

"Sure thing."

"Hurry," I say. "Henry got a head start on us. If he drove and took the highway, he could be at his destination any minute, if he's not already there." I shout to Mullaney in the cockpit. "How close are we?"

"We're practically there now."

A loud clap from above. Thick pellets of rain splatter the windshield. Great. That's all we need to assist in our hunt—rainfall.

Marsha says, "If he's coming off I-90, he'd probably end up taking either Algonquin Road or Dundee Road to Barrington Hills. They intersect."

"Take me to the intersection of Dundee Road and Algonquin Road!" I call to the cockpit.

The helicopter swoops low, threatening the meager contents of my stomach. I hate flying.

The chopper slows to a crawl as the rain unloads on us. Below us, beautiful greenscape. Some huge houses. Some subdivisions, too, but I doubt Henry would go for subdivisions.

"Wait—what's that?" I say. "That truck?"

The helicopter lowers farther still, hovering over Dundee Road, according to the cockpit monitor.

"Zoom in on that truck!"

She does. I watch her monitor. The top of the truck is partly open, a horse inside a stall. Not our guy.

A sports car drives past. A green SUV.

We move slowly toward the intersection with Algonquin Road, crawling and hovering, as vehicles of all shapes and sizes, makes and models pass us. Henry and Jericho could be driving anything. We have no idea what we're—

A white panel van slowly drives along Dundee Road.

That brings back a memory from six weeks ago.

"Mullaney, that white van! Can you zero in on it?"

The helicopter lowers farther. We can't be but twenty, thirty feet above traffic. The pilot knows how to handle this bird, letting the van move slightly ahead of us so we can focus on it as it passes under us.

A logo on the side of the van. My heart does a flip.

"Baird Salt!" Mullaney calls out.

The same logo, same type of van Donnie Delahunt drove.

"That's him; that's our guy!" I shout. "Mullaney, call it into all units with coordinates! Suspects will be armed—a possible hostage situation!"

"All units, this is Air 2! All units, this is Air 2! We have a visual ID of our suspects in a white van heading northeast on Dundee Road…"

CHAPTER 108

"ALMOST THERE," Henry murmurs to himself, driving along Dundee Road in Barrington Hills.

A crack of thunder as the threatening sky makes good on its promise. Henry sets the windshield wipers to work on the heavy raindrops. Thank God it didn't rain earlier; it would've backed up the highway considerably.

Mason, his head in his hands, silent for the better part of half an hour, looks up at his surroundings. "Are we...we're...this is the same..."

"Yeah, we're headed back to the same place where you picked up the drone and the flatbed truck last night," says Henry.

Mason looks at Henry. "She was...there...all...all along?"

"She's on that estate, yeah."

That must kill Mason, knowing how close he was last night.

"Doesn't matter now," says Henry. "What matters now is that it's 12:31 p.m., Mason. Time to validate the money transfer."

Mason shakes his head. "Not till I see...see her."

"Fuck that. Transfer it now. I'm taking you to her. We're almost there."

"N-no. No."

Henry draws the sidearm from his CO belt and aims it at Mason. "How 'bout I shoot you right now, and both you *and* Veronica die? How's that sound?"

Mason closes his eyes, his body trembling, sweat dripping from his face. "You...won't," he says.

Shit. Henry's bluffing, and Mason's no dummy.

"You try to fuck with me, Mason, and I'll kill you both."

Whatever. They'll be there in five minutes. Five minutes, and if Veronica's still alive, this will all be—

Something catches Henry's eye in the side mirror. Something moving—

A helicopter, too low.

A *police* helicopter. Trailing them.

"What the *fuck* is that?" Henry hisses. "No. No. Fuck, no!"

He floors the accelerator, veering into oncoming traffic, fishtailing on the freshly wet surface, passing other vehicles, blowing through an intersection, and just barely avoiding a collision.

The chopper follows him, keeping pace.

"Is that...the cops?" Mason asks.

"The cops catch us, you never find your sister, Mason. Don't forget that. Transfer the fucking money *now*!"

Mason starts typing into his phone.

"You're transferring it?" Henry shouts, gripping the steering wheel, the van doing seventy.

"Yes," Mason says, still typing.

Up ahead, the turnoff. Henry screeches the van into a left turn and pulls up to the gate. He rolls down the window and plants his pass against the sensor.

The gate slowly opens. He drives to the right, kicking up dirt on the road, winding around past the barn where the drone and the flatbed truck were held.

"Did it transfer?" Henry shouts.

"Y-yes. Yes."

Up ahead, a two-story eight-bedroom country house. Henry screeches the van to a stop, nearly sliding into the garage door.

"We gotta go fast, Mason, you wanna see Veronica."

Henry gets out of the car as the police chopper flies overhead, lowering to the ground. The CO's gun still in his hand, Henry fires at the chopper twice.

He's no sharpshooter by any stretch, but he hears one of the bullets hit, somewhere around the tail or the engine. The helicopter spins and rises.

"Let's go!"

Henry runs toward the house. He can already see the chopper struggling to lower itself onto the lawn, not far away.

Henry gets into the house, Mason following, and locks the door behind him.

They race down the hallway into the study, a room filled with bookshelves. Mason can see a fireplace and cozy reading chairs.

Henry goes to the corner bookshelf and pulls on it. It opens off the wall like a heavy door. He pulls it all the way open, perpendicular to the wall, the books on the shelf fastened in place.

On the wall, an elevator, with a thumb-activated pad next to it.

Henry puts the gun against Mason's head. "Show me the transfer or you're not getting in that elevator."

Mason holds up the phone and shows him, his hand shaking:

<< Status: $20,000,000 Transfer approved >>
<< Confirmation # 21JLE17411529 >>

Henry takes a picture of the screen with his phone. "Good," he says to Mason. "Now go. Stay down there till I come back."

Mason presses Delahunt's severed thumb against the sensor. The elevator door slides open.

Mason steps in, holding his gym bag full of medicine for Veronica, and pushes a button. The elevator doors close.

Just as Henry hears a thumping at the front door of the house. Good luck trying to breach it.

The hum of the elevator as it descends into the basement.

Henry pushes the shelf flush against the wall again, concealing the elevator.

He hears the crash of a window shattering. Someone breaking through the front window.

Is that you, Billy?

He finds the thermostat on the wall—or what appears to be a thermostat—opens it up, and pushes a button.

He grabs the remote next to the fireplace. It's not for the fireplace.

Then he opens the sliding glass door onto the balcony, runs the length of the balcony, jumps to the ground, and heads toward the woods in the back.

CHAPTER 109

WE ROCK and spin and yaw as the pilot in Air 2 regains control of our chopper after that gunshot hit the tail, tossing us around like we're in a dryer at a laundromat. Pro that she is, the pilot winds the chopper to the ground, fighting the wind and rain.

I'm out of the chopper before it's fully touched down on Henry's front yard, between some barn and the house, the adrenaline overcoming my dizziness and nausea. I slip on the wet grass, then get my footing and rush to the front door. Locked. I kick at it, slam against it, but it's way too heavy.

I run over to a window and jump through, leading with my shoulder, falling onto a love seat and then to the carpet, a shard of glass cutting into my back, another on my thigh. I come up with my gun out and listen.

Noise in the back. A door sliding open?

I run down the hallway into a room that looks like an office, a study. Nothing out of place save for the sliding glass door being open, the wind whistling in. I look out and see Henry, running through the yard, disappearing into thick woods.

"Veronica Tracy!" I shout. I hear nothing, but the rest of my crew isn't far behind, so I'm going after Henry.

"This is Command. Suspect went out the back of the house!" I yell into my radio to Mullaney, up in Air 2, and to Soscia, who's also on the channel. "Looks like heavy woods."

"Roger that, Command. We'll pick him up on the FLIR," Mullaney responds.

"This is Chicago 1," says Sosh. *"We just got through the main gate."*

"Look for Mason and his sister, Chicago 1!" I shout. "They're still in the house! And clear that barn, too!"

My Glock in my right hand, radio in my left, I run onto the balcony and jump down to the lawn below, heading for the trees.

Just like I chased Donnie Delahunt into the woods. Henry set up both of his stash houses the same—a large estate with a gate in front and heavy woods in the back for an escape route. Always an escape route. The same playbook.

"Command, we've got the suspect on infrared," Mullaney says through the radio. *"He's heading due west through the woods."*

"Which way's west?" I'm turned around, no sense of direction right now.

"Just run straight, Command. We'll follow you and turn you if we need to."

I dash into the woods. The heavy tree cover and the dark sky and rain leave me in almost complete darkness.

I don't have my Maglite, so I latch the radio to my belt and use the flashlight on my phone. A poor substitute, the beam of light far narrower and the range much shorter, but at least I can see the tree roots and branches in front of me while I run.

"We're tracking him, Command. He's not going any-where."

But that's the thing. He's going somewhere. Always an escape plan. The same playbook.

"Chicago 1 approaching the house," Sosh says.

I run through the woods, dodging tree trunks and branches, slipping on leaves, jumping over massive roots. Feeling like I'm right back where I started, chasing a suspect through woods that he knows better than I, but that didn't stop me from catching up to Delahunt, who only got away because—

I stop dead in my tracks. Drop my phone and reach for the radio on my belt. "Sosh, are you inside? Is there a light flashing in the corner of any room?"

"You mean like an intruder alarm?"

"It's not an intruder—"

Boom.

I turn in the darkness as the sound of the blast re-verberates through the woods. An orange ball of flame pops out of the roof of the house as the stone walls collapse and tumble inward with a sickening crunch, the massive country home immediately reduced to a pile of rubble.

"Sosh! Sosh, can you hear me? Sosh!"

No.

"Rodriguez! Turner!" I shout. "Chicago 1, do you copy?"

Jesus, no.

"Chicago—" My voice breaks. "Chicago 1, do you copy?"

Please tell me my entire team—my entire team isn't—

"No no no—"

I start running back to the house when I see, through the spreading smoke, more than a dozen squad cars speeding up to the explosion. Every squad from the Carpentersville-Algonquin search arriving now to this estate.

I stop running. I'm playing right into Henry's hands, a page right out of his escape book. He wants me to go back to the house, as I did after Donnie Delahunt caused the first explosion.

I look in both directions. My team needs me.

But there are plenty of cops to help. Only one can catch Henry.

"I'm coming for you, asshole." He doesn't get to kill Carla and the rest of my team and get away with it.

"Air 2, this is Command. Go back and assist the patrol units in the search-and-rescue," I say. "You copy?"

"Copy that, Command. You're still in pursuit of the suspect?"

"I sure as hell am."

I latch my radio to my belt and click it off. I won't be able to hear Henry in these woods with all that noise from the radio. I'm already half blind; I can't be half deaf, too.

I find my phone on the ground, light up the flashlight app, and start running again.

He's not getting away this time.

CHAPTER 110

HENRY RUNS through the woods, a path familiar to him, a path he's practiced several times over the years. A good intelligence officer always prepares for the worst.

Harney's fast, Delahunt told him after Harney caught him at the other stash house in April. *Caught up to me in a heartbeat.*

That's a problem, because Henry is a lot of things, but he's not fast. He can only hope that Billy Harney's lack of familiarity with the terrain will slow him down.

He hopes even more that the detective stopped chasing him when he heard the explosion, that he went back to the house to help fallen comrades. It worked for Delahunt. Maybe it worked this time, too.

But he can't count on it.

His lungs burning, his legs weak, Henry doesn't dare stop running, but he slows to a jog and works the remote control he took from the fireplace. He hears it up ahead in the small clearing, the gentle rotation of rotor blades. Nice to have your vehicle ready and waiting for you.

He peeks back and sees the beam of a flashlight not far away. Not far away at all. Fuck, Billy *is* fast.

So fast that Henry isn't sure he can get aboard the chopper before Billy reaches him.

CHAPTER 111

I RACE through the woods, mostly protected by the tree cover from the rain, finding some kind of cadence, the tree roots like an obstacle course, occasionally stumbling, my phone flashlight keeping me from any major mistakes. I'm running blind, no idea of the destination, only knowing that there must be one somewhere. Henry isn't just idly running. He has something set up.

I slow to a jog when I hear something. The *thwip-thwip* of copter blades. Overhead or on the ground? Is that Air 2 or...does Henry have a helicopter waiting?

Sure. That's it. That's his escape plan.

Wishing Air 2 was covering me now, not back at the house searching for survivors. But I can't think about that right now. Can't·think about my team under a rubble of fire and rock. *If you let him escape, you'll never forgive yourself.*

Up ahead to the right, sounds like. I change my direction, angling that way, glide past a couple of trees, and see, up ahead, a break in the darkness.

A clearing. A helipad carved out of the woods. A

helicopter, the blades rotating, ready for liftoff, heavy rainfall pummeling its dome.

I'm too late.

Fuck it. I run all the same. It's only forty, fifty yards.

I could've run that in ten seconds on a track in high school.

Maybe sixty seconds through this wet, marshy obstacle course.

If he gets off the ground, he's gone, I think as I run with everything I have left, my chest on fire. He'll have something figured out. Some way to disappear in that copter.

My phone buzzes in my hand.

I look down at the phone and see the caller ID for Sosh. Still with the earbuds firmly embedded in my ears, I push the button to answer the phone, nearly dropping it as I approach the clearing, the helipad.

"Sosh, you're—"

"Harney—"

"—alive! What about Gina and Mat?"

"—your radio."

"What? Henry's in a helicopter—"

"Billy, he's—"

"—about to lift off!"

"—the helicopter!"

The chopper begins to rise slowly, rocking back and forth. Five, ten feet off the ground, heavy rain plinking off it.

I stop ten yards away, plant my feet, rain pummeling my face. I squint through the rain and take aim at the cockpit.

"What?" I shout.

"He's right behind you!" Sosh shouts in my ear.

For one beat, I freeze.

Then I dive to the ground as two bullets whiz past

me. I push myself up and sprint, spraying three shots in the general direction from which the gunshot came just to force Henry to run, buying myself precious seconds to make it through the clearing to the cover of a massive tree on the side of the helipad.

"Air 2 is tracking your heat signatures!" Sosh shouts through my earbuds. *"I'll relay Henry's position! We're on our way—hang tight!"*

"Okay," I say, out of breath, unsure if Sosh can hear me.

"If you're...if you're facing the house, he's at your eleven o'clock!"

My head throbbing, adrenaline in overdrive, rainfall pelting me in sporadic drips as it finds its way through the tree cover above me. I peek around the tree trunk. If Henry's at my eleven o'clock, he's almost directly facing me under tree cover about twenty yards away.

Forming the third point of the triangle, equidistant to my right and to his left, the helicopter in the narrow clearing, hovering five feet off the ground in the punishing rain, courtesy of some remote-control device Henry must have.

All sound is drowned out by the white noise of the helicopter blades and the heavy rainfall. I'm lucky I can hear Sosh in my earbuds at all.

I can't see any better than I can hear. The trees where Henry is hiding are shrouded in darkness. He could be waving hello to me and I wouldn't know it. He could be pointing a gun at me and I wouldn't know it.

That thought makes me tuck back behind my own tree cover.

I have the advantage. The cavalry is coming, probably a dozen officers heading my way. Time is on my side, not Henry's.

And if I can't hear Henry, then Henry can't hear

me. Or my radio. "Sosh, I'm switching over to the radio now!" I say. I kill the phone call, hold the phone in my gun hand, and reach for the radio at my belt with my free hand. I click it on, unlatch it, and raise it to my face. "Air 2, this is Command. Talk to me one-way. Give me his location if I'm facing the house. Keep the updates coming. I'm blind down here."

"Roger that," says Mullaney from Air 2, watching Henry on her monitor.

I latch the radio back to my belt, the volume turned all the way up.

"He's still at your eleven o'clock," she reports.

The helicopter slowly lowers, rocking from side to side but finally landing its skids on the concrete helipad.

Henry put the chopper back down. He wants to get on it. He needs to get on it. It's his only chance.

And I'm in his way.

So what's his move?

CHAPTER 112

TIME ON my side, I wait, my gun aimed at my eleven o'clock, at the trees where Henry is hiding. Radio latched to my belt, phone in my free hand. I should put the phone in my pocket.

"He's still at your eleven o'clock, Command, but...it looks like he's on his phone," Mullaney says through the radio. *"We're picking up heat off something he's holding."*

He's on the phone?

My phone buzzes in my hand. I look at the face. Don't recognize the name.

He's calling me? I click on the call as I stuff the phone in my pocket to keep my hands free, ready for a distraction.

"You're done, asshole!" I shout, hardly able to hear my own voice. "You wanna go peacefully, or is it gonna be a blaze of glory?"

Through my earbuds, Henry's voice: *"Can I interest you in a deal, Billy? How 'bout we split the money fifty-fifty?"*

Yep, a distraction. I steel myself.

"He's on the move!" Mullaney warns me through the radio. *"Your twelve o'clock. Your one. Your two o'clock!"*

He's east of me, and he's moving to his left, to the south. I line up my weapon in that direction, my two o'clock. It's directly in line with the helicopter. If he's trying to ambush me, he's going the wrong way, taking the long way around the helipad.

But that's not what he's doing. He's gonna make a run for the chopper.

I inch forward slowly from the tree toward the clearing, the helipad. I'm losing my cover, but if Air 2 tells me he's running for the chopper, I'll beat him there.

Rain hitting me harder now. I squint and aim my weapon in a two-handed grip.

"He stopped, Command. He's flat on the ground. Keep your cover!"

He's flat on the ground?

"Get back to cover, Command!" Mullaney shouts at me. *"He's aiming his weapon at you!"*

No. He can't hit me from here. The chopper's in the way.

Then... what's he doing? What am I missing?

"A blaze of glory it is, Billy," says Henry. The connection goes dead.

I jump at the sound of gunfire. One shot, another.

Clunk. Clunk.

Another. *Clunk.*

I shuffle left, gun ready, but as I thought, the helicopter's between us, blocking the shots. Is he trying to shoot through the cockpit at me?

Clunk.

Wait. No.

I spin and run back toward the trees. He's not shooting at me at all. He's aiming at the fuel supply—

The explosion rocks through my body, lifts me off my feet, spinning me. My back slams against a tree, then the ground rises up and thumps into my shoulder, my ribs. I roll over on my back, a bright orange glow surrounding me, intense heat, no sound but a high-pitched ringing in my ears.

I can't breathe.

I don't care if I'm afraid. I'm willing to risk it.

I'm willing if you are. What are we waiting—

Whump, the ground vibrating, a piece of the helicopter landing nearby.

I suck in air in desperate, greedy, painful gulps. I turn my head, and a shiver of pain radiates down my back.

Then I cough, and something pops in my ears.

"—mand, do you copy? Command, do you copy?"

My radio, latched to my belt. I reach for it, trying to keep as still as possible, every movement pure torture.

The world swirling around me, pelting rain and putrid smoke and incinerating heat—

"Billy, do you copy? Billy!"

I manage to unlatch the radio and raise it to my face. "Air 2...this is Com—"

"Command, this is Air 2! Do you copy? Do you copy, Command?"

"I'm...here, Air...I'm—"

"We lost you, Command! Do you copy?"

"I cop—copy—"

"Command, there's heat everywhere! He used the heat of the fire to blanket his own heat signature! Do you copy?"

"I...copy, Air 2. Do...you—"

"Command, this is Air 2, do you copy?"

My radio's busted, the button jammed. I can hear them, but they can't hear me.

"It looks like one giant sea of white down there, Command! We've lost you and the suspect. Who the hell is this guy?"

He's a former military intelligence officer. Who planned an escape by helicopter.

And knows how to improvise.

CHAPTER 113

HENRY COVERS himself as the helicopter explodes, burying his face in the grass, hands over his head. It's not a perfect solution, but sometimes you have only shitty choices. *Plan B don't come with no warranty,* they used to say in the agency.

A wave of heat passes over his back, hot as an oven. Debris flies everywhere, bouncing and clanking in all directions but not hitting him directly. He peeks up at the orange ball of flame, the thick charcoal plumes of smoke, a jagged piece of the cockpit door in flames not far away.

Mission accomplished. He's now invisible to the police copter's forward-looking infrared system.

He gets to his feet and heads northwest, to his right, away from the house, running through the woods toward the neighboring horse farm. It's not as dark in the woods now, thanks to the fire, but it's still dim enough to prevent his being easily seen by anyone on foot. The police chopper above — that's a different story. The farther he gets from the scene, the less the heat radiation will cover him and the more visible he will be to the chopper's infrared.

He can hear his own gasps as he runs, nothing left, his chest burning, rainfall hitting him in intermittent bursts through the trees, the ground turning muddy and sloshy.

Five minutes, he figures, is all it takes him. He clears the trees and jumps the fence to the neighbor's property, the rainfall pounding him. He doesn't dare look up or stop to listen for the chopper blades. He doesn't dare look back for flashlights coming after him. He just runs through that small corner of the neighbor's property before he jumps another fence.

Onto more real estate he owns, nearly five acres. He's never set foot in the aging house on the property. But he *has* set foot in the garage, most recently last week, after Billy Harney showed up at his office with that audio recording but before they found Marlene dead—that window of time, one afternoon, when Henry got ready just in case.

And "just in case" happened.

He reaches the garage and punches in the code on the keypad. The door grinds open. He steps inside, invisible under the shelter from the police copter.

He nearly collapses to the floor. So out of breath, heart pounding so hard that he isn't sure what will kill him first—exhaustion or a coronary. But he can't stop now. He gets inside the SUV, silver and shiny, finds the keys inside the glove compartment, and starts it up.

What are the odds, he thinks, that the police would have already set up a perimeter all the way over on this side of Barrington Hills?

He can't imagine they could be that fast. Then again, he doesn't know *what* they know. How the hell did Harney even know to find him up here?

But everything's a risk now. It's a bigger risk to stay here.

He pulls out of the garage and starts down the long driveway, activating the windshield wipers against the heavy rainfall.

CHAPTER 114

MASON HOLDS Veronica's head in his lap, gently stroking her hair like Mama used to do whenever Veronica had a flare-up. Humming the song that Mama always used to sing to her, "You Gotta Be."

He wishes he could sing to her, not just hum.

"Wake up, V," he whispers.

It's been nearly ten minutes since he found Veronica after entering the underground chamber, spotting the hole she'd made in the bathroom wall and finding her lying at the base of the ladder in this tunnel. Nearly ten minutes since he injected her with the cocktail of emergency medicine, the steroids and glucose and saline.

She was unconscious. Still alive, but her breathing shallow.

His phone is on the floor, flashlight aimed up to provide some indirect lighting in the otherwise dark tunnel. Veronica's face, cast in shadow, looks pale and haunted. She looks...he can't even bring himself to think it.

It takes time for the mix of medicines to work their magic. But it's never taken this long.

"*Please,* V," he whispers. "Please wake...up."

And then what? What do they do when—if—Veronica revives? That's what Mason's been trying to figure out.

He knows this much: there was an explosion above ground not long after he got down here, when he was first discovering the hole in the bathroom wall and the tunnel. It didn't cave in the underground prison, below twenty feet of concrete, but it rocked it hard and killed the electrical power.

Did Henry blow up the house? Probably. Hoping to conceal the underground chamber. And leaving Mason and Veronica down here to die, trapped.

But...*are* they trapped?

The tunnel. It goes in two directions. One of them dead-ends here, where he found Veronica, by the ladder. The other direction...Mason doesn't know.

He shines his light up the ladder to the top, twenty feet above. Whatever's at the top of that ladder must be a way out of here.

Judging from the distance and direction, Mason guesses that the ladder leads up to the barn where he picked up the drone and the truck and the uniforms yesterday.

He was standing right above her yesterday, and he didn't know it.

He had the chance to save her yesterday, and he didn't.

"Please...wake up," he whispers, his voice quivering.

Above them, vibrations, noise, not directly overhead but nearby. More police, more law enforcement. And maybe fire trucks?

They're looking for Henry, but they'll be looking for Mason, too. Mason's not just a money launderer now. He's an accessory to a jailbreak. And who knows if anyone died in that escape? Jericho did, so that's at least one.

Mason will go to prison for the rest of his life.

"We'll go…somewhere…somewhere warm, some-where warm," he whispers into her ear. "You al—always w-wanted to go…somewhere warm."

He checks his phone. Fifteen minutes now. It's never taken this…

He has to do something. If this medicine cocktail hasn't revived her by now, a hospital is her only chance. He has to get help. The cops up above. Up that ladder, wherever it leads, to the barn or whatever.

He'll probably never see Veronica again. They'll take Mason into custody and lock him up forever. But at least Veronica will have a chance to live.

"I'll be…right back," he says. "Gonna get you…get you some help."

He gently lifts her head.

Veronica stirs, coughs.

Mason doesn't move. "V? V, it's me."

Veronica's eyelids flutter. Then she opens her eyes.

Mason strokes her cheek and forces a smile on his face. "I'm here," he says, voice quivering, his eyes filling. "You're gonna…be okay."

CHAPTER 115

I LIE by the trees, immobilized, a blanket of thick gray smoke surrounding me, drenched by the heavy rainfall that manages to penetrate the tree cover in a few spots, including the place where I happen to be lying. But I'll take the rain right now. The constant slapping is keeping my foggy brain alert. And it's probably preventing a full-scale forest fire.

My useless radio crackles at me. They're searching for me. They should look for Henry, not me, but I can't tell them that. The Talk button on my radio's jammed. My phone is pinned under me in my pocket, and I can't roll over without help.

I feel like I've been hit by a truck. My ribs must be broken, the way they're stabbing me. I have a shooting pain down my back whenever I even think about moving. And I got my bell rung pretty good, too.

The worst part is that Henry's getting away. I don't know where or how. All I know is he would've gamed this out.

"Harney!"

Through the smoke, Gina Turner skids before me

and brings her face close to mine. "You okay, Billy? You get shot?"

"I'm okay. Where'd he go?"

Gina looks me over, then raises her radio and calls in our location.

"Back pain?" she asks me. "Concussion? Broken bones?"

"Where'd he go?"

"You first," she says. "You know how this works."

"I'm okay. I got…close enough to the tree cover before it blew. Where did Henry go?"

"Dunno. Air 2 lost him with all the heat from the fire."

"Help me up."

She takes a moment, thinks it over. Ordinarily, she wouldn't move someone with a possible spinal, but she can't leave me here with the smoke and the fire.

"Okay," she says. She stands up, grabs both my hands, and pulls me to my feet. It would probably qualify as torture under the Geneva Convention, but I'm upright. My balance is for shit. I almost fall back down, but Gina catches me, and now she's taking no chances, grabbing my hand and leading me along like a child.

I run bent at an angle, every movement feeling like my brother Brendan pile-driving his elbow into my back after pinning me. Every breath like I'm being pierced with a hot poker. Rain peppering my face. Dirty hot smoke filling my nostrils.

Thanks to Gina, we make it around the blaze, or what I assume is a blaze from the heat and the billowy smoke; I can't actually see fire anymore.

"Can the fire department make it back here?"

"From the air!" she shouts. "Rain's helping a lot!"

My back spasms so intense, the stabbing in my ribs so excruciating, I drop to the ground and release Gina's hand.

Just as Sosh and Rodriguez run up to us. "You okay, boyo?" Sosh shouts over the din. "Thought we'd lost you!"

I thought I'd lost all of *them*. "Where did he go?" I manage.

Sosh doesn't know. None of us does. Henry has all the advantages now. A time gap of a solid ten minutes, knowledge of the terrain, probably some car or chopper or drone or goddamn time machine to escape in.

"The patrols are combing the woods?" I ask.

Sosh nods. "We're trying to set up a perimeter, too!" he shouts. "You need a medic."

"I'm fine! Just help me up."

Sosh and Gina each take a hand and pull me upright again.

"You're not fine," Sosh says into my ear. "Don't be an idiot."

He's right. I can't run. I'm no help on the ground. "Radio the chopper," I say. "Tell them to land. I'll be okay in there."

Sosh and Gina serve as my escorts as we make it back toward the house, Rodriguez radioing the chopper to land.

"What about Mason?" I say, not having to shout as we move clear of the wreckage in the woods. "Veronica? Jericho?"

"Veronica, don't know," says Sosh. "Probably still inside the house, under the rubble."

"Get the cadaver dogs—"

"We will, but they're still putting out the fire. It's way too hot to search yet."

"And Mason? Jericho?"

"You said Mason ran into the house with Henry?"

"Yeah, I saw him."

"So he's probably same as Veronica."

Shit. Veronica's an innocent in all this. And Mason? He's no saint—he laundered money for Jericho and stole Henry's money for Jericho—but still, he feels to me like someone who just did what he was told. And everything he's done since last week has been to save his sister.

"And Jericho?"

"Nothing confirmed," Sosh says, "but a patrol unit said the van has blood and brain spatter in the back seat. Figure Henry shot Jericho and dumped the body?"

"Probably." And now Henry's waltzing away.

"We'll get BOLOs at the airports and bus terminals," says Mat Rodriguez.

"Right," I say, but I'm not optimistic. Henry has another way out. I just don't know what it is.

As we get back to the house, the smoke and the heat are too great for us to enter the backyard. The other officers have beaten a different path, closer to the barn, about fifteen, twenty yards south of the house.

We follow that route and make it into the clearing, getting pelted by rain as soon as we leave the tree cover. The county has set up a mobile command vehicle just inside the gate to Henry's property. We start toward it.

I pull out my phone to call Marsha and see that I've just missed some calls.

Three of them. In the last four minutes. From the same number.

The chopper isn't quite ready for me. So I have a minute.

"Catch up with you," I tell my team as they run to the mobile command.

The barn sits empty, off to the side of the property.

A good place for me to get shelter while I return that phone call.

CHAPTER 116

"NEXT, AT the bottom of the hour: eight prisoners escape from a Cook County jail with a manhunt under way in the northwest suburbs."

Henry leans forward, both hands white-knuckling the steering wheel, peering through a foggy, rain-battered windshield, keeping his eyes on the road as he turns onto 83. His wipers doing overtime, the tires sloshing on the slick road. Conditions are treacherous, and the absolute last thing he needs is to slide off the road and require assistance. Everything is taking twice as long, but he doesn't dare speed, doesn't dare stop, doesn't dare even *think* about trying to use his phone while driving.

The heat blasts in the car. Took him half an hour to stop shivering, his uniform soaked from the rainfall during the chase in Barrington Hills. He didn't want to take the time to change clothes. Nothing like spending ninety minutes wearing drenched clothes stuck to your skin.

"At least two are dead, two prisoners still at large, and a manhunt under way in the northwest suburbs after a daring

escape this morning from a Cook County jail on the south side of Chicago…"

The headlines must repeat every half hour on this station, because this is the third time he's hearing this since he left Barrington Hills. Drones, trucks, and vans, oh my! Explosions and fires and helicopters and man-hunts! A news radio station's dream.

"Authorities credit the heavy rainfall with preventing a broader fire that could have spread throughout the heavily wooded northwestern suburb."

Yeah, well, good for those assholes and their freakin' horse farms. And thanks to several of those stuffy pricks for investing in the Henry Arcola Escape to South America Fund, currently valued at twenty million dollars.

"And breaking just now: authorities believe they have discovered the body of one of the two remaining escaped inmates, reputed top gang leader Jericho Hooper, behind a restaurant on Chicago's northwest side…"

So they found the body and already figured out it was Jericho. That was fast. The Dunham CO uniform he was wearing probably helped with the quick ID.

It's hard to read road signs in this downpour, but then he sees the Stateline Inn, so he knows he's crossed the border into Wisconsin. He breathes a sigh of relief. It feels like a victory. The private airfield is just a few miles up the road now, past Salem.

He makes it there without incident. He pulls the car up to the private hangar and types in the code. The door slides open. He drives his SUV inside, into the large hangar.

His Cessna sits, ready for him. Next to it, a large portable fuel tanker.

He rolls his neck. That drive was exhausting, his head craned forward the whole time to keep on the road, worrying about police choppers and license-plate readers and traffic blockades.

But it was well worth it. Now he's tucked away here, invisible and safe and dry.

Just one phone call and he's ready to fly.

CHAPTER 117

HENRY DIALS the number as he gets out of the SUV, parked inside the hangar. It's past nine thirty at night in Switzerland, but someone always answers.

He gives his name, account number, and passcodes to the banker. "I need to move some money," he says. "I want to transfer twenty million US dollars into four different accounts in equal amounts," he says.

"The accounts are with us, sir?"

"Or one of your affiliates."

"Very good, sir."

He still can't shake the shiver from these damn wet clothes.

But thinking about his money always warms him up.

"Sir, the funds are insufficient for transfers of that amount," the banker says.

"There shouldn't be a time lag," says Henry. "The transfer was guaranteed. It came just after twelve thirty my time today."

"The transfer from today is not the problem, sir. The transfer went through."

"So what's the problem? The transfer was for twenty million US dollars."

"No, sir, it was not."

He feels a creeping, rising panic. "Of course it was. I saw the transfer order with my own eyes. Twenty million US dollars."

"The original transfer order, yes, sir."

"What do you mean, the *original* order?"

"The one initiated yesterday, Monday, at 12:31 Central Daylight Time, was in the amount of twenty million US dollars. It required a twenty-four-hour security hold until today at 12:31 p.m. your time."

"And? What happened to it?"

"It was canceled, sir."

"No. No, it wasn't." His hands trembling, Henry finds the photo he took of the transfer confirmation from Mason's phone, just in case this very fucking thing happened:

<< Status: $20,000,000 Transfer approved >>
<< Confirmation # 21JLE17411529 >>

Henry puts the phone on speaker. "I have confirmation of a twenty-million-dollar transfer of US dollars."

He reads the confirmation number to the banker, his heart pounding.

"Sir, the original order was canceled today, Tuesday, at 12:34 p.m. your time. And a new order was initiated simultaneously. The confirmation you read me was confirming the *new* transfer order, initiated and executed today."

Twelve thirty-four today...

When he and Mason were in the van. While the chopper was chasing them and Henry made Mason transfer the money. Mason typing away on his phone, while Henry was dodging and weaving his way to the estate with a police copter on his ass.

He looks again at the confirmation Mason showed him:

<< Status: $20,000,000 Transfer approved >>

"New, old, I don't give a shit—the transfer was for twenty million dollars!" Henry shouts at the phone. "I'm literally looking at a screenshot of it."

"Sir, the new transfer order was not in the amount of twenty million US dollars," says the banker. "It was for twenty million Colombian pesos."

Henry blinks.

"What? He switched the...currency?"

"Yes, sir."

Henry bends at the knees, struggling for air. "I see a...a dollar sign," he says, his voice giving out.

"I think I understand the confusion," says the banker. "The currency symbol for the Colombian peso is the same as the US dollar sign."

Henry can't breathe.

In the van, during the chase, Mason switched the currency on the transfer order from US dollars to one of the weakest currencies on the planet.

"Show me...his transfer history," he manages.

"Sir, I cannot show you the other account holder's history. I can text you yours, if you don't have it pulled up."

"I...haven't had a chance..."

Ten seconds pass like ten hours. Then the text message appears:

<< Transfer of USD$ 20,000,000 Pending validation >>
<< Pending transfer of USD$ 20,000,000 CANCELED >>
<< Receipt of COP$ 20,000,000 CONFIRMED >>

COP$. The Colombian peso.

"But...the security...the twenty-four-hour hold," Henry says. "You can't modify a transaction...that fast. It would've needed twenty...twenty-four..."

"Well, sir, as you know, the twenty-four-hour security hold only applies to transfers in excess of one million US dollars. The original transfer was well above that threshold. But the modified transfer was far below it. So it could be made instantaneously."

No, this can't...

"How..." Henry sets the phone down on the hood of his SUV, planting his hands on the hood for balance. "How much was the transfer?" he asks, his eyes closed.

"Sir, the transfer of twenty million Colombian pesos, in US dollars, amounted to five thousand ninety-four dollars and seventeen cents."

That motherfucking stuttering freak transferred him five grand and kept the rest of the twenty million for himself?

Henry punches out the phone, his heart hammering, struggling for air.

He pounds the hood of the SUV—"Fuck fuck *fuck*!"—then opens his eyes and thinks.

This isn't over, you little fuck. I'll kill you and *your sister. After I get my money back.*

Later tonight, he decides. The fires at the estate have already been tamped down. They'll search for Mason and Veronica, but they'll never find them, trapped below twenty feet of concrete in an underground chamber. Once nightfall comes, they'll give up until morning.

But Henry—Henry can reach Mason and Veronica whenever he wants. He has two different ways to do it.

The easy way: through the barn and down the ladder to the chamber. Veronica and Mason wouldn't know this—none of the girls ever did—but there's a hidden door into the underground chamber through one of the closets. Henry will pop in, grab Mason, and get this problem fixed.

Or, if the cops are still covering the front of the estate, there's the rest of the tunnel. The tunnel runs nearly the length of the entire property. There's an escape hatch in the woods.

So all Henry has to do is sneak into the woods and find the hatch. Then he can climb the ladder twenty feet down and walk to the chamber where Mason and Veronica are trapped. The cops, standing sentry twenty feet above him, will never know.

"This isn't over," he says, standing up straight.

"Actually, it is."

Henry spins, nearly falls backward.

Detective Billy Harney, gun drawn, walks toward him. "Don't move, Henry. I'd take any excuse to shoot you."

Henry's eyes dart around. Police officers coming from behind the fuel tanker, from out of the Cessna itself.

They were waiting for him.

He looks at Billy. "He called you."

"Turn around," Billy says. "Hands behind your back."

The detective cuffs Henry's hands and removes Henry's weapon from his holster. "This would be the gun used to kill Corrections Officer Heppner, I take it," he says. "And Jericho Hooper."

Henry shakes his head. "He fucking called you."

"On the bright side, Henry, you can always try to break out of prison. But sounds like your money won't get you so far anymore. Couldn't help but overhear that there was a misunderstanding with a wire transfer."

Henry's head drops. A dozen cops surround him.

"Sorry—I should have called the go order sooner,"

Billy says. "But I couldn't resist listening to that call. Oh, and Henry?"

Henry turns his head toward Billy.

"I got your note," says the detective. "And yeah, I *am* having fun now."

CHAPTER 118

MASON STANDS at the top of the ladder, his heart pounding. He listens and hears nothing. He shines his phone light above. There is a hatch in the ceiling. He turns the latch, hears a *click,* then feels cool air against his face.

He is still for a moment, listening, but he hears nothing. He climbs onto the last rung and pushes open the hatch. Sticks his head above ground.

It smells like the remnants of a fire. He's in the woods. He doesn't dare shine his flashlight yet. He climbs out and stands. He sees no flashlights, no indication that anyone's out here.

He tried the other ladder first, the one right by Veronica. As he thought, it led into the barn. He could hear people outside the barn, busy at work with machinery. Cops, he assumed.

So he followed the tunnel in the other direction. As best he can tell, his eyes adjusting to the darkness, he's on the opposite end of this massive property. Nothing but trees and the smell of fire and ash.

He climbs back down, closing the hatch. Down twenty

rungs for twenty feet. Then he hustles back to Veronica through the dark tunnel, using his phone flashlight. He finds her sitting up, her back against the wall, drinking one of the vitamin waters Mason brought in his bag.

She looks much better now. The second round of shots has her looking more like herself. Not nearly all the way there, but out of immediate danger.

"Is it safe?" she asks him.

"As safe as…as can be. Can you…can you walk?"

"How far? A mile?"

"Maybe…little less…but about that."

"And then we climb a ladder?"

"Yes. Yes."

"Help me," she says.

Mason slings the bag over his shoulder and helps Veronica to her feet. She leans on him heavily as they move forward. "No rush," he says.

It's near midnight. A few minutes here or there aren't going to make much of a difference.

"There *is* a rush," she says. "You aren't going to prison. Not if I can help it."

He told her everything. They had plenty of time down here for that story. Including Jericho's death. She didn't take it well. But she's tough, like Mama. She immediately took charge and told Mason they had to move forward, not look backward, if they wanted to survive.

"We can…stop," says Mason, after a few minutes. "If you wanna…wanna rest."

"Keep going," she whispers.

"We can't…come back," he says. "Ev-ever."

"I know we can't. It's okay."

They move forward, Veronica doing okay under her own strength. They'll have to rest once they reach the ladder. And probably rest once they're in the woods.

Because eventually, those woods will end, and they'll be on foot in the middle of the night.

They'll hide out until morning. He'll call someone from the Nation for help. He'll get some fake passports. He'll move that twenty million dollars around. He'll find some way to get to Mexico, for starters.

And they'll never look back.

"Somewhere warm, right?" Veronica grunts, out of breath.

He pats her arm. "Somewhere...somewhere warm," he says.

CHAPTER 119

I GET out of my car, still on the phone with Sosh.

"No bodies so far," he tells me.

"So Mason and Veronica aren't there. Above ground, at least."

"They say no. They're still searching. You go to the hospital?"

"Yeah, I'm good," I say. "Nothing to do for cracked ribs or a sore back. Just bandage me up and give me pain pills. Pills are helping."

"You really think Mason and Veronica are below ground?"

"I think that was Henry's stash house for all those girls. So where did he stash them? Knowing Henry, I wouldn't put it past him to have something under-ground. So tell search and rescue to keep at it until they're sure, one way or the other."

"It's almost midnight."

"I know what time it is." I ring the doorbell.

"Don't know about you, but I'm going to the Hole," he says. "It's been a long fuckin' day."

"That it has." I've been tossed and turned inside a

helicopter like I was in the spin cycle. I've been shot at. I've been blown off my feet. And I got the shit beaten out of me by a tree. All in all, my sixteen-hour shift is ready to be over.

"Join us?"

"Got other plans," I say. I punch out the phone.

The door opens. Mia, hair pulled up, in a Bears jersey. "Oh, thank God," she whispers, as if to herself.

"Michelangela."

"You're okay? I saw it on the news. I was going to— I didn't want to call while you were in the middle of…I didn't want to be like a worried wife or something, y'know?"

"Yeah, about that." I put out my hands, like I'm about to say something profound, so this better be good. "Look, I…I don't think this is working."

"What's not working?"

"Us," I say. "Mia, I thought I was gonna die today, and the only person I could think about was you."

She takes a breath. More than she was expecting on a Tuesday night.

"I think we're trying way too hard *not* to mean something to each other," I say. "Maybe we should take our hands off the wheel and see where it goes."

"Yeah?" She chews on her lip. "Scary."

"Yeah, I know, but not as scary as missing out."

I exhale. I can't imagine what I look like. I never got all the dirty smoke off my face. My clothes are ripped and stained and reek of smoke. I probably could've changed clothes or run a comb through my hair before showing up.

"You look like hell," she says, in case I hadn't noticed.

"You should see the other guy." The standard comeback.

She gives me that smirk, those magical blues eyes

lighting up. She saunters up to me, in that sultry Marilyn Monroe way that turns me to jelly, until her lips are nearly against mine.

"I don't want to see the other guy," she whispers. "I want to see my boyfriend."

"Then we better hurry before he shows—"

She presses her lips against mine before I can finish the joke.

WEDNESDAY

CHAPTER 120

"RIGHT IN here," the guard tells me.

I take a seat on my side of the visitation table, moving gingerly, my back in revolt, my ribs no better, a nasty headache. But I capped off the night at Mia's, so nothing's gonna kill my mood today. Not even him.

They bring Pop into the visitation room, no shackles, the guard with a friendly hand on his back. My father is all gray now and wearing a beard, but he has some more weight on him and more color than the last time I saw him, half a year ago.

I said it would be the last time. I said I was done with him, that he wasn't my father anymore, that he meant nothing to me.

But he kept calling me. And I started taking those calls.

Including the one he made yesterday afternoon.

"You need anything, Danny?" the guard says to Pop.

"No, I'm good, Joey, thanks." Pop gestures to me. "You want something, kid? A Coke, some coffee, anything?"

I just look away.

The guard glances over at me. "This one of your boys, eh? I see where he got his good looks."

"His mother," they say together.

The guard leaves. Pop looks at me. I stare back.

"Danny?" I say. "Joey? A Coke, some coffee? What, do you run this place now?"

Pop always had a knack for co-opting people. It's probably how he made chief of d's to begin with. He commanded respect and engendered fear, all at once. Some people just have that quality, I guess.

"You look good," he says to me. "Beat up, but good. Heard you got a nice solve."

"How'd you know?" I say.

"It's all over the news."

"That's not what I meant, and you know it."

"Ah." He rubs his beard.

"If you think this makes us even, it doesn't. Not even close."

He opens his hands, his eyes bugging out. "You're welcome."

"How'd you know? How'd you know where Henry kept that plane?"

"You forget how long I was a cop?"

"Henry didn't have a sheet," I say. "He didn't even have a file."

"A *file*. For Christ's sake, boy. Not everything's in a *file*."

"You protected him, didn't you? He was one of the many sex-trafficking scumbags you protected. And the people you protect, well, you make sure you know *all* their secrets, right? Just in case."

He looks away. I've gotten to him, I can tell. The emotion, at least the way Pop shows emotion—the steely face, sure, but his color changes and his eyes glisten.

"Unbelievable," I say. "You're unbelievable."

"Think what you want about mc," hc says. "I won't give you a quarrel. But I tried to protect you. I tried to keep you away from that piece of shit."

I draw back. "What does that mean? You tried to…"

Then I get it. I remember.

"That day you called and told me to take on this new task force within SOS, focusing on the gangs," I say. "You called me about one minute after Wizniewski offered it to me. You were behind it. You were trying to get me off Delahunt's trail. Because Delahunt led to Henry."

"And Henry destroys people," he says.

I do a slow burn. And shake my head in wonder. How does Pop still have so much reach?

"Don't get involved in my life," I say. "I don't want you in—"

He slams his hand down on the table. "I don't get involved yesterday, Henry's halfway to Brazil or some fuckin' island by now. The fuck did *I* get out of it? Nothin', that's what I got. Nothin'."

So the guy does one good deed and all is forgiven? I don't know what else to say. I push myself out of the chair.

"Billy, don't leave. Please."

The look on his face…I don't think I've ever seen. And when was the last time Pop used the word *please*?

He runs his hand through his hair. "A guy provides for his family and makes no apologies for it. All you kids, your mother, you never wanted for anything. I made sure of that. Maybe I made a deal with the devil. Maybe I did. But I kept all of you out of it. I made sure you were provided for and safe and free from what I did."

"Yeah, okay, Pop, maybe when we were kids, but you…did a few other things you're leaving out—"

"I know I did." He jumps out of his chair, knocking

it over, a loud clanging. "I know, better than you'll ever know, what I did. After your mother died. After your mother died, it all got…"

He goes quiet a moment, turns his back on me. He's probably crying. He never wanted us to see him cry. Crying meant weakness, and one thing Pop never, ever showed was weakness.

"She was my compass, kid. When she was gone, I…I don't know. I lost my way."

"That's no excuse for what you've done, Pop."

"I know it isn't. I'm not making excuses. The things I've done to you, they can't be forgiven. Ever. I just want you…"

I wait for the punch line, some of the venom draining from me. God, what is it about blood and family? Why am I even remotely giving him a pass? After everything he did to me, why am *I* the one feeling sorry for *him*?

Why do I let him punch my buttons?

"What?" I say. "You want me to what?"

His back still to me, his head drops. On our best day, we weren't a touchy-feely family—at least the boys weren't.

"When you…when you remember me," he says, "remember that I was trying to help you. And I still want what's best for you. Along with all the bad, remember that, too." His head turns slightly, still not facing me. "Can you do that?"

My body shaking now. I don't know whether to hug him or strangle him. I want to do both in equal amounts. But he knows this is the last time we'll see each other. He knows I only came today because of Henry, that I'll keep the promise I made and never visit him again.

This is goodbye.

"I can do that," I say.

He raises a hand. Meeting adjourned. He won't turn

around. He doesn't want me to see him with tears on his face. I don't particularly want to see it, either. The Harneys don't hug and cry and share. We hide, suppress, and conceal.

I show myself out. I don't shed a single tear until I've left the prison grounds.

CHAPTER 121

"BIL-LY GOAT! Bil-ly Goat!"

"Okay, let's set some ground rules," I say, holding the mike at the Hole in the Wall as the chant gains steam. "First, there ain't gonna be another Billy Goat. I'm hanging up my disco shoes. I know, I know," I add as they moan in abject sorrow. "I figure I should quit while I'm on top. It's time to focus on my real passion, early-morning birdcalls.

"Second of all, you hold up a camera while I'm up here, I'm t'rowin' youse a beatin.' And I'll pistol-whip anyone who posts something on YouTube. I've had enough of being an internet sensation. I haven't been this 'viral' since I went to the Russian bathhouse on Montrose.

"Let's welcome back Mia," I say, the coppers cheering. "Most of you remember her as your favorite bartender, who just left for her internship at a fancy law firm. From a young age, Mia knew that she wanted a career where she could help others and make the world a better place. But she decided to be a lawyer instead."

Soscia laughs the hardest. Mia, standing next to him, elbows him and wags a finger at me.

"Lanny Soscia wanted to be a lawyer until he realized you had to *pass* the bar and not stop in for a pint.

"I told Mia, don't be one of those bad lawyers who lets cases drag on for years. Be a good lawyer who makes them last even longer.

"But hey, she's willing to date me," I say. "Who says lawyers don't do pro bono work?"

I can do lawyer jokes in my sleep. I end with the one about the Hindu priest, the rabbi, and the lawyer whose car breaks down on a country road by a farm. It doesn't end so good for the cow and pig.

When I'm done, I see Gina Turner in the crowd.

"Had to see it for myself," she says. "You actually get up there and tell jokes. I wouldn't have the stones, personally."

"So was the GPR any help?"

The search-and-rescue team has found no signs of life in the rubble that was Henry Arcola's house in Barrington Hills. The cadaver dogs didn't find any dead bodies, either. Mason and Veronica Tracy aren't in that rubble or anywhere in the woods. So a few hours ago, the team used ground-penetrating radar to search beneath the surface.

"GPR located a structure about twenty feet underground," Gina says.

"Like a cave or chamber."

Her head angles. "More like a tunnel, they think. Seems to go beyond the house."

"A tunnel system. I could see Henry doing that. The question is whether the tunnel leads to another exit besides the house."

"Right. If it does, Mason and Veronica may have adiosed."

Now, that would be something. Henry Arcola hasn't said a word to us since his arrest, but that phone conversation with the Swiss banker that I overheard—it sure sounded like Mason pulled a fast one on Henry and pocketed the money.

For all we know, Mason and his sister could be skipping away with twenty million dollars for their troubles while Henry Arcola rots in prison, counting his Colombian pesos.

"We're assuming it's still a search-and-rescue," Gina says. "Just in case she's down there and in need of assistance."

"Absolutely. Do that. Keep me posted. And Gina—great work on this case. Glad to have you on the team."

"You said it wouldn't be boring," she says. "And it isn't."

My phone buzzes in my pocket. I answer before it goes to voice mail.

"Where are you?" Patti says to me, sounding shaken.

"I'm at the Hole."

"I'm almost there. What did you say to him today?"

"What did I—to who?" But she can only mean one person.

The line goes dead.

What did I say to Pop this morning? I said plenty, and little of it was pleasant.

And he talked about how I would…

How I would remember him.

Was that goodbye more literal than the way I took it?

No, Pop didn't—he wouldn't—

Patti bursts through the front door. I'm already halfway there, trying to meet her. Her eyes scan the room until they make contact with mine.

I can see it on her face. An expression she reserved for our father. The two of them always had a thing that was different from the way it was with the boys. She was his princess, and he was "Daddy" to her.

"What did you say to him today?" she asks. "What did he say to you?"

The same question that's running through my mind. Did I push him too far?

"How'd he do it?" I ask.

"Nobody knows. They're still trying to figure it out."

"They're still...so it might not be suicide? He might have died of natural causes?"

She steps back from me. "What? Daddy isn't dead."

"Then...what? What did he do?"

"You haven't heard? He escaped," she says. "Vanished without a trace."

ACKNOWLEDGMENTS

A very special thank you to Chief James Kruse (ret.), DuPage County Sheriff's Office, for his advice about police tactics and procedure. Any mistakes or creative departures were those of the authors.

—D. E.

ABOUT THE AUTHORS

JAMES PATTERSON is the most popular storyteller of our time. He is the creator of unforgettable characters and series, including Alex Cross, the Women's Murder Club, Jane Effing Smith, and Maximum Ride, and of breathtaking true stories about the Kennedys, John Lennon, and Princess Diana, as well as our military heroes, police officers, and ER nurses. He has coauthored #1 bestselling novels with Bill Clinton and Dolly Parton, told the story of his own life in *James Patterson by James Patterson*, and received an Edgar Award, nine Emmy Awards, the Literarian Award from the National Book Foundation, and the National Humanities Medal.

DAVID ELLIS is a justice of the Illinois Appellate Court and the author of nine novels, including *Line of Vision,* for which he won an Edgar Award, and *The Hidden Man,* which earned him a 2009 Los Angeles Times Book Prize nomination.

JAMES
PATTERSON
RECOMMENDS

JAMES PATTERSON

THE BLACK BOOK

& DAVID ELLIS

THE BLACK BOOK

I have favorites among the novels I've written. *Kiss the Girls*, *Invisible*, *1st to Die*, and *Honeymoon* are top of the list. With each, I had a good feeling when the writing was finished. I believe this book — *The Black Book* — is the best work I've done in twenty-five years.

Meet Billy Harney. The son of Chicago's chief of detectives, he was born to be a cop. There's nothing he wouldn't sacrifice for his job. Enter Amy Lentini, an assistant state's attorney hell-bent on making a name for herself — by proving Billy isn't the cop he claims to be.

A horrifying murder leads investigators to a brothel that caters to Chicago's most powerful citizens. There's plenty of evidence on the scene, but what matters most is what's missing: the madam's black book.

JAMES
PATTERSON

TEXAS
RANGER

★

& ANDREW BOURELLE

TEXAS RANGER

So many of my detectives are dark and gritty and deal with crimes in some of our grimmest cities. That's why I'm thrilled to bring you Detective Rory Yates, my most honorable detective yet.

As a Texas Ranger, he has a code that he lives and works by. But when he comes home for a much-needed break, he walks into a crime scene where the victim is none other than his ex-wife—and he's the prime suspect. Yates has to risk everything in order to clear his name, and he dives into the inferno of the most twisted mind I've ever created. Can his code bring him back out alive?

JAMES PATTERSON

The FBI, DEA, and Miami police are all looking for her.

LOST

AND JAMES O. BORN

LOST

Nothing makes a detective more motivated than when it's their own backyard that's threatened. And for Detective Tom Moon, Miami is about to turn into a hunting ground.

As the new leader of an FBI task force called "Operation Guardian," it's his mission to combat international crime. But as the enemy zeroes in on a target dear to Tom, they're not playing by anyone's rules.

THE BESTSELLING AUTHOR OF THE DECADE

JAMES
PATTERSON
& J.D. BARKER

THE
COAST TO COAST
MURDERS

THE COAST-TO-COAST MURDERS

Nothing brings siblings together more than sharing a terrifying past. Both adopted, and now grown, Michael and Megan Fitzgerald trust each other before anyone else. They've had to. Brought up in a rarefied, experimental environment, they were sheltered from the world's harsh realities, but it also forced secrets upon them.

In Los Angeles, Detective Garrett Dobbs and FBI agent Jessica Gimble have joined forces to work a murder that seems like a dead cinch until there's another killing. And another. And not just in Los Angeles— the spree spreads across the country. The Fitzgerald family comes to the investigators' attention, but Dobbs and Gimble are at a loss—if one of the four is involved, which Fitzgerald might it be?

For a complete list of books by

JAMES PATTERSON

VISIT
JamesPatterson.com

Follow James Patterson on Facebook
@JamesPatterson

Follow James Patterson on X
𝕏 @JP_Books

Follow James Patterson on Instagram
@jamespattersonbooks